WEB OF
PASSION

WEB OF
PASSION

Anne Dunhill

MICHAEL O'MARA BOOKS LIMITED

The characters and events in this book are
fictitious. Any resemblance to any persons, alive
or dead, is entirely coincidental.

First published in Great Britain in 1993 by
Michael O'Mara Books Limited
9 Lion Yard
Tremadoc Road
London SW4 7NQ

A CIP catalogue record for this book
is available from the British Library

ISBN 1 85479 198 2

Typeset by Florencetype Ltd, Kewstoke, Avon
Printed and bound by Clays Ltd, St Ives plc

For A

CHAPTER ONE

March 1972

'Janie, this is Alex Oliver who's just moved into the house opposite. Alex, this is my best friend, Janie Orsini. I'll go and bring up the tea.' Virginia smiled briefly at them both and went downstairs.

Jane felt a warm glow of affection for her. How lovely that Verge still thought of her as her best friend even though she now lived in Italy. She felt like getting up and following her. She'd been in the middle of feeding her baby son when the doorbell had rung. It was a bit much to expect her to entertain a strange man under such circumstances, although this one, on reflection, didn't look as if he'd prove to be too hard going. Tall and slim, with black curly hair, he was like a painting of the god Pan peeping mischievously through the foliage with the greeny brown lights of the forest reflected in his eyes. Perhaps it would be rude to leave him alone. Verge did have the au pair waiting in the kitchen to help her, and anyway, how much use would she be to her with only one free hand?

'Is that your baby?' Alex's smile was surprisingly sweet as he looked quizzically down at the all-too-alert Filippo.

'Yes he is.' Jane found herself smiling back at him. 'It's a historic moment actually – the first meeting between Philly and Benjamin –' She indicated Virginia's ten-month-old son, who was lying asleep on a beanbag on the other side of the double drawing room. 'Verge and I

1

have known each other since we were children, you see.'

'Yes. She's told me so much about you.'

Jane's smile wavered. She wondered exactly what Verge had told him. As a former, much-publicized film starlet, Jane had had what was generally regarded as a colourful past, culminating in a sensationally brief first marriage, and subsequent liaison with an Italian count. Virginia, on the other hand, had been with her husband, the Hon. Robin Askew, since she was eighteen, even though it had taken her five years to get him actually to marry her. Now, with motherhood, Jane and Virginia's lives had resumed the parallel course which had begun twenty years ago and continued uninterrupted during their schooldays, but Jane had an uneasy feeling that Virginia still lost no chance of recounting the lurid details of Jane's past to her more stuffy friends in order to point a moral and adorn a tale.

'Oh dear,' she risked a slight grimace and a dismissive laugh.

'You're married to an Italian, aren't you?'

'Er, yes.' So Virginia hadn't told him that she and Giorgio weren't actually married. Or had she? Before becoming pregnant Jane's speciality had been an almost defiant honesty in the face of all enquiry, but mother-hood had blurred the guidelines a bit. The thing was that the term 'husband' described Giorgio so much better than the term 'lover'. Two and a half years of rigid monogamy – and when, she asked herself now, had it begun to seem rigid? – and major sulks if she ever even talked about, let alone to, another man had made their relationship so much the most respectable she had ever experienced that the phrase 'living in sin', although technically correct, couldn't help but seem ludicrously inappropriate.

Philly started to wriggle. Jane felt the milk welling up in her breast. 'Would you mind awfully if I fed him?' she said in desperation. 'I was halfway through, you see, when you arrived, and I don't think he'll settle unless I finish.'

'Of course not,' he said easily. 'I'm sorry to have inter-rupted you.' He sat down on the sofa beside her and smiled expectantly.

He's expecting me to whip out a bottle, she thought to herself. He's going to be terribly embarrassed. At this point Philly the angelic started the first tentative wails which she knew would build up in a rapid crescendo of weeping if she allowed them to continue. Alex was promptly forgotten. Turning her back on him, Jane flung Philly's baby shawl over her shoulder as camouflage, and quickly undid the poppers of her denim shirt.

Once Philly was settled and sucking greedily, Jane risked a quick glance over her shoulder to see if Alex was looking at her. He tactfully wasn't, but the movement of her head caught his attention and he turned so that their eyes met. Once again she thought what a nice smile he had. He could only have been in his late twenties, but it made him look more like a teenager. He had been drumming his fingers on the arm of the sofa, and she couldn't help noticing the extraordinary beauty of his slim, sensitive hands. She wondered why it should be so much less embarrassing to feed Philly in front of a man she found attractive than it was in front of men she didn't. Surely it ought to be the other way round?

'Do you and your wife have children?' she asked him.

She knew he was married. Virginia had given her a quick biography earlier when the doorbell had rung. 'That'll be Alex,' she'd said. 'He and his wife are the ones we go to the opera with. They've just moved into the house opposite and have got the plumbers in. He asked if he could come over this afternoon for a bath.'

'No we don't,' he replied. 'We'd like to but it's a bit difficult. My wife's ill a lot.'

Jane was surprised. She'd been imagining them as a youthful Mr and Mrs Perfect. Pretty, blonde wife three years younger than him and six inches shorter. The sort of girl who'd got two A levels and lost her virginity at eighteen, she would have done a secretarial or cookery course and used her skills professionally for a year or two to fill in time before getting married and becoming the perfect hostess to Alex's business associates. A sort of counterpoint, couple-wise to the dark, half Polish Virginia and the blond, very English Robin. But then that relationship, whatever surface smoothness it had now acquired, hadn't been all roses either.

'Oh I'm sorry.' She wasn't really. She was rather intrigued. Later she would ask Virginia about it, but for now she supposed she'd better be tactful. 'Verge says you go to the opera a lot,' she added lamely.

'Yes. Robin and I were at Oxford together. We lost touch for a while, but then we bumped into each other at the Royal Opera House and found we were going to all the same productions so decided we'd try and book tickets on the same nights. Julie and I came here to dinner and really liked the area. We'd been living in a flat in Fulham before and were looking for a house anyway. Then this one came up almost directly opposite. Look,' he pointed out of the window across the wide, tree-lined crescent which meandered up to Holland Park. Jane craned her neck obediently. Philly's shawl slipped, but she replaced it immediately and didn't think Alex had seen anything, 'it's the one with the light on up at the top. We're living there at the moment with a camping stove while the builders gut the rest of the house.'

'They're huge houses aren't they?' Jane remarked. She remembered having been astounded when Virginia and Robin had first bought theirs and given her and Giorgio the guided tour. Tall and imposing, with two large rooms on each of the five storeys, the house had seemed ludicrously large for a childless couple, especially taking into account Virginia's professed socialist principles. She wondered what Alex's wife was doing now. Getting ready perhaps for the evening out for which her husband was about to bathe himself. She continued to gaze absently out of the window, half expecting to see her pacing to and fro in front of the curtainless windows.

'They are big,' he agreed. 'It's a nightmare if you get to the front door and realize you've forgotten something and have to climb up sixty-four stairs to find it. Where do you live?'

'Well, we're looking for somewhere in London,' something to put in Jane's name in case anything should happen to Giorgio before they could marry, 'but our main home's in Venice. We live on the *piano nobile* – that's the first floor – of an old palazzo on one of the quiet little canals in Dorsoduro. Do you know Venice?'

'Hardly. I spent a couple of nights there one summer when I was at Oxford. A friend and I were driving round Italy. It must be an incredible place to live.'

'It is. I don't know what it'll be like with a baby, though.'

'What does your husband do?'

'He's an antique dealer.'

'What a perfect job to have in Venice. I adore Italian furniture. I can't think of anything more wonderful than to be able to collect it.'

'Ah, but that's the mistake everyone makes about antique dealers.' Jane's smile was tight. 'Thinking they love antiques. It's rather like thinking nannies love children whereas I'm sure they can't possibly or it would break their hearts every time they changed jobs.' She looked down for a moment at Philly's black head. His lips puckered in a gentle fluttering movement. The sucking had almost stopped now. His eyes were shut and his plump, clenched fist lay possessively against her breast. 'If antique dealers really loved antiques they wouldn't be able to sell them, whereas I'm constantly getting up in the morning and finding one of my favourite pieces has gone missing. My husband even sold our bed to pay for this trip. I'm always expecting to wake up and find myself being lowered out of the window into a gondola because he's sold me as well,' she laughed bitterly.

Alex looked rather surprised. Jane wondered if she'd gone too far. Before her marriage her best friends had always been men. Even now, after living with two jealous men in succession, it was hard for her to get used to the fact that she must remain at all times safely behind the invisible line of what Giorgio would consider propriety. It wasn't that he didn't expect her to look good. Giorgio was proud of her blonde, green-eyed beauty which people in Venice found so exceptional although it had been two a penny in the circles she'd moved in in London, and liked her to bedeck herself in exotic antique clothes and jewellery. It was just that she mustn't ever display a hint of warmth or truth. Gradually she'd learnt to cultivate the art of gracious dumbness. She could get away with it easily enough in Venice because a lot of people still assumed she didn't really speak the language, whereas in fact she'd been completely fluent after six months. Often she had the sensation that while her outward appearance remained unchanged, her spirit was gradually being bricked up alive within a wall of virtue from which it would soon be unable to escape even if it wanted to. Not that it did want to, of course. Having found true love for the first time in her life with the dark cherub who lay sleeping in her arms, all she wanted was to remain on good terms with Giorgio so that the two of them could unite in protecting him. But talking to Alex did make her wonder for a moment what it would be like to be with a man of her own age again, someone she could talk to freely without the risk of causing terrible offence, someone with whom she could be friends.

The door opened and the au pair entered bearing crumpets and strawberry jam, followed closely by Virginia with the teatray. Alex sprang up and took it from her, placing it carefully on the low table in front of the sofa.

'Sorry to desert you both for such ages,' she smiled at Alex. 'Here's tea at last.'

Jane and Virginia had known each other since they were five, though it had taken a while for them to become best friends. Jane, whose birthday was in November, had started school a term later than the rest of her class and had spent her first day there being looked after by a little boy called Bill who lived near her and with whom she had often played in the local park. Boys were accepted in the lower classes of the school, but had to leave when they were eight, so were in very short supply. Perhaps because she was an only child, Jane was as yet unconscious of any difference between the sexes, and had taken Bill's protection for granted. She did not realize that by monopolizing him that first day she was already drawing attention to herself and antagonizing a group of girls who, during the previous term, had set themselves up as the leaders of the class, more because of the lengths of spitefulness to which they were prepared to go than for any outstanding natural abilities they possessed.

Virginia did not really belong to this group, but took care to remain in with it. A small, thin child with dark pigtails, she spent a lot of time staring at Jane with an expression which was difficult to fathom. Years later, when their class was reading *Julius Caesar* and got to 'Yond Cassius has a lean and hungry look', Jane recognized the description of Verge and immediately burst into giggles and was sternly rebuked for being late with her lines: 'Fear him not, Caesar, he's not dangerous; He is a noble Roman, and well given.'

Inevitably, Jane had been behind with her work at first, and Virginia had been quick to join in the general jeers, but one day they had bumped into each other in the park with their respective fathers, and Virginia, after a quick appraisal of Jane's out-of-uniform clothes and her father's car, had been surprisingly nice. As Jane caught up academically and became popular with the other children, Virginia became freer with her public demonstrations of friendship, though she still kept in with the bullies just in case. Jane sometimes wondered why she put up with it, but she never bothered to analyse the situation too deeply. She was a self-sufficient child who spent a lot of her time in a dream world, and friendships with other children were not desperately important to her. Virginia was intelligent and made her laugh, and in spite of her frequent bitchy remarks, or perhaps even because of them, Jane sensed in her a deep devotion to herself that occasionally made her feel vaguely uncomfortable.

At six, Jane had been chosen to play the Madonna in the school nativity play, with Virginia as Joseph. The school suggested that they should rehearse together and thus the tea parties began.

'So how's it all going?' Virginia asked Jane when Alex had bathed and gone, and Philly was sleeping soundly in his carrycot.

'Oh not too badly. I must say it's wonderful being here with you, Verge, and seeing Ben and Philly together. It was so sweet the way they both cried and then ate and fell asleep. They're obviously twin souls. No, it was just that Giorgio and I had a bit of a row today at the registry office. He had to come with me to register Philly, you see, to declare that he's his father, but then when we got there, although he did tell the registrar that he was the father; he refused to sign the declaration because he said his Italian lawyer had warned him it could get him into trouble.'

'So does that mean Philly's got no father on his birth certificate?' Virginia exclaimed.

'Well, we only got the short version. That doesn't mention parents at all. And Giorgio can always add his name later when his divorce comes through. I don't blame him really.' But she obviously did, Virginia thought. 'You can go to prison in Italy, you know, for having a child with someone else if the person you're married to chooses to denounce you. I just wish he'd told me before getting there that he wasn't prepared to sign.'

'How's his divorce going?'

'Well, he got his legal separation last Christmas, as you know, just about the time my divorce came through. But what we didn't realize was that under Italian law you have to wait five years from a legal separation to get your divorce. We thought it was five years from an *actual* separation. So just because Giorgio didn't rush off and get a legal separation the moment the old bag buggered off we've lost two years.'

'But couldn't they have come to some arrangement? I thought she wanted to marry someone else.'

'She did. She left Giorgio for this Spanish diplomat and told him she wanted to remarry as soon as possible. But when our lawyer suggested they backdate the separation she said no. Something must have made her change her mind.'

'Maybe she saw you and thought Giorgio must be worth having after all!'

'Thanks.' Jane laughed. 'More likely she suspected I was pregnant and thought she could screw more money

8

out of him if she resisted. But Giorgio's far too crafty', she went on bitterly, 'to give in to that sort of pressure. I'm sure she'd have agreed to backdating the separation if he'd made her some sort of offer, but he wouldn't. So what if he can't marry me or legitimize Philly for another five years? All he cares about is not giving her a penny more than the law says she's entitled to.' She fumbled around in her bag and got out a cigarette.

'Not smoking again?' Virginia asked her.

'I bought my first packet in nine months today,' Jane admitted. 'I'm not like you, Verge, with no vices.'

Virginia didn't smoke or drink and had only slept with two men in her life, though her husband thought it was only one.

'Tell me about you and Robin,' Jane went on.

'We're OK, I guess. The business hasn't been going too well, though, because of the strike.' Showing unexpected enterprise Robin had abandoned the merchant bank for which he had been destined since birth and gone into partnership with his sister to organize a firm of party planners. He did the accounts, while she supervised the catering. But with the almost daily power cuts caused by the miners' strike, Jane could imagine that people hadn't been too keen to risk throwing an expensive party which might at any moment be plunged into darkness.

'Wasn't it a bore?' Jane agreed. 'We'd been getting all our friends in Italy to send us parcels of candles. I must say it was great being in hospital. They had their own generator so there were no cuts.'

'Still, we've got to support the miners.'

'Have we?' Jane knew she must tread carefully. 'I know it's a terrible job,' she conceded, 'but I do think these bully-boy tactics are awful. What about all the poor pensioners dying of cold, and babies in incubators?'

'Yes but we mustn't allow sentimental considerations put out by the Tory government to blind us to what's really going on.'

'But what is going on? Giorgio says the miners are being paid huge sums of money by the Communist Party to stir things up –' She paused. Virginia's expression had assumed a polite but patronizing sneer. Of course she

9

had been to university and Jane hadn't, but Jane had been cleverer than her at school, and just because Giorgio was twenty years older than them didn't necessarily mean he was always wrong. 'I know it sounds far-fetched,' she went on apologetically. As a child of the sixties she was basically indifferent to English politics. They certainly weren't worth risking her long friendship with Virginia over. 'But Giorgio is very in with all the Italian Communists in Venice, you know. They're dead keen on titles over there.' The slight joke fell on stony ground. It was obviously time to change the subject. 'I'm so sorry about the business,' she said.

'Oh we're all right for money,' Virginia replied. 'The firm only supplies a fraction of our income anyway. The rest of it comes from Robin's gambling.'

'Horses?'

'Yes. You know his uncle has that stud in Ireland. He persuaded Robin to invest in half a racehorse, and the bloody thing keeps winning.'

'But that's great!'

Virginia made a face. 'Not so great when Robin spends the whole season going to race meetings. Have you ever been to one, Janie?'

'Ascot once. Warm champagne, deep-frozen strawberries and high heels sinking into the mud –'

'And you can't imagine how boring the people are. I've stopped going with him now. Besides, it's so much against my principles to earn money that way.'

Not against your principles to spend it though, Jane thought. As well as the au pair, Virginia had a Spanish cleaning lady who came every day, and while they were both dressed in jeans – essential uniform really for young mothers who were liable to be shat or regurgitated upon at any moment – Virginia's were topped by a silk shirt from Christian Dior and a beautiful hand-embroidered cardigan from some lethally expensive boutique in South Molton Street. It seemed so sad that having achieved the aristocratic marriage which Virginia and her mother had plotted and schemed towards for five weary years, Virginia should already be showing signs of discontent. Was nobody happy?

'But it's nice not to have to worry about money when you have children,' Jane said wistfully.

'I know. We're planning to have at least four.'

'Four!' Jane exclaimed. 'And you were the one who always vowed you weren't going to have any. I never really asked you what persuaded you to change your mind,' she added curiously.

'I just did.' There was a definite curtness in Virginia's tone. Jane felt momentarily chilled. 'Oh Janie, I'd love a little girl,' she went on impulsively. 'You know how my mother always wanted boys, and Robin was so pleased about Ben because of the title. If I had a little girl she could be just for me.' The sharp lines of her face softened and her dark eyes glowed.

'I'd love one too,' Jane admitted. 'So Philly wouldn't have to be an only child like I was. Giorgio doesn't want any more, though. But if you're planning to have four you're bound to have a girl eventually. It doesn't look as if I ever will.'

'But of course you must. If Giorgio doesn't agree to it you can just go ahead and do it anyway.'

'Perhaps. I don't know if I'd dare. Giorgio made such an awful atmosphere when I was pregnant.'

'But I thought he was fond of children.'

'So did I. He made such a fuss about his first wife taking his children away. I thought having children would be something I could do for him to make up for it. I told him right from the beginning that I wanted them and he agreed, but then when I got pregnant all he could say was that he hadn't thought it would be so soon. God, it was awful. Like a broken record.'

'But you'd been together two years!'

'I know.'

'And he's fond of Philly now, isn't he?'

'I suppose so. Yes of course he is, how could he not be? But it's funny. When he's angry with me he kind of ignores Philly. As if he was part of me but not part of him. And he said this dreadful thing once –' Jane stopped. She hadn't meant to say so much.

'What?' Virginia asked curiously.

'He said, "Every kiss you give Filippo is a kiss stolen

11

from me!" He said it in Italian, of course, it sounds more dramatic that way.' Jane tried to laugh it off. 'It was almost as if he was jealous of his own son.'

'That's quite common. There's a girl at my baby clinic who told me her husband made her stop breastfeeding her baby after only six weeks because it made him so insanely jealous to watch her.'

'No!' Jane exclaimed. 'Oh well then, it's obviously not just Italians who are like that. Robin's not jealous of you and Ben, is he?'

'Oh no. Robin wouldn't dream of being jealous of me.' There was a distinct note of bitterness in Virginia's voice. 'What did you think of Alex?' she said, changing the subject.

'I thought he was really sweet,' Jane replied warmly. 'He told me his wife was ill a lot. What's the matter with her?'

'Nobody really knows. They think it might be some kind of anaemia,' Virginia shrugged. 'I think she puts it on to get attention. Alex's always having affairs, you know.'

'No!' Jane was genuinely horrified. 'And I thought he seemed so nice and straightforward. I was even wishing', she admitted, 'that I had a nice uncomplicated English husband like him.'

Virginia turned to look at her and smiled maliciously.

Looking out of her kitchen window the following evening, Virginia spotted Alex parking his car and, grabbing her purse and keys, went out to meet him.

'Verge!' He seemed delighted to see her and kissed her warmly on both cheeks.

'Hello, Alex.' Her voice was deliberately casual. 'I was just going out to get myself a takeaway. Robin's in Ireland.'

'Seeing a man about a horse?'

'Exactly.' They both laughed. 'Why don't you and Julie pop over later and keep me company?'

'How sweet of you. I'd better just see how she is. We had rather a late night with Seamus and she was very tired this morning.'

'Well, she's had the whole day to get over it,' Virginia began impatiently, and then pulled herself up. Sweetness and sympathy was the key. At all costs she mustn't show how much Julie irritated her. 'How was Seamus?' she asked. Seamus was a dissolute mutual friend from Oxford.

'Oh pissed as usual. There was another couple there. Sandra and Martin Bailey. Have you met them?'

'I don't think so. What do they do?'

'He's a doctor. I really liked him. He had a genuinely healing quality about him, a bit like an angel.'

'What's she like?'

'Nice tits.'

'Alex!' but she rather liked his being risqué. It seemed to bring them closer together.

'But an awful skin, poor girl,' he added, perhaps knowing that only so much praise of another woman was permissible. 'We thought we might ask them over one evening, so you must come and meet them. They seemed really nice, although Seamus told me that Martin has a bit of a roving eye. Sandra did look rather edgy, I must say –'

'I really don't understand why some women are prepared to put up with that sort of thing,' Virginia said querulously. 'Janie was always having her heart broken too by the most dreadful men –'

'What, your friend yesterday?' She found the surprise in his voice extremely irritating.

'Yes. What did you think of her?'

'She's very beautiful, isn't she? The sort of girl I always wanted to go out with when I was younger but could never get –'

'Of course you could have,' she said, annoyed. Why were men so naive as to be overawed by good looks? 'Poor Janie's had millions of affairs. You could have got her easily. Call me later if you want to come over.'

She nodded curtly and walked away. Alex went in to Julie feeling rather sad.

CHAPTER TWO

January 1973

J ane, surrounded by builders' debris, was sitting on a
folding canvas chair in the middle of the studio she
and Giorgio had just bought at the scruffy end of the
Portobello Road. She had one eye on Filippo, who
appeared to be trying to eat a Fisher Price educational
toy, and one eye on the pathway where she was expecting
Virginia and Robin to appear at any moment.

From the kitchen came the reproachful sound of ham-
mering. Occasionally Giorgio's saturnine profile, straight
off a Roman coin, would appear round the door to check
on the lintel and disappear again without acknowledging
her presence. They were in the middle of yet another of
their alarmingly frequent quarrels.

It was depressing, Jane reflected, to be able to pinpoint
so clearly the exact moment in which things had gone
wrong between them. Until the bombshell of the pregnancy test, which Giorgio's Italian doctor had insisted on
after Jane had visited with him with what she thought was
food poisoning, their relationship had been the longest
and most harmonious she had ever experienced.

Jane had arrived in Venice in the late summer of 1969,
lost and terrified after the break-up of her marriage. She
had the address of an American painter who rented out
apartments in a crumbling palazzo on the Giudecca
which he had been left by an adoring older mistress, and

before long was established in a one-bedroomed flat next to the garden with no idea what she was going to do next but only a fixed determination never to return to her former life in London.

Her landlord, Jonathan, was a blond Adonis whose one foray into heterosexual love had proved so profitable that he had decided never to repeat it. He was permanently surrounded by a seraglio of swarthy, snake-hipped boys dressed in the hand-painted caftans he was designing that summer, and was constantly staging happenings in his garden, where string quartets would play inaccessible music of their own composition while an ever-rolling movie camera recorded the proceedings for posterity.

They were all very kind to Jane, draping her in the caftans, exclaiming over her beauty, and speculating endlessly over which of their eligible masculine acquaintances would be good enough for her. Whenever she could, she would escape to a secluded corner of the garden and lie sunbathing under the fig trees, licking her wounds and reflecting on the worthlessness of her life, until dragged out again to participate in some new event.

After three weeks in the company of Jonathan and his entourage, Giorgio seemed refreshingly normal. They met by accident in the street. Jane and Paolo, Jonathan's current favourite, had been despatched to buy provisions for a cocktail party that evening, and on their return, laden with neatly wrapped paper parcels, had caught sight of a dark, athletic-looking man of about forty mooring his boat outside the local antique shop.

'That's Giorgio Orsini,' Paolo hissed to Jane as they approached him. 'He'll do for you. Come on, I'll fix it.'

'Oh honestly, Paolo!' Jane exclaimed. 'Leave the poor man alone for heaven's sake. Why him, anyway?'

'Because his wife's just left him.' Paolo said triumphantly, 'and he's got a boat, so he can show you round. But you're not to marry him,' he added warningly.

'Why not?' Jane laughed.

'Darling,' Paolo stopped walking and looked round cautiously as if about to reveal some unmentionable vice, 'because he is much too straight!'

Jane, trying desperately not to giggle, submitted herself to the introduction as gracefully as she could. Afterwards she realized that in her current frame of mind Paolo could hardly have picked on a description that would have attracted her more, but for the time being she was unable to meet Giorgio's eye and discovered later that he had read this reluctance as an enchanting modesty which had instantly drawn him to her.

Snatching a sideways glimpse at him as he talked to Paolo in Italian, she received a reassuring impression of studiousness, largely created by the strong glasses he wore, which magnified his blue eyes and made them appear deceptively mild. This was no flashy Latin lover, she felt, but someone who, if she did decide to go out with him, would prove both dependable and kind.

Rather to her relief, Giorgio declined Paolo's invitation to the party that evening, inviting them instead to visit him the following day and see a painting he was restoring by an unknown fifteenth-century master. They arranged that he would pick them up in his boat at ten o'clock.

Jane woke at eight and brewed herself a cup of the strong Italian coffee she had come to love before dressing carefully in a red and white silk minidress and slipping her bare feet into low-heeled white pumps. She had managed to escape early from the party the night before, and was feeling refreshed and optimistic. It was good to be meeting a real Venetian who actually worked for his living. Perhaps he might help her find a job that would enable her to stay in Venice. She'd tried to mention the possibility of working to Jonathan and Paolo, but they'd pooh-poohed the suggestion. With her looks, they said, why on earth should she bother to work? If she waited they would find her a prince to support her. So what if she couldn't pay the rent? Winter was coming, and they'd never find anyone else to take the apartment because of the *acqua alta*. She could stay with them free for as long as she liked.

Jane was sure they meant it kindly, but their effusiveness jarred on her English sense of what was correct, and made her feel uneasy and trapped. She realized afterwards that she had already been looking for an escape route.

At 9.50 she went up to Jonathan's apartment on the first floor. Paolo, bleary-eyed, was in the middle of shaving, and told her to station herself by the window so as not to miss Giorgio's approach. The canal was busy at that time of the day, and he might have difficulty in stopping. Giorgio arrived on the dot of ten, and stopped the big boat outside the palazzo. A wide barge full of ironmongery was attempting to pass at the same time, and its driver started to shout and gesticulate, so Jane flung open the window and using an elaborate semi-comical mime, signalled to Giorgio that she and Paolo would be down in five minutes.

'I fell in love with you at that moment,' Giorgio told her later when their affair had begun. 'An Italian girl would have hidden behind the shutters and pretended not to see me, but you were so open, so honest. I knew then that you were the woman for me.'

Jane, astonished, had attempted to disclaim the credit for merely obeying Paolo's orders, but her protestations had only increased his conviction of her ingenuousness. Finally she had given in and allowed him to keep his misconception since it seemed to please him so much. She didn't realize that in doing so she was paving the way to permitting him all the other misconceptions which would inevitably follow.

The palazzo in which Giorgio lived had been in his family since the seventeenth century. His father had died ten years before, leaving seven children from different, acrimonious liaisons. Giorgio, as the eldest son, had inherited the palazzo, but not the income necessary to maintain it. He had therefore converted it into apartments, keeping the main one for himself and selling off the others.

Jane's first thought as she entered the high-ceilinged drawing room with its marble floors, Persian rugs and vast balcony overlooking the canal, was that it was far more like a museum than a home. Every inch of wall space was covered with paintings, bookcases, antique plates and framed portions of tapestry, hung in an inspired disorder with little regard to period or coherence.

The painting they had come to look at, a pietà, stood on an easel in the centre of the room with Giorgio's work tray and stool beside it. The Madonna was not the fresh-faced young beauty of more traditional works, but a careworn, elderly woman with greying hair and lines of grief etched on her features as she gazed down at the pale body of her dead son.

Paolo started to coo over the artist's technique, the beauty of the perspective and the menace of the lowering sky whose colours Giorgio's restoration had so expertly revealed, while Jane, embarrassed at being so ignorant about art, wandered over to the balcony and stood gazing in fascination at the patterns of light reflected from the water which danced on the ceiling above them.

Later, when the men had moved away from the canvas and gone into the kitchen to make coffee she went softly back to stare at the face of the Madonna. Mingled with her grief, Jane now saw, was a smile of tenderness that seemed to encompass all the years in which she had bathed and clothed her son as a helpless child only to bring him to this point where, helpless once more, she must bathe and clothe him for his tomb. More touching even than the tenderness, her smile showed an unques-tioning acceptance of the rightness of the principle which had led to his death, even though, in her humility, she appeared not fully able to comprehend it.

A rush of tears came to Jane's eyes. She had suffered a miscarriage at three months shortly before her marriage had ended, and was still feeling emotional about it. The painting seemed to show her for the first time exactly what it meant to be a mother.

Giorgio, entering the room silently with her coffee, saw her expression before she was able to turn away. Once more he misunderstood. He saw her tears as an appreciation of the artist's greatness rather than a sympathy with the emotion of his subject. It led him to think he would be able to make her his pupil.

*   *   *

Jane knew this because he told her so the following day after they had become lovers. He had arranged to take her and Paolo on a boat trip to the islands, but Paolo had cried off at the last moment leaving Jane, unsuspecting, to step into the boat alone. For Venetians the season was now over, but by English standards it was still high summer. Jane wore a bikini under her dress and to Giorgio's amusement was carrying a beach towel and sun cream.

On Giorgio's recommendation they skipped the garish glass factories of Murano and proceeded straight to Burano where they left the boat in the care of a little lady with a lace stall, who smiled toothlessly at Jane and pronounced her *'Molto bella'* when she bought some embroidered handkerchiefs.

Their lunch, at Romano, of shellfish and salad washed down by a deceptively light white wine, was one of the most delicious Jane had ever had. Giorgio's English had an endearingly childlike quality as he told her about the break-up of his twenty-year marriage to a German who had never really liked Venice and who had been making up her mind to leave ever since the birth of their second child, but had only got round to it earlier that year, when she met a Spanish diplomat who had taken her and the two children to live in Paris.

'How sad!' Jane exclaimed. 'You must miss them terribly.'

'Of course. But she say they choose Paris especially for me. I suppose I am lucky she didn't take them to Africa or South America.' he shrugged.

Jane thought how unselfish he was, and what a bitch his wife must be to take his children away from him.

She explained that her marriage too had recently broken up and that because the divorce looked likely to be a messy one she was anxious not to return to England for a while.

'I was wondering if I could get a job here,' she went on. 'I do speak some Italian. I've been in a couple of films in Rome and done some TV commercials in Milan, but I don't really want to go back to that.'

The legend that actresses were bitchy, she reflected,

must definitely have originated in Italy, and as her understanding of Italian had improved, she had been shocked
and mortified to overhear the speculations on her
sexual prowess put forward by motley crew members who
had always seemed so respectful and charming when
speaking English to her face. Venice, by contrast, seemed
infinitely more restful and inviting.

'No, no,' he agreed. 'Why go to Rome? Venice is so
beautiful. I show you.'

'Yes, but I must work,' she insisted. 'I'm OK for money
at the moment, and Jonathan's terribly sweet and says it
doesn't matter about the rent, but I couldn't stay there
unless I paid my way. He did mention some artist friend
of his who was looking for a model. Gigi somebody –'

'Gigi Lupo!' Giorgio scowled. 'A terrible man. You
must not go there. Let me think. I find you something.'

'What I'd really like to do is help people somehow,'
she confessed. 'When I was acting I used to visit old
people in hospitals –'

'Yes, but here old people stay at home with their
families,' he reminded her.

'Well, that's much nicer of course. But there must be
some charities?'

'There is nothing,' he assured her. 'The Americans
and English give money to the Italians to save Venice,
and the Italians spend it all on their own palazzi.' Rather
to her surprise she was to discover later that he was
absolutely right. 'Do not worry, Jane,' he went on. 'I will
find you something. Believe me.' And for the moment
they left it at that.

As they meandered back to the boat after lunch, Jane
felt as if she were floating on waves of white wine and
optimism. How stupid she was to worry so much about
the future when she was young and healthy and safe in
Venice from the nightmare of her marriage. She trusted
Giorgio and felt certain he would help her if he could,
but for the moment all she wanted to do was lie down
in the sun and go to sleep. When he proposed that
they should leave Torcello for another day and just
cruise round the islands, she accepted eagerly, sinking
down gratefully onto the blue and white mattress which

occupied most of the free space on the boat, and in spite of her efforts to admire the view, falling almost instantly into a heavy, dreamless slumber.

She awoke to find that the boat had stopped and Giorgio was beside her on the mattress kissing her passionately. She felt quite unreasonably surprised. Nothing in their previous acquaintance had led her to expect this, but she told herself he probably deserved a kiss after the delicious lunch he had bought her. A moment later his hand was up her skirt. This was really too much. She tried to remove it gently, but to her annoyance it refused to budge and she soon found herself engaged in a desperate struggle.

As he started to fumble with his trousers, she seized her advantage and flung him off her and stood up. This was her cue to walk out, but a quick glance round her showed that the boat was moored in the middle of the lagoon with no land in sight and absolutely no clue as to the direction from which they had come.

'I think I'll go in for a swim,' she tried to keep her voice calm. Perhaps he'd just got carried away for a moment. At all cost she mustn't show him she had been frightened. She slipped her dress quickly over her head and jumped into the water in her bikini.

There was a splash as he dived into the water and grabbed her from behind. He was now naked. She felt his penis rubbing against her buttocks. She swam towards the side of the boat, afraid she would drown. Once there, she raised her arms above her head and sank downwards. She held her breath for as long as possible, but could feel nothing but water. Obviously she was hopelessly out of her depth.

Eventually she was forced to return to the surface, only to find him beside her once more. It was beginning to look, she told herself in astonishment, as if she might actually end up being raped. 'Look,' she said finally, 'will you please just leave me alone for a moment to swim?' and kicking out blindly without worrying unduly which part of him she might be injuring, she turned away and struck out into the green water.

And now what? she asked herself a few minutes later after ascertaining that he had temporarily abandoned his pursuit and was clinging rather dejectedly to the side of the boat. She was a strong swimmer and there was nothing much he could do to her while they were in the water, but the fact remained that she was totally dependent on him for getting back to Venice, and eventually she would be forced to return to the boat.

Of course she could always threaten to report him. She wasn't entirely friendless in Venice, but what if she did so and the case came to court?

'Do you mean to tell me, signora,' his Italian counsel would say with an incredulous smile, 'that you, a married woman, accepted an invitation to go unchaperoned and provocatively dressed into the boat of a married man, and honestly had no idea that he would place a sexual connotation on your behaviour?' Well, she had, that's all, and since she doubted whether the threat of exposure would do either of them any good, she was obviously going to have to think of some other way to salvage the situation.

And what if she did let him make love to her? All through lunch she had been thinking how kind he seemed and that she would probably enjoy herself far more in Venice if she had him to escort her around. Obviously this would mean sleeping with him sooner or later. He was much older than her usual type, of course, but he looked at least ten years younger than his age and had a good, athletic body. The fact that he had been married for so long presumably meant that he knew how to satisfy a woman and it had been nearly two months now since her own marriage had ended. Nearly two months since she'd come with a man. Might it not be rather interesting to see if she still could?

She turned and swam back towards him. He was still hovering by the side of the boat, and as she approached him his face assumed the eager expression of a dog awaiting a command. She grasped at the ladder, and then turned her head deliberately and smiled at him. If she knew her Italians as well as she thought she did, it would be encouragement enough.

She climbed into the boat with self-conscious grace and draped herself artistically across the mattress as if she was posing for a centrefold. She didn't have long to wait. With a quick bound which was as athletically impressive as it was erotically incongruous, he was over the side and on top of her, ripping down her bikini bottoms and plunging into her with a clumsy over-eagerness which boded ill for her own chances of satisfaction. Her temporary sense of being in control of the situation vanished once more as he pounded away. Where was the famed finesse of the Latin lover now, she asked herself as he came inside her after a few short strokes, leaving her bruised and breathless with disappointment.

A moment later he had pulled out of her and, still panting, slid down between her legs and started to kiss her. She felt a moment of acute embarrassment. He couldn't kiss her there. She must taste disgusting, dripping with sea water and semen. She made a movement to push him away, which proved as unavailing as had her earlier struggles, so that after a moment she stopped. Well then, let him if he wants to, she thought. Why shouldn't I get something out of this too? And so she lay back and relaxed, and abandoned herself to her own lonely pleasure.

Afterwards he was like a child in his enthusiasm.

'That was so beautiful, so wonderful,' he told her tenderly, his eyes soft and melting without their glasses. 'The moment I saw you I knew you were right for me. With most women there is something which disturbs – the laugh, the way they walk – but with you, nothing. You were so beautiful and so modest when I met you with Paolo. You would not look at me, so the next day, when you call me from the window, my heart jumped with happiness. And I watch you as you look at my painting. I see the tears in your eyes. I see that you understand art. Jane, I will teach you all I know. We will travel together. I will show you the treasures of Italy. You will be my help and inspiration and I will love you for ever.'

Jane listened to him in astonishment. Did the poor

fool think that just because he had screwed her she was going to fall in love with him? It seemed that he did. There was no doubting his sincerity. She had seen that sick calf's look in men's eyes often enough to realize that he was genuinely besotted with her. Her astonishment melted away and was replaced by an almost maternal sense of compassion. She realized how easy it would be to hurt him, and could hardly bear to listen to his dreams any more, knowing with certainty that she was bound to disappoint them. She buried her head in his chest so as not to have to see the expression in his eyes, and soon they were making love once more.

From this unlikely beginning their relationship grew up. At first, knowing she was not in love with him, she resisted his urgent invitations to move in with him, but eventually, as her money started to run out, she gave in. She was already seeing him every day, and knew that in a small, gossipy town like Venice she could not have gone out with anyone else without causing him terrible offence. There was no one else she wanted to go out with anyway. It would only have meant another undignified struggle, and since she'd got over the hurdle of sleeping with Giorgio and found it pleasant enough, she felt she might as well stick with him. At least his presence protected her from Jonathan and Paolo's plans to market her as a saleable piece of flesh, and by now it was obvious to her that, as a foreign tourist with no qualifications, no job offers were likely to materialize.

Their life together suited her very well. She would sleep all morning while Giorgio went about his business, and in the afternoons they would take a picnic lunch to the lagoon and swim and sunbathe from the boat. As the weather grew colder, they walked endlessly together through the streets of Venice with him pointing out small corners of beauty which couldn't be found in the guidebooks, and stopping for dinner in some delicious out-of-the-way trattoria when they were tired. He introduced her to his family, who welcomed her with the same unquestioning acceptance that he had, telling her how pleased they were that he had found happiness again, and exclaiming over the renewed youthfulness of his appearance.

He kept his promise to show her Italy. They travelled to Florence that October and booked into a *pensione* overlooking the Arno from which they went on excursions to Fiesole and to see the treasures of the Uffizi and Bargello, later winding their way by train to Ravello where they stayed high on the hill in a villa owned by some friends of his. Jane's bedroom had once been slept in by Greta Garbo. It had its own balcony where she breakfasted each morning under the shade of a pergola, before strolling with Giorgio down a terrace lined with sculptures and cypress trees which boasted a spectacular view of the sea. She embarked on a crash course in Italian literature, and thought how different Giorgio was from the characters she came across in the works of Machiavelli and Benvenuto Cellini, and how lucky she was to have found him.

That Christmas, they paid a quick visit to England. Jane introduced Giorgio to her father and a few of her closest friends, all of whom were unanimous in their approval of him and delighted that Jane seemed to be settling down at last. On their return to Italy just, as Jane told herself angrily, when she felt safe and should have been so happy, she inexplicably went into a deep depression, which manifested itself as a terror of death. She couldn't sleep at night for fear that the house would burn down, couldn't go into a vaporetto in case it should sink with her trapped inside the cabin, couldn't walk out alone in case she suffered a brain haemorrhage and fell dying in the street. She became totally dependent on Giorgio, and he rose to her need magnificently, comforting and holding her through her midnight terrors and enveloping her in a blanket of peace, love and security.

As she got better, she started to keep a diary in order to remember all the places to which he had taken her, and almost every entry would end with a small paean of thanks to fate for bringing them together and allowing her to bask in the selfless love of this saintly older man who had, quite simply, been her saviour.

* * *

And then, without warning, everything had changed on a sunny morning in August, two years after Jane's arrival in Venice. She was in the kitchen, tearing up fresh basil leaves to put on the mozzarella and tomato salad. Giorgio was expected imminently, and their friend Helmut Behrens, an immaculately elegant German homosexual of sixty-seven was sitting at the kitchen table in a perfectly pressed linen suit drinking a large whisky and flicking disdainfully through the *Gazzettino*.

'Terrible paper,' he commented in his perfect, almost accentless English, as she walked past him to the balcony where the lunch table had been set for three.

'Oh I know.' Yes, everything was ready. The sauce was prepared, with the huge pan of water simmering on the stove so she could throw the pasta in the second Giorgio arrived. 'But we have to get it because it's the only one that tells you what's going on in Venice.'

'My dear, nothing goes on in Venice. That is why I chose it.' Helmut was a former newscaster who had retired two years before on a large pension which enabled him to rent an apartment in Venice all the year round, while still spending his winters in Germany. 'Nothing that you can read about here, at any rate.' He gave her a wicked smile.

'How was Jonathan's party last night?' Jane recognized her cue. They had actually met through Jonathan, and liked each other instantly. Giorgio, who felt secure because of Helmut's age and sexual proclivities, had put up no objections to their friendship, and had been very helpful in finding Helmut his flat, which was on the same *fondamenta* as theirs. Jane and Helmut shared an enjoyment of the fashionable watering holes, such as Harry's Bar and the Cipriani, which Giorgio professed to despise, and would sometimes sneak off for a quick Bellini or a browse round the boutiques. They giggled endlessly together and exchanged the most unabashed confidences. She had come to look on him as her best friend in Venice.

'Not bad. I met rather a dishy Englishman. A stockbroker, I think. I asked him if he'd like to have lunch with me one day but he said, "No, thank you. I'm married, you see, and he wouldn't like it.'" Jane giggled. 'But why didn't you come?' he went on. 'We were all talking about you. Jonathan said you had become the most beautiful woman in Venice and, you know,' he looked at her sideways, 'I think he is right.'

Jane blushed. 'It's not true, of course, but it's terribly sweet of you to tell me. I'm afraid I don't spend nearly enough time on my appearance compared to Italian women.' But she knew her looks had improved since living with Giorgio. The puppy fat she had battled with during her adolescence had melted away, and she had stopped biting her nails and let her hair grow thick and shining to below her shoulders.

'Perhaps it suits you not to spend time,' he suggested.

'I think you're right,' she agreed. 'It seems so ironic when I remember all those years I spent staring into a mirror when my career depended on my looks, and hating what I saw. Now I just put on my makeup in five minutes and I'm away.'

'And where were you away to last night?'

'Some dealer friend of Giorgio's. He had a painting for Giorgio to restore. He's terribly excited about it. He thinks it might be a fragment of a Tintoretto – or was it a Veronese?' she frowned.

'Don't you care?'

'Not terribly. Oh I know it's awful of me. It's just that I used to get so attached to some of the paintings. There was this pietà Giorgio was working on when we first met. He even let me clean some of the background. I loved it so much. When he sold it I felt as if I'd lost a friend. I know it's unreasonable of me. Giorgio's got to earn a living, after all. I just don't think I have the right mentality for a dealer, so I tend to kind of block out the things he buys so I won't mind him selling them.'

'Doesn't he mind you blocking them out?'

'Well, I think he'd hoped I'd be more interested in his work, but he's very good about it. After all we can still go on buying trips together. I'm perfectly happy to follow him round as long as I've got a good book and can curl up in the sun somewhere and read it.'

'Like a pet dog,' he commented, 'that can be shown off and patted on the head when it gets bored.'

'I suppose I am,' she agreed lightly. It was a pity about Helmut's waspish side, but he was old and lonely and she wouldn't let it annoy her. 'Better that than being kicked in the teeth, I suppose.'

'Oh undoubtedly,' he agreed lazily. 'And does Giorgio share your love of reading?'

'Not really,' she smiled indulgently. 'At first I used to get him some of my favourite books translated into Italian. He was very sweet. He started them all. But then we used to talk about them and he'd get the characters from one book muddled up with those from another. I do see,' she went on, 'that we don't really have anything in common – he's so active and capable, and I'm just lazy and useless – in fact it's really quite amazing how incredibly happy we are together.'

She heard Giorgio's key in the lock and went out to the hall to greet him. She could see at once that something was wrong. He was frowning and looked suddenly haggard and old.

'What is it, darling?' She put her hand on his forehead. 'Have you got a migraine?'

'No, no.' He moved away from her to put down the parcel he was carrying.

'Did you get the painting?' She was puzzled. Could his friend have let him down and decided to sell it to someone else?

'Yes, I got the painting, and then afterwards I go to Franco and get this.' He handed her a piece of paper.

'What is it?' but as she took it she knew. Even before her eyes had focused on the freshly typed 'POSITIVO' which loomed under the medical gibberish at the top of the page. 'Oh my God, it can't be!'

'Oh but it is!' His voice was loud and sarcastic and she recoiled from the smell of alcohol on his breath. But Giorgio never drank before lunch. He seemed so angry. Surely he couldn't be angry with her? She was as surprised as he was. 'Helmut's here,' she said warningly.

'*Porca madonna!*' He banged his head with his fist. 'I'd forgotten.'

'Did you remember the bread?' It suddenly seemed terribly important to concentrate on the small issues in order to avoid having to deal with the main one.

'No,' he said wearily. 'I forgot it.'

'I'll go and get it, shall I?' Jane was glad of the excuse to run away. 'It's not quite twelve thirty. They'll still be open.'

'No, I will go.' He turned and went out of the door without another word, while Jane braced herself to go back into the kitchen, the piece of paper still clutched in her hand.

'I helped myself,' Helmut said cheerfully, pointing to the full tumbler in front of him. And then he looked up at her. 'My dear, what is the matter?'

'I seem to be pregnant. Look.' She handed him the piece of paper. It didn't occur to her not to tell him. He'd have to know sometime after all.

'Well, congratulations!' he smiled. 'Would you like me to be his fairy godmother?'

'Oh Helmut –' She tried to smile. 'Yes. Oh I don't know. It's just such a shock.'

'But why should it be a shock? Don't tell me Giorgio is a *sodomita?*'

'No, of course not.'

Actually their sex life had varied very little from that first occasion in the boat. He would enter her without foreplay and satisfy himself while she waited patiently until he had finished and was ready to bring her to orgasm with his tongue. A bit predictable, perhaps, but at least she knew he would always satisfy her. 'It's just that I haven't had the symptoms.'

'Then why did you have this test?'

'Well, I suddenly started feeling sick about a week ago. I thought it was a stomach upset. Giorgio's doctor made me have the test, but I never thought . . . We joked about it. I said Italian doctors always reduced everything to sex. Oh God!' She sat down and buried her face in her hands.

'Don't be upset, my dear. Were you taking no precautions?'

'I came off the pill about four months ago,' she told him. 'I was having some side effects and my doctor in England advised it. Giorgio and I agreed that we'd use the safe period. I've been using it on and off for seven years,' she added defensively, 'and it's always worked.'

'Just because something works for seven years doesn't mean that it will always work,' he pointed out.

'Well, you're obviously right,' she said bitterly, 'but I can't think . . . There was one day,' she was talking more to herself than him, 'about a month after I came off the pill, when we took a bit of a risk. My period was three days late and I got very frightened, but then it came and I've had two more since then. In fact, I've got one now. But they have been very light. Oh God. Do you think that means I'm three months pregnant?' she asked in horror.

'Maybe. But does that matter?'

'Yes! Oh Helmut, I know you're Catholic and anti-abortion, but Giorgio and I are both married to other people. I don't see how we can . . . The thing is,' she tried to speak calmly, 'that if I was just a few days late I think I could probably bear to get rid of it, but if I'm three months and it's already formed, there's absolutely no way I could do it.'

'Of course you must not do it,' he said firmly. 'You were just telling me how happy you are with Giorgio. You plan to marry one day, don't you?'

'I don't know,' Jane said frankly. She loved Giorgio. Of course she did. But could she really bear to be stuck in Venice for the rest of her life? 'We've never really got any further than thinking about our divorces.'

'At least you are in good company,' he pointed out. 'Every couple I meet here is married to someone else.'

'Well, they do seem to be,' Jane agreed. 'There's such a backlog on divorces because of the act only having come in two years ago.' In a way she had found the social work she'd been looking for when she'd first arrived. Through her doctor in London she had fixed up innumerable Italian friends, including one of Giorgio's sisters, with English gynaecologists and hospital beds.

England was the only European country which allowed any child born there automatically to take British nationality and whatever surname the parents chose. 'I suppose it's a good thing I'm English if I do have an illegitimate baby,' she tried to sound more positive. 'but, oh God, why do I have to be the only woman in the world who has periods when she's pregnant so I don't find out about it until it's too late?'

Helmut drank a mouthful of whisky. 'Has it occurred to you my dear,' he said, 'that each child chooses its parents and that perhaps your baby wants very much to be born?'

Lunch was decidedly sticky. Jane had started to feel very sick, and when Giorgio realized that she had confided in Helmut he shot her such a look of animosity that she felt quite terrified, while Helmut's congratulations to him on his impending fatherhood only seemed to rub salt into the wound. Jane felt quite relieved when Helmut announced that he must leave early.

'I'll call you later after my siesta,' he said to her at the door. 'Perhaps we can go and get the English papers at San Marco and have a cup of tea at Florian's?'

'I'd have loved to, Helmut, but I think I'd better stay at home and discuss things.' She glanced through to the drawing room where Giorgio had flung himself moodily onto the sofa.

'Of course.' He kissed her on both cheeks. 'Be brave, Jane. It will be all right.'

'Yes.' She smiled wanly and shut the door behind him, then straightened her shoulders and walked into the nightmare.

The doorbell rang, and Jane, glad to be relieved from such painful memories, sprang to answer it. Today's row was only a comparatively minor one, and she hoped that the arrival of their friends would enable Giorgio to snap out of his mood without losing face.

'Giorgio darling,' she called brightly. 'Do come. Virginia and Robin are here.'

'Janie!' Virginia was the first to enter, elegantly

31

pregnant in a dark green suede coat and black boots, her subtly hennaed hair swinging and shining in an expensively cut bob. Benjamin, a blond, rosy one-year-old, pushed past her, making a beeline for the toy box, the contents of which he proceeded to tip all over the floor and trample on to the delight of Philly and the annoyance of Jane, who waited in vain for Virginia to rebuke him.

'Hi, Janie.' Robin's recently grown beard was a definite success, disguising his aristocratically weak chin and giving him a new-found air of maturity. He was dressed in jeans and a leather jacket, and since the previous winter had acquired a definite twinkle, the source of which, Jane hoped for Virginia's sake, was not an illicit one.

'Sorry we're late,' he said, after he had kissed her. 'I've been interviewing secretaries all day. The last one was absolutely stunning. Looked just like Bianca Jagger.'

'Did you hire her?' Jane asked, smiling.

'No, I didn't. I simply couldn't have trusted myself alone with her for a moment.'

Jane glanced instinctively at Virginia to see if she minded, and then, realizing how annoying such a look of enquiry would be, turned it into a social smile as she led them towards the kitchen.

It had been some time before Jane was allowed to meet Robin. Jane's mother had died when she was thirteen, and shortly afterwards she had persuaded her father to send her to stage school. Virginia had changed schools at the same time, but she and Jane still managed to meet at least once a week, and sometimes Jane felt that Virginia was her only link with the past and her happy, secure childhood.

At fourteen they had both had crushes on film stars, and had taken it in turns to accompany each other to their beloveds' films. Jane could still remember the shock she'd felt when Virginia had informed her that her idol was homosexual. She had mourned for a while, and then transferred her affections to men of flesh and blood. Virginia, however, had continued to idolize her film star far past the normal age, and to criticize Jane's boyfriends mercilessly until her relationships with them ended, when she would immediately discover hidden virtues in them and occasionally go out with them herself.

As Jane grew up and started sleeping with her boyfriends, she became more wary of introducing them to Virginia. She didn't make a conscious decision not to. It was more of an instinctive feeling that it would be wiser not to court trouble if at all possible. In the past Virginia had been known to ring Jane's men up and then report back to her gleefully that they had asked her out. Now that Jane's emotions were more deeply involved she knew it would be harder to shrug off that type of interference. The difference in their life styles made this avoidance comparatively easy. Jane was getting a lot of work abroad, and when in London would often have to go to bed early in order to get up at five to film. Virginia was still at school, and studying frantically for her A levels.

At eighteen, Virginia auditioned for drama school and was turned down. At this point, in Jane's view, she sold out. Virginia's mother Maria, who had come to England as a refugee from Poland before the war, was a dedicated social climber who was desperate that her daughter should avoid the sort of terrors and insecurities she herself had known as a young girl. She now determined that Virginia should become a debutante in order to capture a suitable husband. The photos of Virginia's film star were taken down from her bedroom walls and replaced by a silver-framed studio portrait of Robin Askew, who was neither attractive nor successful with women but whose elder brother was an earl, and reputedly a confirmed homosexual who would never produce an heir.

Jane had finally been allowed to meet Robin at a small dinner-dance Virginia gave towards the end of the season, when their relationship was safely established. She'd heard vague reports of Maria's plans from Virginia, but had not taken them seriously. Surely it was impossible to give your daughter an English education and then expect her to conduct her life according to a hopelessly outdated pre-war continental set of rules? Even if you did, such an expectation was bound to be doomed to failure. Jane had enjoyed the dance, but with typical vagueness had not caught Robin's surname when he was introduced to her. The next day, when Virginia rang her up to ask her what she thought of him, she had been forced to improvise frantically.

'Robin?' she asked in surprise. 'Your Robin? He wasn't there, was he?'

'Of course he was. He was sitting next to me at dinner. He said he had a chat to you about acting afterwards.'

Heavens. She'd received a vague impression of chinlessness, spots, and a loud whinnying laugh. Christopher, Virginia's brother, had come up and asked her to dance in the middle of the conversation, and she had accepted gratefully.

'Was that *your* Robin?'

'Yes of course it was.'

'Oh Verge, I'm sorry. You must think I'm hopeless. It was just that the music was starting right at that moment and I must have heard his name wrong.'

'Well, what did you think of him?'

'I thought he was very nice.' Jane hoped her voice didn't have a false ring to it. Actually, he had seemed quite nice. It was just that whenever Jane met a man she divided him into one of two categories – possible or impossible – and Robin had definitely belonged to the latter. She did reflect for a moment that if she herself had produced him for Virginia's appraisal, Virginia would no doubt have proceeded to make mincemeat of her. But one of the main differences between the two girls was that Jane had always had a horror of hurting people. She searched frantically for something else to say in Robin's favour, but Virginia spoke first.

'Of course I know he's not good-looking, and he has that dreadful voice, but he's terribly sweet really.'

'I'm sure he is.' In those two sentences Virginia's plea for mercy had been recognized and accepted. Inexplicable as it might seem to Jane, Virginia had obviously decided to obey her mother's wishes.

Strangely, it had not proved easy for Virginia to land

34

Robin. Perhaps the very fact that he had been rejected by a lot of women in the past made him wary of being so avidly desired by Maria and Virginia. He had seduced Virginia and then, a year later, abandoned her completely, and she had gone around looking hunted and desperate. Jane realized that awful as it was to be rejected by someone you loved, it must be even worse to be rejected by someone you didn't.

Virginia had gone to university and eventually started an affair with a good-looking boy in her year, but her mother had caught them in bed together and thrown him out of the house. A concerted family effort was then made to get Robin back. Christopher, Virginia's brother, had invited him to lunch, and Virginia had appeared 'accidentally' at the end, fresh from the hairdresser, in a stunning new dress. Robin hadn't been able to get anyone else in their time apart and was ready to resume the relationship, but this time he wasn't allowed to back out. As a last-ditch attempt at escape he had flown to India to join an expedition that was touring the country in Land Rovers and planning to stay away for at least a year. The leader of the expedition had been felled by dysentery in Calcutta before they could set out, and the party had disbanded. Not knowing what else to do, Robin had returned to London, and some months later a large, engraved wedding invitation had plopped onto Jane's doormat.

But now all these dramas were long forgotten. Marriage and maturity had improved Robin beyond measure. In fact, Jane reflected, if one of the chief rules of her personal code of honour had not been that her friends' men were automatically untouchable, she might even have fancied him herself. From a outsider's point of view the marriage was an undoubted success, and Jane was sure that any secret dissatisfaction Verge might feel would disappear with the birth of her baby, who would surely be the little girl she longed for so much.

To Jane's great relief Giorgio was smiling as he emerged from the kitchen, arm outstretched, to shake their hands.

'Verge, Robin, it's good to see you! Would you like a cup of tea?'

'Why don't you come back to us for tea?' Virginia's eyes had swept the room and found it wanting. 'I got a huge chocolate cake in the market and we can light the fire.'

'Oh how lovely!' Jane exclaimed. She had begun to get cold in the unheated studio, and there was really nowhere for them all to sit. 'We could do that, couldn't we, Giorgio? It's nearly five o'clock.'

'Gianna, you know that I'm obliged to stay here until Joe leaves,' he answered coldly, the Italianization of her name, which she had at first found so romantic, now seeming merely a deindividualization, making her one with all the other foreign girlfriends whose names he had converted to Italian in the past.

'Oh yes, of course. Joe's our Italian builder,' she explained to the others. 'He's absolutely marvellous. He and Giorgio are doing the whole conversion by themselves. But he'll be going soon, won't he, Giorgio?'

Giorgio shrugged.

'Well then, you can come back with us when we've seen the house, Janie, and Giorgio can follow when he's finished,' Virginia said firmly. 'It's only a ten-minute walk. What are you going to show us first?'

Giorgio took Robin into the garden, while Jane and Virginia went into the kitchen to get Ben a drink.

'I think it's going to be great, Janie,' said Virginia, approving the Italian terracotta floor tiles and huge pine dresser. 'Well done.'

'I only found it, and paid the deposit with those shares my mother left me. It was dirt cheap. You know how much property prices have fallen recently. There was a passageway here before and three little rooms, which Giorgio's knocked down to make the studio bigger, but there's a bedroom and bathroom off here which we're going to rent to a friend of ours who teaches at the Italian school in Notting Hill Gate, which should pay off the mortgage. And it's in my name because I can't own anything in Venice until we're married –'

'What's the latest on that?'

'Unspeakable. I meant to write to you about it but I was too depressed.'

'Come on. Tell me about it quick before they come back.'

They went into the living room. Ben was now occupied in throwing particles of educational toy at the walls while Philly watched him enraptured. Virginia gave him his drink which he promptly hurled to the ground.

'Oh dear. I'll get you a cloth, shall I, Benny so you can mop it up?' said Jane crouching down to his level to pick up the plastic cup.

'Oh leave it, Janie,' Virginia said impatiently. 'I'll do it. Go and see Daddy, Ben,' she added and opened the back door and shoved him outside. 'Come on, Janie, they'll be ages.'

Jane's temporary irritation was forgotten in the desire to pour out her woes. 'You remember Giorgio's children were coming to stay with us in August?' she said. 'Well, his wife took it into her head to come too. She and lover boy stayed with a friend of theirs who has a huge palazzo on the same *fondamenta* as ours and rents out apartments. It meant she was walking past our house all the time and we couldn't go to any of our favourite restaurants without getting the waiters to check first if she was there. I was quite keen to just brazen it out but the children begged us not to and I think they were right. She's quite mad, you know.'

'Is she really?'

'Yes. I discovered it runs in her family. Her father was schizophrenic. It got so I was scared to take Philly out in the pram on my own in case she attacked him.'

'My God. Does she look mad?'

'She used to be very pretty when she was young. A bit like Ingrid Bergman, but she sure as hell isn't any more. Do you remember my friend Helmut?' Verge and Robin had spent a fortnight in Venice the previous spring. They'd got Giorgio to book them into a nearby *pensione*, then changed dates twice, driving him into such a black rage that it had taken all Jane's coaxing to persuade him to see them when they finally arrived. She herself had been rather shocked that they'd left Ben in London to

37

spend his first birthday with the au pair, but it had been so wonderful to have them there as allies that she would have forgiven them a far greater sin than that, though she did sometimes wonder if Ben's increasingly disruptive behaviour didn't stem from Verge's alternate spoiling and neglect.

'Helmut?' Virginia asked. 'What, that terribly distinguished-looking German queen?'

'That's right. Oh Verge, he's such a lifeline to me. It was he really who persuaded us that we should go ahead and have Philly, so you can imagine how much he means to me. Anyway, his apartment's in the same palazzo where Giorgio's wife stayed. One day, just after she'd arrived, a parcel came for him which he'd had sent to us for safekeeping because the Italian postmen are so hopeless over foreign names. I decided to take it straight round to him. There was this funny little man standing outside his house on the *fondamenta*, who was staring at me as if I was something the dog had brought in. I thought it was maybe because I was wearing my purple hotpants and boots. Anyway, he just stood there, not even moving aside for me when I rang Helmut's bell, and then followed me in, and I saw this middle-aged woman in the courtyard, kind of blocking my way. I felt quite threatened for a moment, as if they were closing in on me. Then Helmut appeared at his window – he's on the ground floor fortunately – and I said "I've got your parcel for you." I went in and he just said to me, "So it's happened at last," and then I realized the couple were Giorgio's wife and her lover and you know, Verge, I just couldn't believe it. There was my great rival. A hideous fat old German hausfrau!'

Virginia giggled loyally. 'I didn't realize she was German.'

'Well, she pretends to be Danish because apparently everyone in Europe was so anti-German after the war and she couldn't get a job. That was when she met Giorgio and latched on to him.'

'So did she make friends with Helmut?'

'Oh no. She's into confrontation. Poor Helmut had a terrible time once she knew he was friends with me. He was waiting for his telephone to be installed and had to use one in the hall. She used to lie in wait for him and every time he went to use it she'd barge in front of him and say, "*Permesso*". She wouldn't even speak German to him. And the night before the children were leaving, Giorgio took their cases round to her and she unpacked all the clothes we'd bought them – beautiful Italian children's clothes, Verge – and hung them on the wrought-iron grille outside our house. I happened to be looking out of the window and she saw me and shrieked, "*Puttana!*" up at me.'

'What does that mean?'

'Prostitute!'

'Jesus!'

'I know. And it's so illogical. She's living with a married man, so if I'm a *puttana* she must be one too. We heard he'd changed his mind about marrying her though, so I suppose that's why she's in no hurry to divorce Giorgio, in case she falls between two stools.'

'Oh poor Janie!'

'It's not that bad really. I'm sorry to go on like this. I'm afraid I get horribly irrational whenever I talk about her.' Jane tried to laugh.

'I don't blame you. I hope Giorgio backs you up over all this.'

'Well, he was adorable to me after the children had gone, but he didn't do much to defuse the situation when they were there. I had a funny feeling he rather liked the drama of two women fighting over him. Perhaps I'm wrong. He was out most of the time they were there, on buying trips. He says he's got to make lots of money now he's got two families to support, but honestly, Verge, the children spent most of their time in Venice alone with me. That's why I can't understand their mother not being nicer to me. I'd want to be friends with the woman who was looking after my children, wouldn't you? She reminds me of the false mother in the judgement of Solomon. The one who'd rather see the child cut in half than give it to anyone else.'

Their preoccupied expressions changed to smiles as the back door opened.

'Who does the other studio belong to?' Robin asked Jane. 'I was just admiring their washing.' He pointed to a line in the next-door garden, which was adorned with a selection of purple and orange saris and long antique dresses.

'They belong to some religious sect,' Jane told him. 'Indian, I think. They've been rebaptized with wonderfully exotic names like Brahma and Bethlehem, and their religion only allows them to do casual labour, so the men are going to help Giorgio paint the studio and one of the girls has offered to clean for me when we're settled. They're lovely. They have this sort of guru who comes round occasionally who they all seem to worship.'

'Sounds OK. Does he have droit de seigneur?' Robin winked at Giorgio, who looked puzzled.

'Oh don't be silly, Robin,' Virginia snapped. 'And shut the door. It's absolutely freezing in here.'

'And where are you going to sleep?' Robin asked when they had completed the tour of the ground floor.

'Up there.' Giorgio pointed. 'I have built a loggia with two bedrooms. One for Filippo and one for me and Gianna. Come, I show you.'

'Maybe Verge should stay down here,' Jane said anxiously. 'The stairs are very steep and he hasn't put the handrail on yet.'

'No, no. It's OK Gianna.' Giorgio sounded impatient.

'Well, it's all right going up,' Jane admitted, 'but you must be very careful coming down, Verge. I do it crabwise.'

'That's because the treads aren't right.' Robin remarked. 'They're too close together. This isn't the permanent staircase is it, Giorgio?'

But Giorgio, bounding impatiently up the staircase ahead of him appeared not to hear the question. He flung open the landing doors to show them the two bedrooms and bathroom where Joe, the swarthy Sicilian builder, was putting the finishing touches to the tiles Jane had bought that morning.

'Joe, you've finished them already. They look great!' Jane exclaimed.

'Yes, I finish. I go now.' He nodded curtly to Jane and Virginia, who were lingering in the entrance, and brushed past them without meeting their eyes to join Giorgio who was showing Robin the main bedroom.

'Seems rather a sulky piece of work,' Virginia commented.

'I know,' Jane sighed. 'He's usually adorable, but I'm afraid I got him involved in one of our arguments this morning. I got here to find Giorgio'd bought some ghastly cheap tiles from the shop on the corner. I know it sounds pathetic, but I'd set my heart on having mirror tiles. D'you remember my friend Liz?'

'What, the tarty one who was always having affairs with married producers?'

'That's right. She bought a new flat last year, and her bathroom was done in mirror tiles and I thought it was too glamorous for words. I'd told Giorgio I wanted them, but he said I hadn't and he'd already started putting the other ones up and couldn't change them. So I nobbled Joe before Giorgio could get to him and played the sweet innocent, and he said yes, of course he could change them as the cement wasn't dry. I rushed out to get the mirror tiles before he could change his mind, and when I got back Giorgio was absolutely furious. I could tell he'd been having a terrific go at Joe for falling for my feminine wiles, and now Joe will hardly speak to me. Well, you saw.'

'At least you've got the tiles.'

'But the awful thing is that I'm not even sure it was worth it. It's OK for Liz. She needs to look glamorous and spend hours in front of the mirror, but with the sort of life style I lead I'd probably do better just to encase my body in heavy black like an Italian peasant and allow myself to wither away underneath. After all, no one but Giorgio's ever going to see my body again.'

'I wouldn't be too sure of that if I were you,' said Virginia.

'You know you really ought to get Giorgio to change that staircase,' Robin said to Jane as she and the boys climbed into the back of his comfortable BMW. 'Ben tripped as we were going down. Luckily I was able to catch him, but for a moment I thought we were both going to fall.'

'You're right, Robin. I can see it's dangerous and I know I must, but I do dread it. Giorgio had it made like that so he'd have as much space in the studio as possible to show off his bigger pieces, you see. And we've already had one major row today – I've just been boring Verge with the details. I really don't know if I can face another.'

'But he can't be angry with you over something like that. Not if it's genuinely dangerous. After all, it'd be far more of a nuisance to him if you broke your leg and had to lie around for weeks.'

'I know,' Jane agreed unhappily.

'Honestly, Janie,' Verge said, 'I never thought you were such a wimp. You're not afraid of him, are you?'

'Not of him exactly, but his moods. You can't imagine what it's like to live with someone who sulks. It's like a sort of black lava which oozes over everyone who comes into his presence. And yet I don't think he really does it on purpose. I think he can't help himself. It's like that story of the scorpion stinging the frog who was carrying him across the river. Just as they were both about to sink the frog turned turned to him and asked why, and the scorpion replied, "Because it's my nature."'

'Shall I have a word with him for you?' Robin asked.

'Oh would you, Robin?' Italian men have this macho thing about other men's good opinions. If you could convince him it was part of his responsibility as the man of the house to change the staircase . . . You'd have to be very tactful, though, so he didn't think I'd put you up to it.'

'I'll just tell him I nearly fell down the wretched thing. You don't even have to be there if you don't want.'

'Oh no, I've got to be there. If you talk to him alone he can just agree with everything you say and then do nothing about it.'

'Janie!' Virginia exclaimed, turning round to look at her. 'This is getting worse and worse.'

'I know. I seem to be becoming the archetypal scheming woman,' Jane agreed gloomily. 'Don't think I like it. But of course Giorgio has masses of good points too.'

'Yes, but it's when you find yourself having to list the other person's good points that you know the relationship's really in trouble,' Virginia stated.

'How do you know?' Robin asked her.

'Giorgio's taking a long time,' Virginia remarked, cutting Jane a second slice of chocolate cake.

'Yes. He does work terribly hard. I worry about him sometimes. But he's determined to get the studio finished before we go back to Venice,' said Jane.

'When are you going?'

'About April, I think. There's some antique fair Giorgio wants to be back for.'

'So you won't be here when the baby comes?'

'Probably not. Oh, Verge, I'm so sorry. You will promise to ring me immediately, won't you? I do envy you. I'd so love to have another.'

'How does Giorgio feel about it now?'

'Absolutely adamant that we shouldn't. He says I've got my hands full with Philly already and I couldn't possibly cope with another.'

'I think he's right,' said Robin unexpectedly. 'Ben's totally out of control as it is. I dread to think what two will be like. We're definitely going to have a rethink after this one.'

'What do you mean?' Virginia sounded furious. 'You agreed we'd have four. Just because Ben left the bath water on the other day –'

'And brought the drawing room ceiling down. It cost me three hundred pounds to have it fixed.'

'Well, you can afford it,' she said angrily. 'You won so much money last season it was ridiculous. Anyway it won't happen again. What do you mean rethink? If you won't agree to any more I'll just find someone else who will.'

'Ah, the neighbourhood stud, I suppose?'

Virginia smiled complacently. 'He means Alex,' she said to Jane. 'He made a pass at me last summer when we were staying with him at his house in Suffolk. Of course I told Robin about it straightaway.'

'Yes, you did,' Robin agreed pleasantly. 'In fact we never hear the end of this famous pass.'

'Not that I blame him,' Virginia went on, ignoring Robin. 'It must be awful for him with Julie being ill so much. I had to do the cooking while we were there, you know. She just lay in bed most of the time.'

'Julie's a nice girl,' Robin said firmly. 'I imagine she just gets fed up with all the frustrated women who seem to flock round Alex under the illusion that they can look after him better than she can.' He shot her a venomous look.

Virginia didn't appear to notice. 'Yes, a lot of women do seem to fancy him,' she agreed. 'But I don't. He's not my type at all.' She patted her hair.

Jane's eyes met Robin's, and held them for just a second too long.

'I sorted out the staircase all right,' Robin said to Virginia later, as she loaded the dishwasher. 'Giorgio seemed quite reasonable once I'd got started.'

'Oh I expect Janie was exaggerating,' Virginia replied. 'She's never had a clue how to handle men. Of course it must give her a dreadful inferiority complex not being married to him.'

'Well, his family seem to have accepted her,' Robin remarked. 'From what you told me I'd imagined she was just his bit on the side, but they were all over her when we went to Venice. I suppose it's different in a society where you don't have divorce. Giorgio said his sister wasn't legally married to her partner either and had to come over to England to have her baby in order to give it its father's surname.'

'Yes. But what about when Philly gets older and can't inherit the title or anything? Janie pretends not to care about that. She's so hopeless. She said she didn't even realize Giorgio was a count until she'd been living with him for six months!'

'You wouldn't have made that mistake, would you?'

'Of course not,' she said exasperated. 'I'm not a complete idiot who goes around in a dream world. What are you implying anyway?'

'Nothing at all,' he said pleasantly. 'Look, I've got to get ready for my dinner now. We'll probably go on to the club afterwards and have a game or two of chemmy, so don't wait up for me.'

As she turned the dishwasher on, Virginia thought how lucky she was compared to Jane. At school it had seemed that Jane had everything – brains, looks, doting parents and beautiful clothes – and now she had thrown it all away on a bad-tempered middle-aged man who would probably never marry her and it was she, Virginia, who had the degree, the title, the grand house, the bottomless bank account, and soon, no doubt, the daughter on whom she would lavish all the love and acceptance which her mother had never given to her. She had something else too. The very special friendship with Alex who, however many women he might sleep with, would always regard her as his unattainable ideal. He had said something of the sort in Suffolk. She had told Robin he had made a pass at her and so he had. Of course, he hadn't tried to kiss her or anything crude like that because he knew she would refuse, but she could tell from the expression in his eyes how much he longed to. She was glad Robin was going out this evening. Julie was spending the weekend with her parents and Alex must be lonely. What could be more neighbourly than to invite him over to spend the evening with her?

She called him as soon as Robin had left. The phone rang for a long time, and his voice was breathless when he answered. 'Oh hi, Verge.' He spoke with his usual warmth. 'You just caught me as I was going down the path.'

'Are you going out then?' She hoped he hadn't heard the sick pang of disappointment in her voice.

'Yes I am. Sandra's invited me round to see her new flat. I think I told you she and Martin had separated.'

Damn. That calculating bitch Sandra had got there before she had. 'How cosy,' she said acidly. 'Better be careful she doesn't look on you as a substitute.'

He laughed. 'Absolutely no danger there, I promise you.'

'Yes, but I wonder if she agrees with you. You will call me tomorrow, won't you,' she went on lightly, 'and tell me all about it?'

CHAPTER THREE

Sandra's flat was in the basement of a six-storey converted house in a busy thoroughfare leading from King's Road to the river. Alex felt depressed as he walked to the front door. He'd had to park his car a long way away and it had started to drizzle so his velvet suit would be ruined. This was what happened when couples split up, he told himself. The family home which they'd put all their money and hopes into was sold and its occupants banished to transit camps like this one, permanently lined with For Sale boards and skips because the residents never stayed put for long enough to get things exactly as they wanted them. He felt as if fate was sending him a timely admonition.

His depression was eased by the warmth of Sandra's greeting. She was wearing a plum-coloured dress, short and low cut to accentuate the large, firm breasts and slim legs which were her best features. Her shoulder-length chestnut hair looked as if it had just been washed, and in the dim light of the passage the faint scars which remained from her teenage acne had disappeared under a glow of peach-coloured foundation.

He'd brought her two bottles of the Wine Society's best claret, which he knew she liked, and placed them carefully on the table in the hall.

'Thank you, Alex.' She stood on tiptoe to kiss him on

the lips, her musky perfume blending uneasily with the taste of stale nicotine.

'You're looking marvellous, Sandy,' he said warmly, wishing she didn't smoke so much. 'Being single obviously suits you.'

She made a face. 'I didn't have much choice after what that bastard did to me, did I? Bring the wine through, Alex, and I'll show you the flat.'

This was quickly done. The flat consisted of a large sitting room, small, functional kitchen and bathroom, and rather an attractive bedroom with a double bed, and French windows leading out on to a patio. Alex made the appropriate noises of approval, and soon afterwards they were sitting beside each other on the sofa in front of the fire, drinking Alex's wine, while behind them the candles flickered on the dinner table which was carefully laid for two. She had gone to a lot of trouble, he thought, touched. Normally Sandra's dinners were of the no-nonsense, English nanny type. Stews and apple pies on the kitchen table.

'I wanted you to come on your own the first time, Alex,' she was saying, 'because I wasn't sure how Julie would feel about me after my illness.' She looked at him appealingly. Sandra was always so direct, he thought. It was one of the things he'd always liked about her.

'Well, of course she agreed with me that it was appallingly unfair that it should have happened to you,' Alex said.

Martin had returned from a solo visit to the West Indies just before Christmas and infected Sandra with syphilis.

'Yes, but wasn't she terribly disapproving of it all?' Sandra asked.

'Oh no. Not disapproving at all,' he reassured her hastily. It was true, he thought. After the appropriate gasp of horror at Sandra's plight, Julie had announced that it was important that they should both be as supportive of her as they could. As she had said it she had seemed to exude a glow of self-righteousness which had reminded him irresistibly of the French saying that in the misfortunes of our friends there is something not altogether displeasing to us. But perhaps he was being unfair. He couldn't deny that he too had felt rather smug.

Alex could still remember clearly the pang of envy he'd felt when Martin had called him after his return.

'God I had a good time,' he'd said. 'I met this fabulous-looking black girl on my last day. We were sitting by the pool. She was in this incredibly brief gold bikini with a really sensational figure. I kept looking at her sideways, and eventually she caught me at it and gave me the most wonderful smile.'

'Did you talk to her?' Alex asked dutifully.

'Not then. I just kept moving my chair closer and closer to hers. And every time I did it she smiled at me. Eventually there was no one left by the pool but us, and then,' he paused triumphantly, 'I moved in!'

'What did you do?'

'Asked her if she wanted a drink. She said she'd like a shower first so we went up to her room – and that was it! God she was sensational, Alex. I think it was the best sex I'd ever had in my life. Really. To die for!' They had both sighed.

'It was sweet of you', Sandra went on, 'to offer to come and visit me in hospital, but you know I really couldn't bear any of my friends to see me there. It was so sordid, and the nurses were so bitchy to me even though they knew perfectly well that it was my husband who'd infected me. But the worst thing of all was that Martin got off with a much lighter dose than me. They say he's completely cured now, whereas I still have to go back for check-ups in case it recurs.'

He could see she was close to tears. He felt he ought to reach out and comfort her, but her last words had caused him an involuntary shudder of physical repugnance of which he was already bitterly ashamed. He compromised by patting her hand. 'Poor Sandy,' he said soothingly.

'Yes. Poor little Sandy waiting at home patiently while her husband screws his way round the world and brings her home a nice present from his latest conquest,' she said bitterly. 'But I tell you, Alex, he's not going to get away with this again.'

'No, of course not,' he agreed. 'Well, I mean, you've left him –'

'Oh but it's not over,' she said with certainty. 'We've been through this sort of thing enough times for me to know that. No. I'm biding my time, Alex, till I can hurt him the way he's hurt me. I'll find a way. You wait.'

Alex listened dumbly. He felt it was no use making some pompous speech about revenge ultimately rebounding on those who perpetrate it. She must know all that. Much better just to listen and let her get it all out of her system so she could then forget about it and start to get on with her life.

'Anyway, let's not talk about Martin any more.' Sandra made a visible effort to pull herself together. 'I'm sure nothing would give him greater satisfaction than to think of the two of us sitting here discussing him all evening, so let's have dinner and talk about you instead.' She smiled tightly and led the way over to the dinner table.

'So how's Julie?' she asked abruptly, passing Alex a roll and cutting short his appreciative comments on the watercress soup.

'Not very happy at the moment, I'm afraid. I think I mentioned to you that her doctor had decided to put her on cortisone because the swelling in her joints was so bad?'

'Yes. How did that go?'

'It did seem to ease the pain a bit,' he said, 'but the awful thing is that it's made her blow up like a balloon. She's put on about two stone, I'd say. She can't get into any of her clothes, and her face has taken on that funny moon shape.' He shook his head. 'I'm afraid she's terribly upset about it.'

'She must be. It can't be much fun for you either, can it?'

'Well, no. Although I don't really feel I'm entitled to complain. After all, it's so much worse for her.' He took a gulp of wine.

'Yes, but you do have some rights too. After all, you

work very hard and you've bought her that wonderful house and you're only twenty-nine. You shouldn't be having to play nursemaid to a sick wife all the time. How does all this affect your sex life?'

'Oh Sandy –' He reached automatically for his glass and found it empty.

'Come on,' she poured him another one, 'surely you can tell me? After all, you know the most dreadful things about me and Martin.'

'It is very difficult,' he admitted. 'I suppose I got out of the habit of – well – starting anything, because I was afraid of hurting her, so it's usually she who suggests it. But then I get the feeling that she doesn't really want to because she's so tired all the time, but she kind of wants me to want to as a sort of reassurance that I still find her attractive. But then, if I do respond she often winces as though it's terribly painful –'

'But hasn't the cortisone helped that?'

'Well, yes. But the dreadful thing is, Sandy, that now she's so large I just don't –'

'You don't fancy her any more?'

'No,' he said helplessly.

'How long has it been since you made love?'

'About six months, I suppose.'

'Poor Alex. What a tragedy.' She reached across the table and took his hand. 'I'm so glad you told me. You know how fond I am of you both. I'd really like to help you if I could.'

Alex smiled at her gratefully. It wasn't being disloyal to confide in Sandy, he told himself. After all, she was Julie's friend too. She'd just said so. And she seemed to understand him so well – no doubt because she'd been through the mill herself. Verge was a wonderful friend too, of course, but she grew strangely impatient whenever he talked of Julie's illness. He thought it was because her own life had always gone so smoothly. She'd never experienced suffering or illness of any kind so she tended to dismiss them as if they didn't exist. 'You're helping me just by listening,' he assured her.

'Yes, but I'd like to do more than that.' She leaned forward eagerly.

Alex felt suddenly awkward. He squeezed her hand and disengaged his own gently to reach for his glass.

'Then how about giving me some more of that delicious soup?' he said lightly.

'So what do Julie's parents say about it all?' she asked him as he was finishing. 'She does still go to their doctor doesn't she?'

'Yes. You know I was keen for her to go to Martin, but they wouldn't hear of it. Well,' he shrugged, 'they're still maintaining the same line. They say there's absolutely nothing wrong with Julie and keep implying that it's somehow my fault.'

'How ridiculous,' she said impatiently.

'Part of me thinks it's ridiculous, but they keep doing all these tests on her and not finding anything and you know, Sandy, I have begun to wonder more and more recently if I couldn't have caused it somehow.'

'Oh Alex, how?'

'By marrying her,' he confessed. 'I knew, you see, the moment we were engaged that I didn't want to go through with it. She's a very sweet girl and everything, and I was very fond of her, but I just felt I needed more time. But then I had to go off and do that consultancy job in Suffolk and she was in London so we were hardly ever able to meet and talk. And her parents seemed so determined it should all happen that in the end I just allowed myself to be carried along by it all. Then when she got ill I felt as if I was being punished for having been such a coward in not putting a stop to it all before it was too late. I think she must have realized how miserable I was, and that maybe it triggered off some depression in her that made her ill.'

'But hadn't she ever been ill before the wedding?'

'No – I did ask her parents that because we'd hardly seen each other during the engagement. She was supposed to come and join me at weekends, you know, but she kept cancelling at the last minute.'

'And what did they say?'

'They said she'd been fine. She'd only cancelled because there were so many wedding arrangements to attend to.'

'Well, there's something you ought to know, Alex. Martin told me about it when I was in hospital but we weren't sure if we should pass it on to you.'

'What is it?' He was quite surprised by the seriousness of her tone.

'Martin went to a conference recently and met this specialist who said he'd been called in to see Julie before you were married. Martin told him he was a great friend of yours and he said, "I'm afraid that poor young man had no idea of what he was letting himself in for."'

'So you're saying her parents knew she was ill all the time and didn't tell me?'

'It certainly looks like it, doesn't it?'

'But could I verify that?'

'I expect so. Why don't you call Martin tomorrow and get the man's name? Look, Alex, I'm sorry if I've shocked you, but I felt you deserved to know the truth. Have another drink while I clear the bowls away, and then perhaps you wouldn't mind carving the lamb for me?'

'What are you thinking?' she asked him softly.

Alex started. Dinner was over, and the last thing he remembered was sinking down onto the sofa by the fire feeling decidedly drunk while Sandra went into the kitchen to make coffee.

'I think I must have nodded off for a second,' he confessed.

'I think you must have.' She smiled at him and leaned forward to pass him his cup. She had powdered her face he noticed, and reapplied her perfume. The top button of her dress seemed to have come undone and he could see a tantalizing glimpse of black lace at the bottom of her cleavage.

'Are you feeling better now?' she asked.

'Yes, I think I am.' His initial anger over Julie's deception had almost immediately been replaced by sadness that she hadn't trusted him enough to confide in him. But hadn't she been right not to trust him? Would he in fact have married her if he'd known? To be fair to her, he had to admit to himself that he would probably have not. Sandra had wisely not pressed him to talk about the subject any further over dinner. Instead they had talked of her future – she had previously worked as Martin's receptionist and was now looking for a new job – and of his.

For some time Alex had been sustained by a dream of one day being able to throw up his highly successful career as a management consultant, sell his London house and go and live in the country and paint. He had always suppressed this dream before because Julie's parents had found the whole idea too ridiculous. So what if he had shown great talent at school and his art master had encouraged him to think of painting as a career? People like him simply didn't do that sort of thing. They grew up and had highpowered careers and took on wives and mortgages instead. But now, although he had no intention of abandoning Julie, he felt that his loyalty to her need no longer exclude the possibility of pleasing himself.

'Are you going to tell Julie?' Sandra asked, as if reading his thoughts.

'No, I don't think so.' He had been considering it over dinner and decided that as the whole of their marriage had been based on a tissue of lies and deception it would probably be less painful to continue that way.

'I'm glad.' She sat down beside him and took his hand. 'I'm very fond of her, you know. I wouldn't want her to feel I'd betrayed her.'

'I won't tell her,' he promised. 'Oh Sandy, I am grateful to you. I can't tell you how it feels to have that great burden of guilt lifted from me.'

'I know,' she said tenderly. 'That's the only reason I told you, believe me. I couldn't bear to see you so unhappy and denying yourself all the things you want to do and know that I had it in my power to set you free. I'm so glad you're not angry with her, Alex. A lot of men would have been. You really are exceptionally sweet, aren't you?'

He sat up abruptly, letting go of her hand, and reached for his coffee. Sweet. It seemed as if that word had haunted his existence since, as a skinny eight-year-old in shorts, he had been inveigled into passing round canapés at his parents' interminable cocktail parties.

'Oh dear, have I offended you?' She reached forward

laughingly and ruffled his hair. 'What's the matter with being called sweet?'

'I've always found it particularly nauseating, that's all,' he said with what he hoped was dignity, wishing he hadn't chosen a sentence with so many Ss in it.

'But you know, you are sweet, Alex, to have stayed with Julie all this time. You've never been unfaithful to her, have you?'

He looked at her in bewilderment. He didn't really know the answer. There had been the odd fumble at parties, and then that afternoon, two years ago, when Julie was on holiday and a temporary secretary from his office had asked him back to her flat for lunch. Just as they'd got onto the bed together there had been a knock at the door and a pony-tailed man with a bucket had come in and insisted on cleaning her windows. Alex had found this so off-putting that he'd hardly been able to perform afterwards. Did this count as infidelity, he wondered? 'Sort of,' he managed.

Sandra laughed again, and kissed him lightly on the cheek. 'Tell me about it,' she said.

Alex was ashamed to realize how little he had to tell.

Before Julie, his sexual conquests had consisted of an eighteen-year-old Mexican prostitute whom he'd visited while doing voluntary service overseas, and a glamorous third-year student who'd seduced him one afternoon during his first year at Oxford. The following day he'd seen her in the canteen twined round her lecturer boyfriend and they had both turned to stare at him and burst into derisive laughter. Of course there had been plenty of girls at dances and in the holidays who'd been prepared to go nine-tenths of the way with him, but they'd always stopped short of actual intercourse, and he had gradually come to realize that this was what nice girls did. Julie had been the only one who was prepared to go all the way which was why, combined with her parents' repeated enquiries as to what exactly his intentions were towards their daughter, he had eventually been induced into proposing to her.

'I don't want to talk about it,' he said sulkily. He knew from Martin that Sandra had had several affairs since their marriage, usually out of revenge for his own infidelities. Naturally she would be scornful of Alex's inexperience. For a moment he thought longingly of Virginia. She was about the only person he knew who'd had even less sex than he had. He'd told her once about his secretary – carefully leaving out the window cleaner incident – and from that moment she seemed to have become convinced that he was a sort of lethal combination of Don Giovanni and Casanova rolled into one. Short of actually lying, he'd done nothing to disillusion her. He found her image of him extremely attractive, but he knew enough to realize that Sandra wouldn't be fooled by it for a second.

'All right, then don't, love,' she said soothingly. 'But how are you going to manage in future? You're an extremely attractive man, you know, Alex, and you deserve some happiness after all you've been through. You wouldn't be taking anything away from Julie, would you, and if you didn't tell her about it she couldn't possibly be hurt?'

Her words were so exactly what he wanted to hear that Alex felt totally disarmed. He knew suddenly that he was going to tell her his secret.

'You're absolutely right, Sandy,' he agreed, enunciating his words with caution.

'Do you have anyone in mind?' She was facing him three-quarters on. His gaze flickered bemused from her eyes to her breasts. For a moment he couldn't remember which of them he was supposed to be looking at.

'Yes I do,' he replied, feeling pleased with himself.

She sighed and sank back beside him. His arm had been lying along the back of the sofa, and he reached out absent-mindedly and stroked her hair.

'Who is she?' Sandra asked.

'Well, it's all a bit complicated –' he began.

'Is she married?'

'Yes.'

'To a friend of yours?'

'I'm afraid so.'

She turned to smile at him. 'Don't be afraid, Alex. You owe it to yourself to tell her, you know.'

'I have – sort of,' he admitted.

'Have you? What did she say?'

'She seems to want to be with me. She doesn't feel much loyalty to her husband because he's had several affairs, but she's worried about her children.'

Sandra stiffened suddenly and sat up and lit a cigarette. Why did she have to do that? he asked himself petulantly. She'd hardly smoked all evening. It had been so nice.

'What's her name?' she asked him sharply.

'Georgina,' he said proudly. 'Georgina Cunningham. She's married to our local magistrate in Suffolk.'

'Oh yes.' She appeared to be readjusting her thoughts. 'I've heard of her. Julie told me. I thought it was all over.'

'Well actually it never really began. We were all terrific friends, you see, and I can't deny that I fancied her like mad, but then Julie wrote this awful letter to Henry – that's Georgina's husband – saying she thought he should stop her from seeing me, and – well – he did.'

'When was that?'

'About two years ago.' The lunch with his secretary had been his consolation prize, he remembered. Some prize.

'And now you're seeing her again?'

'I bumped into her in the Portobello Road two weeks ago. I couldn't believe it, Sandy. I thought I was over her, you see, but the moment I saw her it all came flooding back.'

'Did you arrange to meet again?'

'Yes. She comes up to London quite a lot to shop, and she'd taken a room at the Cavendish Hotel. I arranged to meet her there for lunch, but when I arrived there was a message in reception for me saying that her mother-in-law had turned up unexpectedly and she was afraid she'd have to have lunch with her instead. She'd had to leave the number with Henry you see, in case anything happened to the children, and we think he'd sent his mother along to check up on her.'

To his surprise and annoyance Sandra burst suddenly into fits of hysterical laughter. Normally Alex had a good sense of humour and he could see, of course, that the situation did have a funny side, but, really, her reaction was way over the top. She actually had tears pouring down her cheeks. He tried to compose his features into a pleasant smile as he waited for her to stop, but looking at him only seemed to set her off again. Eventually he rose to his feet.

'Thank you', he said, 'for a lovely dinner. I think I ought to be getting along now.'

'No.' She flung herself into his arms. 'Look, Alex, I'm really sorry I laughed like that just now,' she gulped. 'Please don't be offended. It was just – well – I'd been imagining something completely different. But look, I do want to help you and show you I'm your friend. I've got an idea. What you really need, don't you, is somewhere to meet Georgina?'

'Well yes. She's talking of getting a flat in London, but then I suppose there would always be the risk of Henry turning up.'

'But is she planning to leave him?'

'She'd like to eventually. She doesn't want to ruin his career, and then there are the children. She thought perhaps she could do it later. When they go to boarding school –'

'Yes, of course. Look, I know this sounds strange as I'm Julie's friend, but I've found in life that if these things are going to happen they're going to happen anyway, no matter what anyone tries to do to stop them. So why don't you and Georgina borrow this flat one day next week? I've got a temporary job so I'll be out all day, and I can leave the key in the window box for you –'

He couldn't speak for a moment. He was too over-whelmed by a sudden erotic vision of the blonde, voluptuous Georgina reaching her arms out to him at last in the pretty little bedroom Sandra had shown him earlier.

'Would you like that?' she asked him softly.

He put his arms round her and kissed her on the forehead. The combination of alcohol, sadness and sudden dazzling hope he'd gone through that evening made him feel close to tears.

'I'd like it more than anything else in the world,' he told her. 'Thank you, Sandy. I think you must be the best friend anyone's ever had.'

CHAPTER FOUR

December 1973

'Verge?'

'Janie! When did you get back?'

'Last night. Oh Verge, it's so wonderful to be in London again. I can hardly believe it.'

'How long are you staying?'

'Probably at least till April. Longer if I can drag it out. Giorgio may have to make a few odd trips, but Philly and I are just going to stay put.'

'When are we going to see you?'

'As soon as possible, please. I'm simply dying to meet Joshua. Does he look like Ben?'

'Not really. There are flashes of family likeness of course, but he's darker and thinner. More like me, I suppose, whereas Ben's the image of Robin.'

'How lovely. One for each of you.' If Verge had felt any disappointment at not having the little girl she had dreamed of she certainly hadn't mentioned it to Jane, and there was no way, therefore, that Jane was going to be insensitive enough to mention it to her. 'What about tomorrow?'

'Lunch?'

'Great. Would you like to come here?'

'No, come to me,' Virginia said. 'It's easier. I've got a nanny now. She can look after the kids while we catch up on the gossip.'

'Gosh, how grand. Is she a starchy number in uniform?'

'Oh no, not a bit. Very laid back. I got her because I was going back to college this autumn to do an MA.'

'Goodness, how brilliant of you. I'm terribly impressed!'

'Don't be. I dropped out after a month. It was terrible, Janie. I found I simply couldn't cope with all the work and the sleepless nights. Anyway, I think my brain's gone.'

'Oh but it'll come back,' Jane assured her comfortingly. 'I expect it was just too soon after Joshua's birth. There's a recognized condition, isn't there, called maternal amnesia?'

'Yes. But it's supposed to go away after the baby's born.'

'Well mine didn't till Philly was at least six months old. You'll be fine, Verge. Wait and see.'

'Maybe. I might try and do it part time next year, but in the meantime there's really not enough for the nanny to do. Actually I was wondering if you'd like to share her, Janie. Two days a week or something, so you could have a bit of free time?'

'It is rather a tempting thought,' Jane admitted. 'My former agent turned up in Venice this summer and looked me up. He said there was lots of advertising work around for young mums and I ought to try and do some commercials while I was over here. If I had a nanny it would give me a chance to go around and see a few people. I'll have to talk to Giorgio, of course. After all, he's the one who'll be paying for her until I get some work. But it would be nice to make some money and not be entirely a kept woman any more.'

'Of course. You talk to him. We'll have an evening with the men soon, anyway. What are you doing on New Year's Eve?'

'Nothing planned at the moment.'

'We were thinking of going to this new restaurant in Chinatown. Do you remember Alex?'

'The one who lives opposite you? Yes, of course.'

'He's just got divorced. We were thinking of making up a party to cheer him up.'

To her surprise, Jane felt a totally irrational thrill of

pleasure. 'Goodness that was quick,' she said enviously. 'How on earth did he manage it?'

'Paid through the nose, of course. So, d'you think you'll come?'

'Yes. I think we'd love to.'

'Great. Come early tomorrow so you can talk to Sarah the nanny and see if you like her, then we can leave Josh with her after lunch and take Ben and Philly to the one o'clock club in Holland Park.'

'God, how blissful. There's absolutely nothing like that in Venice, you know. Only one proper park and it's miles away from us and they don't even let you walk on the grass. Oh Verge, you simply don't realize how lucky you are to live in London!'

Chinese restaurants had certainly come a long way from the grotty establishments Jane had visited in the sixties, where she and her friends used to pass surreptitious joints to each other under the table, perhaps in order to ward off the knowledge that at least one of them was almost certain to be violently ill the following day.

This one, decorated with minimalist chic, was on two floors, connected by a perilous spiral staircase. The walls were white, with framed Andy Warhol prints above the austere, white-clothed tables and steel chairs. Seated opposite Giorgio, with Robin and Alex on either side of her, Jane was alarmed to realize that there were no knives and forks in sight and that she was presumably going to be expected to eat with chopsticks.

Virginia, who had warned Jane to dress formally, was looking tremendously elegant in a beautifully cut, short-sleeved chiffon dress in autumnal shades of brown and gold which reflected the lights in her hair. She had bought it in a French boutique in Sloane Street and confided in Jane that it had cost her £50. Jane had managed to achieve much the same effect by spending £8 in an antique clothing shop in Portobello Road on a thirties black crepe dress printed with horizontal bands of red and blue pansies, while Camilla, the slightly horsey divorcée who had been invited along by Verge as Alex's date, was playing it safe in Laura Ashley.

Giorgio who, like Jane, bought most of his clothes from the Portobello market, was in a maroon, brushed velvet suit with flared trousers and an Indian silk scarf round his neck. Jane thought proudly that he looked just as smart as Robin and Alex, who went to the same tailor in Jermyn Street and who had derived much amusement from the fact that they had both chosen to wear the same navy and grey velvet suit. Alex wore the jacket, with navy trousers, and Robin, who, on seeing Alex, had hastily changed into a black leather jacket, the trousers.

Jane had always found it a bit difficult to sustain a prolonged conversation with Robin. She wondered if it was because she had spent so many years regarding him as merely a quarry to be hunted and vanquished by Virginia, so that now he was caught and apparently domesticated it was difficult to adjust her thinking and relate to him as a person in his own right. She decided to play it safe by asking him about the children – an end-lessly absorbing topic of mutual fascination, and a real lifeline for dinner parties such as these, which looked as if they might otherwise turn out to be rather sticky.

'They're fine,' he said. 'I suppose the good thing about having two boys is that they're so incredibly destructive during the day that at least they go to sleep exhausted at night.'

Jane laughed. 'Not Josh, surely? He's only seven months.'

'Oh you'd be surprised how much havoc even a seven-month-old can create when there's absolutely no discipline imposed on him at all.'

If this was a criticism of Verge, Jane was determined to ignore it. 'Doesn't Sarah clear up after them?' she asked. 'I think she's pretty good.'

'She tries,' he admitted, 'but then she leaves at six, so I usually find myself having to do it when I get home from work. We really ought to get another au pair now that Verge has dropped out of her course. The hours work better and it's much cheaper. It was good of you to say you'd share Sarah. How's it working out?'

'Very well really.' Philly liked Sarah, and it was very

nice to have someone to do the shopping and take him to the park two days a week. The trouble was that although it had been agreed that Sarah would come to Jane on Tuesdays and Thursdays, Verge was always ringing her at the last minute and asking her to change dates. Jane's agent had already lined up a number of auditions for her on the appointed days, and as a result of Virginia's changes, she had sometimes had to ask Giorgio to stay in and look after Philly. He was understandably annoyed about this and said she should just tell Verge that she must stick to their prior arrangement, but Jane felt she couldn't. After all, Verge was the one who had gone to all the trouble of finding Sarah, and she was doing Jane a great favour in allowing her to share her. Jane had lost touch with many of her English friends when she went to live in Italy, and her friendship with Verge meant a lot to her. She felt it was important not to place it in jeopardy by quarrelling over a nanny.

'Virginia said you'd started acting again,' Robin went on. 'How's that going?'

'Well, it's hardly acting,' Jane told him. 'I'm not around for long enough to go for a film or play, you see. It's only TV commercials, I'm afraid. They do pay well, and there's plenty of work around, but things seem to move on so fast in the advertising business. I keep getting sent to see new people I've never heard of, and none of them seems to have heard of me, so whereas before I'd often get asked for on the strength of my previous work, now I find myself just one of hundreds of girls all after the same job.'

'I'm sure you can hold your own with them,' he told her. 'You're looking great. Much better than you did five years ago. You ought to get work.'

'Thanks.' Jane was touched. She'd always thought Robin was completely impervious to her charms. 'Some of them do seem interested in using me,' she admitted, 'but then when I say I'm going back to Italy in April, that often rules the whole thing out.' In fact she had found it infinitely depressing to realize that her nomadic existence with Giorgio rendered her virtually unemployable even in England. If only he would let her have another baby so that she could at least shelve the problem for another year or two . . .

'Oh look,' she went on with a false brightness, 'they're bringing the food. Do you think you could possibly show me how to use chopsticks?'

When he had obliged, and she had mastered them, Jane was further depressed to realize how little she was actually going to be able to eat.

'Did you remember to tell them I was a vegetarian?' she asked him tentatively, as one succulent-looking dish after another was found on closer examination to contain meat or fish.

'Yes, of course. We asked them about it particularly when we booked. They're doing a special set menu for New Year's Eve, but they said it would be no problem at all. Look, you can have some of those beansprouts, and what about one of these rolls?' He picked it up expertly with his chopsticks and took a bite. 'Oh dear. It seems to have fish in it. It's really delicious, though. Couldn't you bend the rules a bit, just for tonight? The food's frightfully good here, you know. We're thinking of using them for some of our parties.'

Jane smiled wanly and helped herself to beansprouts. From what she could decipher of the menu, it was going to be a hungry evening. At least it would suit Giorgio, who loved fish and was prone to migraines if he ate a heavy meal in the evening. She was relieved to see that he seemed to be getting on well with Camilla, who was telling him about a ball she was helping to organize to raise funds for Venice. Jane hoped he wouldn't launch into one of his tirades about the corruptness of charity organizations, but so far at least he seemed to be on his best behaviour. On his other side Verge was smiling tenderly across the table at Alex, her chin resting in her hands, and the gold watch Robin had bought her for Christmas glowing softly in the candlelight.

Jane felt acutely conscious of Alex's presence beside her, though so far, apart from greeting her warmly and asking after her adorable baby son, he had not talked to her. He looked thinner than when she had last seen him, and there were lines of sadness round his eyes, but his smile was as sweet as ever, and she had warmed to the quickly suppressed look of admiration he had given her when they first met. Part of her wanted him to turn his attention away from Verge and talk to her, but part of her dreaded it. It was easy for Verge to entertain him with amusingly bitchy remarks about their many shared acquaintances, but what on earth could Jane, an unemployed actress and unmarried housewife and mother, exiled in a city she no longer enjoyed, find to say to an attractive, newly single man who was just re-embarking on life?

It didn't help that other people's perceptions of her life were so different from her own. She knew that in looking after Philly she was doing the most challenging and important job in the world, but the fashionable attitude was that she was a mere parasite who must be incredibly boring to be content with doing so little. She knew that Venice, with its innumerable bridges, perilous canals, and hostile vaporetto attendants, who refused to allow her to bring the pram on board if the boat was remotely full, was one of the least practical places in the world to bring up children, but people would persist in telling her how romantic and lovely it must be to live there, and how they envied her.

She felt that anything she might find to say to Alex would be as hollow as her stomach was likely to be at the end of the meal, and began to wish passionately that the evening was over. New Year's Eve imposed the uncomfortable necessity of assessing one's life, and hers was definitely wanting. She looked across the table at Camilla and felt a pang of envy. So what if she was plain and horsey and her husband had left her for another woman? What was any of that compared to the priceless gift of freedom to be able to live where she pleased and go out on dates with exciting men like Alex?

'You're not eating much,' he had turned towards her without her realizing and was looking in concern at the small pile of beansprouts on her plate.

'I'm vegetarian, you see,' she explained apologetically, 'and everything else seems to have meat or fish in it.'

'But this won't do, will it?' he said calmly. 'What about

the next course?' He picked up the special menu card which was standing in front of him.

'It's abalone soup,' she told him. 'I'm pinning all my hopes on it, but I don't know what it is, do you?'

'No, I don't.' He turned to a passing waiter. 'Can you tell me if abalone soup's vegetarian?'

'Vegetarian? Oh yes, sir. Abalone very nice Chinese fish!' He seemed delighted at being able to oblige him. Alex and Jane exchanged conspiratorial smiles.

'Don't worry,' she said. 'I'll be OK, honestly. There'll be some rice later, and I can always drown my sorrows in sake.'

Alex was scanning the menu. 'But it's absolutely hopeless for you!' he exclaimed. 'Robin should have checked –'

'He did,' Jane assured him, 'but I expect they just told him what they thought he wanted to hear. Please don't bother –'

She watched in trepidation as he summoned the waiter, dreading a scene such as Giorgio would have made in the days before Philly when Jane could do no wrong. Instead she was soon lost in admiration, as, with a quiet charm which seemed to imply that such an excellent restaurant could not fail to be delighted at being given the chance to rise to the challenge of creating a special meal that would satisfy the unusual dietary requirements of the beautiful lady at his side, Alex managed, through frequent consultation with Jane, to order just the sort of simple rice and vegetable meal she most adored. Her depression vanished, and for the first time in over two years she experienced the warm feeling of being cherished by the man she was with.

'But this is absolutely delicious!' she exclaimed a few minutes later, after taking her first tentative mouthful of the crispy fried seaweed Alex had suggested.

'Isn't it?' he smiled at her. 'To tell you the truth, I rather envy you. How long have you been vegetarian?'

'Four years,' she told him. 'Since just after I went to live in Italy. Giorgio and I went to a place called Arezzo just south of Florence where they have a huge antique market on the first weekend of every month.

Unfortunately they also have an animal market on the same day.'

'And that put you off?'

'Well, I'd always hated the idea of killing animals, but it had always seemed so impersonal before. It's difficult to work up much compassion for a slab of meat on a plastic tray in the supermarket, isn't it? In Arezzo the animals were still alive. There were these two old women I saw holding live rabbits upside down by their hind legs to take home and slaughter. They were just standing there, gossiping together, and their faces were so red and ugly, while the rabbits' faces were so beautiful and full of fear. I just had one of those flashes when you know something's terribly wrong, and that even if the rest of the world condones it and you're absolutely powerless to do anything about it, there's no way that you yourself can ever be part of it again.'

'So you stopped eating meat just like that?'

'Oh yes. I just wished I could have done more. I did persuade Giorgio to buy some pigeons. There were about eight of them, all huddled together in a tiny crate. We took them up to the top of the hill to free them, but it was awful. They must have had their wings clipped. They couldn't fly any more. Just kept flapping around hopelessly and trying to get back into the crate. In the end we had to give them some food and leave them there, but I doubt if they even survived the night.' She reached for her drink and tried to smile at him. 'Sorry to bang on like this. Giorgio says I'm a frightful bore when I get on to the topic of vegetarianism.'

'Not at all. I admire you. I don't think I'd have had the strength of mind. Isn't it terribly difficult socially?'

'Not really. Italian food's absolutely ideal for vegetarians, you see. All that pasta and huge plates of vegetables and wonderful fruit. Of course, nobody there is vegetarian, but they don't seem to mind that I am. They just think I'm a mad foreigner and try to humour me. The only time they did try to get at me was when I was pregnant – saying it wasn't fair of me not to eat meat for the baby's sake – but I was very careful. I read lots of books about it and made sure my diet was adequate.

Unfortunately when Philly was born so big and strong and healthy they didn't stop to think that maybe it was because I was doing something right. They just thought how unfair it was that I was doing everything wrong and yet my child was so much healthier than theirs.' She laughed. 'Excuse the proud mother.'

'Well, you have the right to be. He's lovely. Are you going to have any more?' Alex had been pleased with the way the conversation was going so far. She'd seemed so sad and remote at the beginning of the evening, and he'd enjoyed choosing the menu for her and being rewarded by her brilliant smile. He'd felt she was really beginning to open up to him, and wanted to encourage her to talk more because he found it so enjoyable studying her profile, which reminded him of a Fra Angelico Madonna. He was totally unprepared therefore for the shutter which seemed to descend at his last question, wiping all the animation from her features.

'I don't know,' she said, and drank some more wine. Alex was alarmed to feel an almost tangible aura of sadness oozing from her. He cast his mind round desperately for another topic of conversation.

'But tell me about you,' she went on brightly. 'Verge tells me you're divorced. I was terribly impressed by how quickly you'd done it because my own divorce dragged on for such ages.'

'It was really my parents-in-law who organized it all,' Alex told her. 'My wife found out what I was doing –' he paused.

'Verge told me', Jane said hastily, 'that you were, er, seeing a slightly older lady –'

'Yes. Well, my wife told her parents, and they said I must never see her again or the marriage would be over, and I just couldn't agree to that.'

'But what did your wife say?'

'Not much. She'd moved back with her parents by then and I had to drive down to their house in the country to tell them all my decision.'

'Goodness. It's just like a nineteenth-century novel. Weren't you terrified?'

'Yes, but I felt I ought to do it. It was weird, though,

because my car wouldn't start although it had been fine the night before. Fortunately Verge saw me and very sweetly lent me hers.'

'But did she know what you were going to do?'

'Oh yes.' He seemed slightly surprised.

Jane was silent for a moment. She wondered why she should find this piece of information so extraordinarily chilling. Of course Verge knew far more about the state of Alex's marriage than she did, but was it normal to interfere so actively in bringing it to an end, or was she herself just being ridiculously overscrupulous?

'And then what happened?' she asked finally.

'Once I'd said my piece I was out of the door in ten minutes flat. I had a letter from their lawyer two days later, admitted everything they asked me to, and was divorced in about three months.'

'And have you ever spoken to your wife since that day you went down there?'

'No. I was told it would upset her too much.'

'But if you'd been left to yourselves,' Jane asked, 'do you think you would have divorced each other?'

'I don't know. Julie – that's my wife – was very sweet at first when she heard about Georgina, my, er, friend.'

'How did she hear?'

'Well, it was rather strange . She just seemed to know . About two days after it happened.'

'Someone must have told her,' Jane said with certainty.

'Oh no,' Alex assured her. No one could possibly have told Julie but Sandra, and Julie had denied this categorically.

'How absolutely extraordinary.' Jane remained unconvinced. 'And are you going to get married again?'

'I don't know. My friend's already married, you see, with young children. What we need is time together without pressure to sort out what we really feel, but that's just what we can never get.'

Georgina was adept, he thought, at keeping him at fever pitch. Not, he was sure, that it was deliberate. It was just that nine times out of ten when they arranged a meeting her husband would turn up unexpectedly in the little house she had bought in Chelsea especially for her romantic trysts with Alex. Sometimes she wasn't even able to let him know, and he would spend whole evenings pacing up and down in a frenzy of anticipation, waiting for the call that never came.

'Perhaps if we did,' he went on, 'we might find out that the whole thing was less important than we'd imagined.'

And where, he asked himself in surprise, had this newly realistic attitude come from? To Verge and all his other friends he was constantly maintaining his passionate desire to marry Georgina. Why should he suddenly find himself so reluctant to do so to Jane?

'Perhaps,' Jane agreed noncommittally. She found she didn't want to talk about his feelings for Georgina either. For one thing the thought of Alex being in love with another woman was curiously distasteful to her, and for another she felt a strange sort of compassion for him. Verge had told her that Georgina's husband was far too rich and powerful for her to consider leaving him for a younger man and that she was just stringing Alex along. If this was true Jane felt it would be like mocking him to encourage him to talk about a future which would probably prove to be merely a mirage.

'But if you did end up not being with Georgina,' she went on curiously, 'would you regret having divorced your wife?'

'Oh no, not at all.' Even in his loneliest moments he had never wanted for a second to go back to Julie. In fact he felt almost guilty at how little he thought of her. It was as if their eight years of marriage had never existed.

'And do you think she regrets it?'

'She was sad at first,' he said, 'but once it was all settled I think it was a relief to her. I've heard she's much better now. She's actually gone out and got a job. I'm thrilled for her, of course. but I do find it a bit puzzling because all through our marriage she kept saying she was too ill to work.'

'It's strange, isn't it,' she said slowly, 'how people can be so convinced they want to be with someone who's bad for them? Rather like craving a food one's allergic to. People feel so sorry for them, but in fact it's equally bad for the person at the receiving end, especially if they're quite fond of the person who's pursuing them and don't have anyone else and go along with the whole thing because they think they can make them happy. The trouble is that they don't at all. The other person just senses their lack of love and becomes all sort of tortured and ill with resentment and hostility.'

Alex listened to her in surprise. Had Verge been telling her about him and Julie, or could she possibly have been talking about herself?

'Anyway, it must be a comfort for you to know that she's better, mustn't it?' Jane went on. 'And that at least there are no children to worry about?'

'Oh, but I'd adore to have children,' he said eagerly.

Jane turned to look at him, temporarily abandoning the struggle with her chopsticks. 'Would you?' she asked.

'Oh yes, although I suppose I'm unlikely to have them if I marry Georgina. She's already got three, you see.'

'Yes. I suppose it's not fair to expect someone who's been through it all once to feel particularly enthusiastic about starting all over again.' She must be careful, she told herself, not to sound bitter.

'It's not that.' Alex assured her. 'Georgina told me she'd love to have more children. She'd have to wait a few years, of course, so as not to upset the ones she has –'

'Yes, of course.' Jane averted her eyes. She felt convinced that Verge was right and Georgina was just stringing Alex along. She was beginning to sound like a combination of a female version of Giorgio and the White Queen in *Alice*. Children yesterday and children tomorrow, but never children today. 'At least it's thanks to her that you're free,' she added somewhat inconsequentially.

Alex frowned. Free? Yes, he supposed he was technically. The trouble was that he didn't feel it, enslaved as he was emotionally by Georgina and financially by Julie. Part of the divorce settlement had been that he should buy Julie a house in London. This entailed working frantically at his job and taking on as many new clients as possible. Of course, he could always sell *his* house, but property prices had dropped so dramatically recently that it seemed foolish not to hang on to it. Even if he did sell it he would still need some sort of London base in order to carry on working at his job so he could keep up the payments on Julie's house. Since his divorce his dream of moving to the country and becoming an artist seemed to have receded further than ever.

'I'm not sure how good I am at freedom,' he said lightly. 'I think I'm more like one of your pigeons in Arezzo, trying to get back into their crate.'

'Oh, please don't say that,' she tried to match his tone, 'or you'll spoil all my philanthropic fantasies. Surely there must be some compensations?'

'Of course.' He thought of Georgina. 'But –' At that point Jane's attention was distracted by Robin asking her to pass him the soya sauce. It's just that they have to be paid for so dearly, he thought.

He remembered the day, almost a year ago, of his first meeting with Georgina. He had woken at dawn and looked at Julie sleeping beside him, feeling once more the sense of affection and compassion towards her which had filled him ever since he knew he was going to betray her. The knowledge that he was about to become Georgina's lover had given him a godlike sense of power, convincing him that his love for Georgina would some-how enrich his relationship with Julie so that she too would be able to benefit from his new-found happiness.

There had been an awkward moment the night before when she, perhaps sensing that he was slipping away from her had tried to initiate sex. He had to admit that this had thrown him. They had got through the preceding days so successfully, circling each other with all the polite courtesy of total strangers, and Julie had accepted his alibi for the following day without question. He had got into bed full of relief that there seemed to be no further obstacle in the way of his dreams.

When she turned towards him he had pretended to be asleep, and was thus unable to protest when she slid down the bed, undid his pyjama bottoms and started to suck his penis. He wondered how he could stop her without offending her. It was months now since he and Julie had had sex, and he had so wanted to stay faithful

71

to Georgina. Georgina. At the thought of her he stirred unwillingly and grew hard. Julie opened her eyes and looked up at him in triumph, increasing the speed of her movements. He had to admit she was good at it. Often during the early years of their marriage she had managed to entice him away from his desk by walking over to him, dropping silently to her knees, and unzipping his trousers, and however much his mind had protested, his body had always, eventually, responded. Tonight was no exception. His disgust with himself was mingled with excitement at the thought that perhaps tomorrow it would be Georgina performing these same actions. He gasped and stiffened, twining Julie's dark hair in his fingers absent-mindedly as he thought of Georgina's ash-blonde curls until thought gave way to sensation and he came in Julie's mouth, then lay motionless and full of self-hatred as she ran from the room and down the short flight of stairs to the bathroom, which was still not far enough away to disguise the familiar sounds of retching and flushing followed by the relentless buzz of her electric toothbrush.

He got up early and tiptoed next door into his dressing room where he had carefully laid out his suit and briefcase the night before. He felt it was desperately important to get out of the house without waking Julie so he could preserve his earlier feeling of affection for her without being forced to face the memory of the previous night's fiasco.

It was ages yet before he could go to Sandra's flat, so to salvage his conscience he drove to his deserted office near Cadogan Square, and put in a couple of hours' hard work before going to a nearby café for breakfast. A further intoxicating hour was spent in Harrods, stocking up on champagne, smoked salmon, chocolates, and armfuls of lilies and Christmas roses.

He arrived at the flat just before eleven, glowing with anticipation. Georgina was meeting him there at twelve, and he wanted plenty of time to arrange things. The key was in the window box, just as Sandra had promised him, and there was a note for him in her writing taped to the bedroom door. He presumed it must contain instructions about what to do with the sheets or the doorkey when he was ready to leave, and decided to read it after he had unpacked the food.

It took longer than he'd thought to get the sitting room looking exactly as he wanted it, with the table laid for two, a vase of Christmas roses in the centre and the huge bunch of lilies resplendent on the coffee table. The champagne was safely in the fridge, and the smoked salmon laid out on plates in the kitchen ready to serve. Casting a last approving look round the room, he went to open Sandra's note.

Darling Alex, it read. *Please don't go into the bedroom because I've taken an overdose. I'm sorry to spoil your lunch, but I just can't bear to go on like this any longer. Forgive me for involving you, but I didn't want to give Martin the satisfaction of finding me dead.*
Thank you for having been such a wonderful friend to me.
Sandra

Half an hour later when Georgina, swathed in red fox fur and *Ma Griffe,* stepped out of her taxi, she was surprised, but not displeased to find Alex standing on the pavement outside the flat.

'Darling,' she exclaimed over her shoulder as she paid the driver, 'how wonderfully indiscreet of you to wait for me here! Were you afraid I'd get lost?'

She turned and flung her arms round his neck, excited rather than hurt by how stiff and awkward he felt in her embrace. He certainly had a lot to learn about adultery, she thought, and she had an idea it was going to be rather fun teaching him. She stood on tiptoe and bit his earlobe.

'Let's hurry up and go inside,' she whispered. 'I'm freezing. I've got absolutely nothing on underneath my coat.'

Alex stared at her dumbly. The silence, which had just begun to seem awkward, was mercifully broken by the siren of an approaching ambulance which rounded the corner at top speed and screeched to a halt beside them.

*   *   *

'I'm sorry.' Jane turned back to Alex. 'I didn't hear what you said.'

He dragged his thoughts back to the present with an effort. 'Oh it was just something about being technically free but not able to feel it – although I doubt if you can understand that.'

'Yes, of course I can,' she said quickly. 'You see Giorgio and I aren't actually married –' and why on earth, she asked herself, had she told him that? Since Philly's birth she had always been so careful not to mention the fact to strangers in case they were shocked.

Seeing his almost comical look of astonishment she tried to cover it up. 'I imagined Verge must have told you,' she said lamely.

'No, she didn't.' Was his astonishment disapproval, she wondered, or could it just possibly be pleasure? 'I had absolutely no idea,' he said.

CHAPTER FIVE

March 1974

I t was a Friday afternoon, and Jane was fumbling in
her purse for some money to pay Sarah with before
dashing off to tea with Virginia. Giorgio was out at an
auction, but the studio, which he had long since transformed into a corner of a museum, was as immaculate
as if he were about to step in at any moment with an
important group of clients. It contained so many taboo
objects that Jane found it easier, while Philly was awake,
to spend most of her time in the kitchen. He was a
sweet and obedient child, but it seemed unreasonable to
dangle temptation in the shape of small sculptures or
ceramic vases constantly in front of him. Anyway, she
preferred her own domain, which was light and cheerful,
with French windows opening on to the small paved
garden, and a large pine dresser with their brightly
coloured Italian dinner service arranged artistically
on the upper shelves and Philly's toys stashed away discreetly in the cupboard at the bottom.

'Don't bother about waiting till six or anything, Sarah,'
Jane was saying. 'I probably won't be back till later, so
if you'd just finish clearing lunch and put Philly's
dungarees in the drier you can go home after that.'

'Thanks.' Sarah was a divorced mother of thirty-
seven who looked ten years younger than her age and
always managed to dress neatly and fashionably while
spending very little money on clothes. Only a slight lack

of animation in the expression of her pale blue eyes and small mouth prevented her from being really attractive. 'I feel quite guilty taking it from you for only half a day's work. It seems silly I'm not at Virginia's today to help with the tea.'

'I know. That was the original plan, of course, but Verge wanted to change and have you yesterday – anyway, it doesn't really matter. So – I'll see you on Tuesday, all being well. Are you bringing the girls?' Sarah had two thin, pale, excellently behaved daughters of twelve and eight whom Philly adored and Jane too had become genuinely fond of, and welcomed to the house as extra playmates for him whenever they were off school.

'If that's all right. They will be on holiday by then, but they're perfectly all right on their own.'

'I know. They're wonderfully capable, aren't they? I do think you're a marvellous mother Sarah.'

'Thank you,' Sarah's thin lips broke into a smile. 'I suppose I had to be really.' At twenty-three she had married a good-looking Irishman twenty years older than herself, who was charming when sober, but became violent and abusive after visiting the local pub which he had begun to do with alarming frequency after the birth of their second daughter. Legend had it that Sarah had walked out on him seven years before with the two girls and only thirty shillings in her pocket.

'Yes I know, but I don't think I could have done it on my own.' Jane was genuinely full of admiration for Sarah's courage, which had been rewarded shortly afterwards by her husband dropping dead from a heart attack and her regaining possession of their flat and quite a nice little sum in life insurance.

'Oh I expect you could have if you'd been desperate. You just can't imagine it because you're lucky to have a good man to look after you.'

'Perhaps.' Rather to Verge's disapproval. Jane had long ago confided to Sarah the fact that she and Giorgio weren't married. 'Yes, he is a good man,' she admitted. In spite of Giorgio's sulks and constant criticisms of her, Jane knew he still loved and valued her and would be devastated if she left him. 'If only he'd just let me have

76

another baby.' Jane's longing was rapidly building up into an obsession and as Giorgio remained unmoved by either pleading, logic or tears she was forced to seek relief by confiding endlessly in her women friends.

Sarah squirted some Fairy Liquid into the washing-up bowl. 'What I don't understand,' she said, looking at Jane sideways 'is why you don't just go ahead and have one anyway.'

'Don't think I haven't thought of it,' Jane replied. 'It's just that I suppose I'm afraid of what it would do to our relationship. He was absolutely furious when I became pregnant with Philly, you see, and that was a genuine accident.'

'Well, if he blamed you when the accident was genuine, wouldn't it serve him right if you had a deliberate one this time?'

'Yes, I suppose it would. The trouble is I don't think I could get away with it. He knows I've got a coil, you see.'

'It's not a hundred per cent safe, you know.'

'Well, they *say* that, but it is really, isn't it? I mean, I've never actually heard of anyone with a coil getting pregnant have you?'

Sarah looked at her in surprise. 'Virginia did,' she said.

'Oh no, she definitely had it removed before Josh.' Jane protested.

'I know. It was Ben who was the accident.' Sarah had sensitive hands and always wore rubber gloves for washing up. Jane gazed at her deft, scarlet-coated movements in fascination.

'Are you sure?' she said.

'Absolutely. I have a coil too, you see, and I used to think I was a hundred per cent safe as well. Virginia told me about Ben to stop me getting too complacent. Why don't you ask her about it this afternoon?'

On her way to Virginia's house, Jane tried to analyse the hurt she was feeling at what Sarah had told her. She and Virginia had been so close recently. OK, so they'd had a moment of rivalry as teenagers, but now that they were both married – or almost – what reason could Verge have for keeping such a secret from her? Jane had been

77

perfectly honest about Philly being an accident, so why shouldn't Virginia have been prepared to tell her that Ben was?

Jane had long ago discovered that she was temperamentally unsuited to lies or deception. At sixteen she'd had three regular boyfriends, all of whom had professed to be madly in love with her and, not wanting to offend any of them, she'd been forced to spin a huge web of deceit which had resulted in such ludicrous situations as having to sit through the same movie three nights in a row because she hadn't dared admit to numbers two and three that she'd already seen it with number one. It was when she'd found herself having to write down the complicated alibis she'd invented for herself that she decided enough was enough. It had taken a while to disentangle herself without hurting anyone, but from the age of eighteen, she prided herself on the fact that she'd given up all but the whitest of lies. The elimination of falsehood from her life had been like a huge burden falling off her back, and as a surprising bonus Jane had discovered that she could tell men the most outrageous and unflattering truths about herself and, providing she kept a smile on her face, they would merely hug her and say how wonderfully original she was or else laugh and assume she was lying. Honesty had proved so successful for her that she assumed others too, and most especially her best friend, Virginia, must have made the same liberating discovery. It occurred to her suddenly that perhaps Sarah had somehow got things wrong. She resolved to speak to Virginia about the matter at the earliest possible opportunity.

Tea at Virginia's house without an attendant nanny wasn't quite the civilized affair Jane had grown accustomed to. There was no question of going up to the drawing room. Instead they were confined to the kitchen, their conversation interspersed with yells and thuds which wafted through the double doors leading to the next-door playroom where Ben and Joshua had already covered every inch of floor space with toys. Ben was now busy denuding the wall shelves, the

78

contents of which he hurled systematically into the central pile. Philly took one blissful look at the chaos and dived beatifically in.

'Aren't they sweet?' Jane was momentarily distracted. 'People always say they love looking at their children when they're asleep, but I think what I enjoy most is watching Philly when he's totally absorbed in playing with his friends. Isn't it lovely that they all get on so well together?' At that moment one of Ben's missiles hit Joshua on the head and he burst into noisy sobbing. Virginia, who was looking distinctly less glossy than usual, went to the cupboard and produced three tubes of Smarties, which gained them instant silence.

Virginia poured Jane a cup of tea and sat down at the table opposite her, passing her a plate of toasted buns. 'How much longer are you here for, Janie?' she asked.

'Well, actually I'm making a political stand,' Jane remarked with her mouth full. 'You know I told you they were having a referendum on divorce in Italy? Well they've fixed it for May the twelfth and I've told Giorgio I'm not going back until it's over, and then only if they vote to keep it.'

'Oh but they will, won't they?'

'I don't know. You'd think so certainly. There are so many thousands of other couples in the same position as us. One quarter of the population apparently. But I've been getting worried recently. Italy's run by the Christian Democrats, you see, and they're presenting the divorce law as some sort of dreadful Communist plot to disrupt the nation. Like vote for divorce today and tomorrow you'll have Moscow battering at the gates. Even quite civilized people of Giorgio's age have been telling me that although they're in favour of divorce in principle, they're going to vote against it in the referendum because they don't approve of this particular law.'

'But that's crazy –'

'I know. I actually brought a dinner party to a standstill the other night by accusing a client of Giorgio's of voting to condemn my son to permanent illegitimacy. He was frightfully embarrassed. I don't think he knew. But he didn't say he'd change his mind.'

'What will you do if they vote against it?'

'I just won't go back. I couldn't live in a country that was so uncivilized as to condemn thousands of children like Philly to a sort of legal limbo. Besides, it's awful for me too. I have no official status either. At first I had to go to the police every three months and be ogled by the entire force, who knew perfectly well I was Giorgio's mistress, and treated me as if I were a prostitute. Now Giorgio's done a deal with one of them. He comes to our house with the forms and Giorgio slips him the odd antique and he extends my visa. But I can't go on like that for ever.'

'No, I can see you can't. But what will Giorgio do if you don't go back?'

'He'll have to live here. He could still work. He's got several friends who are dealers here and just go back to Italy now and then to sell things. It would mean I could have a career too, and eventually, once he'd established residence, he could get an English divorce and marry me here. Oh, Verge, it would be so wonderful –'

'But has he agreed to do that?'

'No, he hasn't. He's convinced they'll vote to keep divorce and refuses to talk about it until after the referendum. I suppose he's got a point. Anyway it's all fixed. He's leaving here at the end of April and stopping off in Paris to see his children, then going on to Venice to vote. If it's yes to divorce, Philly and I will fly out as soon as possible.'

'And if it's no?'

'Then the battle starts. He thinks I'm being unreasonable, you see. He says marriage is just a piece of paper and he made his commitment to me when we agreed to have Philly – which is all very well now that Philly's little, but which'll cause all sorts of problems later with his education and so on.'

'Oh God. Perhaps it's just as well you didn't have another one.'

'I know.   All this referendum business only came up in January, of course, but I've obviously put the matter on hold since then. I'm certainly going to have another try, though, if they do vote to keep divorce.' She paused.

'I was talking about it to Sarah today,' she went on. 'She thinks I should just have my coil removed and not tell Giorgio.'

'Does she?' Verge got up and went over to the kettle and poured herself some more tea. 'Have another bun, Janie.'

'Thanks.' Jane waited until it became obvious Virginia wasn't going to say any more. 'Verge –' she began.

'Yes?'

'Sarah told me today that you had a coil in when you conceived Ben. It's not true, is it?' Their renewed closeness over tea had almost convinced her it couldn't be.

There was a shriek from the playroom. Ben, having finished his Smarties, had decided to wrest Joshua's packet away from him. Joshua, his face and T-shirt smothered in chocolate, was not prepared to take this lying down. Virginia rose to her feet in fury and strode over to Ben.

'God, you're a little pig sometimes,' she shouted. 'Give Joshua back his Smarties at once or I'll send you to bed,' and she gave him a resounding slap on his dungareed bum.

Jane, momentarily transfixed, felt like cheering. Verge had always professed herself to be totally against discipline of any kind for children and classed smacking as 'physical violence'. Ben, having cottoned on to this fact, seemed to spend most of his time testing his mother with new excesses. Jane felt that he was basically rather a sweet child, but that Verge's unwillingness to impose rules and structure on his existence had resulted in a deep insecurity which manifested itself in increasingly thuggish behaviour. Now, although his eyes filled with tears and his jaw dropped open in an expression of utter astonishment, Jane could sense that his underlying emotion was one of relief at having for once received his just deserts.

A moment later Verge had spoilt it all by sinking to her knees in front of him. 'Oh God, I'm sorry, Ben,' she said. 'Mummy didn't mean to hurt you. I was just upset. Mummies do get upset too, you know, sometimes. Will you forgive me, darling?' and she put her arms round him and hugged him.

Jane glanced instinctively at Ben's face. He had stiffened in his mother's embrace and his eyes, which met hers over the top of Virginia's head, were full of fear and bewilderment. Jane turned away and reached in her bag for a cigarette.

When Virginia returned to the tea table a few minutes later she was visibly shaken. 'My baby book says that if you do lose control for a moment and smack them you should always apologize to them immediately afterwards,' she explained.

Jane took drag of her cigarette. 'Who's it by?' she asked.

'Oh some woman doctor. She's very highly qualified.'

'Really? Does she have children?'

'No. I don't think so.' For a moment they sat in silence. 'Verge,' Jane persisted, 'was it true what Sarah said?'

Virginia took a mouthful of tea. 'Yes it was,' she replied. 'The reason I didn't tell you at the time was because I thought it would be so awful for Ben if he found out he hadn't been wanted.'

'Oh no, surely not!' Jane exclaimed. 'After all he must know how much you love him now.' The words sounded hollow even to her own ears. Verge didn't bother to reply. There was another awkward silence. 'Didn't you tell anyone?' Jane asked.

'I did tell my mother,' Verge admitted. 'She was all thrilled about my pregnancy, you see, because she'd been on at me for ages to provide Robin with an heir and I didn't want to give her the satisfaction of thinking I'd done it to please her.'

'And you told Sarah.' This was what Jane found the most inexplicable. In fact it made her feel extraordinarily wary, as if their whole friendship was one-sided and based on a sham.

'Oh well, I felt I had to,' Verge said dismissively. 'She's such a tart, you see. I thought it was my duty to warn her so she could take extra precautions.'

'What, Sarah?' Jane asked in amazement. 'But hasn't she just got this one boyfriend that she met on the day trip to France last autumn? I thought they were practically engaged.'

'She may just have one at the moment, but before him there was a new one practically every night. She used to pick them up in her local pub. I once asked her how many men she'd had and she told me she'd stopped counting at three hundred.'

'Good God! Are you sure? She doesn't seem at all the type.'

'I know. Yes, of course I'm sure. I used to get the gory details every morning. She says black men are the best. It's something about the smell of their skins. Apparently once you've been with them you never really want to go with a white man again.'

'Goodness,' said Jane lamely, thoroughly side-tracked by these sophisticated revelations. She had already noticed a tendency in Verge to surround herself with people she regarded as highly promiscuous, while obsinately maintaining her own isolated virtue in the midst of their activities. It had occasionally made Jane wonder if Verge wasn't something of a voyeur. 'Didn't it bother you?' she added curiously.

'Not really. I'd rather the children were looked after by someone who was getting it every night than by some warped old spinster who'd take out all her frustrations on them.'

'Well, there is that, I suppose,' Jane agreed dubiously. 'But what about her children? Did they know what was going on?'

'Oh yes. She used to take the men back to her flat with her, you see.'

'Oh dear,' Jane thought how much she would have hated it if her own mother had brought home a string of lovers. She felt full of compassion for Sarah's children. 'But they seem so well-adjusted,' she said.

'Do you think so? I find them very sly and odd. They're always giving me funny looks when I come in and whispering about me when they think I'm not looking. I've told Sarah I don't want them to come here in the holidays any more.'

Jane felt a flash of indignation, but she knew that if she defended the girls and told Verge it was cruel of her to force Sarah to leave them alone all day, it would antagonize her against them still more. 'I actually find they're a wonderful help in entertaining Philly,' she said cautiously.

'Maybe, but that's Sarah's job. I don't pay her just to bring her own children here and feed them at my expense.'

Jane reached in her bag for another cigarette. She kept her eyes lowered deliberately so Verge wouldn't see the anger in them. Keep calm, she was telling herself. Don't say anything. It won't do Sarah or the girls any good. After all, Sarah's got to go on working for Verge when you go back to Venice.

'Is something the matter?' There was a definite challenge in Verge's voice, as if she were spoiling for a fight. They'd had terrible arguments as children, Jane remembered, although it was years now since they'd quarrelled.

'Oh no.' Jane forced herself to return a relaxed smile. 'I suppose I was just a bit surprised by what you told me about Sarah. Did you really say three hundred?'

'Yes, and she was so pathetic about it too. Each time she has a new man she's convinced he's going to be the love of her life, and then he lets her down and she picks up another one and within a few days she's making wedding plans with him.'

'How awful.' Jane couldn't imagine anything sadder. She felt genuine compassion for Sarah.

'You're not shocked, are you?' Verge said maliciously, presumably implying that someone with Jane's past didn't have the right to be shocked by anything. She was definitely trying to annoy her, Jane decided.

'No, it doesn't shock me,' Jane replied. 'I just find it terribly sad.'

'Well, she shouldn't be such an idiot as to sleep with them all, should she?' Verge said impatiently.

'I don't know,' Jane replied. 'I'd have thought there was safety in numbers actually. I know I always found that sleeping with lots of men seemed to anaesthetize me against falling in love. I think I'd be far more vulnerable now, after having been faithful to Giorgio for five years.'

'*Have* you?'

'Yes, of course. Haven't you to Robin?'

'Yes I have.' Verge had been about to add, 'But that's different,' but then, realizing it probably wasn't, decided to keep quiet.

'Not', Jane went on, 'that I could ever have competed with Sarah's score.

'*Couldn't* you?'

'Good God, no. Giorgio's number twenty-nine. It seems kind of incomplete, doesn't it? Thirty would be more significant.'

'Really? Is that all?' Virginia seemed genuinely surprised. Jane felt another flash of irritation. Presumably Verge had been going round for years telling people she'd had more men through her than the Hyde Park underpass.

'Well, what about you then? You've only had two –'

'One,' Virginia said quickly.

'But what about Johnny,' Jane asked, 'the one at college, after you'd split up with Robin? You told me your mother caught you in bed together.' Surely she couldn't have forgotten the hysterical phone call she'd made to Jane late that night after her parents had gone to sleep? Jane had been in bed with rather a dishy cameraman at the time, but she'd been touched by Verge's almost unprecedented distress and vulnerability, and had done her best to be supportive.

'She did,' Virginia replied, 'but we hadn't actually done anything together . My mother came in too soon.'

'Oh I see.' What Jane saw was that for reasons known only to herself, Verge had decided once more to rewrite history. It was her second proof in one day of Verge's lack of trust in her, and made her feel she needed to get away from her in order to think things out. The opportune arrival of Robin a few moments later made the perfect excuse to leave. Her offer of help in clearing was refused, so she scooped Philly up, kissed Virginia and Robin unenthusiastically and went home to Giorgio.

Two hours later, when the playroom had been tidied, the children dispatched to bed and Robin, bathed and changed, had gone off to his club to gamble, Virginia made her way wearily upstairs and lay down on her bed, with a cold flannel on her forehead to relieve the sharp pains which were stabbing relentlessly at the back of her eyes. Had she been foolish, she wondered, to tell Jane that lie about Johnny? In her fury at having been caught out by Jane earlier she had been unable to think straight, and had just said the first thing that came into her head. Jane had seemed to accept her story all right – almost too easily, in fact. But after all it had happened years ago, and Jane had no proof. If she ever went to Robin with the story it would just be a case of Jane's word against Virginia's, and Virginia had so thoroughly discredited Jane in Robin's eyes already that she knew which of them he would believe. Besides, she reminded herself, she and Robin were safely married now with two children, and even if she had only induced him to marry her by pretending he was the only man she had ever slept with, he couldn't now divorce her just because he found out that she'd had a fling with a boy at college eight years before.

Johnny had been so tall and blond and good-looking. He'd exuded the same sort of golden aura as Jane, the same casual academic brilliance, and the same danger-ously light-hearted attitude towards sex. Virginia had told him she was a virgin, even though at that point she'd been sleeping with Robin for about a year. This was because her mother had told her she'd never get anyone worthwhile (by which she meant rich and titled) to marry her unless he believed he was the first. She'd tried to tell herself that maybe it was true. Robin had been almost as inexperienced sexually as she was, and was painfully clumsy and inept. They hadn't been able to make love very often because they were both still living with her parents, and whenever they had she'd found it painful and difficult. Perhaps she really was technically a virgin. She'd said this once to Robin, and he'd been furious and told her that of course she wasn't. Unfortunately Johnny hadn't believed her either, and had insisted on finding out.

They'd chosen an evening when her parents were going to Glyndebourne and the house was empty. Johnny shared a room in student digs in Cromwell Road so there would have been no privacy there. He'd brought a pile of records round to play on her stereo in the chaste white bedroom where Robin had never been allowed to intrude, and when she'd emerged from the bathroom, modestly wrapped in a full-length red and white cotton negligée which she'd bought to take to houseparties during the season, she'd found him lying on her bed in just his underpants, listening to The Doors.

He didn't hear her come in, and she stood in the doorway for a moment looking at his body. He was only nineteen, a few months younger than her, and not yet fully developed. His torso was thin and white and hairless like a girl's, and he looked curiously vulnerable without his clothes. Verge was overcome by a wave of tenderness for him. The concept of making love to a man purely because he pleased her physically was entirely new to her but for a moment, looking at Johnny, it flashed through her mind that perhaps for once this would be an evening when she was actually going to get more out of sex than just gritting her teeth and thinking of the title.

She'd walked over to him and knelt on the floor beside the bed, and he'd smiled at her and kissed her on the lips and drawn her in beside him under the covers. After the initial tussle with the negligée, which he'd been kind enough not to laugh at, she was surprised and enchanted to feel the softness of his skin against hers. It was a summer evening and the sun was still shining through the muslin curtains onto her bed. Virginia closed her eyes and remembered the afternoon, years before, when she and Jane had gone up to the roof terrace with their homework to sunbathe.

Greatly daring, Virginia had suggested they take all their clothes off and sunbathe nude, and when Jane, giggling, had obeyed, Verge had insisted on rubbing oil over her in order to protect her fair skin from the sun. She'd started with her back, kneeling beside her and using gentle circular movements until Jane had stopped chattering and Verge had felt her relax and lie passive under her hands.

'Why don't you turn over and let me do your front?' she'd suggested with deliberate casualness, and to her surprise and

*triumph, Jane had rolled over obediently, her eyes tightly closed
and her arms folded modestly across her chest at first, but soon
dropping to her sides as Virginia's hands moved insistently
upwards over her diaphragm and out, with a fanning movement, so that they were cupping Jane's little breasts.*

Verge caught her breath as Johnny's mouth closed
softly round her nipple, and her hands clasped his head
automatically and twined themselves in his long blond
hair. She found it miraculous that a man could be so
gentle – as if caressing her was an end in itself rather
than a perfunctory text book preliminary to the main
action. For once she forgot to tense herself when his
hand moved downwards between her legs. This was no
future husband who had to have his favours strictly
rationed so that he'd eventually become desperate
enough to propose to her. They were just two teenagers
lying together innocently in the sunlight who'd accidentally stumbled for the first time on the miracle of sensual
pleasure.

*Jane's nipples had hardened under Verge's exploring fingers,
and her face had taken on a rapt expression of almost religious
intensity.* Virginia moaned and opened her legs, remembering the sense of power and tenderness which had
overwhelmed her. She drew Johnny's head upwards and
kissed him on the lips, as she had longed to kiss Jane, and
when his cock slid inside her she was so moist and ready
for him that it seemed merely a natural extension of
his caresses, and she was flooded again with the sense
of sweetness and anticipation that she'd felt on that
summer afternoon with Jane, and thereafter only in
dreams.

Her pleasure had been shattered on this occasion, as
on the previous one, by the shrill foreign tones of Maria,
her mother, screaming at her in Polish. Verge had been
so sure she and Johnny were safe that she hadn't even
bothered to lock the bedroom door. Later she found out
that her parents' windscreen had shattered on the
motorway and they'd been forced to stop at a garage
and get it repaired. They could have gone on to
Glyndebourne and seen the second act of the opera, but

had decided against it. They only went there to see their friends and have dinner with them in the interval. They often missed the last act anyway.

Maria broke into English and ordered Johnny out of the house. He asked Virginia if she wanted to go with him, but she begged him to leave, and in the end he obeyed. Maria had kept her up for another hour or so shouting what a filthy little whore she was and how stupid to throw herself away on a nobody when Maria was sure she'd get Robin back if she hung on long enough. She asked if Johnny had made love to her, and Virginia had denied it. She felt totally broken by the scene, and by the realization that whenever she tried to go against her mother's wishes she came unstuck.

Virginia knew there were great plans under way to throw her in Robin's path again. Maria reckoned that if Robin saw Virginia was still in love with him and didn't have anyone else, he would be bound to marry her in the end. He was a gentleman. He had been to public school. He couldn't do anything else. Virginia wasn't so sure. There was a streak of coldness, almost cruelty, in Robin that frightened her sometimes. She felt he could see through the casual friendliness that Maria showed towards him and sense the tigress hunger that lay underneath. She believed that this was the real reason he had broken off with her, but of course she would never dare say such a thing to Maria. Maria was so sure she could get him back. Virginia was frightened to think of how angry she would be if the attempt failed.

She wasn't too happy to think of it succeeding either. She felt that if Robin did marry her it wouldn't be because he loved her, but because he couldn't get anything better, and that part of him would be pleased by the fact that she and her family had been prepared to grovel in order to get him, and would take great pleasure in seeing them continue to grovel for the rest of their lives. But that was hypothetical. Everything might change if he married her, and at least Maria would be pleased with her, and it was certain that her life at home would be intolerable if she didn't try. It was really as simple as that. She would be sorry to give up Johnny, but perhaps they could still be friends.

Johnny, however, had not seemed to want to be friends. He nodded to her whenever they saw each other in the canteen, but never made any effort to speak to her alone. He couldn't call her at home, of course, because of Maria, but as far as Virginia knew, he hadn't even tried. It reminded her of Jane's behaviour after the sunbathing incident. They had both gone away for their school holidays shortly afterwards, and not seen each other until the start of the autumn term. Virginia had been glowing with health and longing to see Jane again, but on the first day of term Jane had been distant with her. She had avoided being alone with her, and, most ridiculous of all, had chosen a desk as far away from hers as possible. Inside, Virginia had seethed with resentment, but she pretended not to notice anything, afraid that if she picked a quarrel she would lose Jane for good. Jane wasn't able to remain standoffish for long, and soon their friendship had been back on its old footing, but the moment on the roof when Virginia had so nearly been carried away by her love for Jane was never mentioned by either of them again.

These two incidents had been enough to prove to Virginia that sexual passion was both bad and dangerous. As the years went by she had looked on scornfully as Jane became embroiled in a series of turbulent romances. She had minimized Jane's triumphs and emphasized her disasters and reiterated to herself, even in the face of direct evidence to the contrary, how deeply unhappy Jane must be.

For as long as she could remember, one of Virginia's chief preoccupations in life had been to score off Jane. At school, maddeningly, her attempts had been doomed to constant failure, but with her marriage to Robin she had evened the score triumphantly and when Jane's first marriage had failed after only a few months, and she had retired, defeated, to Italy, Virginia felt as if she had taken a giant leap towards the supremacy she had been fighting towards for the past seventeen years. Jane had however returned, seemingly unbowed, with Giorgio in tow, and however much Verge might tell herself it didn't really count because Jane and Giorgio weren't married, she felt the edge of competition keenly enough to make maintaining the fiction of her perfect marriage an absolute necessity to her. She might grumble to Jane occasionally about Robin's racing – it was also, after all, a way of showing off to her about how much money he was making – but it was important to her that Jane should know nothing of her own failures, such as the messy, unplanned pregnancy, which she felt obscurely had reduced her to Jane's own level of a woman at the mercy of nature, or the reminder of a past lover which she was afraid of her husband finding out. To be faced with Jane's knowledge of both these secrets in one day had made Virginia feel extraordinarily insecure and full of impotent fury towards her friend.

One of the worst things was that she had absolutely no one she could confide in. Her thoughts turned longingly to Alex. She couldn't tell him, of course, but she always found his company extraordinarily soothing, and she planned to ask him round to dinner anyway, but had put off ringing him because she hadn't wanted him to come round while Jane was there. He and Jane had seemed to be getting far too cosy lately. The trouble had started on New Year's Eve, and since then they had met twice more at dinner parties, and to Virginia's annoyance, had spent most of the evening deep in conversation with each other, seemingly oblivious to the rest of the assembled company.

She reached for the phone by the bed and dialled his number, allowing it to ring long after she had abandoned all hope that he might answer it. Her fury increased. It was Jane's fault. How dare she worm her way in like that and screw up her friendships? And how dare she talk to her nanny behind her back and get her to blurt out her secrets? The pain behind her eyes was throbbing unbearably. She sank back on to the bed and started to plan her revenge.

The phone rang late on Monday afternoon, just as Jane was about to get Philly up from his nap.

'Jane? It's Sarah.'

'Sarah! I didn't recognize your voice. Is something wrong?'

'Virginia's just sacked me.'

'No!' In the background Jane could hear Philly's imperious chant of 'Mamamamamam'. She had to go to him. She was afraid he might climb out of his cot and fall. 'Why?'

'She told me she didn't need a nanny any more. She said the hours didn't work and it was too expensive and she was going to get an au pair.'

'Oh I am sorry. But she's given you proper notice, hasn't she?'

'Well, I'm afraid I was so upset by her manner that I just walked out.'

'Oh dear. Poor Sarah. I do understand.'

'The thing is, Jane, that I can't afford just to work two days a week for you. I'm going to have to look round for a full-time job –'

'Yes, I can see that.' Because of her longing to get to Philly, Jane was being a bit slow on the uptake. A sudden horrible thought struck her. 'But you will be here the week after next, won't you, when I do my commercial? Giorgio's going to be away, you see –'

'Well, I don't want to let you down, Jane,' Sarah replied, 'but I don't know how I'm going to manage.'

The full extent of Verge's betrayal hit Jane at last. Verge knew perfectly well about her commercial, which she had been talking about for weeks. 'Sarah.' she said, 'I've got to go and get Philly up now, but come to me tomorrow as planned and we'll think of a way round it. I'll see you don't lose out, I promise you.' It was obvious to Jane that she was going to have to employ Sarah full time. It would take up most of her earnings, but she couldn't be without someone now, just as she was on the brink of getting work. Damn Virginia, she thought.

'Oh thank you, Jane,' Sarah sniffed. 'I'm sorry to be so upset. It's just that Virginia was so nasty to me. I think,' she added, 'that she was absolutely furious with me for telling you about Ben being an accident.'

'Oh God. I suppose I shouldn't have said anything to

her, but I thought that as she'd told you it couldn't be a secret.'

'So did I,' Sarah agreed. 'Besides, Virginia's always telling me you're her best friend. I couldn't see any possible harm in you knowing. Jane –'

'What?' Jane asked impatiently.

'I don't know if you realize it, but Virginia really is extremely jealous of you, you know.'

CHAPTER SIX

April 1974

E ver since Sandra's abortive suicide attempt the year before, Alex had been zealous in accepting her invitations, even when they came at the most awkward moments.

It had been a long time before he'd felt he could relax in her company again, although mercifully she had never reproached him for saving her life, nor even complained at his going against the wishes expressed in her letter by summoning Martin to her hospital bedside. It had seemed to give her a grim sort of pleasure, when she finally regained consciousness, to find the two of them sitting beside her, both abject with their separate remorses and full of the desire to atone for the grief they had caused her. She and Martin had been reconciled, and had moved into an attractive new flat overlooking one of the canals in Little Venice. Alex was on his way there now, battling against the lunchtime traffic and wondering desperately how he was going to get back to the office for his four o'clock meeting.

Her summons had come that morning at ten, and he, alarmed by the sharp note of hysteria in her voice, had found himself promising meekly to be at her flat at one. What could have gone wrong now, he asked himself. She and Martin had seemed so happy recently, and had even been talking about trying to have a baby. Sandra had given up her job because Martin reckoned it might be work stress that had so far prevented her from conceiving, and she had told Alex how much she was enjoying being a lady of leisure, buying things for the flat, eating the special high protein diet which Martin had worked out for her, and putting up her feet in the afternoons and listening to classical music.

Alex looked at her searchingly when she opened the door to him. She was wearing a purply blue Indian cotton dress which he had once admired, and was carefully made up and smiling tightly, though there was no disguising the slight puffiness round her eyes. Her manner, however, was light and social and Alex found himself playing along with it. If there was really anything wrong, he told himself, she would be bound to come out with it eventually, and if there wasn't he would only upset her by asking her what the matter was. Perhaps, he thought hopefully, she had now resolved the problem, whatever it had been. Surely Martin couldn't have been such an idiot as to go after another woman just when he was trying to get his wife pregnant?

He followed her into the sitting room which was furnished with beanbags and low, soft sofas running along the walls. The flat was open plan, with all the rooms merging into each other, and Sandra and Martin's large, low bed. smothered with mirrored Indian cushions, could be glimpsed through the double doors at the far end. Since giving up work. Sandra had acquired two silver Persian cats to keep her company, a brother and sister, who, at Alex's suggestion she had named Siegmund and Sieglinde. The more docile Siegmund came and sat on Alex's knee as he sank into the longer of the two sofas, while Sieglinde, desperate to attract his attention, clawed her way, yowling, up the white, hessian curtains, and when this didn't work, took a flying leap onto the sofa next to Alex, causing him to jump and almost spill the large Bloody Mary which Sandra had smilingly handed to him.

'My God, Sandy,' he said after taking the first sip, 'this is absolutely lethal. I don't think you'd better give me any more after this. I do actually have to be back at the office at four.' He thought it was only tactful to say this at the beginning so that if she did have anything to tell him she wouldn't get all offended if he broke off in the middle.

'Don't worry,' she smiled at him reassuringly. 'I'll make sure you don't get too drunk. Perhaps we'd better eat at once then, so you won't have to rush.'

Lunch – spinach quiche, with a green, leafy salad and nutty bread – had been laid in the kitchen. Alex, who had never allowed his romantic vicissitudes to affect his appetite, wolfed it down appreciatively, exclaiming with delight when, for dessert, Sandra went to the fridge and produced a huge bowl of strawberries and cream.

'Sandy, you're a genius!' he exclaimed. 'Where did you get them? They're the first I've seen this year.'

'Me too. We'd better make a wish, hadn't we? Let's make it something practical, though, that we both think we can get. I've already decided exactly what I want,' she smiled at him.

'Oh all right then.' He knew that to her mind that excluded Georgina, but he was so relieved to find her in such a good mood that he didn't allow himself to be offended. 'It's lovely to see you so happy,' he went on incautiously. 'I was quite worried about you when you rang this morning.'

'Yes. Well, I had had a bit of a shock.' She was heaping the strawberries on to his plate as she spoke, and for a moment her hand trembled and she dropped one of them onto the table. 'Can you bear to hear about it?' she asked.

'Yes of course.' It couldn't be that bad, he reasoned. Not if she was in control enough to have prepared this delicious lunch for him.

'I was going through the pockets of Martin's suit this morning,' she told him, 'so I could take it to the cleaners, and I came across this letter in the inside pocket. It was from Seamus.'

'Oh yes?' For a moment Alex had feared it might be from a woman. 'Martin went over to Ireland to stay with him last weekend, didn't he? How is the old bugger?'

Sandra looked at him sharply. 'Why did you call him that?' she asked.

'Just a manner of speech. I don't think I meant anything special –' He put down his spoon. Oh no, he thought.

'Did you know he was homosexual?' she persisted.

'Well there were rumours at Eton, but then there were about almost everybody. I never heard anything at Oxford. He was always too busy getting pissed out of his skull.'

'It was a revolting letter,' Sandra stated. 'All gushing and flirtatious, saying how lovely it had been to see Martin and going on and on about some walk they'd taken together, and how they'd lain down in the heather afterwards under the stars –'

Alex was feeling a bit sick. 'Seamus was always very keen on astronomy,' he remarked feebly.

'Oh come on, Alex.' Sandra allowed her anger to flash through for a moment. 'Surely you can't think I'm that naive –'

'But he didn't actually say they'd done anything, did he?' Alex asked hopefully. To him this was even worse than a woman would have been. He'd always looked on Martin as one of his best friends. Alex had never really got on with hearty, competitive men such as Robin Askew or Henry Cunningham, far preferring the company of their wives. But Martin, in spite of his numerous female conquests, had always seemed so gentle and sensitive. Alex actually liked him better than he did Sandra, although he'd always been careful not to show it. If Martin were secretly gay the implications were too horrendous to contemplate.

'No, he didn't,' Sandra said. Alex heaved a sigh of relief. 'Not in so many words. But it was definitely a love letter. At the beginning he called him "Darling Martin," and,' she paused dramatically before delivering the *coup de grâce*, 'the M of Martin was the most revolting drawing of a pin man bending over with his bum in the air.'

Alex felt a wave of revulsion which he was immediately ashamed of. 'Oh God,' he said faintly. Then: 'Sandy I do see that it must have been a shock to you, but although it does look as if Seamus might have been after Martin, I'm sure Martin would never have agreed to anything like that –'

'I rang him,' she said, 'after I'd calmed down a bit, and asked him. The bastard admitted everything. He said they'd drunk a lot at dinner and gone out for this walk and it had just seemed like the right thing to do at the time. He even had the gall to say I ought not to mind about it because at least he wasn't being unfaithful to me with another woman.' She shrugged. 'How about some coffee?'

Seated on one of the low sofas stroking Siegmund while Sandra poured out his coffee, Alex gave a surreptitious glance at his watch. Only two o'clock, thank goodness, and as Sandra was still maintaining her admirable state of calm there seemed no reason why he shouldn't get to his meeting on time. He allowed himself to relax back into the sofa. It really was unbelievably comfortable. The sort of sofa which once you sank down into it you began to feel you never wanted to get up again.

Sandra finished her ministrations and sat down beside him. 'So tell me about you and Georgina,' she said softly.

Alex smiled at her. 'I wish there was more to tell,' he said. 'I'm afraid this month has just been the usual series of cancelled appointments. I think the Royal Opera House have become rather suspicious of me because I'm constantly standing outside the Box Office just before curtain up trying to sell my spare ticket. We have an agreement you see, that if she's not there by seven fifteen she's not going to come.'

'Oh but how awful for you!' Sandra exclaimed. 'When they cost so much money. Surely she could let you know before that?'

'Well, I have tried to explain to her that I wouldn't mind nearly so much if I knew in good time, but of course I do understand that it's not her fault if Henry turns up unexpectedly. He seems to have some sort of sixth sense that she's meeting me, you see. And of course it's equally awful for her to be all dressed up and ready and then to have to invent all sorts of lies to calm him down.'

'Why doesn't she just tell him the truth?'

'She feels he's not ready for it. It was such a blow to him that Labour won the election, you see. All his business interests are at stake, and she thinks it would be too cruel to abandon him now. Besides, she couldn't leave the children. The youngest daughter's only eight now. But she'll be going to boarding school when she's eleven –'

'So she's expecting you to carry on like this for another three years?'

'I suppose so. But she says, and I agree with her, that three years is nothing if it means that afterwards we'll be able to spend a whole lifetime together –'

'But it'll be a bit late for children, won't it?'

'Well, women do have children when they're over forty, but I wouldn't really mind if she didn't. Her own children are so sweet that I'd be perfectly happy just to be a stepfather to them.'

Sandra made an impatient gesture. 'How saintly of you,' she said. 'I wonder if you'll feel the same when you're forty and Georgina's going through the menopause. Don't you think you might have some regrets then about all you've given up for her?'

Privately Alex was convinced that there would never come a time when he wouldn't feel privileged to be with Georgina, but his women friends seemed to find this idea so irritating that he decided to be evasive. 'Verge is always saying that too,' he told her. 'I really can't say, Sandy.'

'Oh poor Alex. And how are you ever going to find out when she keeps you hanging around like this? When did you last see her?'

'Three weeks ago. It was one of the times I wasn't expecting her. I've given her the keys to my house, you know, and it was about eleven o'clock. I was lying in bed reading when I heard the front door slam and then her footsteps walking across the hallway and up the stairs. She just came into the bedroom without saying anything and started to undress slowly in front of me, almost as if she was doing a striptease.' He smiled at the memory.

'And nothing since then?'

'No.' He shook his head. 'Nothing.'

'Poor love, you must be so lonely.'

'I have made a point recently of going out more,' he said defensively. 'Verge and Robin have been wonderful in that respect. I have an open invitation to go round there any night when I'm on my own.'

'But isn't Robin away a lot?' Sandra asked suspiciously. Alex had invited the two couples to dinner one night feeling sure they'd get on like a house on fire but strangely enough the evening hadn't been a conspicuous success. Martin had adopted a slightly satirical air towards Robin, whom he seemed to regard as the archetypal upper-class twit, while Robin had become increasingly patronizing as the evening wore on over what he afterwards termed Martin's 'hippy attitudes'. The two women had been studiously polite to each other and then lost no time in ringing Alex the following morning to bitch about each other, Sandra sneering at the contrast between Verge's designer clothes and militant left-wing principles, and Verge dismissing Sandra as a loser and hopelessly neurotic.

'Yes, he is,' Alex replied, 'but then Verge very sweetly invites me over to take pot luck with her.'

'I bet she does. Martin and I are both convinced she's got a terrific crush on you.'

'Oh no.' Alex laughed dismissively. It was true that Verge's sharp black eyes always took on a soft melting expression whenever she saw him and that she had started to turn her head slightly when he greeted her so that his brotherly kiss should land on her lips, but Alex regarded this merely as a sign of the warmth of her friendship. 'In fact she's always introducing me to other girls,' he added. This was true, although he'd noticed that whenever he seemed to get on with them Verge would immediately start to criticize them unmercifully.

'Anyone nice?'

'There was rather a sweet girl called Camilla, whom she produced for me on New Year's Eve. Camilla actually invited me to stay a weekend with her parents in the country. Unfortunately they'd organized the most ghastly tennis tournament on the Sunday. I was Camilla's partner in the doubles and she got frightfully cross with me when we lost.'

Sandra laughed. 'Who else?'

'Well, she's got the most beautiful friend called Jane.

She's married to an Italian, but he's often away. I gather he buys paintings at Christie's and Sotheby's and smuggles them back to Italy and sells them at a vast profit. She's Verge's best friend. They were at school together. She spends most of the year in Italy, but sees a lot of Verge when she's in London. As a matter of fact I took her to the opera last week.' He was still feeling rather pleased with himself over that one. It was one of the evenings when Georgina had cancelled early. He'd gone round to Verge's for an early drink and found Jane there. It transpired that she was on her own too, and he'd just come straight out with it and asked her. To his amazement she had accepted.

'What did you see?'

'*Otello*. It was wonderful. She'd never been to the opera before, but she loved it. She'd studied the play at drama school – she used to be an actress you know – and she had all these interesting ideas about it. I did rather enjoy being there with such a beautiful woman,' he confessed. 'I watched her as she left to go to the loo, and everyone was turning to stare at her.'

'But it would be hopeless, wouldn't it, if you got involved with another married woman?' Sandra asked quickly.

'Oh yes. Although in fact she's not actually married. He's waiting for his Italian divorce, you see.' Sandra looked suddenly wary. 'But of course they live together and have a two-year-old son,' he went on, 'so it's the same thing. Anyway, she's not in the slightest bit interested in me. I've never actually met a girl before who seems so totally disinterested in flirting.' He stopped, feeling rather peeved. Sandra laughed.

'Poor Alex.' She slid her arm along the back of the sofa and started to stroke his hair. It felt nice and relaxing. He turned his head and smiled at her.

'Anyway she's going back to Italy at any moment,' he said. 'I probably won't see her again.'

Sandra tickled the back of his neck. 'Well then, perhaps I'd better comfort you,' she said, deliberately reaching round with her other hand and starting to stroke the inside of his thigh.

Sandra's voice was so soothing and her gestures so quietly authoritative and redolent of the professional medical assistant that at first, when her hand crept up to his groin and, Siegmund, displaced, jumped angrily to the floor and chased his sister up the curtains, Alex hardly registered what was happening. It was only as his cock began to stir and Sandra, with a low laugh, dropped to her knees in front of him and coolly unzipped his flies, that he managed to bring out a token protest.

'But, Sandy – what about Martin?'

'What about him? You surely can't think I owe him any loyalty after what I've told you?' Even as she spoke, she was calmly undoing his belt and trouser buttons and reaching inside his Y-fronts for his penis.

'No, but I'm his friend –'

'Yes, and you're my friend too.' Her right hand, clasping his penis, had started to move gently up and down, while her left hand cupped his balls. 'My very dear friend, who needs comforting, just as I need comforting. Look, why don't we just forget about Martin and Georgina for this afternoon and have a nice time together?' and she smiled briefly up at him before bending her head forward and sliding her lips round his cock.

Alex allowed his head to sink back on the cushions as the pleasurable sensation took over. She's really very good at this, he thought dispassionately, as her movements became more rapid. She seemed genuinely greedy for him, as if trying to absorb as much of him as possible, and he was touched by her generosity. Sandra, he was sure, would never gag or run to the bathroom afterwards, as Julie had. She was right of course, about their owing no loyalty to Martin or Georgina. Georgina had admitted to him at the beginning of their affair that she still slept with Henry occasionally out of pity, and although he had been hurt, it had seemed to him that as a married man himself, he had no right to protest. After his divorce he hadn't liked to broach the subject again, perhaps for fear of receiving the wrong answer. As for Martin, Alex, like Sandra, had felt obscurely betrayed by the knowledge of his affair with Seamus. It seemed suddenly important to him to prove his own masculinity and it wasn't as if it was the first time Sandra had committed adultery. For a moment his eyes snapped open.

'Are you going to tell Martin?' he asked.

As she continued to suck him he thought at first that perhaps she hadn't heard. He was just about to repeat the question when she stopped, with apparent reluctance, and then ran her tongue slowly up the length of his cock so that he shivered with pleasure.

'No, of course I'm not,' she said lightly, 'and you're not going to tell Georgina either. This afternoon's just going to be our lovely secret, and no one's going to get hurt. Shall we go into the bedroom?' She rose to her feet, and when he didn't follow her immediately, pulled playfully at his cock so he was forced to stand up and follow her somewhat sheepishly through the folding doors, which she shut firmly behind them.

The bed was even softer and squidgier than the sofa.

'Why don't you lie down, Alex –' sensing his hesitation, she once more adopted the soothing, professional tone of the doctor's receptionist 'and let me undress you?'

He lay back slowly and allowed her to straddle him as she undid his shirt and slipped it off his shoulders, following with his trousers and pants. His misgivings had not diminished his erection and he was rather hoping she might suck him again, but instead, still smiling at him, she undid the buttons of her dress and gave him a tantalizing first glimpse of the firm, rounded breasts he had so long admired, before sinking forward on top of him so that they brushed silkily against his face.

Alex reached up and started to caress them, while Sandra, lifting her skirt, began to rub herself against his penis. She was naked under her dress, and Alex wondered for a moment if she had been planning the whole thing before his arrival, but then as she sat up again pulling her dress over her head and slipping his cock inside her with practised ease, he was overtaken once more by pleasure. This, after all, was the sort of situation he had dreamed about as a schoolboy – effort-less seduction by an experienced woman who knew exactly what she wanted and was prepared to take over without any preliminaries or fumblings on his part and bring them both to unconditional pleasure. She made such an erotic picture as she writhed on top of him with her breasts swinging and her hand caressing her own clitoris that he was unable to hold back, and soon felt himself coming inside her.

'Shall I run you a bath?' Her voice was as casual and friendly as before, and she'd tactfully allowed him enough time to recover his breath but not enough to let the silence become awkward while he sought vainly for excuses as to why he hadn't satisfied her and how on earth he was going to get away.

'Why yes, I'd love a quick one. Thank you, Sandy. I – er –'

'Just give me five minutes,' she smiled briefly and walked out of the room.

The bathroom opened conveniently out of the bedroom and when Alex trailed in a few minutes later modestly wrapped in the Indian cotton bedcover, he found Sandra already ensconced in the lemon-scented bubbles.

'My goodness,' she smiled at him. 'You look just like a bride. Come and join me, Alex, and I'll wash your back for you.'

He climbed in front of her, facing the taps as she directed, and felt her legs wrapping round his waist as she soaped him from behind. Before long he felt the gentle pressure of her breasts nudging against his back as she slid her arms round him and started to soap his penis. His good resolutions about getting to the office on time were forgotten once more. The fact that he couldn't see her gave him an irresistible sense of helplessness and abdication of responsibility as she kneaded and caressed him, and when she stood up and held out a towel for him, he was only too ready to follow her back into the bedroom where she pushed him on to the bed, thrust her lemon-scented cunt into his face, and taking his rigid cock into her mouth, writhed and wriggled her way to orgasm against his lips.

'And now,' she whispered, when her gasps and moans had subsided and she had slithered off him and pulled him over on top of her, 'I think you'd better fuck the living daylights out of me.'

To Sandra's credit, he was dressed and ready to leave by 3.35. She had even made him a cup of tea.

'Thank you, Sandy.' He was pleased to hear his voice striking just the right note of affectionate friendliness, though he wasn't quite able to bring himself to meet her eyes. 'It was perfectly wonderful, though I must say I'd never imagined we'd end up doing what we did –' He hoped she would infer from this that he had absolutely no desire to repeat the experience.

'Oh hadn't you? she replied. 'I'd imagined it often,' and she stood on tiptoe to kiss him on the lips.

As he got into his car Alex found himself wishing he could have another bath before returning to the office. Perhaps it might help him to stop feeling so intolerably dirty.

CHAPTER SEVEN

May 1974

'So you think I should get the silver rather than the gold?' Virginia asked.

Jane considered the matter seriously. 'Well, I think they'd go better with jeans,' she replied. They were standing in the middle of a mêlée of exasperated women at the boot counter of the magnificent Art-Deco Biba emporium in Kensington High Street, which had opened the previous year. Virginia and Robin were going to spend the weekend in the country with Alex. He had promised them some sailing, and Virginia had decided she would need wellingtons. Jane had mentioned that Biba were doing them in luminous silver and gold and they had promptly dashed off guiltily together in Verge's Renault 5, leaving the children in the charge of Verge's new au pair.

'It looks as if we're going to be here all night,' Verge said impatiently a few minutes later as the two beautiful, immaculately made-up salesgirls carried on an absorbing conversation together, seemingly oblivious to the supplicating gestures of their would-be customers. 'Just as well Carmen's so good with the children.'

'She's sweet, isn't she?' Jane agreed warmly. 'I think you've found a real treasure there, Verge. I'm so glad for you.'

'And how's Sarah?' The pretext of catching the salesgirl's attention gave Virginia a good excuse for not looking Jane in the eye.

'She's fine,' Jane agreed readily enough. There had been a distinct coolness between Jane and Virginia for a few weeks after Sarah's sacking, but they had made up their quarrel at Joshua's first birthday party.

'Was the reference I did for her OK?' After her initial spite, Virginia had seemed ashamed of her bitchiness and anxious to atone for it.

'Yes, she was thrilled with it.' Jane had accepted Verge's gesture gracefully, knowing it was the nearest she or Sarah would get to an apology. It was a pattern which had been familiar to her since their schooldays.

'Has she got another job yet?' Virginia asked.

'She's been offered one looking after a six-month-old baby whose mother works full time,' Jane told her. 'She's promised to let her know on Tuesday after the referendum.'

'Oh God, I'd forgotten,' Verge turned and looked at Jane stricken, and an olive-skinned woman in a Missoni dress promptly sidled in front of her. 'It's this weekend isn't it?'

'On Sunday,' Jane agreed. 'Look out, Verge, you've lost your place,' and she stepped determinedly behind the counter and touched one of the astonished salesgirls on the shoulder. 'Would you mind seeing if you've got a pair of the silver boots in size seven?' she asked her pleasantly.

'Gosh, that was brave of you, Janie,' Virginia said admiringly ten minutes later when the boots had been bought and paid for and they were making their way past the potted palms to look at the children's clothes upstairs.

'Well, I was just so appalled by the rotten service. And that woman queue-barging was the last straw,' Jane replied. 'They're always doing it in Italy and it drives me mad.'

'You're really quite an operator, aren't you, deep down?'

'Not really,' Jane sighed. 'That is, I seem to be able to operate things for other people, but I'm afraid I'm an absolute wimp when it comes to standing up for myself.'

'That's because you don't compete,' Verge announced, her tone neutral enough for Jane not to be sure whether she was making a statement of approval or criticism.

By now they had reached the children's department and Jane had fallen with joy on some turquoise and lime striped cotton Bermuda shorts and matching T-shirt top.

'Aren't these divine?' she exclaimed. 'They'll be absolutely perfect for Venice this summer. You know I've persuaded Giorgio to take an apartment on the Lido this year, so we can avoid the sirocco? That is if we go.'

'Oh you'll go OK,' Virginia insisted. 'All the newspapers are saying the referendum's going to be a walkover.'

'You're probably right,' Jane agreed. 'It's just that I don't dare assume anything until it's all over and the votes are counted.'

'When's that going to be?'

'Monday evening, Giorgio thinks.'

'I'll ring you on Tuesday morning then.' Virginia said. 'We're probably going to be in the country till Monday anyway. Are you going to get that outfit? It looks a bit small to me.'

'Yes it does. It says age two but Philly's so big he's more like a four-year-old. I'll see if they have anything larger.'

This proved to be easier said than done. There was no salesgirl in sight, and when Jane finally tracked one down, she was told unhelpfully that if the item wasn't on show, it meant it wasn't available. She returned crestfallen to Verge.

'It does seem a shame,' she commented. 'They have all these lovely designs, but somehow they're never in the size you want.'

Virginia was examining a purple Babygro. 'I know, they're absolutely hopeless,' she agreed. 'Robin says there are rumours they're going to go bust. What do you think of this?'

'Glorious,' Jane replied. 'Josh'll look wonderful in it, like a little cardinal. Oh and look at this tiny black nightdress. I can't stand it, Verge. It makes me feel too broody. I'm going back to the toddlers' section.'

When they finally left the store an hour later, they were laden with carrier bags.

'Isn't it fun shopping together?' Jane remarked as they loaded everything into the boot of Verge's car. 'Rather like being teenagers again – urging each other on to new excesses except that now we're buying clothes for our kids instead of ourselves.'

'Well, I did get my boots,' Virginia reminded her as she started the engine. 'I'm really pleased with them, I must say, though it's a pity they're probably going to end up covered in mud.'

'Does Alex have his own boat?'

'Yes, he does. His house overlooks a tidal marsh, and he keeps it in a creek there. It's not very big. Hideously uncomfortable if you're crewing. You have to keep ducking so the silly boom doesn't hit you over the head.'

'Where do you sail to?'

'There's an island. At least it's only an island at high tide. Other times you can walk across to it. There's a bird sanctuary at one end, and some quite nice sandy beaches on the far side that you can swim from if you can stand the cold.'

'It sounds idyllic,' Jane commented.

'Only for some,' Verge retorted. 'Robin and Ben love it, but I've never been able to stand swimming in the English sea. Do you remember that time I came to stay with you in Kent when we were about ten? I was terribly impressed because you could swim in that arctic sea for hours, whereas I went bright blue after five minutes.'

'I remember your teeth chattering,' Jane said. My mother was quite worried about you. She made us go home early.'

'I suppose it was because my parents always used to take me abroad when I was little,' Virginia remarked. 'And now we've reversed roles, and you're going to be spending your summer in a lovely civilized cabana on the Lido while I rough it in the North Sea.'

Jane laughed. 'How civilized can you be when you're running around after a two-year-old all the time?' she asked. 'Although I admit Italian women seem to manage it. They loll around all day on sunbeds getting perfect tans and issuing commands to their husbands and never seem to go near the sea at all. I always feels like a savage compared to them, with my red English skin and dripping hair. I should think an English beach would be a tremendous relief. At least nobody gives a damn how you look.'

'No, they don't, do they?' said Virginia disapprovingly. 'Oh well then, you ought to get Alex to invite you to Suffolk.' Was Jane imagining it, or was there a challenge in her tone?

'But why on earth should he?' Jane asked lightly. 'I hardly know the poor guy.'

'You seem to be getting on pretty well to me,' Virginia remarked. 'Robin was convinced you were going to end up in bed together that night you went to the opera.'

Jane laughed. Thank goodness, she thought, that finally, at the age of twenty-seven, she'd given up blushing. 'Really?' she asked.

'Well, you must admit it was pretty cool the way you just walked off together.'

'I hope you didn't mind. It was just that I had to make a split-second decision because of the tickets. Gosh, the opera was wonderful, Verge. It was quite a revelation to me. I'm definitely going to try and get tickets for La Fenice this summer.'

Virginia wasn't the slightest bit interested in Jane's impressions of the opera. 'Yes, but what about you and Alex?' she insisted. 'How did you like him?'

'I already told you,' Jane said truthfully. Verge had rung her early the following morning and insisted on a blow-by-blow account of the evening. 'I like him a lot. In fact, if it wasn't for Giorgio and Philly – oh and Georgina, of course – I'd be seriously tempted.'

'You don't need to worry about Georgina,' Verge said quickly. 'I don't think he's seen her for weeks. He didn't spend the whole evening talking about her, did he?'

'No, in fact I don't think he mentioned her once.' And she hadn't mentioned Giorgio either, she thought.

'Well, there you are,' Verge said triumphantly. 'But didn't he make a pass at you at all?'

Jane smiled to herself. Verge was obviously cross-examining her to see if her later version of the story tallied with the original one. What a good thing she had given up lying when she was eighteen. 'I told you,' she said patiently. 'He asked me if I'd like to come in and have a cup of coffee, but as it was nearly midnight I said I ought to get back to Philly. Anyway,' she added truthfully 'I didn't feel he really expected me to say yes. I think he was just being polite.'

When she'd got home and found both Philly and Liliana, the lodger, who'd been babysitting, fast asleep, she'd been seized by a sudden sharp regret at having refused Alex. She'd looked his number up in the phone book and dared herself to call him – it was only a two-minute drive from her house to his – and say she'd changed her mind. She'd actually gone as far as lifting the receiver, but then something – was it loyalty to Giorgio, she wondered or just plain cowardice? – had stopped her. She'd gone to her solitary bed and lain awake until three, thinking about what they might have been doing together if only she'd been brave enough to accept his invitation.

'You sound as if you wish he had meant it,' Virginia said slyly.

'Well, yes I do. Or rather I did. But I suppose it's better this way. After all, nothing could have come of it with me going away so soon.'

'Do you really fancy him then?'

'Yes,' Jane admitted.

'You should have him then,' Virginia said lightly, 'so you can tell me what he's like.'

Jane turned to look at her. 'But wouldn't you mind if I had him?' she asked her. 'Are you sure you don't fancy him yourself?' At that moment she had completely forgotten Verge's trickiness over men when they were teenagers. She was thinking of her more as one of her actress friends who had been totally open and unabashed in their conversations about men, and amongst whom the light-hearted comment, 'Hands off him, darling, he's mine,' had been universally and unquestioningly accepted.

'Absolutely sure,' Virginia replied instantly. 'I don't fancy him in the slightest.'

This was good enough for Jane. 'Then maybe I will one day,' she said. If the Italians voted to abolish divorce and Giorgio refused to move to London she would, after all, be free. The thought was both terrifying and exhilarating. 'But, Verge –'

'Yes?' They were just pulling up outside Virginia's house.

'You won't tell him about this conversation, will you?' Jane knew, of course, that a true friend such as Virginia would never be disloyal enough to humiliate her by letting Alex know she was suffering from anything as pathetic as a crush on him, but something made her ask the question anyway.

'Oh no, of course I won't,' Virginia agreed readily, and she snapped off the ignition and pulled the handbrake up smartly with a jerk.

Jane's phone rang at about ten o'clock on Monday evening. Philly had long since been put to bed and she had been pacing nervously round the house, chain-smoking, ever since. She was currently occupied in making herself a cup of tea to replace one she had made only minutes before and then mislaid somewhere around the house.

'Gianna?'

'Oh Giorgio, have the results come?' Jane suddenly felt quite faint. It was a wall phone, designed to allow her to carry on cooking while she talked, and there was no chair handy. She sank down onto the floor and sat on the cold terracotta tiles.

'It's no.' he told her.

'No to divorce?' she gasped.

'No. No to abolish divorce.'

'You mean they're keeping it?'

'Yes of course they are keeping it. The nos were always ahead. There was never any chance they would abolish it, but I wait till now to give you the official result.'

'Oh Giorgio, I'm so happy!'

It was true, she thought. How many moments are there in life when happiness is a tangible emotion rather than a mere absence of pain? When the blood in one's veins is replaced by a flooding of liquid light? For Jane this was one of them. Giorgio had been away for more than two weeks now, and she missed his physical presence. The fear that she might never be able to marry him had given him the charm of unattainability so that she forgot his sulks and criticisms and remembered only his kindness and dependableness, while the dangerous physical attraction she felt towards Alex had faded, now that she had not seen him for some time, into something she thought she had perhaps only imagined, and would be able to keep under control. She felt as if fate had intervened and decided her future for her.

'Helmut is here,' Giorgio told her. 'He sends you his love. We are going to have a glass of champagne together.'

'Oh send him mine!' Jane had a sudden longing to be with them both. What was she doing here alone, when she and Giorgio should be celebrating their victory together? With hindsight the stand she had made seemed merely ridiculous. 'I'm going to have some too,' she told him. 'I put a quarter-bottle in the fridge this morning, even though I was afraid to hope too much –'

'But no.' His impatience, she told herself, was merely a sign that he too had been worried about the outcome of the referendum, whatever he might say now. 'How many times did I tell you –'

'I know, darling, and you were absolutely right. I can't wait to see you, and I'm going to go along to Alitalia first thing in the morning to book my ticket.'

Virginia rang Jane early on the Tuesday morning as she had promised.

'How did it go?' she asked.

'Oh, Verge, how sweet of you to ring. It's OK, thank goodness. They voted to keep divorce.'

'There you are. What did I tell you? That's really great, Janie. I'm so glad for you.'

'You only just caught me actually,' Jane went on. 'Sarah's here to look after Philly, and I was just going off to get our plane tickets. But tell me quickly about your weekend. Did you wear your boots?'

'No. We couldn't sail after all because the weather was so ghastly, but it was quite fun. Oh and by the way,' she continued with deliberate casualness, 'I told Alex you fancied him.'

All the happiness and anticipation Jane had been feeling since the previous night melted away as completely as if they had never existed. 'Why on earth did you do that?' she asked.

'But I thought you wanted me to,' Virginia replied innocently.

'No!' Jane protested. 'I asked you specially not to.'

'Oh well then,' Virginia said airily, 'I suppose I must have misunderstood.'

Jane blamed herself. If Virginia had realized she was going against her wishes in talking to Alex, she obviously wouldn't have told her anything about it. It therefore followed that the mistake had been genuine, which meant it was Jane's fault for having been so silly and indiscreet as to confide in Virginia in the first place.

'What did he say?' she heard herself asking.

'He gave this huge grin and said something like "*Aha!*" I said, "Honestly, Alex!" and he said, "Well, she's very pretty, isn't she?" and asked me for your telephone number. I thought I ought to warn you,' Virginia went on sanctimoniously, 'because he's probably going to ring you and ask you out.'

Jane digested this bitterly. It made her feel like a call girl. 'Well, it's too late,' she said flatly.

'Why? When are you going?' Virginia asked.

'Tonight,' Jane told her impulsively. She had actually been planning to go the following day, but now she was determined to leave as soon as possible in order to escape temptation. Once she was back in Venice, she thought, Virginia and Alex could sneer at her as much as they liked. She would be safe from both of them.

'Then I suppose it'll have to wait until you come back.' Was Jane imagining it, or did Virginia sound distinctly relieved?

'Yes it will,' Jane said shortly. 'Anyway, I expect it'll all have blown over by then. Look, I'd better go, Verge. I really must get on.'

'OK. You will call me later, won't you, and let me know what's happening?'

'Yes, of course.' Jane put the phone down and then instantly took it off the hook in case Alex should call her before she got out of the house. She knew that if he did, even under the present humiliating circumstances, she would be totally unable to resist him, and might even yet commit herself to something foolish. There was only one way, she thought, of ensuring that she was totally protected from him, and that was for her to return to England in December pregnant with Giorgio's child. As a sex object she would become automatically taboo, and the guilt she would feel at having tricked Giorgio would be bound to make her transfer all her loyalties to him. She had already been toying with the idea since hearing the result of the referendum. Virginia's phone call had merely served to convince her that it was the best way to save her relationship with Giorgio and safeguard Philly's future.

She picked up the dangling receiver and clicked it in the socket to obtain a line before resolutely dialling the number of her doctor.

Jane and her doctor were old friends and consipirators. He had first endeared himself to her by prescribing the pill for her when she was seventeen without bothering to accompany the prescription with the usual mandatory lecture. When she was eighteen he had earned her undying gratitude by assisting at the removal of her appendix and ensuring that the resultant, almost imperceptible scar was placed well below the line of even the tiny bikinis she was sometimes required to wear for glamour shots. Later he had inserted her first (and his first) IUD – a shared experience of such gruesomeness that their subsequent bond reminded her somewhat of the rapport between reluctant executioner and teenage martyr. Since then, she had run into him in fashionable restaurants, discussed with him the merits and disadvantages of fashionable drugs and wept on his shoulder when her first marriage was breaking up. After moving in with Giorgio, she had sent him a stream of Italian patients. The women were invariable delighted with his care and universally declared him to be *simpaticissimo*, while the men voiced no objections to spending hours in his waiting room undergoing the ministrations of his receptionists who were famous, without exception, for being amongst the most charming and beautiful girls in London. Giorgio's sister, in gratitude for his help in organizing the delivery of her illegitimate child, had presented him with a large, futuristic landscape of the Piazza San Marco, carefully chosen by Giorgio, which hung behind the desk of the gracious consulting room in Eaton Place where he now sat chain-smoking, with his usual refreshing disregard for health warnings and listening attentively to Jane's story.

The phone buzzed just as she was finishing, and he picked it up and launched into a conversation with a distraught mother whose baby was running a temperature of 104°. Jane sat back in her chair and listened to him. There was something so soothing about Bobby, she reflected. He was only about ten years older than she, but he had an ageless, Buddha-like quality, with his thick, curly hair and slight stockiness. However rotten one was feeling when one went to see him, one was immediately healed and reassured simply by entering his presence.

She herself was feeling flustered by her visit to Alitalia, where she had queued for ages and then failed to obtain the tickets she had been hoping for in order to make her escape that evening. At least she had managed to get them for the following night, and Sarah had promised to be around next day to help her, while Liliana, the lodger, had offered to babysit if she wanted to go anywhere on her last evening. Jane had accepted. Determined to be out of contact to Alex and Virginia, she was planning a solitary visit to the cinema.

'I'm so glad you still smoke, Bobby,' she said as he put the phone down. 'Would you mind if I had one too?'

'Of course not, darling.' His deliciously husky voice seemed to sink an octave each time she saw him. Jane imagined fondly that it was due entirely to good living and dissipation. He held out his packet to her and snapped open his lighter.

'Everyone I meet nowadays seems to be giving it up and lecturing me about how healthy they are,' Jane remarked. 'They make me feel like Frederick the Great. You know, when his guards hesitated in the charge and he screamed at them, "Dogs, do you want to live for ever?"' Bobby chuckled comfortably. 'Though of course one does read all these awful articles about smoking,' she went on. 'What do you really think about it, Bobby?'

He appeared to consider the matter seriously. 'I think you shouldn't read,' he said at last.

Jane was delighted. Bobby would never let her down.

'Do you think it would be too awful of me to have my coil removed without telling Giorgio?' she went on.

He frowned, and flicked through her file. 'But haven't you had it removed already?' he asked.

Jane stared at him. 'No,' she said, 'I had this one put in about two years ago, just after my postnatal.'

'Oh yes, April 1972, and no record of its removal,' he went on flicking. 'I'd assumed that perhaps you'd had it done in Italy.'

'Oh no,' Jane said. 'Contraceptives are illegal in Italy, you know. I mentioned it once to my Italian doctor, and he hadn't even heard of the IUD. Anyway, why should I have?'

Bobby was looking bewildered. 'Well, simply because most women do when their husbands have vasectomies,' he said.

Jane couldn't help feeling rather hurt. Until that moment Bobby had always made her feel that she was unique, but now he was obviously confusing her with another patient. 'Giorgio hasn't had a vasectomy,' she said.

Bobby's eyes widened. He looked as if he was about to contradict her, but instead he checked himself and pressed his buzzer.

'Bring me Count Orsini's notes, will you?' he said to his receptionist.

His phone rang again. Jane started to make a mental list of the clothes she was going to take to Venice. She felt perfectly calm. It was unreasonable, she told herself, to suppose that doctors weren't capable of making mistakes.

Just because Bobby had never happened to have done so before didn't mean he was infallible. The latest beautiful receptionist, a swanlike brunette, glided in and laid the file on the desk in front of him. Jane smiled at her. Bobby opened it and started to look through it while continuing his conversation.

'Very well then, my dear, I'll see you at three o'clock,' he said and put the phone down. There was a slight pause before he looked up at Jane. 'Giorgio had a vasectomy performed by Tristram Holland-Bennett at his consulting rooms in Devonshire Place on the nineteenth of March 1973,' he told her, taking a piece of paper out of the file and sliding it across the desk to her.

Jane was still convinced there had been a mistake. Perhaps there was another Giorgio Orsini – it wasn't such an unusual name after all – and his notes had been sent to Bobby instead of Giorgio's. She opened her mouth to say so, and then saw from the paper that the patient's address and telephone number were the same as theirs. Bobby seemed to be speaking again. She tried to focus her mind on what he was saying.

'Giorgio rang me last year to ask about the possibility of being sterilized,' he told her. 'I recommended Holland-Bennett, but told him he'd need to get you to sign a consent form before he had the operation. Do you mean to say he didn't tell you anything about it?'

'No,' Jane said helplessly.

'And I don't seem to have seen you since January 1973 when I visited you at home about Filippo's earache,' he went on, ransacking the files once more.

'No, I don't think you have,' Jane agreed. 'We're both so disgustingly healthy, you see,' she added, trying to smile.

'But it's not allowed!' Bobby, the unshockable, for once seemed positively confounded. 'Let me ring Holland-Bennett.'

As he dialled the number Jane tried to work out how Giorgio could have done it. Last spring had been the time when she had first started to talk seriously to him about having another baby. He'd had the operation in March, just before going back to Venice. He would have had to have it in London, of course. It was illegal in Italy. She wondered idly if she could report him, but then remembered she couldn't report anybody. She had no status in Italy. She didn't really exist.

'Holland-Bennett's in the Seychelles,' Bobby told her, 'but the receptionist found Giorgio's file. The consent form's been signed by a J. Orsini. She thinks Giorgio took it away with him and brought it back on the day of the operation.'

'He must have forged it,' Jane said dully.

Bobby walked over to her and put his arm around her shoulders. 'Are you all right, darling?' he asked. 'You seem to be taking it remarkably calmly.'

Jane discovered that she was in imminent danger of crying. 'That's because it hasn't really sunk in yet,' she explained. 'But I don't understand. How could he have had an operation without me knowing?'

'It's only a very minor one,' he assured her. 'It's done under a local anaesthetic, then the patient rests for half an hour and has a cup of tea and goes home.'

Jane started to laugh, but something went wrong in the middle. She reached blindly for the box of Kleenex on Bobby's desk and blew her nose loudly. 'And is it reversible?' she asked.

Bobby looked serious. 'It can be, but it's only successful in a small percentage of cases. Patients are always advised to look on it as permanent.'

'I see.' That meant she'd never have another child, Jane told herself, but somehow she couldn't quite believe it.

'I must say,' Bobby went on, 'that much as I've always liked Giorgio until now, I do consider that he's behaved quite outrageously badly over this –'

'To be fair, I suppose that what I was planning to do in having my coil removed was just as bad.' Jane said quickly.

'But that's entirely different.' Bobby exclaimed. 'It's quite natural for a young woman of your age to want more than one child. Besides, it's a compliment to Giorgio –'

'Well, that's how I see it,' Jane agreed eagerly. 'I think

that wanting someone's child is the greatest possible proof you can give of your love for them, but Giorgio doesn't agree with me,' she added dismally. 'He sees my love as a sort of finite object, like a cake. He thinks that if I cut off a slice for Philly and then a slice for another baby there'll eventually be none left for him. Perhaps it's my fault for neglecting him since I had Philly. But I have tried –'

Bobby patted her shoulder. 'I really don't think you need blame yourself over this,' he told her.

'Oh I don't,' she assured him. 'I think it's important that I should try to understand his motivation, but that doesn't stop me from realizing he's behaved like an absolute cunt.' She gave a forced smile.

Bobby laughed. 'That's better,' he said approvingly. 'And now what are you going to do?'

'I don't know.' Jane had started to feel helpless again. 'I've got my plane tickets, you see, and we've taken a flat on the Lido for the summer – I was so looking forward to it – and my nanny's got a new job. Besides, I've hardly any money left.'

'You'll have to go back and have it out with him,' Bobby told her. 'He may have behaved badly, but you owe him a chance to explain after – what is it? – five years. What I really meant was do you still want your coil removed?'

'Oh that,' Jane laughed bitterly. 'Sorry, Bobby, I'm really not thinking properly at the moment. I suppose I might as well. I'm not exactly going to be needing it now, am I?'

'No. Not much point in risking your health if there's no likelihood of pregnancy, I'd say,' he said briskly. 'Why don't you just go behind the screen and get ready while I wash my hands?'

Jane did as he told her. She felt doubly betrayed. She thought the official line was supposed to be that the coil had no side effects, and now Bobby had just implied that it did. Her anger against Giorgio redoubled. He could at least have told her afterwards that he'd been sterilized, so she could have dispensed with the hassle of contra-ception. You bet she was going to have it out with him. If he wouldn't agree to try and reverse his vasectomy she'd threaten to get pregnant by somebody else. Hardly aware of what she was doing she took off her tights and pants and lay down on Bobby's couch.

CHAPTER EIGHT

J ane was alone in the house when the telephone rang. She had come home at lunch time, exhausted by the emotions she had gone through that morning, to find a note from Sarah saying that as it was such a lovely day she was going to give Philly a picnic lunch in the park and bring him back around three.

Jane was glad. She felt totally unable to face anyone, even her darling Filippo. She was sure Sarah would see instantly that something was wrong, and that if she questioned her she would be bound to blurt out the truth, which would then get back to Verge. Verge was so black and white where advice was concerned. Jane was sure that if she knew what had happened she would say Jane should leave Giorgio. Probably she would be right, but for Philly's sake Jane felt she must at least give Giorgio a chance to defend his actions and salvage their relationship if he could. If he succeeded, it would be best that none of their friends should know what had happened. Possibly the operation could be reversed. If Giorgio would agree to attempt that, Jane felt that she could still forgive him, even if the attempt was not successful. Bobby had been right, she thought. She couldn't make a decision until she saw Giorgio and found out what he really wanted to happen to their relationship.

All her hopes were now pinned on the apartment they

had taken for the summer. Giorgio would still have to work, of course. The summer months were particularly busy ones for Venetian antique dealers because of the tourist trade. But they would have their evenings and weekends together away from the distractions of Venice, and Jane would be rested and refreshed by her days on the beach. Possibly they might be able to rekindle something of the relaxed happiness they had known in their early days together. If this didn't work, the apartment would still be useful as a neutral ground on which to meet and make arrangements – Jane hoped amicable ones – for their separation. Jane would then return to London in the autumn, enrol Philly in nursery school, and re-embark once more on her career – a prospect less daunting than it might have been had she not already enjoyed a small success in getting work that spring.

It was at this stage in her mediations that the telephone rang.

'Jane? This is Alex Oliver.'

A few hours earlier she would have been reduced to a state of palpitating hysteria. Now she felt perfectly calm. It was inevitable, she told herself, that he should call her just at this moment.

'Alex! What a nice surprise,' she said warmly. That's right, she thought, pile it on.

'I was ringing you because I've got some tickets for the opera tomorrow night and I wondered if by any chance you'd be free to come with me.'

Jane was touched. She liked him better for the subtlety of the invitation. After what Verge had told her she'd been expecting something more on the lines of, 'Why don't you come over to my place, babe, and get your gear off?'

'Oh Alex, I'd have loved to,' she said regretfully, 'but I'm going back to Venice tomorrow.'

'What a shame.' At least he had the grace to sound genuinely disappointed rather than merely irritated by the setback to his sexual agenda. 'I didn't realize you were going so soon. I don't suppose', his voice contained a wobble of nervous eagerness that endeared him to her still further, 'that you're free tonight by any chance?'

Jane caught her breath. So this was it at last. And if she were to commit this enormity, she asked herself, wouldn't it only balance the enormity that Giorgio had committed and enable them to meet each other on equal terms? Or was she just using the idea as a pretext because she wanted to see Alex more than anything else in the world?

'Yes,' she said. 'As a matter of fact I am.'

She thought she heard him gasp. If she had been in a more rational frame of mind she might have been surprised that the great seducer of Verge's descriptions seemed to be even more nervous about this than she. As it was, she felt totally unable to do more than speak in monosyllables and agree to whatever he suggested. 'How would it be then,' he managed finally, 'if I bought some food and you came round here for an early dinner?'

Why not, Jane thought. After all, they were both adults. They both knew why she had agreed to see him. This way at least there would be no messing around, no coy invitations to coffee, no need for her to pretend to make a decision that they both knew she had made already.

'That sounds lovely,' she said.

'Wonderful. Would you like to come at seven thirty? Will that give you enough time to pack?'

Jane looked at her watch. It was only two and she already knew what she was going to be taking. 'That should be fine,' she said. It crossed her mind to ask him not to tell Verge she was coming, but she thought it would make the episode seem even more sordid than it was already. Besides, if he was the practised adulterer that Verge claimed, he would surely have wit enough to be discreet about it.

'Wonderful,' he repeated. 'So I'll look forward to seeing you then.'

'Yes. Goodbye,' she said and put down the phone.

Virginia's call was not long in following. It caught Jane in the middle of a burst of activity. The knowledge that she was about to embark on such a potentially disastrous course of action, far from depressing her, had filled her with an almost unbearable sense of exhilaration. She felt as if she were eighteen again. What did youth consist of, after all, but doing things you knew you would regret bitterly the following morning? Her suitcase lay open on the floor, and she had ransacked her cupboards and thrown her summer clothes into a reckless pile on the bed. She was eager to finish as soon as possible so she would have the rest of the afternoon in which to make herself beautiful for Alex.

'Has Alex called you yet?' Virginia demanded.

Jane laughed to herself. Trust Verge not to bother with anything as boring as preliminaries. 'Yes he has,' she told her. 'He asked me to go to the opera tomorrow evening, but unfortunately I couldn't.' And it's not a lie she told herself.

'Are you still leaving tonight?'

'No, tomorrow,' Jane replied. 'I couldn't get tickets for today.'

'And I suppose you'll be busy this evening, packing, et cetera?'

'Yes,' Jane said. Especially et cetera, she thought.

'I mustn't keep you. Best of luck, Janie, and you'll write to me, won't you, and tell me how you're getting along?'

'Of course I will.'

'I'll see you in the autumn then. Give my love to Giorgio.'

'Yes, of course. And mine to Robin and the boys. Goodbye.'

Now that she was off the hook Jane started to feel vaguely guilty, but not enough to make her regret for a second that she had not confided in Verge. How could she make love to Alex if Virginia knew what she was doing? It would be like having her in bed beside them watching every movement they made. She thought back to the moment all those years ago when Virginia had started to caress her while they were sunbathing. What would have happened if Virginia's mother hadn't summoned them when she did? And why, in spite of all the confidences they had exchanged since, had they never been able to bring themselves to talk about that?

She knew of course, with hindsight, that Virginia had been in love with her at school. Why else would Virginia have copied her clothes and interests so slavishly and tried to bust up her friendships with other girls by telling Jane the nasty things they had said about her? But all that was over long ago. They were both grown up and married now, and Virginia no longer stared at her with a lean and hungry look. She told herself she was just being silly and morbid. Fear him not, Caesar, he's not dangerous.

The idea of Virginia being involved in her relationship with Alex was making Jane feel so uneasy that she decided not to think about it any longer. Going over to her pile of records she chose George Harrison's beautiful 'My Sweet Lord' and put it on the stereo, then flung herself with renewed energy into her packing.

Virginia would have liked to ring Alex at his office, but she didn't quite dare. Instead she waited impatiently at her kitchen window till she saw him arrive home by taxi, rather later than usual, laden with carrier bags from Justin de Blank. Grabbing a letter which she had written several hours before, she went out to join him on the pretext of catching the last post.

'I hear you invited Jane to the opera tomorrow,' she said to him teasingly. 'You were an idiot you know, to leave it so late.'

Alex smiled. 'Oh but it's all right,' he said quickly, 'because she's agreed to come and have dinner with me tonight.' He was looking so proud of himself that she felt a sudden almost uncontrollable urge to hit him.

'How nice,' she said tartly. 'Well, don't do anything I wouldn't do.' She was so shocked and angry that she hardly knew what she was saying.

'I'll try not to.' If possible his smile grew broader. 'But I don't think I'd better promise. It's wonderful to see you, Verge, but do you mind if I go in now? These bags are so heavy that I'm terrified they're going to burst and spill champagne all over the pavement.'

The church clock struck 7.30 as Jane turned the corner into Alex's road, causing her to jump violently. She had come to her assignation on foot. Normally somebody

who had no difficulty at all in arriving half an hour late –
as required by the laws of Italian hospitality, where
people who turned up on time were quite likely to
find their hostess still in the bath she had found herself
ready so ridiculously punctually on this occasion that
she had decided not to risk a taxi for fear of turning herself into that universally unwelcome of guests, the early
arriver.

Jane was quite surprised by her own eagerness. She'd
had plenty to occupy her that afternoon, but her happiness and excitement at the thought of seeing Alex had
seemed to give her boundless energy so that the tasks
had melted away as if by magic. Her cases were packed
and labelled in the hall ready to be collected by one of
her neighbours from the religious sect, who was giving
her a lift to the airport. Philly was bathed and fed, and
she had read him his bedtime story and sung him his
bedtime songs before kissing him goodnight, tucking
him up with his toy koala and tiptoeing softly out of his
room. Philly had always been wonderful about going to
sleep. She'd never had to sit by him or rock him for
hours as other mothers claimed they had to, and from
the age of two and a half months, he had always slept
through the night. For a moment she lingered in the
doorway. It was, after all, something of a momentous
occasion, and she wondered suddenly at her total inabil-
ity to feel any guilt. Might not some people look on her
betrayal of Giorgio as a betrayal also of Filippo? Even as
the thought came to her she dismissed it utterly. It was
impossible that she should ever betray Filippo. She *was*
Filippo and could no more be untrue to him than she
could to herself. She blew him a last kiss and shut the
door gently behind her.

For the first time since their contentious installation,
the mirror tiles in Jane's bathroom were put to good use
as she scrubbed and scrutinized every inch of her body.
Virginia had told her that Alex was highly experienced
with women, so however shy she might secretly be feeling
at making love with a new man for the first time in five
years, she must take care not to show it and to appear
totally carefree and uninhibited. She was anxious to

make herself as perfect as she could for him, as any sign of timidity or reticence would be bound to bore him.

However long Jane lay in the sun, her skin never got darker than a slight peachy glow. Now, in spite of several weeks of reasonable weather and many brave attempts to sunbathe on the patio, she was still annoyingly white. At least she was in good shape. No one looking at her would be able to tell she'd had a child. She'd remained remarkably tiny for the first months of her pregnancy and lost all the weight she'd gained within a few weeks of Philly's birth. There wasn't a stretch mark in sight and her little breasts were as rounded and smooth-nippled as a virgin's. As an actress she'd attended body conditioning classes, and had kept up a small daily routine of exercises which she'd later combined with her postnatal ones to keep her in shape. Few people exercised at that time, but Jane had always enjoyed the godlike sensation which walking the world on well-toned muscles conferred. She could do the splits, stand on her head, and put her nose on her knees with her legs straight. In the summer she walked round Venice for hours each day, and in the winter she swam regularly at their local pool. Filippo would splash valiantly through the duckling sessions in the small pool and then sit contentedly at the side in his arm bands while Jane did her lengths in the big pool. Her buttocks and the inside of her thighs were firm and hard, and her stomach, though never as flat as she would have liked, was rounded and taut and resembled, as Giorgio had told her, rather to her annoyance as she had never much admired the German masters, that of Cranach's Eve in the Uffizi.

Since becoming vegetarian four years before, Jane had scrupulously stopped using French perfumes, which she had been told involved some dreadful, nameless cruelty to animals. She now used Penhaligon's Violetta, which she had been assured was made solely from flowers, and found, to her delight, that people commented on and admired it far more than the expensive brands she had once favoured. Her bath water was cloudy and fragrant with the drops she had sprinkled into it, and she mixed it with the baby cream which she used as a moisturizer and rubbed liberally all over her body, then sprayed the toilet water into her newly washed hair, which she had allowed to grow that winter and which now hung, damp and golden nearly to her breasts. Later, when it was almost dry, she would put heated rollers in the ends, just for a few seconds, so it would hang in big, loose curls.

She wrapped herself in a giant-size purple bathtowel and padded barefoot into the bedroom to do her make-up. She had never liked dressing-tables, which so often obscured the natural light, and plonked herself down on the bed which was directly underneath a large skylight, and covered in a chocolate lace bedcover she had dyed herself and scattered with satin cushions. Her makeup, when she wasn't working, was very basic: translucent powder over her face and neck to give it a pearly glow, peachy rose blusher to highlight her cheekbones, deep, indigo shadow applied with a delicate brush to give a soft, smudgy outline to her eyes, lashings of black mascara and a soft smear of wine-coloured lipstick to accentuate her full mouth.

She had already decided what she was going to wear, and had laid out the clothes on her bed. At one stage Virginia had advised her to wear tight jeans when she saw Alex to show off her figure ('Georgina's short and dumpy,' she had said, 'and can't wear anything but caftans') but he had already seen her in jeans lots of times, and tonight she felt like being more romantic. The fashions of the time – preposterously flared trousers and garish shirts with long, droopy collars – were gener-ally so hideous that Jane preferred to opt for antique or ethnic clothes. Tonight she had chosen a three-quarter length dark green Mexican skirt from the Portobello Road, embroidered with wine and gold daisies, which she wore with a biscuit silk shirt left over from the sixties, which had a high neck and full Russian-style sleeves. Shoes were a huge problem for vegetarians – if she wore leather there was always someone who would sneer at her for not living up to her principles – so she had been thrilled to find a pair of high-heeled navy canvas boots in Kensington Market to go over her navy tights.

When she was ready, Jane pinned a Victorian cameo brooch at her throat, and flung a pale green silk shawl round her shoulders. It had been left to her by her grandmother, and was fringed and embroidered exquisitely with white roses. She had an antique raffia clutch bag she had bought in the market, which she filled with keys, lipstick, perfume, cigarettes, and violet cachous to sweeten her breath, before going downstairs to say goodbye to Liliana, a dark, serious woman in her thirties, who was sitting at the desk in her room frowning over some papers she was marking for the following day.

She gave quite a start when she saw Jane, and rose to her feet.

'*Ma come sei bella!*' she exclaimed.

Jane laughed. 'I'm going out to dinner with a friend,' she said in Italian, remembering too late that it would have been wiser to opt for English, where the word 'friend' was genderless. 'Here's the phone number, in case you want me.' She knew, of course, that nothing was going to happen to Filippo, but she knew equally that the one way to make it happen would be to go out without leaving a number. She had rung Venice earlier and given the details of her flight to Giorgio's assistant. She was fairly confident Giorgio wouldn't call, but even if she hadn't been, she would still have left the number.

Liliana took the piece of paper without comment, but as she eyed Jane up and down her serious features were illuminated by a gleam of feminine solidarity. They had never become close – Liliana always kept herself very much to herself and disappeared to Italy for long periods in the holidays – but she had occasionally been witness to some of Giorgio's blacker moods, and Jane had intercepted the odd look of sympathy from her and felt that they were kindred spirits.

'*Brava,*' said Liliana, and kissed Jane approvingly on both cheeks.

Meandering through the market on her way to Alex's house, Jane passed by her favourite flower stall, which was just closing down for the night. The men called to her that they were selling off their stock cheaply, so she stopped, laughing, on impulse, and bought an armful of white lilies to give Alex. If he seemed surprised that a woman should bring flowers to him rather than vice versa she would tell him it was the custom in Italy to take flowers to somebody the first time you visited their house.

As she neared Alex's street, she started to walk more slowly, with frequent glances at her watch. The big hand didn't seem to be moving at all. Could it be broken? She stopped, and put it to her ear to see if it was still ticking. The striking of the clock, once she had got over her fright, was a relief to her. Once she had made up her mind to do something, Jane found waiting anathema. Now at last she had received the signal she needed to go forward.

When she was only about six doors from Alex's house she heard the sound of a car coming down the road behind her and glanced instinctively over her shoulder. Her happiness gave way to terror as she recognized Virginia's black Renault 5. Without stopping to think, Jane pressed herself against the side of a parked van for shelter. What could Virginia be doing returning home at this time, she asked herself. And how was she going to get to Alex now if Virginia was going to be standing on her doorstep in full view of his house? She took deep breaths to try and control her panic. What on earth would people think of her if they came down the road and saw her pressed, trembling against the van? She peered round the side of it, but could see nothing. In the distance somewhere a door slammed, and behind her a man in a pinstripe suit rounded the corner and started to walk purposefully towards her. Jane straightened her back and shifted the lilies from her right arm to her left. Perhaps if she buried her face in them Virginia wouldn't be able to recognize her from the other side of the road. Forcing herself to appear casual, although she was secretly longing to bolt like a rabbit, she somehow covered the few remaining steps to Alex's house and rang appealingly on his doorbell.

Virginia had lent her car to Robin that day because his own was being serviced. Of course he would have to come home just at that moment she told herself, and interrupt her vigil by the window. She greeted him perfunctorily and, as soon as she could dispatched him upstairs to say goodnight to the boys, before rushing back into the kitchen.

She was just in time. She felt quite cold at the thought of how nearly she had missed them. They were standing on Alex's doorstep together. His hands were on her shoulders and he was kissing her on both cheeks. How beautiful they looked together. He so tall and dark, and she so blonde and slim and just the right height for him, so she didn't even have to stand on tiptoe, but could just turn her cheek graciously and accept his kiss.

Virginia advanced shamelessly towards the window to get a better look, but after a moment they drew apart. Alex put his arm round Jane to draw her into the house, and a moment later there was nothing left for Virginia to look at but the unwelcoming blackness of Alex's front door.

Virginia waited. In a moment he would turn his ground-floor light on and she would be able to see them sitting at the dining table. She willed him to hurry up. The street was wide, and the reflections on the windows made it impossible to see inside his house unless the lights were on. Damn these long summer evenings. What on earth could they be finding to do together in this irritating semidarkness?

Virginia's pretext for lingering in the kitchen was the casserole she was preparing for dinner that evening. The onions were already chopped and sizzling in the pan with the herbs, and she forced herself reluctantly to start on the carrots. She and Robin were eating together then he was going off to join a group of racing friends to gamble – so he said.

This had become the pattern of their lives recently. If they weren't entertaining or going to the opera it was extremely rare for them to spend an evening at home together. Virginia sometimes wondered how she had allowed herself to be placed in this position. She was no doormat. She was perfectly able to maintain authority amongst her women friends and domestic staff, most of whom she sensed, not without a certain pleasure, were slightly afraid of her. She wasn't timid with men either. All Robin's bachelor friends liked her enormously, although they never seemed to fall in love with her. Why then, she wondered, should she be so afraid to ask Robin why he never stayed at home with her in the evenings?

Robin was what her parents' generation would refer to as a man's man – uneasy in the company of women, and far happier spending his leisure time at his club or with his racing cronies. In a way this suited her because, aside from planning their social lives and those of the boys, they actually had very little to say to each other. Their physical relationship was practically that of brother and sister. They regularly went for months without having sex together, and although Virginia found this a relief because Robin's lovemaking had always been so unsatisfactory to her, she had an uneasy feeling that it would not be considered normal among her married friends. Even Janie had told her once that Giorgio's sulks never lasted more than a few days because he could always be counted on to want sex with her at least twice a week. During her second pregnancy Virginia had become aware, from the half-overheard comments and sly sniggers of some of Robin's friends, that his trips abroad generally included visits to the sorts of clubs and bars frequented by ladies of the night. Virginia could understand only too well why he would be attracted to them. The fact that he could visit them in the company of his male friends would make him feel secure, and there would be no need for him to make the painful effort to establish any rapport with them before the act, or attempt a stilted conversation with them afterwards. Certainly they would never reproach him, as she done in the beginning, with not having brought them to orgasm.

Sharp tears stung at Virginia's eyes, and she glared fiercely at the innocently sizzling onions, before wiping them away impatiently with a kitchen towel. She told herself she had nothing to complain about. Robin was prepared to pay well for her lack of interference in his life style. She was always beautifully dressed in the latest fashions, and paid regular, soothing visits to the hairdresser and beauty parlour. She also spent lavishly on the boys, dressing them in expensive French and American children's clothes which they tore and filthied, and buying them the latest toys which they proceeded to smash and trample on. When they did this, Virginia would simply buy more to replace them. She found shopping for the boys a more acceptable activity than spending time with them, as well as being a suitable way of assuaging her conscience for not doing so.

She had also persuaded Robin to let her try for one last child. Originally she had put about the statement that she wanted a large family as a bluff to mislead people so they wouldn't suspect Ben's birth had been an accident. Since Josh's birth, however, her desire for a daughter had become as great an obsession as Jane's for a second child, though she would never have dreamed of telling anyone because it would have been so humiliating in the event of failure.

With this end in view, Virginia had cut out a magazine article which was supposed to give its readers an 85 per cent chance of choosing their baby's sex. The procedure was fairly simple and she was confident she could carry it out without Robin knowing. He had been so keen to have sons to inherit the title that she knew he would see her desire for a daughter as subversive, and jeer at her if the method didn't succeed. Basically all she had to do was douche with a solution of white vinegar and water immediately before intercourse, and make love in the missionary position on days eight to twelve of her menstrual cycle. The article did, however, state that frequent intercourse was more likely to produce girls, citing the example of a Persian ambassador with 100 wives at the court of St Petersburg who produced 202 girls to only 57 boys. It was this last factor which was most likely to prove a problem. Virginia had come off the pill the previous month and was now just coming to the end of her fertile period. Soon she and Robin would have to get started, but how, she wondered, was she to persuade him of the necessity of frequent ejaculation without giving herself away? If only, she thought sourly, she could be sure he visited prostitutes. She could then relax in safety and leave all the dirty work to them.

She wondered suddenly if Jane and Alex had gone up to his drawing room for a drink before dinner. Hastily she threw the carrots into the pan and went to the fridge to get out a packet of mince to put in with the vegetables. Once they were safely on she would be able to turn the gas down to minimum and leave them to simmer for half an hour while she went upstairs to get a better look.

Jane, sitting demurely on the sofa beside Alex in the rapidly gathering dusk, took a sip from her champagne glass, and glanced covertly at the decor of his drawing room. Having spent the last five years living in the middle of the Italian Renaissance, she was intrigued and cheered by the colourful blend of contemporary fabrics and Victoriana. The walls of the room were fashionably covered in chocolate-brown felt hung with brightly coloured theatrical designs. The sofas and chairs were upholstered with Liberty prints and there was an abundance of potted plants in the wrought iron jardinière which stood next to the pink marble fireplace. She thought how much Giorgio would have disapproved of the youthful Englishness of Alex's taste, and liked it still more.

'I do think you've done the room nicely,' she said at last. 'It's strange, because it's an exact mirror image of Virginia and Robin's drawing room, isn't it, and yet you've made it completely different. Being here's making me feel rather like Alice Through the Looking-Glass.' She turned and smiled at him, and he, greatly daring, took her into his arms and kissed her on the lips.

Jane felt a great sense of relief and homecoming. Since her arrival they had been constrained and awkward with each other, and she'd been so afraid they would squander the few hours they had together eating food they couldn't taste and making superficial conversation. She had always been shy about expressing her emotions and found it easier to communicate physically the feelings she was unable to put into words. Once she and Alex had become lovers, she thought, and were relaxed and at ease with each other, there would be time for them to become friends. She had forgotten temporarily that she was leaving next day and that consequently they would have no time at all.

'Will you come upstairs with me?' he murmured a few minutes later, as the possibility of breaking off their embraces and sitting down demurely at the dinner table together became increasingly more remote.

'What about your girlfriend?' The last thing Jane wanted to do was stop kissing him, but if he told her he was still in love with Georgina, she knew that she would.

'I don't know,' he said honestly. 'I haven't seen her for nearly two months.'

'Yes but have you ever been unfaithful to her before?' She was angry with herself for the word 'before', but it had slipped out involuntarily.

'Once,' he said, 'about a month ago. With an old friend. It was something that won't be repeated.'

Jane sighed. However hopeless his affair with Georgina might be, she wouldn't have wanted to be the first person to cause him to be unfaithful to her. She twined her arms round his neck and pulled him gently towards her so she could whisper in his ear. 'All right,' she said. 'I will.'

Mixed with his jubilation, Alex was conscious of a sudden moment of panic. He realized that this was the first time in his life that he had gone after a girl he really wanted and actually been accepted by her, at the moment when he wanted her, and with no strings attached. Of course he would never have dared approach her in the first place if Virginia hadn't assured him she would be a pushover, but he had still not really allowed himself to believe it would happen. He had too many uncomfortable memories of the girls he had dated when he was young. Girls who had stopped him at the last moment and made him feel their surrender was dependent on some unmentioned commitment which he did not feel ready to make. In spite of Virginia's goading he had still half expected that the evening with Jane would end in that way.

He wondered suddenly if he was going to be able to

satisfy her. Since his marriage, the women he had slept with – his secretary, Sandra, even Georgina – had all seduced him. Of course he had wanted Georgina desperately, but it had never occurred to him that he might actually possess her until her whispered invitations to stay with her and her husband at their country house where they would have 'lots and lots of lovely opportunities to be alone together' had finally nerved him to risk the first tentative embraces to which she had responded so warmly and absolutely. Although hardly aware of it himself, he had rather come to expect the woman to make the first move. He found it comforting because it lifted any sense of responsibility from him, and made it easier for him to perform satisfactorily.

There was no such comfort to be found in his union with Jane. He had instigated the situation and now she was entitled to expect him to carry it through. As they walked up the stairs to his bedroom, he started to feel quite panic-stricken. The fact that she was by far the most beautiful woman he had ever been to bed with only made things worse, as did the knowledge, gleefully related to him by Virginia, of her vast sexual experience. What if she just lay there like a statue and expected him to ravish her? How would he begin? Like a silent movie, the sexual failures from his past ran themselves in slow motion before his eyes. The episode with his secretary when he had wilted so disastrously after the appearance of the window cleaner, the times with Julie when he had ground away for hours, conscious that he was causing her pain but unable to bring their joint ordeal to an end by coming. By the time they reached the bedroom he found he was quite trembly with panic.

Hardly knowing what he was doing, Alex walked over to the window and drew the curtains before switching on the bedside light, and then wondering immediately afterwards if it would have been more tactful to leave the room in darkness. Georgina, he remembered, had chosen darkness at their first meeting. It had taken some time for him to convince her that he loved her more, rather than less, for the flaws in her thirty-eight-year-old body, and that her vulnerability over her lack of physical perfection helped to redress some of the vulnerability he felt over her wealth and social importance. Suddenly he wished passionately that she was there to take charge of the situation.

When he could avoid it no longer, he turned reluctantly to face Jane, and found her still standing in the doorway staring at the vast cane bed, which, with its matching bedside tables had been a wedding present from Julie's godmother. He and Julie had chosen it together at the Bedding Centre in Sloane Street. As they left the shop she had remarked that it would last them a lifetime. He could still remember the surge of black gloom which had overcome him at her words.

'What an enormous bed you have,' Jane said smiling.

'Oh Julie's taking that,' he blurted out naively. He had actually been contacted that morning by her lawyer with another of his interminable lists.

Jane's eyes widened mischievously and she took a step backwards in pretended awe. Immediately Alex rushed over to her. Had he been tactless in mentioning Julie? His fear of impotence vanished, overcome by the greater fear that Jane might change her mind and leave.

She was unprepared for the strength with which he caught her, and stumbled against him, nearly falling. A moment later they had collapsed together, laughing, on his vicuna bedspread.

'I hope she'll get good vibes from it,' Jane said later, when she could catch her breath between kisses, and she sank back laughingly on the pillows and held out her arms towards him.

Virginia slipped stealthily upstairs to the drawing room and entered it quietly, shutting the door behind her. Thank goodness there was no sign of Robin. Probably he was still on the top floor reading Ben a bedtime story, while Carmen, she knew, was getting ready for her evening out. Virginia walked over to the window and peered avidly across at Alex's house. His kitchen remained obstinately in darkness, and there was no light in his drawing room either. Virginia couldn't understand it. It was at least half an hour since Jane's arrival. Surely they should be having their dinner by now. Another thought struck her. It couldn't be possible, of course, but maybe she should check it out anyway. She left the room and ran up the next flight to her bedroom, quite surprised by the sudden feeling of constriction in her chest, and the way she had to pause on the landing to catch her breath.

When she was feeling better, she pushed the door open and advanced once more to the window. She saw immediately that her hunch had been right. Alex's bedroom curtains were drawn. There was no question of his having left them drawn that morning. Virginia had already been upstairs after bumping into Alex that evening. She had sat at her dressing-table while Carmen was giving the boys their bath, pretending to apply fresh makeup, but secretly hoping to catch a glimpse of Alex getting changed for dinner. The curtains had definitely been open then, which meant that in the thirty minutes or so that Jane had been in Alex's house, they had somehow become so carried away by their disgusting passion as to ignore all the rules of polite society, abandon the elaborate dinner Alex had bought and rush upstairs like two animals on heat in order to fall on each other in Alex's bedroom.

Virginia put the blame entirely on Jane. Alex would never have done such a thing of his own volition. Look how respectful he had always been with her. But what could Jane have done to bring Alex to such a state of abandonment? She herself might not have any intention of letting Alex make love to her, but she had to admit she had been as encouraging to him as she knew how and yet, since that moment in Suffolk when he had told her how much he admired her – which she had rushed off and reported so triumphantly to Robin – he had given her no further hints of his enslavement.

Probably he was in awe of her. That must be it. That and the fact that she was married. Naturally he would be afraid of falling in love with another married woman after the way he had been hurt by Georgina. Of course Jane was married too – at least as far as Virginia knew, Alex thought she was – but there would be no question of his falling in love with her. Jane was just a tart. Someone Alex could use as a convenience to satisfy his sexual needs. Virginia had to admit she had been taken aback by the eagerness with which he had asked for Jane's telephone number when she had told him about her stupid crush on him. It wasn't at all what Virginia had intended. She had told him Jane liked him because she wanted reassurance. She had thought he would laugh at Jane, and that they could turn her into a joke together for being so stupid as to imagine someone like Alex would ever be interested in her. Virginia's mouth tightened. Well, they could still do that. After Jane had gone back to Italy she would dredge up all the discreditable episodes she could remember from Jane's past – or even invent a few if necessary – in order to show Alex what a fool he had been to like her. Talking about Jane to Alex could also prove to be a very useful way of bringing their conversation round to the topic of sex, she told herself, and her thin lips spread into a malicious little smile.

The light snapped on and Virginia jumped and spun round to face Robin who was standing in the doorway looking almost as startled as she felt.

'What on earth are you doing skulking here in the dark?' he asked her curiously. 'What are you looking at?' And he came over and joined her at the window.

Virginia decided to tell him the truth. 'I was looking at Alex's house,' she admitted. 'Janie's gone round there for dinner, and I just noticed there were no lights on downstairs and his bedroom curtains are drawn. He must be screwing her already.'

'That was quick work,' Robin sounded genuinely intrigued. Virginia felt quite pleased with herself for having caught his interest. Bitching about their friends had always been one of their chief pleasures as a couple. Robin's views of human nature became yearly more pessimistic and cynical and to please him Virginia had honed and sharpened her natural intolerance for others' frailties to achieve glittering heights of verbal malignity. 'Do you wish it was you in Janie's place?' he asked her with a grin.

Virginia's eyes widened, but she took care not to display any further signs of shock. Robin had always enjoyed stating the unmentionable and she had long ago taught herself not to flinch when he did it because to do so would merely drive him to further peaks of sadism. 'Not particularly,' she said lightly. 'Do you wish it was you in Alex's?'

Robin chuckled. 'Well, she could probably show me a trick or two, couldn't she, if all the things you've told me about her are true?'

'Oh I wouldn't count on it,' Virginia was careful to speak casually. 'I've always imagined that she probably just lies there and lets men use her till they get bored with her and throw her out.'

'You mean you think you're better at it than she is?' Was she imagining it, or did he sound as if he was sneering at her?

'Well yes, I think I probably am,' she replied defiantly. 'After all she's never managed to hang on to anyone for longer than a few months, has she? Apart from Giorgio, of course, and he's so old he's probably desperate –'

'What do you think you do that's better than her?' he asked pointedly.

Virginia sighed. During her long fight to retain her seeming virginity before marriage, she had become something of an expert at hand jobs. She had managed to keep Robin at bay that way for nearly six months, as well as deflecting the advances of numerous other men she had known before him or during her time at college. Once she got started, she quite enjoyed it. Men always seemed so embarrassed and ashamed of themselves afterwards that they generally abandoned their futile attempts to give her pleasure, thus sparing her the inevitable sense of disappointment.

'Shall I go and get the baby lotion?' she asked.

'No don't bother about that. Come here and lie down.' He had already taken off his jacket and hung it over the chair and was now unbuttoning his trousers.

Virginia hesitated. It was approximately day sixteen of her cycle. She thought she was safe, but she really ought to check that she was out of the boy-making period before allowing Robin to have sex with her. 'You know I'm not using anything,' she reminded him. 'We were planning to start trying next month.' She was so surprised by Robin's unwonted eagerness that for once she didn't have any of her usual excuses ready.

'Then look on it as a dress rehearsal.' Robin had removed his shoes and trousers, and was standing between her and the bed in his shirt and socks. She averted her eyes from his erection.

'All right.' She turned to draw the curtains. It looked, she told herself, as if nothing less than a blow job would deflect him. At least it would be an orgasm to chalk up towards her goal of getting a girl.

'No, don't do that.' He was behind her at the window now, his hands resting on the sill on either side of her, and his cock nudging insistently at her buttocks. 'Look. Isn't that a crack in Alex's curtains?'

'Where?' Virginia craned forward. Robin lifted her skirt and pulled roughly at her tights and pants till they straddled the middle of her thighs. 'Robin –' she started to turn towards him.

'There! The far window. Can't you see Janie lying on the bed starkers? I thought you said she was a natural blonde.'

'She is!' The vision of Jane as a teenager, glowing and golden in the sunlight, and hers to do with as she wanted, was suddenly so overpowering that she hardly noticed when Robin, finding the right place for once, slid his cock into her vagina from behind and started to thrust at her with increasing urgency.

'How do you know?' he asked, and came inside her.

'Because – honestly, Robin, I don't believe you could see anything at all.'

He withdrew from her, grinning, and started to pick up his clothes. 'No I couldn't,' he agreed, 'but the thought that I might be able to made you extremely wet, didn't it? You ought to ask them to let you watch next time. They'd probably enjoy that,' and putting on his dressing-gown, he walked cheerfully off to the bathroom.

Virginia straightened her clothing and glanced in the dressing-table mirror to check on her hair and makeup.

Later, when they had eaten and Robin had gone off to his club, she would put on her Janet Reger nightdress and lie in her pretty brass bed caressing herself with the baby lotion which Robin had earlier rejected. Why were men always so clumsy and coarse? She had long ago accepted the fact that she would never find one who would make love to her as beautifully and sensitively as she did to herself.

Jane, drowsy and heavy with the glow of postcoital rapture, was struck by a sudden, horrible thought.

'Oh my God,' she said, stiffening.

'What is it?' Alex, still inside her, lying in her arms on top of her, with his head resting in the hollow of her shoulder, was marvelling at the sense of closeness he had felt to her when they were making love. As if they had known each other always instead of being virtual strangers. And of the way in which she had banished his fears of impotence and inadequacy and made him feel like a god.

Jane moved away from him, taking care, even in her pain, to do it tenderly so he would not feel rejected, and sat up with her knees bent and her head clutched in her hands.

'I meant to tell you,' she said. 'I'm not using any contraception. Giorgio's – had a vasectomy you see,' she didn't feel ready to spoil their happiness by introducing the dark topic of Giorgio's treachery, 'and I don't have anything. I simply can't believe I could have been so careless.' She turned and looked at him, stricken, and he sat up hastily and put his arm round her shoulders and kissed her on the cheek.

'Don't worry,' he said gently. He didn't feel in the least bit angry with her, and anyway he was perfectly certain they would be okay. Look how long he and Julie had tried for a child – and Sandra and Martin. Her sudden vulnerability made him feel almost unbearably tender towards her, and he started to kiss her on the lips.

Jane's mouth opened under his, and she twined her arms around his neck. The smell of his skin evoked powerful memories. Already, in the short time he had

143

been her lover, he had managed to erase her five years with Giorgio as completely as if they had never existed. Jane knew that she and Alex were right for each other as she and Giorgio had been wrong, and longed to sink once more into the soft whirlpool of oblivion he was offering.

'But you don't understand.' She forced herself to push him gently away from her. 'It's the thirteenth day. The most dangerous day of the month. I've only once made love on the thirteenth day before, and I got pregnant.' For a moment she was haunted by the ghost of the child of her first marriage which she had lost at three months.

Alex stared at her bewildered. No other woman had ever spoken to him about these things. He hardly knew what she was talking about. His attempts to make Julie pregnant had been clothed in silence. After a few years of childlessness his father-in-law had taken him aside and told him that he and his wife had come to the conclusion that Alex ought to have some tests. Alex had dutifully masturbated into a glass bottle and been announced fully fertile. A further period of silence had followed, after which it had been announced that Julie was going to have some tests, and after that a minor operation to clear an obstruction in her tubes. By then Alex and Julie had drifted so far apart that their lovemaking had virtually ceased. He wondered now if it was a coincidence that the moment Julie had been pronounced fertile had also been the moment their sex life had ended for good.

Jane saw that he hadn't understood the urgency of the situation. 'Is there an all-night chemist we could go to?' she asked him.

Alex's mind spanned the hostile regions of Ladbroke Grove. 'No, I don't think so,' he said. 'I believe there might be one in Westbourne Grove which shuts at ten, but it's nearly that now –' He hesitated, struck by the extraordinary rapidity with which the hours had flown.

'Could we try?' Jane was already on her feet. The moonlight, shining through the gap at the top of the curtains, illuminated the gentle curves of her perfect little breasts and buttocks. Alex thought how much he would hate to leave the comfort of her arms and scramble into his clothes in order to dash to a sordid, neon-lit destination where they would be forced to explain their dilemma to a group of incomprehending Indians. He sprang out of bed and took her in his arms, and as he did so the clock started to strike.

'Listen,' he said. 'It's too late.'

Jane's whole body seemed to sag. Alex tightened his grip in order to support her. 'Then I don't know what to do,' she said forlornly, and hid her face against his shoulder.

Alex stroked her hair. He felt overcome by a mixture of protectiveness and desire. He knew in that moment that if she was really pregnant he wanted her to have the child. 'Don't do anything,' he said.

Jane's soul leaped to meet his in a great thrill. She lifted her head and looked him in the eyes, and he smiled back at her, lovingly, comfortingly, but still, she could see, not really comprehending the awesome responsibilities of the situation. He means it now, she thought, but he still doesn't think it's really going to happen.

Jane knew, as Alex did, that their lovemaking had been something exceptional. Not in terms of technical virtuousity or multiorgasmic splendour – he had, in fact, been surprisingly diffident and tentative for the great seducer of Virginia's descriptions – but in terms of recognition and communion – the feeling that they had been everything to each other in a previous incarnation, and would come to be everything again to each other in this one. Her sceptical side had tried to deny it, telling her she was merely exceptionally aroused because he was the first new man she'd had in five years, but her soul had told her they were made for each other, and that the least damaging thing they could do would be to join hands and walk off over the horizon together – stopping, of course, to collect Filippo and take him with them – and let the world scream and shake its fists at them as it would.

Even knowing this, however, and knowing that she would one day give Alex the children he wanted and be a loving and tender mother towards them, she could not feel that it was right for them to conceive their first child now. Other, more tepid lovers might require the birth of a child to unite them, but in her and Alex's case she saw instantly that a child, in their complicated situation, could only be a wedge that would drive them apart.

Jane would have been even more worried if she had known of Alex's inexperience. She imagined that at some point in his life he must already have been in this situation, and that he was fully aware of the danger they were in and the commitment he had made to her in telling her to do nothing further to prevent conception. What she didn't realize was his almost total ignorance of such matters. Alex was convinced that once intercourse had taken place, nothing more could be done. He had seen Jane's desire to visit the chemist as mere panicking on her part, and an enterprise that was doomed to failure. He didn't realize that by telling her not to do anything he had made any commitment to her at all. And so they stared at each other, incomprehending, Jane full of astonishment at the recklessness of the proposition she thought he had made to her and Alex full of tenderness at what he thought was her unnecessary panic over a minimal risk.

Jane was the first to break the embrace. 'I think I'd better go to the bathroom,' she said, almost apologetically. Beautiful and romantic as she had found Alex's words, she thought it important that one of them at least should maintain an element of sanity. He let her go reluctantly, and she walked naked down the short flight of stairs to the bathroom, where she turned on the bidet as high as she could and let the water run cold inside her, praying all the time that it wasn't going to be too late.

When she returned, he was sitting up in bed with the sheets covering the lower part of his body. She stared at him with pleasure. Undressed he reminded her of Michelangelo's *David*, youthful and perfect in the Piazza della Signoria by moonlight. He smiled and held out his arms to her and she went to them gratefully, snuggling up to him under the sheets with her head sinking automatically into the newly familiar hollow of his shoulder.

'Alex.'

'Mm.'

'I just want to say again how sorry I am. I find it so extraordinary that I didn't say anything to you. I almost wondered if I mightn't have done it on purpose – subconsciously I mean. I wouldn't have done it consciously, of course.'

'Of course not,' said Alex soothingly, starting to stroke her left breast.

'So if I do turn out to be pregnant,' she went on, 'I promise you I won't hold you responsible. I will have an abortion if you want me to.'

'Oh please don't talk about it now.' Alex was quite surprised at the horror the word 'abortion' aroused in him.

'I'm sorry.' Jane slid her arm around his neck and started to stroke his hair. 'I've really spoilt our lovely evening, haven't I? My only excuse is that I was completely thrown just before I got here by seeing Verge's car driving down the street. I know it sounds silly, but I felt quite panic-stricken at the thought she might see me.' She had in fact been trembling when he'd opened the door to her. He'd noticed her hand shaking when he gave her the champagne and asked if anything was the matter, but she'd laughed it off and said it was nothing.

'But Verge knew you were coming to see me this evening,' Alex said. 'I told her myself. I bumped into her earlier, you see, and I was carrying all the things I'd bought for our dinner –' the dinner they had never eaten, which still stood in lonely state on his dining table, with Jane's lilies resplendent in a vase at the centre.

He felt her stiffen in his arms. She thought how angry Verge would be with her for having deceived her, and buried her face in her hands. 'Oh God,' she said faintly.

'I'm sorry.' Alex took her hand and turned her face gently till she was looking at him. 'I didn't realize it was supposed to be a secret from Verge. She's always telling me you're her best friend, you see –' although actually he didn't remember her having done so for a few months now. Not since the New Year's Eve dinner when he and Jane had first started to get on so well together. 'I didn't think you'd mind her knowing,' he concluded lamely. 'After all, she's so sweet, isn't she?'

Jane hoped she hadn't made her surprise too obvious. She herself was often accused of being naive about people – most notably by Virginia, in fact – but she still didn't see how anyone who knew Verge well could possibly describe her as sweet. Of course, she couldn't say this to Alex. It would seem so odd and disloyal after his speech about her being Virginia's best friend. Besides she didn't really have anything to go on except this strong animal instinct of danger which would only sound ridiculous if she attempted to put it into words.

'I wouldn't exactly describe her as sweet, would you?' she ventured carefully. 'Very amusing, of course, and – well – acerbic –'

'Oh but she's been terribly sweet to me,' Alex said eagerly. 'She and Robin have had me over to dinner endlessly in the last year. I can't tell you how lonely I would have been sometimes if it hadn't been for them.'

How cosy, Jane thought, and how bitter to realize that tomorrow she would be in Venice and that the dinners with Verge would be carrying on without her. She remembered her happiness at the beginning of the evening and marvelled at how quickly it had all been transformed into sadness and fear. Turning, she slithered softly on top of him, rubbing the length of her body against his and feeling him grow hard instantly between her legs. If conversation between them was to be so fraught with danger, she thought, they would just have to seek solace in the magic of their lovemaking.

He started to kiss her on the lips, but she broke away from him and slid gently down his body before smiling mischievously up at him.

'Would you like me to suck your cock?' she asked.

CHAPTER NINE

Alex bounded eagerly up the steps to his front door. It was nearly twelve, and Jane had agreed to visit him for a last lunch before leaving for the airport at four.

He had spent the morning at his office in an erotic haze, beaming on colleagues and secretaries alike, and coping with all the petty work problems which had lately come to seem so infuriating, with effortless goodwill and patience. The sorting of his mail and correcting of his latest report on the location of a new distribution depot for a large chain of breweries had been illuminated by haunting visions of Jane's Madonna-like beauty as she lay naked in his arms performing acts which he had been brought up to think of as dirty and unmentionable with such gentleness and sweetness that for the first time in his life they had come to seem not only natural, but also curiously innocent.

He had tried to tell her this last night, after she had satisfied him, as she lay with her head still resting on his groin and her arms encircling his buttocks. He had drawn her up towards him till she lay in his arms and told her that it was the most beautiful thing that had ever happened to him in his life and then, when she only smiled at him and gently stroked his hair, had been prompted by jealousy to add: 'But I suppose that's thanks to your experience.'

She had lain very still for a moment, recognizing Virginia's contribution to this remark. 'I don't think', she said at last, 'that making love well's necessarily a sign of vast experience. Often it can be enough just to have one good teacher.'

'Which you had, I suppose?'

'Oh yes,' she said, and sighed.

'Was it Giorgio?'

'Oh no.' Making love with Alex had unfortunately only emphasized the unsatisfactoriness of Giorgio's love-making – the way he managed to enter her at just the wrong angle so it was always slightly painful and unpleasant – and, what she now found most extraordinary of all, the fact that she had never been able to tell him this.

'Who was it then?'

'My first husband,' Jane told him. 'The whole thing was a disaster emotionally, but I'll always be grateful to him for what he taught me about my body.'

'What did he do?'

'I'll have to be careful how I answer that,' she said smiling. 'When Giorgio and I were over here one Christmas before Philly was born, I did some voluntary work for a Housing Association. I was talking to one of the girls there about my first marriage, and how it lasted less than a year, and she asked me the same question. I said, "He used to beat me up," and she looked a bit embarrassed and said, "Oh no, I meant what did he do for a living!"' She laughed.

Alex was horrified. '*Did* he beat you up?'

'Yes. And in answer to your first question, if that was what you were asking, he was a film director. Mostly experimental arty stuff which it was very difficult to get distributed. I think my relationship with him was one of the factors that made me want to get out of the business entirely. That was why I fled to Venice, where they don't have a film industry.' She had started to shiver. Alex pulled the bedclothes over them both and then took her into his arms again to warm her.

'I think what I was actually asking was what he taught you about your body.' Alex wasn't sure he wanted to know, but felt compelled to ask the question anyway.

'Oh that,' Jane laughed. 'It was nothing particularly mysterious. Just a question of taking the trouble to find the right places, and then applying the right pressure to them once you did. Basic stuff that people often get wrong because they can't bring themselves to talk about it.' She wondered now if, in not trying harder to talk to Giorgio, she had been punishing herself. Trying to show herself she could live without sensual pleasure, only to be reminded by Alex that she couldn't. 'And the way to suck people properly –' she smiled at him.

'Well, he certainly succeeded there.' Alex had to fight to keep his voice as casual as hers. In his limited experience of sleeping with married women, the etiquette seemed to be for them to pretend either that their husbands were monsters – Martin – or pathetic lackeys – Henry. In admitting, to a husband who apparently really had been a monster, a debt of gratitude because of what he had taught her about sex, Jane showed a devastating degree of honesty that Alex felt uncertain he could ever match. He had the uncomfortable, but also strangely exhilarating sensation that he was following her into uncharted waters where the rewards of discovery would always be counterbalanced by the fear of being swept irretrievably out of his depth.

'Thank you,' she said. 'It's very nice of you to say I have a talent, even if the application of it does have to be strictly limited. When we were on our honeymoon, my husband took me to a prostitute in Paris, and watched us make love together. When he was washing afterwards she asked me if I'd like to go back and work with her the following day and make lots of money. I didn't do it, but I did feel terribly flattered that she thought I was good enough.'

Alex felt a mixture of outrage and almost unbearable excitement. 'He took you to a prostitute and watched you make love together?' he repeated, dazed. Other women he knew had told him they fantasized about that sort of thing, but he couldn't think of a single one who would actually admit to having done it, nor could he begin to reconcile such depravity with her earlier, equally casual statement about doing voluntary work for charity which was also the sort of thing other people talked about but never did.

'Yes. Haven't you ever had a threesome with two women? It was terribly fashionable in the sixties.' All Jane's instincts were urging her to be gentle and romantic with him. Making love to him had made her feel pure and reborn, like a virgin again, but she told herself that a romantic approach would only bore the sophisticate of Verge's descriptions, who must surely at some point have experimented with exotic sexual combinations. She was determined at all costs to keep their minds off the possible tragedy that was hanging over them, and knowing nothing of his inexperience, imagined that this would be the best way to do so.

'No,' Alex said. 'I always had too much trouble getting one woman to even think about getting two.'

Jane, convinced he must be teasing her, laughed and held him tight. 'Well, I don't think it ever really works in practice,' she said. 'It's hard enough, isn't it, for two people to fancy each other equally? I don't actually think it's possible for three. I'm glad to have tried it and got it out of my system, but I didn't want to do it again. I think that's really why I moved in with Giorgio,' she went on. 'Because he's so absolutely straight sexually, and I needed to prove to myself that that was enough for me. And it was.' She looked troubled. 'For nearly five years. Until tonight. Oh Alex, I know they say married women always tell their lovers that it's the first time they've ever been unfaithful to their husbands, but it's actually true in this case. I almost wish it wasn't. If I'd had more practice at it I'd never have been such a fool as to take that awful risk.' She looked at him appealingly for a moment and then shrugged her shoulders. 'But you don't have to believe me unless you want to.'

'Of course I do.' Why should she lie about this, he thought, when she had already admitted to so much worse? Repulsed, and at the same time more violently excited than he had ever been in his life, he felt a sudden longing to tear into her and crush her and fuck her until all her other lovers were eradicated from her memory and she belonged only to him.

As he entered the house Alex saw a solitary letter on the mat, which must have arrived by the second post. Its pale blue envelope and tall, spiky handwriting proclaimed it instantly to be from Georgina.

Only two days ago he would have fallen on it with rapture. Now he felt strangely reluctant even to pick it up. Why does she have to write to me now, he asked himself, just when I'm happy?

He told himself he must be practical. Jane was leaving tonight. She was going back to Giorgio. They had discussed the possibility of Alex going out to Venice to see her, but he already knew from his experience with Georgina how wildly unsatisfactory it would be to be treated once more like an Edwardian chorus girl in St John's Wood, waiting passively in his hotel while Jane juggled desperately with her domestic routine in order to grant him the odd, fleeting assignation. Jane was leaving and Georgina was staying. However frustrating, their relationship might be, he couldn't just let it go now after the huge emotional investment he had put into it. He hesitated for a moment, then bent down and picked it up.

Darling, it read. *This must have been the longest and the worst. Rosie's been staying with us. Jocelyn's just left her and she sits around all day in her misery, trying to understand why she still loves someone who treats her so thoughtlessly. Her terrible unhappiness has made me think of my own selfishness, and yet I do so very much miss you. The garden was so beautiful last weekend that I thought of you constantly and imagined I was there with you. I haven't had a moment to myself for so very long. The house has been full with Eddie Aldeburgh, Hamish R-S and a drunken Russian ballerina who defected to Italy, married the inevitable prince, and has now left him. Tomorrow it will be half term for the children and another week will be gone. I've no idea when I shall be in London next, but I think of you all the time and wonder what you are doing. Hope we are still speaking? Love G XX*

For once Georgina's soufflé-like mixture of a proclaimed desire to see him, excuses for not seeing him, and name-dropping didn't quite work its magic. Before, he would have been struck by the nobility of her self-renunciation, inflamed by her longing and desperately jealous of the exciting social circles in which she seemed to move. Now he merely felt befuddled. What exactly, he wondered critically, was she actually trying to say to him? He would have liked to read the letter more carefully, but Jane was due at twelve, so he put it away reluctantly in the drawer of his desk and resolved to pore over it later.

His thoughts returned to it, inevitably, as he set about the unrewarding task of removing last night's carefully wrapped banquet from the fridge and arranging it once more on the table. It had effectively destroyed his happy mood of anticipation and left him with a dull, unreasoning resentment for them both – Georgina for stirring up his emotions just when he'd thought he was getting over them, and Jane for being due to arrive at any moment so he wouldn't have time to read the letter again and sort out what he really felt.

The doorbell rang just as he'd finished, but before he'd had time to go upstairs and wash as he'd planned. Jane was waiting on the doorstep, eager and rapturous, but as her eyes met his the light in them went out and her smile hardened and became social and artificial. Alex, instantly contrite, took her into his arms and breathed in her scent of violets, then drew away, still holding her hands, and stared at her in appreciation.

'How beautiful you look,' he said wonderingly. 'And I do love your outfit.'

'They're workman's overalls,' she told him. smiling. 'I got them in a shop in Vauxhall Bridge Road and dyed them myself.' They were now a sludgy beige, and she had belted them in with a wide canvas belt which emphasized her tiny waist.

'Well, you certainly make an extremely sexy workman.' He undid the top button and found to his intoxication that she wasn't wearing a bra, but as he started to caress her she caught his hand in hers and drew gently away from him.

'Alex,' she said, 'I was remembering this morning that I'd read an article a few months ago about something called the morning-after pill. It was for people who'd taken a risk the night before and wanted to make sure they weren't pregnant. I rang my doctor this morning, but unfortunately he'd gone away till the end of the week.' Bobby was tremendously popular with all his patients and was always receiving glamorous invitations to yachts and stately homes. Jane understood only too well why people should enjoy having him as their guest and had never resented his frequent absences until now. 'There was an answering service dealing with his calls,' she went on, 'so I poured out my story to them, but all the sniffy woman at the other end could do was say she'd never heard of it and ask me scathingly if I was a private patient. I was wondering if your doctor might be able to help.'

Alex frowned. 'I do have a great friend who's a doctor,' he said, thinking of Martin. 'He works for a busy National Health practice, but unfortunately they'd be shut at this time of day. His wife used to work as his receptionist,' he went on dubiously. 'She might know if it was available or not.'

'Do you think you could ask her?' Jane said eagerly. 'Would she be at home?'

'Yes.' Alex had done his best to forget about his lunchtime escapade with Sandra, but now it returned to haunt him in all its lurid detail. She had rung him several times since then, but so far he had managed studiously to avoid seeing her on her own. He began to regret having mentioned her to Jane. 'Or there's Julie and my old doctor,' he went on, 'but I suppose that might get back to her family –'

'Try your friend's wife,' Jane urged him. 'She wouldn't mind, would she?'

'Er, no.' Alex felt thoroughly caught in his own trap. 'But let's have a drink first, shall we or some lunch?'

'Let's have a glass of wine,' Jane said, 'and call her at once. I'd need to get a prescription probably, if there was anything, so I'd have to get on with it because of my plane.' Her face clouded.

Alex, feeling thoroughly hunted, led her into the dining room. It looked particularly attractive in daylight with its lime-green walls hung with theatre designs of an opium den featuring riotous overblown poppies and kimonoed Chinamen in cubicles smoking their pipes under the impassive gaze of a cross-legged Golden Buddha. He had taken a lot of trouble with the table, which he had spread with a burgundy-coloured cloth which set off his olive and saffron Italian dinner service and hollow-stemmed Victorian wine glasses engraved round the rim with vine leaves and clusters of grapes. He felt a little hurt that Jane didn't seem to notice how nice it looked, but merely accepted her glass of wine in silence before taking a nervous gulp from it.

'Won't you have some quiche?' he asked her. 'I've got cheese or spinach. I made sure they were both vegetarian.'

'Thank you.' She made an effort to seem more relaxed. 'They look delicious. I'd love some in a minute, but couldn't we just make the call first? It would be such a relief.' She was beginning to feel slightly baffled by his obvious reluctance to act.

'All right,' he said rather crossly, and then seeing her chilled expression, hastily disguising his annoyance with a social smile. 'I–I've left my address book upstairs.' This was true, though in fact he knew Sandra's number by heart. 'Why don't you help yourself to some food while I go and make the call?' He nodded at the table curtly and walked out of the room.

Jane sat down slowly and cut herself a small slice of quiche. It was still frozen, and tasted vaguely of sawdust. She had to drink more wine than she really wanted in order to get it down. She was feeling helpless and uneasy. Everything seemed to be going wrong today, and she couldn't understand what she had done to cause it. She had thought Alex would be so pleased at the hope of salvation she was offering him, but instead he seemed merely irritated. It crossed her mind to wonder if the friend he was calling could be the one he had mentioned the day before that he'd had the brief encounter with, but she decided at once that it couldn't. No one of Alex's experience, she thought, could possibly be so naive as to have suggested such a thing.

Alex went into the bedroom and locked the door cautiously behind him. The errand he was on now was a far cry from the erotic visions which had sustained him that morning as he'd plumped up the pillows and spread the fur cover enticingly over the bed. He felt as if he were going to his own execution, and the breathless eagerness in Sandra's voice when she realized who was calling only added to the sinking feeling of doom. As he poured out the story to her, the silence at the other end of the line seemed to echo disapprovingly in his ear. When he'd finished there was a long pause.

'Do you mean to tell me,' Sandra said at last, 'that you've only slept with her once and that now she's trying to tell you she's pregnant?'

'Only that she might be. Her husband's had a vasectomy, you see, so she doesn't use any contraception. She'd been meaning to tell me but, well, she was a bit upset at nearly running into Verge. She hadn't told her she was coming here –'

'I must say she sounds like the most frightful liar to me,' Sandra interjected acidly.

Alex swallowed. After their conversation last night he had come to the conclusion that Jane was the most honest woman he had ever met. On the other hand it *was* a bit odd that she should have been so anxious to keep her visit a secret from Virginia. 'Not necessarily,' he said. 'After all it's natural that she should want to be discreet. She is married –' his voice tailed off dubiously as he wondered if he hadn't just confirmed the fact that he had been trying to deny.

Sandra sensed his uncertainty and changed her tone to one of saccharine sweetness. 'Alex darling,' she said softly, 'you mustn't be offended by me saying this, but you know you really are a little bit naive as far as women are concerned. Don't get me wrong. I think it's terribly sweet. It's one of the reasons I'm so fond of you. But unfortunately there are certain types of women around who wouldn't be above taking advantage of you. You're quite a catch, you know, Alex. You're single and tremendously attractive, and you have that lovely house and an awful lot of money from your job. This woman's probably desperate to settle down and get some security. I expect she knows her Italian will never marry her, so she's trying to latch on to you because you're so sweet and gentle. Believe me, Alex, one simply doesn't get pregnant just like that. Look how long Martin and I have been trying. If she really is pregnant, it's far more likely to be someone else's child which she's trying to pass off as yours because she thinks you're a soft touch.'

Alex felt quite cold with horror for a moment. He'd always thought that it must be the worst thing in the world to believe one was the father of a child, and then discover it belonged to someone else. He even seemed to remember having said this once to Sandra and Martin. 'But she's not saying she's pregnant,' he protested. 'Only that she took a risk last night and wants to know if there's anything she can take to prevent it if she should happen to be.'

'Well there isn't,' Sandra said flatly. 'There's absolutely nothing. A woman who's had a child already certainly ought to know that much. I must say, Alex, I find it extremely hard to believe that someone of her experience could just have forgotten to tell you something as important as the fact that she wasn't using any contraception. *I'd* never dream of having an affair with someone unless I was absolutely sure it was safe.'

Yes, but you're an old pro at the game, aren't you, he thought as he digested the bitter fact that there was nothing he and Jane could do. He realized now what a disastrous mistake it had been to call Sandra and put himself at the mercy of her vitriolic tongue. 'Yes I know,' he said, 'but she was upset. She's never done anything like this before –'

'Oh come on, Alex.' The note of sarcasm in her voice reduced him to a state of fury made worse by the fact that he was wholly powerless to do anything about it. He couldn't afford to quarrel with Sandra in case she told Martin about their affair, and since her suicide attempt there was also the constant fear of once more pushing her over the edge. 'You really mustn't', she went on, 'allow yourself to be fooled by that old story. It's the oldest trick in the book. Married women always tell their lovers they've never slept with anyone else since they met their husbands, but you surely can't be such an idiot as to actually believe it.'

'I suppose it must be true sometimes,' he said sulkily.

Sandra gave an artificial little laugh. 'Yes, Alex, but not in this case, I'm sure. After all, you hardly know her, do you? She can hardly pretend it's a great love affair. Alex, you must promise me to be firm with her. Ask her what she wants to do if she is pregnant. I can assure you that if it's a genuine mistake she'll tell you she wants to get rid of it and go back to her Italian. It's the only fair thing she can do anyway, isn't it? For the sake of the child she already has? Oh Alex, can't you see how selfish she must be to take a risk like this when she's got a child? It seems so unfair that women like that are able to have children when I can't –'

'But Jane's a wonderful mother,' he burst out. He thought of her beauty and tenderness as she fed Filippo on Virginia's sofa at their first meeting, and the times he'd seen them leaving Virginia's house hand in hand, laughing together and absorbed in a world of their own. He'd always envied their closeness, and compared it to his own distant relationship with his pretty, social butterfly of a mother who had left him entirely in the care of a nanny until he was seven and could be decently packed off to boarding school. 'You don't know her,' he added lamely.

'Alex,' Sandra asked softly 'what about Georgina? When you and I made love that time I was prepared to go through with it in order to comfort you because I could see how unhappy you were.'

Alex grunted in astonishment. Was that really how she had seen it? As he remembered it, she had practically raped him, but he supposed it would hardly be gallant to point out the fact now.

'I understood', she went on, 'that what you felt for Georgina was true love, and I admired you for it, Alex. If I've ever seemed to question your feelings for her, it's only been to find out if they were genuine or not. A lot of people found it difficult to understand how you could leave Julie for her when Julie was so sick, but Martin and I have always defended you. We could see that you and Julie were wrong for each other, and what an exceptional woman Georgina is, with all those charity events she organizes and all those committees she sits on. But oh, Alex, if you were to leave Georgina now for a fling with some actress you've only just met, what on earth would people think of you? After you broke up your marriage for Georgina and led her to think you were offering her a future. Alex you can't be so cruel as to do that to her.'

Alex was astonished at the way in which these sentiments, which sounded so right when he expressed them himself, could sound so wrong when coming from Sandra. 'But, after all, she's let me down too, Sandy,' he pointed out. 'Lots of times.'

'Yes, but surely you can understand how torn and guilty she must feel about loving you? I'm sure it's just that she *genuinely* cares about her children, and that soon she won't be able to resist seeing you again. Haven't you heard from her at all?'

'As a matter of fact I had a letter from her today,' he admitted.

'There you are,' Sandra said triumphantly. 'You see, Alex, I really do know the way other women's minds work. Are you seeing her soon?'

'I don't know,' he said wearily. 'She didn't say anything definite.'

'You will, Alex. Believe me. She won't be able to resist you much longer. But for goodness' sake get yourself disentangled from this other woman first.'

'I don't need to,' Alex replied with some bitterness. 'She's going back to Italy this evening anyway.' He looked at his watch and saw that they'd been talking for nearly ten minutes. 'I must go, Sandy. Jane'll be wondering what's happening. I'm sorry to have bothered you with all this – and even sorrier you can't suggest anything for her to take,' he added, trying to end the conversation on a lighter note.

'There's nothing at all, I'm afraid. And, Alex –'

'Yes?' he replied reluctantly.

'Promise me you won't commit yourself to anything – for Georgina's sake.'

'All right,' he said. However unpalatable it was to be lectured, he admitted to himself that the strange enchantment he felt in Jane's presence might well disappear once he saw Georgina again. It was important for all their sakes that he should at least find out. 'Not that I think there's any real risk.' He was too modest to believe that Jane might genuinely be in love with him, and still felt it was unlikely that she could have become pregnant so quickly. 'I'll call you in a day or two,' he added.

'Yes do, Alex. We must have lunch.'

Alex shuddered. ''Bye, love,' he said hastily.

'Goodbye.'

His hands were trembling as he replaced the receiver. Thank God, he thought, that he had made the call in private. However, even knowing that Jane couldn't possibly have overheard it, he still felt himself unwilling to face her. If only, he thought unreasonably, she hadn't been so insistent on his ringing Sandra. It was dreadful to think that Sandra was now irretrievably involved in the situation. He knew her well enough to realize that she wouldn't rest until she had squeezed every last drop of information out of him, and dreaded the series of cross-examinations which would inevitably ensue. It took him several more minutes to calm himself sufficiently to walk downstairs to the kitchen.

Jane was sitting at the table where he had left her. She had pushed her plate to one side and was reading, or trying to read, that morning's copy of the *Guardian*. She looked up eagerly as he came in, her eyes full of hope, and then seeing his expression, dropped them again and went on reading the article.

Alex pulled up a chair beside her and put his arm round her. She didn't look at him again, but leaned her head against his shoulder and put the paper down.

'What did she say?' she asked.

'She said there's nothing.'

'Well actually there is,' Jane said. 'I definitely remember reading about it, but I suppose it's not generally available yet. It's supposed to be quite dangerous, you see. Not the sort of thing you could take every month, but effective in cases of emergency – where the woman's been raped and so on. Not that I was.' She attempted a smile. 'Oh if only I'd kept the article, but at the time I thought it was the last thing I'd ever be needing . . .' Her voice trailed off and she slid her hand into his. Alex squeezed it, thinking how small and delicate it was for someone of her height, and how icy cold.

'Do you really think you're pregnant, Janie?' he asked. 'Surely it's far too soon –'

She gave him a sharp look, and he reddened and looked away. Had he sounded peevish, he wondered? Could she have caught some echo of Sandra's words in his voice.

She sighed and spoke patiently: 'Of course it's far too soon to know definitely,' she agreed. 'It's just that last night was the most dangerous night of the month, as I told you.' She attempted to laugh. 'Well, at least I've tried everything I can think of. Now I'm just going to have to put it out of my mind until I can know for sure. Let's talk about something else, shall we? Can I cut you a slice of quiche?'

Much later, after they had made love three times, and, somewhat astonishingly to Alex in the circumstances, recaptured and even surpassed all the tenderness and bliss that they had known the previous night, Jane announced that she would have to go.

'Oh not yet, surely?' Alex was half-asleep on the fur bedcover, blissfully entwined in her legs and arms and breathing in her scent of violets.

'I'm afraid so. It's nearly half-past three.' She started to disentangle herself from him, but he pulled her back.

'I feel very guilty at letting you go,' he said.

She moved restlessly. 'Don't feel guilty,' she said. 'You are letting me go, and that's that.'

'But would you stay if I asked you to?' he said wonderingly.

'I don't know. Maybe not.'

'Janie look at me.' He turned her face towards his, but she kept her eyes lowered. 'What do you really want to do?'

'Alex, please don't let's play games with each other,' she begged.

'I'm not playing games,' he protested. 'Please tell me.'

She hesitated. The sense of wrongness she had felt on entering the house had been terribly compounded by the mysterious phone call he had made. He had, however, been adorable to her at lunch, and she had almost thought things were all right again until, just as they had started to make love, he had produced a condom from his bedside drawer and said to her smilingly, 'I think I'd better put this on, hadn't I, so we don't make two babies instead of one?' Her rational mind had tried to applaud his sense and practicality, and pointed out that he was only trying to protect her, but her heart had lurched sickeningly and told her that for reasons beyond her understanding he had changed his mind about wanting her child.

Since then, however, the magic of their physical communion had wrought its powerful spell once more, so much so that she was almost prepared to believe she had imagined the earlier sense of an invisible enemy that was thrusting itself between them. Was she brave enough, she wondered, to do what she had never done in her life before and admit to a man that he was more important to her than he had yet declared her to be to him? It went against everything she had ever learned about the art of love, and if it had just been for herself she would never have done it. But she told herself a child's life might be at stake. She was leaving that night and it might be her only chance to speak. She had promised Alex the night before that if he wanted her to she would have an abortion. She would never break her promise to him, even if he was to go back on the commitment he had made to her. She knew from her experience with Giorgio how bitter it was to have a child by a man who didn't really want it, and would never go through it again with someone else, especially someone she loved as much as she did Alex. If she didn't speak now, he might never realize that, much as she regretted what had happened, she wanted to keep the child. She knew suddenly that she couldn't go back to Venice without telling him.

She looked at him at last, for a long moment, and then said casually, 'Well then, I think you should marry me and take on our child and another child you hardly know,' and she gave him a challenging little smile.

Alex felt outraged. Sandra had been right, he thought. She *was* trying to trap him. He found the word 'marry' particularly disturbing, conjuring, as it did, visions of in-laws and wedding lists and legal wrangles from which he was only now just beginning to disentangle himself. Why should she require marriage from him, he wondered, when she had been prepared to have Filippo without it? Did she trust him less than she did Giorgio? Georgina had always proposed that they should merely live together. He had found the idea wonderfully romantic and appealing, not stopping to think that as a married woman herself she would be powerless to marry him anyway. He wasn't sure what he had been expecting Jane to say, but it certainly wasn't that. He had expected tears perhaps, and pleading and protestations of love. They were all things which would have moved him, even though he would probably have despised both her and himself afterwards. He hadn't expected this cool challenge. My God, he thought, she's not like a woman at all.

'I'm sorry,' he heard himself say indignantly, 'but I couldn't possibly get married again without knowing the person really well.' He sneaked a look at her. She didn't look upset. She was still smiling with a sort of grim satisfaction as if she had been proved right. He was annoyed to hear a note of pleading creep into his voice. 'I was so unhappy for seven years in my last marriage, you must understand –'

'Never mind, Alex. I do understand.' She had gone against her own rule, she thought, and been punished for it. And now, however much she might love him, she would never ever open up to him again. It didn't occur to her to mitigate her plea. Having had one illegitimate child, she would never be prepared to go through all that suffering and legal complication again with another man. She didn't stop to think that with an Englishman, someone who wasn't already married to a vindictive wife, the whole process would be simpler and more tolerable, nor did she remotely understand his conception of marriage as a minefield of bourgeois trappings, which, if she had, would have horrified her as much as him. 'Let's just forget about it,' she said.

She sounded almost sorry for him, he thought, bewildered. It was as if she had rejected him for his lack of courage, not he her. He wanted to go on talking to her to make her understand him. He needed to feel she respected him. 'I know I shouldn't have made love to you,' he said.

'Why not? It was handed to you on a plate.'

He almost gasped. He had never heard a woman talk with such brutal honesty about herself. It didn't seem natural.

'Oh Janie,' he said feebly.

She got up. 'I *must* go, Alex.' She talked as if it was the end of a polite social occasion. He watched helplessly as she put on her clothes. Seeing her slim body disappearing into her overalls only made him long to rip them off her and start making love to her all over again. 'Goodbye bedroom,' she said when she was finished.

Alex seized on this remark as a way of delaying her. 'You haven't seen over the house yet,' he said. 'Let me just show it to you before you go.' He put on his clothes quickly, feeling cheered by the prospect. He was proud of all the work he had done on the house. As a way of keeping himself occupied after his divorce, he had resumed the decoration of the top floor, which contained two bedrooms and a bathroom. Georgina had promised to help him with it, but had somehow never had the time, so he had gone round the manufacturers himself collecting endless samples of wallpapers and carpet and curtain materials, and pinning them together to see if they would go with his collection of paintings.

Jane trailed after him obediently as he showed her the rooms. For the main guest room, where he sometimes slept on nights when Georgina failed to turn up, he had chosen an oppressive print of blue waterlilies, strangled by a background of brownish reeds. He found it particularly comforting on those nights to lie in bed and imagine himself drowning painlessly under a heavy blanket of brown water.

Jane exclaimed enthusiastically over the beauty of the rooms with their high ceilings and spectacular views over the leafy crescent which led up to Holland Park. She also admired his paintings, but made no comment about his carefully chosen decor. Alex realized with a sinking feeling that although she might be too polite to say so, she didn't really like it. 'Oh well,' he thought resentfully, 'she's going back to Venice tonight. I don't have to bother about pleasing her.'

'It's a beautiful house Alex,' she said thoughtfully as they went downstairs, 'but I find something a little sad about it. It's as if it needed to be lived in more.'

He didn't reply. It was a comment which had been made to him before, but on this occasion it struck warning bells. Jane noticed his expression as they reached the landing and felt instantly stricken. Could he have imagined that she had been proposing to move in with him? She felt overcome with embarrassment at the thought, and they made their way down the rest of the flight in an uncomfortable silence, which continued, almost unbroken, as they got into his car and he drove her the short distance to her home, parking the car discreetly round the corner so she wouldn't be seen by her neighbours.

'Thank you for lunch,' she said. Her smile didn't quite work this time, and she turned away from him and fumbled blindly for the door handle.

Alex took her in his arms and heard himself saying, 'I could always fly out for the weekend if you needed me.'

'Could you?' He was dismayed by the sudden radiance of hope in her expression. He could just imagine Verge and Sandra's comments if he told them he was going to Venice.

'Well,' he hesitated, 'if you really needed me, I suppose –'

'Don't worry. I won't ask you to. But it was a very nice thought.' She held him close to her for a moment and then slipped out of the car and disappeared round the corner without once looking back.

CHAPTER TEN

S peeding across the lagoon in the grey twilight with
Giorgio at the helm of the boat and Filippo lolling
sleepily beside her on the striped mattress, Jane was
struck by a sudden acute awareness of the beauty of the
city she had inhabited so reluctantly since Filippo's birth.

It was as if, through adultery, she had been reborn into a
new, painful world of childishly heightened emotions and
corresponding depths of despair. People she had known
for years seemed suddenly like strangers to her as she
wondered how they would react if they knew her guilty
secret, and whether they would cast her off in disgust.
Things and places which she had taken for granted before
knowing Alex became suddenly unbearably precious now
that she felt her days among them might be drawing to a
close. It was useless to tell herself that technically it wasn't
adultery because both she and Alex were free. She had
thought of Giorgio as her husband for too long for
the words to have any meaning. She felt all the guilt of an
adulteress, and all the compassionate affection for the
husband who did not yet know she had betrayed him, and
who had seemed so happy to see her when she and Filippo
had finally emerged through customs, swinging his son in
the air until he was almost hysterical with giggles, and
putting a protective arm round her shoulders before
summoning a porter to carry their suitcases the short
distance from the airport building to the boat.

Jane had felt quite unreasonably pleased to see him. After saying goodbye to Alex she had been sustained through the sad process of leaving London by all the last-minute preparations for departure and the need of keeping up a cheerful appearance in front of Filippo while saying their goodbyes to Sarah and Liliana. On the plane, however, once they had eaten what they could of their suppers and Filippo had fallen asleep with his head in her lap she had sunk into a fit of utter despair. How would she survive without Alex, she wondered. She had promised to ring him to say she had arrived safely, and they had agreed that they would write to each other with a view to Alex coming out to Venice to see her for his summer holiday. But would he still want to come, she asked herself, once he was out of her company and back in the clutches of Georgina and Virginia? If they could have spent more time together she was confident that he would shortly have become as convinced of their exceptional compatibility as she had been right from the moment they had first made love. But with her away and their relationship at the mercy of the extraordinary inefficiencies of the Italian postal and telephone systems, who knew what hostile influences might whisper their poison into his ears? Even if he did come to see her, how would their relationship fare under the cloak of conceal-ment and deception? Jane's nature was wholly unsuited to a clandestine relationship. She was proud of her love for Alex and wanted it to be open and carefree and visible to the whole world. Much as she longed to see him, she knew deep down that it would be better for him not to come, and the knowledge filled her with despair.

The plane, approaching the customary pocket of turbulence above the Alps, started to shake alarmingly. The seat belt signs went on and the passengers were told to return to their places. Jane rested her hot head against the cool window and stared out at the jagged, snow-capped mountains, praying suddenly that they would crash and that she and Filippo would sink painlessly together into eternity so he could die in his carefreeness and innocence and be spared the tumult and moral dilemmas of ever growing up.

They had not crashed, however, and Jane had accepted that for the time being she was condemned to battle on. The boat was now entering the city through the Fondamente Nuove, slowing down abruptly to conform with the speed limit which decreed a snail-like crawl through the narrow canals so as not to disturb the ancient foundations of the city with the backlash of waves from the engine. Every inch of the route was familiar to Jane, from the side canals near SS Giovanni e Paolo to the long stretch of the Grand Canal with its lowering sixteenth-century palazzi, now mostly broken up into offices or apartments. She had visited many of them with Giorgio for dinner parties or local festivals such as the Regatta Storica in September when the glitterati of Venice would gather on balconies to coo momentarily over the passing procession of ornate antique boats before returning inside to resume the more urgent business of drinking and gossiping.

At San Trovaso they turned abruptly right by a small white palazzo with a gondola painted on the front. They were nearly home now. As they pulled up outside their house a group of boys who had been playing football in the local *campo*, abandoned their game and came rushing towards the boat with cries of welcome. Jane knew and liked them all. Often when Giorgio was working, she would take a book and some toys for Filippo and sit in the *campo*, watching with one eye while he tried valiantly to join in their games. He had become a great pet with the local boys, none of whom seemed to be aware, as English boys would have been, of any barriers caused by age or language. They were always ringing Jane's doorbell to bring him little gifts or ask her if they could take him on short excursions. Two of the older boys, Paolo and Marino, would sometimes baby-sit for him if she and Giorgio had a late dinner. Filippo was overjoyed to see them, and stretched out his little arms to them trustingly as Jane lifted him onto the bank.

Marino, a blond, blue-eyed pocket Adonis of fourteen, whose father ran the local bar, scooped him up affectionately and held him aloft while the others crowded round and exclaimed at how big and strong he had grown during the winter months in London. Filippo giggled delightedly, and Jane felt her eyes filling with tears at the warmth of their welcome.

Only Giorgio seemed unmoved by the scene. He tied the rope of the boat carefully to its mooring ring and tilted the engine out of the water before turning to unload the suitcases. Jane, assisted by helpful hands, sprang out of the boat to receive them, but was pre-empted by the group of boys, who, forming a willing chain, soon had everything safely deposited at their front door.

'Can we take Filippo to the *campo* with us, signora, and show him my new bike?' Marino asked eagerly.

'I think that would be lovely, don't you, Giorgio?' Jane said. 'It would give me a chance to unpack his things and get everything ready for bedtime. We've had our supper on the plane, so he should only need a glass of milk before he goes to bed.'

'But I have already prepared his supper,' Giorgio said reproachfully, his features, which had seemed young and carefree at their meeting now settling into a stern mask of disapproval. 'I spent the afternoon making a vegetable risotto for you both, and I wish you to put him to bed immediately as my friend Desnoyer is coming round at nine o'clock.'

Jane's heart sank. Desnoyer was a rich Parisian who had recently bought an apartment in Venice which Giorgio was helping him to furnish. He was probably only in his mid-fifties, a few years older than Giorgio, but always managed to convey the impression that he had never been young. He always referred to Jane formally as 'La Signora', and never spoke to her directly, addressing even the most trivial remarks to her through Giorgio till Jane wanted to scream.

It was in the presence of acquaintances like Desnoyer that she felt the age gap between herself and Giorgio most acutely. She wondered if all younger women with middle-aged partners started out protesting blithely, as she had, that the age difference between them didn't matter at all, until one day a chance remark or an evening spent with boring contemporaries of their partner caused the trap door to snap open over the abyss and make them aware, in one sickening second of realization, that in fact it mattered very much indeed.

'Does he really have to come this evening?' she protested. 'I'd been so looking forward to settling in quietly.'

'Yes, he does,' Giorgio informed her coldly. 'He's leaving tomorrow, and I have a *Marriage at Cana* by Francesco Trevisani which he has told me he will make a decision about this evening.'

'Well, couldn't he have seen it at the gallery this afternoon?' Jane asked sulkily. Giorgio had recently acquired an antique shop in one of the small side streets leading from the Via XXII Marzo to the Fenice, and now spent most of his days there. He always came home religiously for lunch, but apart from that Jane hardly saw him until the evening as he liked to leave the house before she and Filippo were awake and return for supper at about 8.30, when Filippo had gone to bed. In many ways this was a relief, but it made a marked contrast to the early days of their relationship when she and Giorgio had hardly been out of each other's company for a second.

'He was busy today,' Giorgio said flatly. 'Besides it is better for him to see the painting hanging in a home. These rich borghesi have little imagination. But he is a most cultivated man, and one of my best customers.'

'Of course,' Jane agreed casually. 'It's just a pity that he also happens to be such a frightful bore.' She watched in some trepidation as Giorgio's mouth tightened like a trap, knowing from past experience that she would pay for the remark later.

The boys were still grouped round them, listening, rather like spectators at a tennis match, to their exchange, which had taken place in English. Seeing from her watch that she only had twenty minutes left before Desnoyer's arrival, Jane took Philly abruptly from Marino's arms and explained in Italian that he would have to go to bed because Giorgio had a customer arriving.

Philly, sensing that he was to be thwarted in his adventure, started to struggle and protest that he wanted to go with 'M'wino'.

'Naughty Filippo,' Giorgio said sternly. 'Go with mummy at once. *Che brutto!*'

Filippo, tired by the flight and accustomed from his weeks in London with Jane and Sarah to nothing but gentleness and approval, promptly burst into tears. For a moment Jane glared at Giorgio, but then realizing bitterly from long experience that if she continued to defy him the chief casualty of the situation would only be their son, lifted Filippo high in the air until he started to gurgle with laughter, and then ran with him up the steep staircase to the apartment crying joyously, 'Come on Philly, let's go and see if all your toys are still there!'

'Toys, toys!' Filippo echoed enthusiastically.

'Yes, darling.' Arriving at the door of the apartment, Jane put him down breathlessly and then knelt beside him and kissed him. 'Isn't it exciting?' she said with a slight break in her voice. 'We're home!'

Jane had been spoiling for a fight all evening. There had been another scene at supper when Filippo refused to eat his risotto and Giorgio, attempting to force feed him, had made him cry until he was sick. Desnoyer had arrived just as Jane was clearing up the mess, which had at least given her a chance to retreat to Filippo's bedroom with him. She had then, most unusually, had to spend three-quarters of an hour trying to settle him. Every time he had seemed to be dropping off, there had been a burst of loud, foreign laughter from the drawing room which had caused him to turn restlessly and start to grizzle. Jane knew that he was only longing to sleep, and that by tiptoeing anxiously into his room every time he made a sound she was actually disturbing him and making him more unsettled, but she didn't dare let him cry because she knew that Giorgio would blame her for it afterwards if he failed to clinch his deal. Eventually she ventured, barefoot and dishevelled, into the drawing room and asked the men if they would mind being a little bit quieter. Desnoyer, after his initial surprise at not seeing the perfectly groomed houri to whom he was accustomed, was actually quite nice about it. Giorgio, however, though he merely suggested walking Desnoyer back to his apartment with the painting in order to see how it would look on his wall, was quite obviously furious.

After they had gone, Jane sat motionless on the floor outside Filippo's room for half an hour, not daring to move in case she woke him. Her thoughts were full of rebellion. For the past two days, on and off, she had been wondering how she would broach the topic of Giorgio's vasectomy, which she had decided would have to wait until Filippo was asleep, so it could then, she hoped, be discussed by them in a civilized manner with no interruptions.

Now at last the moment had come and there was no Giorgio to discuss it with. Obeying an impulse which she knew she would probably regret, Jane walked softly to the phone. Often there was a two-hour delay on calls to London, but now, at nearly 10.30p.m.,there was a chance she might get through straightaway. She had so far managed to avoid moaning about Giorgio to Alex, partly because she had not wanted to intrude on their bliss by introducing such a topic, and partly because the guilt she felt at deceiving Giorgio had made her forget his faults and bathe his memory in a glow of guilty affection. Now, however, the urge to let off steam to someone was irresistible. She picked up the receiver and placed the call.

As she had hoped, there was no delay and she was put through straightaway. Her heart started to beat wildly as she heard the first ring and she had to take deep breaths to calm herself down and plan what she was going to say. As it continued to ring, however, she realized he must be out. Her eager anticipation was replaced by a jealous annoyance that he should be out enjoying himself while she, just by telephoning him at a time when Giorgio might return at any moment, was risking her whole future for his sake.

The bored voice of the operator broke in on her meditations.

'No reply from London, signora. Do you wish me to try the call later?'

Jane thought fast and decided she didn't dare. Giorgio had already been out longer than she'd expected. 'No thank you,' she said.

'You wish to cancel the call?'

'Yes. I'll cancel it.'

Jane put the receiver down and lit a cigarette. Why had she come back here, she wondered, when she longed only to be in London? Giorgio didn't want her. She and Filippo were only a nuisance to him. She had thought at the time that she was doing him a favour by providing him with a son to replace the children he had lost with his first wife. Now she realized that any vestiges which he might have felt when young of a desire for family life had long since been expunged by his first family. He had been too old to start all over again with nappies. He had wanted Jane to be his daughter as well as his mistress, sprung ready-made and nubile like Venus rom the foam, to worship him and submit to him in everything.

If he had ever really cared about children he would never have allowed his older ones to depart in the first place. Sure, his wife had found a lover – and how well Jane could understand her motives now when faced by the granite wall of Giorgio's sulkiness and disapproval – but Giorgio had admitted to her long ago that he had been the first to be unfaithful. During the long years of his marriage he'd had a succession of mistresses. Mostly foreign tourists whom he'd picked up during the summer months when his wife had been away in Germany with the children visiting her family. For all Jane knew he'd been unfaithful to her too. She didn't really think so, but she had absolutely no way of knowing for sure. No one in Venice would ever tell her, and Giorgio himself, motivated as he was by a consuming desire always to appear in the right in any argument, would certainly never confess to it.

Sometimes, before Filippo's birth, they had discussed the topic of fidelity. Giorgio had always maintained stoutly that if Jane were unfaithful to him it would be the end of their relationship. Jane had tried to tax him with unfairness. If he believed in fidelity, how could it have been right for him constantly to betray his first wife and yet expect the marriage to continue? At this point he had always flown into a violent rage, so they had never been able to resolve the argument. Until Alex, Jane had told herself it didn't really matter. She was perfectly content with Giorgio, and had no intention of being unfaithful to him anyway.

Now, however, the subject returned to her like an inspiration. What if she simply told Giorgio that she had a lover? He would be mortally offended and throw her out immediately, and that way the decision would be made for her without any agonizing on her part as to whether or not she was doing the right thing. She could return to London with Filippo. If Giorgio wouldn't help them she had a little money saved from her commercials, enough to last her the summer, and in the autumn Filippo would be old enough to start at playschool and she could go out and get a part-time job. Acting would probably prove too precarious for a single mother, but she was healthy and could type and drive a car and speak two languages fluently. She wouldn't mind how menial a job she got if it meant she could support Filippo and herself and be free once and for all from Giorgio's tyranny.

She stubbed out her cigarette with determination. The future was starting to look positively rosy. What a good thing Giorgio had been so unreasonable this evening, she thought. She would never have had the heart to confess to him in cold blood. Not because she was afraid of him, although she was, but because she would have shrunk from dealing such a mortal blow to his masculine pride. How lucky also that she hadn't even unpacked. She and Filippo could leave tomorrow with the minimum of fuss, and once they were settled back in London she could call Alex calmly and tell him things hadn't worked out with Giorgio and she had decided to leave him. She wouldn't put any pressure on Alex. They could just date normally and see what happened. Now that she was back in Venice her fear of pregnancy had receded. The burst of optimism she had felt on reaching a decision made her convinced suddenly that she was bound to be lucky. Surely, she thought, fate couldn't be that unkind to her.

When Giorgio returned she was sitting self-consciously on the drawing room sofa rereading *Anna Karenina*. She had retrieved her shoes, tidied her hair, and spent some time applying a fresh makeup. Who was it, she tried to remember, who'd said, 'I have a feeling this is going to be the sort of conversation a girl needs to be wearing her lipstick for'?

Giorgio's eyes softened for a moment as he looked at her. He seemed to be about to say how nice she looked, but then, remembering she was in disgrace, checked himself and composed his features into their familiar, contemptuous mask. Jane's defiance rose at the sight. Couldn't the idiot see that if he'd ever given her any encouragement or praise in the last two years, she wouldn't have needed another man?

'Did he buy the painting?' she asked.

'Yes,' he admitted reluctantly, 'in spite of your intrusion. I have told you, Gianna, many times, what an important client he is to me. You should know by now that it is important to keep your son under control on these occasions.'

'I do,' Jane agreed. The sudden rush of anger she felt at his use of the phrase 'your son' made her feel positively exultant. She could almost find it in herself to be grateful to him for giving her the strength she needed to destroy him. 'But since, unfortunately, I can't seem to control him, I think it's far better, don't you, that *my* son and I should return to England as soon as possible?'

Giorgio looked at her for a moment and then shrugged his shoulders insolently. The implication was clear. This was an empty threat, already made by her many times in the past, but never, unfortunately, carried to fruition. The wine glass he had been drinking from earlier was still standing on the table. He picked it up and went into the kitchen to get another drink.

Jane sprang up and followed him. 'Well,' she said angrily, 'don't you think it would be better if we went back, so you could entertain your clients in peace?'

Giorgio poured himself a glass of wine and drank it down in one. 'Oh come on, Gianna,' he said wearily.

'I mean it.' She was annoyed to detect a slight quiver in her voice, and swallowed before speaking again. 'I've found someone else, you know,' she told him.

They stared at each other for a long moment. He believes me! she thought exultantly, and felt a deep flush of triumph creep up her neck and suffuse her cheeks and forehead.

'Who is it?' he said at last. 'Alex?'

Jane's mouth dropped open in astonishment. In the past he had often made jealous scenes about men they had met, but he had never once uttered a word of complaint about her growing friendship with Alex or the many evenings they had spent at Verge and Robin's house talking only to each other. Jane had thought at the time that he couldn't have noticed. Now she wondered if, sensing a genuine threat for the first time, he had been too afraid to speak. The thought made her feel a sudden painful compassion for him, and at the same time it struck her how stupid she had been not to prepare a story in advance. Naturally he would want to know who her lover was.

'No!' was all she could manage now. She went to the cupboard and took down a glass for herself so he wouldn't be able to read her expression. 'It's someone you don't know. Someone I met –'

'Through Virginia?'

'Er, yes.' He knew she'd been spending a lot of time at Virginia's during the weeks he'd been away. The Askews were always entertaining and it seemed reasonable that she might have met a stranger there. 'But she doesn't know about it,' she added hastily. 'She just happened to introduce me.' As she spoke she was trying hastily to conjure up the image of a fictitious lover who would deflect his thoughts from Alex. She thought wildly of Count Vronsky, and her lips twitched into a nervous smile. A second later she jumped violently as he hurled down his wine glass, which whizzed past her and shattered noisily in the sink. He took a step towards her, and stood over her, red-faced and rigid, with clenched fists.

'*Puttana!*' he spat.

Jane felt suddenly frightened. Long days spent scrambling in and out of his boat and the constant lifting of heavy pieces of furniture had kept Giorgio admirably fit and strong. If it came to a physical confrontation between them, she knew with certainty that she would be the loser.

A disjointed memory flashed into her mind of an evening spent with Verge and Robin watching the movie *Life at the Top* on TV. After the scene where Joe's friend Mark makes a hasty exit from Joe's house having been caught screwing Joe's wife, Giorgio had commented menacingly to no one in particular: 'I think that man was extremely lucky.'

'Giorgio would have killed him, you see,' Jane explained brightly, and there had been a short silence broken by the nervous explosion of Robin's high-pitched aristocratic giggle.

She told herself it was important not to let him see she was afraid. Summoning up all the righteous anger which she had so far held in check, she said, 'Well then, what about you? Sneaking off and having yourself sterilized a year ago, and allowing me to make a fool of myself all this time, begging and pleading with you to have another baby? What about you, pretending to be concerned about my health and nagging at me to give up smoking, and then letting me suffer agonies each month with the coil and watching me bleed for ten days because you were too cowardly to tell me what you'd done? You knew, didn't you, that if you told me I'd leave you and find another man? Well I have. I went to Bobby yesterday to have my coil removed and he told me about your operation, so last night I went out and screwed the first man I could find –'

Jane stopped suddenly as she realized, somewhat to her surprise, that what she had just said was true. Until then it had seemed more dignified to pretend to herself that she'd slept with Alex purely because she wanted him. Now, although of course she *had* wanted him, she knew that she would never have gone to him on her last night if she hadn't been driven into his arms by her desperate humiliation and bewilderment over Giorgio's betrayal. Her eyes filled with tears of self-pity, and she groped blindly for a kitchen towel. Giorgio, who had been staring at her dumbly, turned abruptly on his heel and walked out of the room. A moment later she heard the front door closing behind him.

And now what? At first Jane was too overwrought to do more than sob helplessly into the kitchen towel, muffling the noise as much as possible so as not to wake Filippo. After a moment, however, she told herself sternly that crying was a luxury she couldn't afford if she was to remain clear-headed enough to organize their departure. She lit another cigarette, walked determinedly to the front door and shot the large bolt across it. If Giorgio were to return suddenly she wanted warning. She also wanted, more than ever now, to ring Alex.

This time she was told there would be a twenty-minute delay. Damn and blast it, she thought. Had all the Englishwomen in Venice suddenly decided to ring their lovers? She told the operator she would wait and replaced the receiver, then jumped up and went into the kitchen to get herself the drink which she had never got round to pouring earlier. If the doorbell rang she would just have to get through to the operator again quickly and cancel the call.

The wine, a young Tocai Friulano, was fruity and delicious, and revived her spirits wonderfully. Gradually, guiltily at first, but with an ever-increasing sense of euphoria, it began to dawn on Jane that she was feeling most extraordinarily happy. In making her confession to Giorgio, now that the initial fear and shouting were over, it was as if she had unloaded her heavy burden of guilt and passed it all over to him. Whatever might happen to her now, and even if she never saw Alex again, she was free for the first time in five years, and the sense of it was suddenly both delicious and dangerously intoxicating.

With her happiness came a new sense of magnanimity towards Giorgio. Tenderly she picked the pieces of his glass out of the sink and wrapped them painstakingly in a newspaper, then ran the tap carefully over the enamel to make sure there were no fragments remaining. When everything was clear she poured herself another glass of wine and went back into the drawing room to sit by the phone.

Just as she had almost given up hope it started to shrill, suddenly and shockingly, in her ear. In her rush to pick it up before it could wake Filippo, Jane realized ruefully that perhaps she wasn't quite as much in control of herself as she'd imagined. Her hands were shaking so badly that she could hardly lift the receiver, but still the dizzying sense of happiness remained.

'*Pronto,*' she said quaveringly.

'London on the line, signora,' said the operator briskly, and Alex's number started to ring once more. Jane took a nervous drag at her cigarette and steeled herself once more for disappointment.

'Hallo.' For a moment Jane's throat seemed to close up as she realized it was him.

'Hallo, Alex?' she said. 'It's Jane.' She thought it was only courteous to announce herself in view of his large entourage of female admirers.

'Janie!' The warmth in his voice was unmistakable and infinitely reassuring. 'How *are* you?'

'Well, I'm not quite sure,' she admitted. 'I've just had a bit of a row with Giorgio, you see. He's found out I've been having an affair.'

'I know,' Alex said, to her astonishment. 'I was over at Verge's house, and she's just had the most extraordinary phone call from him.'

'Oh my God,' she said faintly. He must have made the call from the gallery. But how on earth had he managed to get through so quickly? And trust him to do something stupid and melodramatic like that. 'What did he say?' she asked.

Alex thought back. All in all it had been rather an awkward evening. Dinner, the leftovers of a slightly over-cooked casserole, hadn't quite been up to Verge's usual standard, and there was a definite edginess between Verge and Robin that in the end had started to make him feel positively uncomfortable.

After dinner Robin had announced that he was going out to gamble. Alex had tried to leave too, but Verge had persuaded him to stay for coffee, and then once he was safely installed on her sofa, imprisoned by his enormous coffee cup, had immediately started to pump him about his relationship with Jane.

'Now, Alex, you've simply got to tell me,' she had said. 'What was it like?'

'Very, very good indeed,' he replied defiantly, wondering how soon he could escape. He took a large mouthful of coffee, then realized to his annoyance that it was still far too hot to drink. It seemed to burn at him reproachfully all the way down his oesophagus and into his stomach.

Something like rage had flickered across Verge's face for a moment, but she had hastily composed her expression to one of humorous sarcasm. 'I suppose it would be, wouldn't it?' she commented. 'With all the men she's had.'

Now it was Alex's turn to feel rage. She was behaving exactly like Sandra, he thought, unable to see anything but the reflection of her own sordid mind in what had been one of the tenderest, most beautiful experiences he had ever had. The bleep of her telephone had come as quite a relief. It gave him a chance to gulp down the rest of his coffee and invent excuses for a rapid escape. He had already been on his feet when she returned, pale and angry, from the call.

He tried to remember her exact words to repeat to Jane. 'I think he said something like, "Did you, as my friend, assist in Gianna's adultery?"' he told her.

'Oh God,' Jane said again, the very ludicrousness of the phrase stirring an unwilling compassion in her once more. Poor Giorgio. His English, never perfect at the best of times, always seemed to become particularly convoluted at moments of crisis. How she wished, for both their sakes, that he hadn't exposed himself like that to Verge and Alex's scorn. 'What did she say?' she asked.

'I think she told him not to be ridiculous, at which point he slammed down the receiver,' Alex replied. His own reaction to the call, he remembered, had been one of extraordinary elation. Did this mean, he had wondered, that Jane would be coming home? Verge had soon deflated him, however, by insisting that Giorgio would almost certainly follow her and make frightful scenes. He could be very dangerous when aroused, she told him, and might well resort to physical violence against Alex. Temporarily carried away by Verge's obvious fear of Giorgio, Alex had left her house in a distinct state of agitation. On the doorstep she had delivered her parting shot.

'How on earth,' she had said, 'could Janie have been such a fool as to let him find out?'

'How did he find out?' Alex asked her now.

'I told him,' Jane replied.

'You told him?' Jane felt suddenly chilled by the cold note of astonishment in his voice. 'I must say,' he went on reproachfully, 'I can't help rather wishing you hadn't involved me –'

'I didn't,' she said with dignity. So he was a Judas after all, she told herself. Not only a Judas, but a coward as well. 'I just told him I'd met someone else. I didn't say it was you. You needn't be afraid,' she went on sarcastically. 'You don't have to be involved at all. I just told him because I wanted to get out. And I have. I'll be coming home tomorrow, and I don't give a damn what happens to me. I don't care if I starve in the streets. This is the happiest moment of my life and no one can take it away from me. I'm free!' Her moment of triumph was shattered a moment later by a ring at the door.

'Oh heavens,' she said agitatedly, 'there's someone at the door. I think it must be him. I'll have to go, Alex. I'll talk to you soon. Goodbye.' She replaced the receiver hastily.

It turned out not to be Giorgio but a concerned neighbour who had seen that the light was still on. He'd noticed that Signor Orsini had left the engine attached to his boat. This was most unwise with so many thieves around. Normally the signore brought it into his house every night. Did the signora think he had forgotten?

Jane sighed. In many ways Venice was remarkably suburban. Everyone always seemed to know exactly what their neighbours were up to. Normally, as in this case, their interference was well meant, but to a

Londoner like herself it could at times be extremely claustrophobic.

Inspired by the new magnanimity she had felt towards Giorgio since her confession, she eventually went downstairs with the neighbour and located the trolley which Giorgio used for transporting the engine from the *fondamenta* to the house. The neighbour lifted it off the boat and they wheeled it together into a small storeroom which Giorgio owned on the ground floor.

Returning to the apartment, Jane became aware at last that she was absolutely exhausted. Leaving the bolt of the door unlocked, she retired to her bedroom and undressed herself hastily before falling instantly into a heavy, dreamless sleep.

She woke with a start at 6.30, appalled at what she had done and assailed by the most hideous pangs of conscience.

Tiptoeing into Filippo's room to ensure that she hadn't, by her rash confession, brought down some terrible curse upon them both, she felt her throat closing up with love and remorse at the sight of his tousled black head and plump, dimpled fists clenched possessively round his much-loved and slightly battered koala. She told herself sternly what a terrible thing she had done in depriving him of a father – even such an unsatisfactory father as Giorgio – purely in order to gratify her own sensual passion for a man who had proved last night to be utterly unworthy of the mistaken idolatry which she had nurtured (and, if she were honest with herself, still nurtured) towards him. What sort of summer would she be able to give Filippo, alone and penniless in London, compared with what he might have had in Venice with his friends, or later on the Lido, visiting the beach each day and growing bronzed and healthy in the warm sea and sunshine?

He was quite likely to sleep on till eight, so she decided to bath and dress herself before he woke, in order to be ready for any eventuality. First, however, she must have her cup of tea, without which she felt incapable of facing the exhausting and emotionally draining day which lay ahead of her.

As she entered the drawing room she noticed at once that Giorgio had returned and was ensconced on the sofa underneath an inappropriately festive multi-coloured blanket. His eyes opened as she looked at him, and she felt a further pang at the drawn look of misery in their expression.

'Gianna?' he said bewilderedly.

'Yes –' she hesitated for a moment and then went over to him. 'Philly's asleep,' she said softly. 'I was just going to make myself a cup of tea.'

He sat up. He was still dressed in his shirt and underpants, with wildly dishevelled hair which he ran his hands through absent-mindedly in an attempt to flatten it.

'Sit here for a moment, will you?' he asked her.

Jane sat beside him. She saw him looking round helplessly for his glasses, which were lying on the table beside his wallet and keys.

'Do you want these?' she asked, and reached out and handed them to him.

'Thank you. Gianna, was it true what you said to me last night?'

She hesitated. How easy it would be to save herself and deny it. She could say she'd invented the story to punish him for his vasectomy. It was obvious from his expression that he would be only too willing to believe her. Wouldn't it perhaps be the kindest solution for everyone? She swallowed. 'Yes, it was,' she said.

He was silent for a moment. She saw to her horror that his eyes had filled with tears. 'Helga did the same, you know,' he told her.

Jane was astonished. Helga was his wife who, according to him, he had consistently deceived for so many years. 'What, with José?' she asked him.

'No. A long time ago. Before José. Someone she met in Germany. I found a letter from him after she returned. She used to keep them hidden inside her books.'

'So she was the first to be unfaithful?' Jane asked. 'It wasn't you?'

'No. She was the first. She told me she wanted to leave me. It was only afterwards that I found someone else.'

'I see.' Jane found this admission unbearably pathetic.

It upset all her ideas about him. One of her own justifi-
cations to herself for being unfaithful to him had been
the knowledge of his consistent infidelities to Helga. She
had felt she was striking a blow for betrayed wives every-
where. 'What happened?' she asked. 'Didn't it work out?'

'No,' he answered. 'He only wanted her for sex.
He wasn't interested in the children, so in the end she
decided to stay with me.'

Jane went cold all over. Was this to be her fate too? To
throw in her lot with a man who was only interested in
her body and who would regard her beloved son merely
as an encumbrance?

Giorgio might not show much affection towards
Filippo, but at least he was his father. Wouldn't it be
better for her son's sake to stay with him?

'Why didn't you tell me before?' she asked helplessly.

'I was ashamed,' he said. 'Just as I was ashamed to tell
you of my operation. It's not an easy thing for an Italian
to have himself sterilized. People here would laugh at me
and say I had castrated myself.'

'Then why did you do it?' she asked indignantly. 'I
didn't ask you to. You knew how desperate I was to have
another child.'

'I know, Gianna, but I was afraid. I saw how much you
changed when you had Filippo. You had no time for me
any more, only him, and you were so sick all the time,
and so exhausted. I felt that two children would be too
much for you. With one child it is possible still to travel
and do things together, but with two everything changes
again and the woman must stay at home with the children and cannot be a wife to her husband. I did it,' he
said pleadingly, 'because I loved you.'

Jane was silent. She knew, and had always known,
in spite of, or perhaps even because of, the relentless
hostility he had shown her since Filippo's birth, that
Giorgio was still in love with her. How tragic, therefore,
that it should take a crisis like this to make him finally
admit to it. Could he be right in what he said about two
children being too much for her? Her desire for a
second child had been so powerful and unreasoning that
she hadn't stopped to think how she would manage to

cope with the prostration and sickness of the early months of pregnancy while having to run around all day after a lively toddler like Filippo. And what if she should be pregnant now by Alex, she thought suddenly. How much less able would she be to cope, alone and abandoned in London?

'Gianna –' he said tentatively.

'Yes.'

'You said last night that you went to Bobby to have your coil removed. Could it be that you are now pregnant by this other man?'

Jane caught her breath. It was as if he had read her thoughts. She saw it as a further sign of his concern for her. She felt suddenly as if no one, since the death of her mother, had ever known her so well as Giorgio, or cared for her so deeply. 'I don't think so,' she said evasively, unable suddenly to meet his eye.

Giorgio sighed. 'You are so impulsive, Gianna,' he said. 'Like a child sometimes the way you rush into danger, and yet so shy and timid at others. Did you not think of the risk you were taking?'

'I forgot,' Jane admitted. 'I was so upset,' she added defensively, 'by the news of your operation –'

'But what will you do', he asked, 'if you are pregnant? Will this man accept your child?'

'Oh I shouldn't think so,' Jane said, trying to sound nonchalant. 'I mean, I hardly know him. But I don't think we need worry about that just yet.'

'But I do worry,' he told her. 'And if you go back to England I will accompany you in order to find out this man's intentions towards you –'

'But you can't do that!' Jane exclaimed in panic. She had a horrible vision of him camping on Verge and Robin's doorstep until they agreed to reveal the name of her lover, and then lying in wait for Alex and beating him up. And what would she do if he came with her? She wouldn't be able to see Alex at all!

'Certainly I can do that,' he said calmly. 'You are my wife, after all, and the mother of my son.'

'But we're not married,' she protested.

'Of course we are married,' he told her. 'What does a

piece of paper matter? I made my commitment to you when you gave birth to my son.'

'But you don't love him,' she said desperately, daring, for the first time, to voice the accusation which had haunted her since Filippo's birth, and which had been her chief cause of complaint against Giorgio.

'I don't love him?' The astonishment in his voice sounded completely sincere . 'Of course I love my little black-haired boy who is so like you. I am his father. I would give my life for him.'

Jane sighed. At last she had the reassurance she needed, and how ironic that it should have come too late. Or was it too late?

'Do you want us to stay with you then?' she asked tentatively.

'Of course I want you to stay,' he replied instantly. 'I had always imagined we would spend the rest of our lives together. You can't think that I would have changed towards you so quickly.'

'But you always said you'd leave me if I ever had any-one else,' she reminded him.

'Oh Gianna, there are times when one says many things one does not mean. You have made me very unhappy, but I can understand why you did what you did.'

'But if I do stay,' she persisted, 'will you consider having your operation reversed? Not now, of course, but later, in the winter say, once Filippo's started at nursery school? It would mean so much to me.' Her voice broke suddenly. Could it be, she wondered, that her affair with Alex was not to be the great love she had imagined, but merely the means that would bring her and Giorgio to a new closeness and understanding? In the last few minutes he had shown her a gentleness and affection that had been absent from their relationship for years. It made her remember the times, before Filippo, when they had been so close, and led her to hope that they could one day recapture them and make a new start together.

He sighed. 'Very well, Gianna,' he said. 'If it means so much to you. I will see if anything can be done when we next go to London.'

She reached out timidly and put her hand over his. 'Thank you,' she said simply. 'So you don't want me to do anything about leaving? You'd just like me to unpack today and carry on as normal?'

'Not quite as normal,' he said sadly. 'That can never be. But let us try to put this thing behind us and see if we can continue together.'

Later, when he had gone to the gallery, she booked a call to Alex.

'I just wanted to tell you,' she said, 'that I won't be coming back to London today after all. Giorgio and I have talked about it and he wants me to stay with him. He told me a lot of things that he probably ought to have told me long ago which have – well – made me feel differently towards him.'

Alex, who had completely got over his panic of the previous night, and who had woken up full of optimism and excitement at the thought of seeing Jane again, felt suddenly bitterly hurt. So she was just like Georgina after all, he told himself, building up his hopes to a fever pitch and then bringing them down again with a crash just when they seemed to be within his grasp. Knowing from his long experience with Georgina that to remonstrate with her would only alienate her further, he forced a note of cheerfulness and sympathy into his voice.

'I'm sure you're right,' he told her.

'Yes.' Jane felt suddenly bitter. Didn't he even care enough about her to sound disappointed? Perhaps he was relieved she wasn't coming. Now he could carry on with his cosy dinners with Verge. 'Oh, Alex,' she asked sadly, 'why do people always wait to tell you these things until it's too late? I find it so sad.'

'I know,' he said soothingly, 'but husbands tend to do that sort of thing, you know.'

'Do they? Well, you're the expert. Alex, I won't keep you now. You must have to go to work, but you will write to me, won't you?' She didn't know if this was strictly within her pact with Giorgio, but talking to Alex had made her realize that she couldn't bear to let go of him completely. Perhaps, she told herself unconvincingly, they could just become very good friends.

'Of course I will,' he said. 'Do you still want me to come out and see you?'

In spite of her good resolutions her heart gave a sudden leap. 'Oh it would be lovely,' she said, 'though I don't know how we'd manage.' She felt instinctively that after her confession Giorgio would be bound to watch her like a hawk. 'Anyway write to me,' she urged again, 'and we'll see.'

'All right,' he agreed. 'And Janie – thank you for ringing me.' Georgina, he thought, would probably not even have bothered to do that.

'Of course,' she said in surprise. 'I mean I had to after what I said last night. And thank *you* for being so understanding. Goodbye, Alex.'

'Goodbye,' he said.

Mingled with his disappointment at not seeing her, was a sense of shame at the harm he had unwittingly done her. Her attempts to sound brave and cheerful had not fooled him for a moment, and it seemed to him suddenly that wherever he turned he left a trail of destruction in his wake. Should he write to her, he wondered? She had chosen to stay with Giorgio, and now perhaps he owed it to her to allow her to work out her relationship with him in peace. Making love to her might have been the most beautiful thing that had ever happened to him, but he had already committed himself to Georgina and it was unthinkable that he should be the means of destroying two families. One was quite bad enough.

Helmut called in to see Jane later that morning. He complained bitterly about the sirocco, but still contrived to look as immaculate as always in an Yves St Laurent safari suit and cream panama hat. Filippo had been borne off by Paolo and Marino to play in the *campo*, and Jane was looking forward eagerly to unburdening herself to her friend. It had seemed to her for some years now that Helmut had been subtly inciting her to rebel against Giorgio and she felt confident of his unconditional approval. In any case he would have to know about Alex because she had already arranged for him to write to her at Helmut's address.

'Would you like some coffee, Helmut?' she asked.

'No thank you, my dear,' he said firmly. 'I'd prefer something cool.'

'How about lemonade then?' she suggested. 'I made it this morning for Filippo. It's just lemons and sugar. Very pure.'

'Certainly not,' he replied disapprovingly. 'I'll have a large whisky, please, with ice.'

He sank gracefully into an armchair, and eyed her speculatively as she walked, smiling, to the drinks tray. She had made a special effort to look smart for him – Helmut disapproved strongly of jeans – and was dressed in an uncharacteristically expensive sea-green linen dress with cut away shoulders, from Venice's smartest boutique, the Duca d'Aosta. She had bought it in a fit of pique the previous summer to console herself during one of Giorgio's more spectacular bouts of sulkiness.

'You are looking extremely lovely today,' he told her as she handed him his drink.

She smiled. 'Well, if I do, it's purely because of you. You always look so elegant yourself that I feel I have to dress up in order to compete.'

'But it's not just the dress.' He studied her face, looking almost puzzled for a moment. 'It's you yourself,' he concluded. 'You have a strange sort of glow about you. What on earth can you have been doing?'

'Something very naughty, I'm afraid,' she admitted. She sat on the sofa opposite him and took a sip of the despised lemonade.

'My dear!' He looked quite startled. 'Not what I think?'

'I'm afraid so,' she nodded, and proceeded to pour out the whole story. The relief of having someone to confide in was so exquisite that she failed to notice the fact that he had grown unaccustomedly silent. Actually it was something of a reversal of roles for her to be recounting her escapades to him. She had spent most of the previous summer trying to advise him on the various stages of his pursuit of one of the waiters from the nearby *gelateria* on the Zattere. Before that he had been in love with a twenty-two-year-old baritone from Israel who had moved his rucksack and guitar into Helmut's flat for a few months and then spent most of his evenings in solitary pursuit of Venice's almost nonexistent nightlife, while Helmut, abandoned at home, had bombarded Jane with despairing late-night phone calls. The fact that Helmut had been through the mill himself was one of the reasons that had convinced Jane to confide in him. She felt that few people could be better equipped than he was to offer sympathy and advice.

Shortly after finishing, however, she was to discover how wrong she had been.

'This has come as a great shock to me,' he told her bluntly. 'I really don't know what to say.'

Jane felt thoroughly taken aback by the coldness of his tone. 'But you will let him write to your address, won't you?' she asked anxiously. 'I'm afraid I've already said that he can.'

'Oh I suppose so,' he told her ungraciously. 'But I don't like it. I don't like it at all. Giorgio has been so good to me.'

Jane flushed. If Giorgio had been good to him it was only as a result of her nagging. He was actually rather disapproving of homosexuals as a general rule, although to be fair to Helmut, she supposed he couldn't be expected to know that. 'Well, he hasn't been good to me,' she pointed out. 'Not until this morning, that is,' she corrected herself. 'You were always telling me last summer that you couldn't understand how I put up with him.'

'Yes, but after all, you are a married woman,' Helmut reminded her.

'Actually I'm not,' Jane pointed out.

She was only just saved from losing her temper by the arrival of Filippo, red-cheeked and thoroughly overexcited by his outing with the boys. Helmut, never an overt lover of children, drained his whisky hastily and stood up to take his leave. Jane saw to her consternation that he was looking suddenly old and tired.

'I wish,' he said to her reproachfully, 'that you had not told me.'

Jane followed him dutifully to the landing and stood watching him as he started to descend the stairs. She felt suddenly forlorn. It was as if all their old friendship and camaraderie were departing with him.

A moment later the door slammed behind her and she realized to her horror that Filippo, annoyed perhaps by their lack of attention, had shut her out of the apartment. Feeling thoroughly overwrought by now, she burst into tears.

Helmut turned and looked at her in disapproval. 'Oh don't be so silly,' he said coldly.

For two weeks Jane and Giorgio waited together for her period. She felt for him during this time rather as a nurse might feel towards a severely shocked patient whom she was guiding, gently and kindly, to recovery. He wasn't always docile. Occasionally there were flare-ups, such as when he caught her listening to the love duet from *Otello* with a faraway expression on her face, and seized the record off the turntable and shattered it against the back of a chair. He knew by then that Alex was her lover. Jane had told him one night, about a week after her return. He had promised beforehand that he would not be angry or seek revenge in any way, and so far he had kept to his promise. Afterwards they had made love for the first time since her confession. Jane had suggested it out of pity for the obvious anguish he was suffering, and he had accepted gratefully, and actually been much gentler and more sensitive than usual, so that she might even have enjoyed it had she not been conscious all the time of his dark desperation.

They made love again a week after that, on the night her period was due. This time Giorgio was more violent, and she encouraged him to be so in the hope that it would bring on her bleeding. Afterwards she kept waking in the night and going to the bathroom to see if it had started, and each time she returned to the bed she was aware that Giorgio was lying awake in the darkness waiting in vain for the news that would save them both.

For four more days they waited. The weekend was particularly agonizing, with Giorgio at home all day, watching her mutely while she did the chores and played with Filippo and went through the charade of being a devoted wife in front of their friends, knowing all the time that inside her was a time bomb waiting to explode.

One thing that struck Jane most particularly was the fact that Giorgio was far nicer to her now she was expecting Alex's child than he had been when she was expecting his own.

CHAPTER ELEVEN

June 1974

O n the Monday Jane decided that she must ring Alex. Because of the usual long delay she was unable to reach him at home and decided in desperation to call him at his office.

'Alex,' she said, when she finally got through to him, 'I'm desperately sorry to ring you at work, but I felt I ought to let you know that my period's five days late and I think I must be pregnant.'

'Yes, I can see that,' he said brightly. 'Look, I'm afraid it's a bit difficult for me to talk at the moment, but I'll call you back in fifteen minutes if that's OK.'

Oh God. Alex had probably never had to telephone Venice in his life before. How could she begin to try to explain to a novice that even with direct dialling from his end it generally took at least forty minutes to get through? On the other hand she couldn't insist that he should stay on the line if he had someone in the office with him.

'All right,' she said. 'But if you don't get through I'll call you at home at six o'clock this evening.' She didn't dare make it any later. It would be seven o'clock her time and Giorgio had recently taken to popping home at odd moments during the day as if to check up on her.

'I'll get through,' he assured her. 'I'll just be a few minutes, I promise you,' and he replaced the receiver.

* * *

Jane sat huddled by the phone waiting for it to ring. She was using the bedroom extension and had closeted herself in the room with Filippo, who couldn't understand why they weren't out for their customary morning walk and who, quickly becoming bored with rearranging the shoes in Jane's wardrobe, proceeded grumpily into the bathroom where he started to unravel the toilet roll.

Jane eyed him unseeingly, and Filippo, sensing that something was very wrong, started to whine and cling to her and try to pull her out of the room. Jane, doing her best to speak calmly, kept repeating to him that they had to stay indoors that morning because Mummy was waiting for an important phone call, but she had started to feel herself dangerously near to losing control. For several days now she had been nervous and on edge, and now, as the minutes ticked by and it became increasingly obvious that Alex wasn't going to call her back, a thousand nightmare possibilities started to flash through her mind. Perhaps there hadn't been anyone in his office after all and he'd just used it as an excuse to get off the line. Perhaps he had no intention of calling her ever again, and was just going to abandon her to her fate.

Contrary to the propaganda put out by Virginia, Jane was not the sort of woman that men grew tired of. To be pregnant at twenty-seven by a man she hardly knew yet was madly in love with, and who now appeared to have abandoned her, was an entirely new situation for her and one she felt totally unequipped to deal with. Temporarily oblivious to Filippo's tuggings, Jane buried her face in her hands and told herself that apart from the death of her mother, this was the worst thing that had ever happened to her in her life.

Alex got home at 5.30 to make sure he was in time for Jane's call. His office was open-plan, so it was impossible to talk about anything there without it being overheard by all his colleagues. The phone in the conference room, to which he sometimes retired to make private calls, was attached to the main switchboard and he'd had an uneasy feeling for some time that the office receptionist, a friend of the temporary secretary he'd had the brief affair with, was in the habit of getting her kicks by listening in to his calls. In any case, the conference room was also the room into which clients were automatically shown when they called in to visit the office. The last thing he wanted was to have to break off his conversation with Jane in order to shake hands with some suave representative from the Charisma Clothing Company.

Nearly opposite the office was a hotel where calls could be made from a private booth in the lobby and paid for afterwards at reception. He had already used it occasionally to ring Georgina. Alex had gone there immediately after speaking to Jane and placed the call to Venice only to be told that there would be a two-hour delay. He looked at his watch. Just after eleven, and at 12.30 he was meeting a client from the country, whom he couldn't put off, for lunch at San Frediano. He decided he would have to cancel the call. It upset him a lot to think of Jane sitting waiting by the phone, but at least she had given him an alternative plan of action.

Inside Alex was feeling strangely elated at the thought that Jane was expecting his child. His mind told him it was awful because of Giorgio, but deep down he couldn't help feeling rather excited about it. Not knowing what else to do he returned to his office and sat down at his desk and impulsively dashed off a little letter to her, as if by doing so he could somehow compensate for the fact that he hadn't be able to return her call. In it he spoke frankly of his confusion. He said how much his time with her had meant to him and how important it was that they should meet as soon as possible and talk properly about what they wanted to happen in the future, as it was vital that they should be entirely in accord before making such an important decision. When he had finished he slipped out again immediately and posted it. What he really wanted, he reflected as he walked to his lunch date, was to spend time alone with her in order to allow their relationship to develop and find out whether the exceptional closeness he had felt towards her was real or illusory. But wouldn't that be selfish? he asked himself. If he wanted her to go ahead and have the child, wouldn't he be obliged to offer her an immediate commitment.

Variations on this theme reverberated through his head for the rest of the day, making him virtually unaware of his surroundings. Just as he turned the corner of his street, he was overtaken by Virginia's car which drove past him, stopped, and then reversed neatly into a small space almost directly outside his house.

Virginia sprang out, her progress only slightly impeded by a large quantity of Harrods bags, and started to wave at him frantically. Alex continued to walk towards her unseeingly, so she waited until they were practically nose to nose, and then said curiously, 'What on earth are you doing home at this time of the day?'

Alex jumped as he focused on her for the first time. She was looking particularly alert, he noticed, like a dog on the scent of a rabbit. Her features seemed to have grown sharper recently and more drawn, and her dark eyes were glinting hungrily for information.

For the past two weeks Alex had done his best to avoid Verge. This was because every time he ran into her she attempted to cross-examine him about his relationship with Jane, and he felt strongly that it was something he wanted to handle direct rather than, as Verge seemed to wish, by proxy. He had fallen back on the male standby of throwing himself into his work, with a vague idea of clearing his desk so he could visit Jane in Venice with a clear conscience. Now, when confronted directly by Virginia, he felt strongly, and most uncharacteristically, that he should lie to her. Being utterly at a loss for a story, however, he was unable to think of anything better than an approximation of the truth.

'I've come home early because I'm expecting a phone call from abroad,' he told her.

'It's not from Janie, is it?' she asked immediately, almost quivering with excitement.

He sighed. 'Yes, as a matter of fact it is,' he said, trying to speak casually.

'But, Alex –' she had been examining his features closely, and now her black eyes softened and a look of genuine concern came over her face. Alex felt touched. He remembered what good friends she and Robin had always been to him and told himself he had been wrong

197

to be so irritated by her interest in his affairs. '– you look as if you've had the most terrible shock. What's happened? Are you all right?' She put her hand comfortingly on his arm.

'Yes, yes, I'm fine,' he assured her.

'But you look *awful*,' she insisted. 'I can tell something's happened. Why don't you come in with me and have a cup of tea and tell me about it?'

For a moment he was tempted. The predatory look had completely disappeared now, and her expression was soft and supplicating. He suddenly felt a desperate need to confide in someone and who, he asked himself, could be better equipped than Verge to give him dispassionate advice? She was Jane's best friend, after all. He shook himself. No, once he went in, he knew he would be drawn into a spider's web of complicity from which it would be virtually impossible to escape. He told himself he must go back to his house alone and give himself time to think. 'No thank you,' he said. 'I'd better be getting back. I don't want to miss the call now I'm here.'

'But what on earth can this mysterious call be about?' she burst out. 'It's not *that*, surely, that's making you so upset is it? After all you hardly know Janie, do you? She was just a one-night stand, wasn't she?'

Foolishly he hesitated, and she was on to him immediately. 'It is, isn't it?' she insisted, and then softened her voice and spoke to him cajolingly. 'Oh come on, Alex. Please tell me. Surely you can trust me, can't you?' Her eyes didn't quite meet his as she spoke, but a wistful smile played around her thin lips and her well-manicured hand caressed his sleeve tenderly.

It was the note of hurt in her voice that finally cracked him. 'She thinks she may be pregnant,' he confessed.

Virginia jerked backwards. 'But that's ridiculous,' she said. She was now virtually certain that she too was pregnant as a result of Robin's surprise assault on her the night she had been watching Alex's window. If this was true it would mean that she and Jane had conceived on the same night, and worse, that while she, because of the position Robin had chosen, and the fact that she'd had no time to douche with vinegar beforehand, was most probably expecting another boy. Jane, because of Alex's vigorous sex life, might well be expecting a girl. Virginia knew suddenly and with absolute certainty that this was something she was not going to allow to happen. 'She's not trying to say it's yours, is she?' she asked incredulously.

'Well yes,' Alex replied. 'It can't be Giorgio's. He's had a vasectomy, you see.'

Virginia laughed. A dirty, triumphant laugh, that for a moment made Alex feel as if he'd had a glimpse into hell. 'No he hasn't,' she said.

'What?' Alex stopped short incredulously, and, sensing his sudden uncertainty, Virginia was quick to seize her advantage.

'Let me come in with you for a moment,' she said. 'You really oughtn't to be alone, you know. You look quite ill. How long have you got before she calls you?'

Alex looked at his watch. 'Half an hour,' he admitted.

'Well then, we'll have a cup of tea together and talk it over,' she insisted, and walked up his steps determinedly in front of him.

Alex felt too bemused to do anything but trail after her. The house, when they entered it, felt extraordinarily cold and forlorn. Alex switched on the kettle, and then jumped, baffled, as it clicked angrily back at him a few seconds later.

'There's no water in it.' Virginia took the kettle purposefully from him and filled it from the kitchen tap. 'Sit down, Alex,' she said firmly, 'and let me do it. You're really not in a fit state to do anything at the moment. Not that I blame you,' she added disapprovingly.

Alex sat down obediently. His helplessness in the kitchen had become a sort of joke between them which it pleased Verge to perpetuate. Often, on weekends in Suffolk, she would cook for everybody while Robin took the children down to the beach or watched the racing on television, and Alex came and chatted to her in the kitchen, leaning elegantly against the pine sideboard with a delicate, long-stemmed wine glass in his hand. He was always offering to help, and saying how much he wanted to learn to cook now he was on his own, but basically, Virginia realized, he didn't have a clue how to start. Sometimes she complained to Robin about how irritating she found it to have Alex hovering round her, but secretly she relished the attention, and the unbelieving admiration in his eyes as she made stocks and sauces, and whipped up mysterious desserts in the blender. She was a good cook when she wanted to be, but she always surpassed herself at Alex's house. She knew his kitchen well by now, and moved around in it gracefully and deftly, preparing her masterpieces with the skill of a sleight-of-hand artist, making light of her achievements, but never allowing Alex to lend her a hand in case he should discover just how simple an art good cooking really was.

Alex was guiltily aware sometimes of exaggerating his own helplessness in order to flatter Virginia by emphasizing her capability. Today, however, he had no need to exaggerate. He felt genuinely incapable of so much as putting a tea bag into a cup.

'Did you say Giorgio hadn't had a vasectomy?' he asked her, dazed.

Virginia smiled at him as she placed the cup of tea in front of him. 'No, of course he hasn't,' she said gently. 'Can you imagine an Italian agreeing to do a thing like that to himself?'

'Well, no. But then why on earth should Janie have told me he had?'

'Alex,' she paused, 'what I'm going to say about Janie may sound disloyal because of her being such an old friend of mine, but you're an old friend of mine too,' she reached out for a moment and squeezed his hand, 'and I think that what she's trying to do to you in this case is so unfair that I owe it to you to tell you the truth. You do see that, don't you?'

'Yes, of course,' Alex said automatically. He knew, or thought he knew, that women always stuck together, and couldn't help feeling flattered that Verge thought him a good enough friend to be prepared to break this mysterious bond for his sake. At the same time he felt quite alarmed. What on earth, he wondered, was she going to tell him?

'What you've got to understand,' she said, 'is that Janie's reputation's so bad because of all the men she's had – just to give you some idea, I remember her telling me once that she'd stopped counting at three hundred – that she obviously can't get anyone decent to take her on any more, so I'm afraid she uses the oldest trick in the book, and forces them into it by getting pregnant. She did it with Giorgio, you know. She pretended Filippo was an accident. Honestly, how could he have believed it from Janie? Someone whose whole *raison d'être* for the past ten years has been screwing! Men are such fools sometimes. Of course I thought it was pretty awful of her then, but I didn't say anything. I didn't know Giorgio, you see. But I do know you,' she smiled at him tenderly, 'and I can't just stand by and let her get away with it again.'

'So you do think it's mine?' In spite of himself Alex couldn't help a note of eagerness from entering his voice. Virginia heard it and her face hardened.

'No, Alex, I'm afraid I don't' she said. 'You see, Janie told me a few weeks ago that she was planning deliberately to have her coil removed in order to trick Giorgio into having another child. That, incidentally, is how I know the vasectomy story isn't true. I'm not sure why she wanted to do it. Perhaps she was afraid Giorgio was getting tired of her or something. Naturally,' she said self-righteously, 'I told her what an awful thing that would be to do. I happen to think that it's essential for a child to be wanted by both parents and reared in a stable home, and I made that absolutely clear to Janie at the time, which is, I suppose, why she must have gone ahead and had her coil removed without telling me.' And she pursed her thin lips disapprovingly.

'So where do I come in to all this?' Alex burst out.

'Well, I can only guess, of course,' she said, 'but you must admit it's the most likely explanation. I think Janie must have had her coil removed and conceived a child by Giorgio, but then got cold feet remembering how angry he was with her last time, and taken advantage of the fact that you'd come on the scene to pretend it was yours. She's not actually married to Giorgio, so she can't force him to support the child if he doesn't want to. On the other hand, you're single and she knows how rich you are, and probably imagines you're quite gullible. You can understand really, can't you, how you'd seem to her to be a better bet?'

Alex started to shiver. And he had actually believed she was fond of him! If only he hadn't been such a fool as to write to her. He tried desperately to remember what he'd put in the letter. Had he compromised himself irretrievably? But there was still something wrong with Verge's theory –

'But then why did she decide to stay with Giorgio?' he asked.

'Oh, Alex,' Virginia smiled patronizingly, 'someone like Janie would never walk out on a secure setup like she has with Giorgio unless she was absolutely certain she had something better lined up. After all, who on earth would take her on now without the sort of heavy emotional blackmail she's trying to use on you? If you'd offered her anything permanent, I'm sure she would have left him like a shot, but thank goodness you were too sensible for that.' She gave him an approving glance which Alex tried unsuccessfully to feel he had deserved. 'At the moment she's probably busy playing you both off against each other. She may have told Giorgio she had a fling with you in order to make him jealous, but I'm quite certain he believes the child to be his.'

'But I suppose it could be mine, couldn't it?' he almost pleaded.

Virginia started to grow impatient. Why was he still harping on about that after all she had told him. 'Well I suppose it *might* be, if you want to take pot luck,' she said acidly. 'But it really is far more likely to be Giorgio's, you know. Or someone else's,' she added.

'But she hasn't slept with anyone else since she's been with Giorgio,' Alex protested. 'She told me she hadn't.'

Virginia's lip curled. 'I suppose she would have told you that, wouldn't she?' she said patiently. 'But, you see, I happen to know with absolute certainty that she has.'

After Verge had gone Alex sat huddled in his drawing room waiting for Jane's call. He tried to plan what he would say to her, but the horror of what Verge had told him had made his mind go completely blank. Had Jane really just been using him? he wondered, and all his old adolescent feelings of inferiority and unattractiveness came flooding back to haunt him. He told himself bitterly that no one half as beautiful as Jane had ever been interested in him before, so it stood to reason that she must have had some ulterior motive in making love to him. Verge was absolutely certain of it, and she was Jane's best friend. She had known her for years, so naturally her summing up of the situation was more likely to be correct than his own.

He reminded himself that he had already been duped into marriage once, and that at all costs he mustn't let it happen to him again, not just now, when he had made up his mind to leave his job and take up painting as a career. He told himself that everything would be all right if he could only keep his head and be very, very careful, but inside he felt desperately lonely and unloved, and full of a shivery sense of foreboding.

Jane trailed through the narrow streets with Filippo in his pushchair. She turned backwards to bump him up the bridges and then forwards to bump him down again. She was heading for the main post office at Rialto, next to which were some telephone cabins where one could dial London direct – the only place in Venice where it was possible to do so. One could talk for as long as one liked there and then pay for the call afterwards.

Terrified of being late, she had arrived ridiculously early, and been forced to hang around with Filippo, looking blindly into shop windows. Finally she had sat down at an outdoor café in the Campo San Salvador and ordered a coffee, which she knew would only make her sleep worse than ever, and a Coca-Cola for Philly, which was bound to stimulate and over-excite him.

Arriving at the phone booths on the dot of seven, she found a queue of people had formed in front of her. Just as she and Filippo were nearing the front of the queue, he announced that he wanted to pee. Jane, terrified of missing Alex altogether, implored him to wait. A moment later they were both ushered into a booth.

'Hallo.' Alex's voice sounded faint and deeply unhappy – completely different to the positive tone he had used that morning. It occurred to Jane instantly that he'd been got at. But by whom?

'Alex, it's Jane.'

'Yes. I'm so sorry about this morning.' He explained about the hotel and the two-hour delay. 'I wrote to you,' he added, 'when I couldn't get through to you. Silly of me, I suppose. I knew I'd be speaking to you long before you got the letter.'

'Silly but nice,' Jane said warmly, feeling quite light-headed with relief that he hadn't abandoned her after all.

'Yes, I suppose so.' He sounded troubled again.

'Don't worry about it,' she went on. 'It's often like that. But I've discovered this place near Rialto where I can dial London direct. I'm there now. It's great. We can talk as long as we like.' Just speaking to him was making her feel better by the second. In fact it was quite ridiculous, given the circumstances, how happy it made her to hear his voice.

'Good.' She was glad to hear that he was sounding happier too. She must be having the same effect on him. His voice was firmer now and more positive. 'Oh Janie, do you really think you're pregnant?' he asked.

'Yes, I'm afraid I do. Of course, I'm only a few days late. If I had a test now it would probably be negative and they'd tell me to come back in six weeks or something, but I know myself well enough to be sure.'

'And how do you feel about it?' he asked.

'Stunned of course, but I seem to be bearing up.' In fact she was so happy to be talking to him at last that she had quite forgotten her misery of the preceding days. 'Giorgio's being very kind to me.' she went on. 'He knows, you see. He suggested that I should just have an abortion without telling you about it, but well, I didn't want to do that. I'd feel somehow as if I was putting myself in his debt for the rest of my life if I did.'

She paused. She felt it was important that Alex should

know about the child, but at the same time she didn't want him to feel that she was throwing herself entirely on his mercy. He had recoiled so absolutely from the idea of marriage when she had suggested it in London that she didn't want to make him feel she was pressurizing him in any way. She was also determined to let him know how well Giorgio was behaving, and that he at least loved her and wanted to keep her, even if Alex didn't.

'Yes, I see,' he said soothingly, but in fact he was feeling more and more bewildered. Surely Giorgio hadn't been told the child was Alex's? Perhaps he believed it could belong to either of them and this was why he was anxious for Jane to get rid of it. Now he was actually talking to Jane he found it hard to believe she could have lied to him so blatantly about Giorgio's vasectomy. Could he have misunderstood her? He tried vainly to think of a way in which he could broach the subject tactfully.

'Janie, ' he asked at last, 'what do you really want to do?'

Jane hesitated. Although she would never have chosen for it to happen this way, now that she was pregnant she wanted the child very much indeed. Part of her desperate unhappiness over the last few days had been due to the fact that she couldn't say this to Giorgio. She knew that marriage to Alex was out, so there was no way she was going to suggest that again. She had come to think, however, that after all it wouldn't be so bad to have the baby as a single mother. Very young children didn't really need fathers, she told herself. She could see that fathers might come in useful as authority figures when the child grew older, but in her experience women were actually much better than men at coping with pre-school-age children. Women had the necessary gentleness and compassion to cope good-humouredly with menial chores such as washing and nappy changing, and the necessary patience to listen to the endless succession of unanswerable questions, whereas men – and by men she meant Giorgio – most emphatically didn't. If she were to have the child on her own, however, she would need to ask Alex for money. She couldn't go ahead with the pregnancy if there was any risk of Filippo suffering as a result. She hesitated to say this to Alex, however, because it was so utterly foreign to her nature. It would be the first time she had ever asked a man for money in her life.

'I'm not sure,' she said at last. 'What do *you* want to do, Alex?'

'I haven't had time to think properly,' he admitted. 'But I do think it's terribly important that we shouldn't rush into anything.' Could they have blood tests, he wondered, or would they have to wait until after the child was born?

'Yes, of course.' Jane felt chilled by his words. But they did have to rush, she thought. If he wasn't prepared to stand by her he must tell her now, immediately, while the child was still a sightless blob of jelly. There was no way he was going to force her to get rid of it later, once it was properly formed.

To add to her distress, Filippo had started to clutch frantically at her jeans, and was saying, 'Mama, peepee. Mama, peepee,' in a frantic crescendo.

'Alex,' she said apologetically, 'it's awful, but I think I'll have to go. I have Filippo with me, you see, and he needs to go to the loo.' He was beating at her legs now and wailing. 'Yes, darling,' she said desperately, 'just a minute. Please. Oh, Alex, I'll ring you again in a few days –'

For a moment Alex forgot all Virginia's good advice and threw caution to the winds. 'I can fly out to see you this weekend if you want,' he said eagerly.

'Thank you,' she said. 'Yes, darling, Mummy's just coming. I'll call you again in a day or two, shall I? Goodbye, Alex.' She was just about to grab Filippo and hurry outside with him when his clutching stopped and he burst into tears of rage and mortification. She felt a warm wetness splashing her bare ankles and looked down in guilt and horror at the rapidly spreading puddle at their feet.

Later that evening Alex rang the Baileys, hoping to discuss the situation with Martin. He had become very close to them again in the last fortnight. Sandra, on hearing that Jane had chosen to stay in Venice with Giorgio, had been particularly sweet to Alex, and this had lulled him into believing that she had got over their brief affair, and that they could now return to being the very good friends they always had been. He was still careful not to see her on her own, but the passage of time had assuaged much of the guilt he felt towards Martin, as well as the revulsion he'd felt on hearing of Martin's relationship with Seamus.

The three of them had spent several very enjoyable evenings together, during which they seemed to have recaptured all their old cosiness. He told himself that the Baileys were really much nicer than the Askews because it was possible to talk to them about emotions without being told one was being ridiculous. He had really enjoyed talking to Martin about Jane. This was partly out of satisfaction at, for once, being the one with something exciting to recount, but mostly because Martin had been so sympathetic and understanding when he told him how confused he felt. Until then, he had always imagined that nothing could destroy his love for Georgina, but sex with Jane had been so wonderful that it had seemed to eclipse Georgina from his memory altogether. Sandra had been present at these discussions, but had generally remained silent, hunched on the sofa chain-smoking, and occasionally springing up to get something from the kitchen whenever Alex's praises of Jane became too lavish.

Martin was out when Alex rang, but Sandra scenting a secret, put on her most beguiling manner and refused to let him off the line until he had told her everything. At this point she exploded and told Alex that what Jane had done was absolutely outrageous, that the only decent thing she could possibly do was to have an abortion, and that he must be sure to be really tough with her and not allow her the slightest loophole through which to escape what she had to do. No, Martin wouldn't be back in time for him to call him that evening, but he could take her word for it that when he did come back he would echo her sentiments exactly. It was out of the question that Alex should allow a comparative stranger with whom he had slept on only two occasions to muck up his life for him, when he had absolutely no moral responsibility in the matter whatsoever.

As she walked home from Rialto, it struck Jane suddenly that it was imperative for her to return to London immediately. It was impossible to decide anything with Alex unless she could talk to him face to face, and completely unfair to Giorgio to remain any longer under his roof while she was expecting another man's child. She hadn't lost her reason entirely, and knew that she probably owed it to the men in her life to have an abortion, however little she might want one for herself. She had a sudden hope that if she got back to London quickly enough, there might still be something she could take that would bring on her period in such a way that she would never know for sure whether she had been pregnant or not. That would probably be the least agonizing situation for everybody.

She walked unseeingly, as if in a trance, responding absent-mindedly, if at all, to Filippo's chatter. Now that she had made up her mind she was desperate to be gone. Giorgio had a friend who worked for Alitalia, who would probably be able to pull strings and get her a seat for the following day. She was sure that Giorgio would agree with her that it was the only thing to do. She decided to tell her friends that she was going home for a minor operation. It was best, she thought, even in these impossible circumstances, to stick as close to the truth as possible.

She rang Alex again on the Wednesday morning. 'I'm in London,' she said.

'When did you arrive?' he sounded startled, and, to her mind, wary. He'd had Virginia on the phone to him again the previous evening, reiterating the fact that the baby couldn't possibly be his, and that he'd simply got to persuade Janie to get rid of it. This, combined with Sandra's attack, had made him feel rather as if he'd had both barrels of a shotgun emptied into him at point-blank range.

'Very late last night,' she told him. 'Too late to ring.' In fact she had arrived at about ten, but had forced herself not to contact him out of loyalty to Giorgio, who had been so good about the whole thing, moving heaven and earth to get her and Filippo on to a flight, and agreeing, after much serious discussion, that it would be unfair to extract a promise from her not to see Alex. 'Alex – can you talk?'

'Yes I can.' Once more she sensed something cagey and dubious in his tone. 'I'm in the conference room, you see, doing a report.'

'Well, I went to see my doctor first thing this morning. I had to go, because Filippo woke with a temperature, but he said it was nothing serious. Anyway he's referred me to a place called the Pregnancy Advice Bureau, and I'm going there this afternoon. I think, don't you,' she went on brightly, anxious to show she was putting no pressure on him, but at the same time praying he would contradict her, 'that it's probably best if I have an abortion?'

'Yes I'm sure you're right,' he said automatically, surprised at what a pang the words gave him when he should have been overwhelmed with relief that she was being so reasonable.

'I shall have to see two gynaecologists first,' she was quite proud of herself for managing to keep her voice so steady, 'but this place is run as a charity, so it won't cost very much.'

'I see.' But in fact he didn't see at all. If she had become pregnant deliberately in order to trap him, why was she now proposing to get rid of the child? Perhaps her innate sense of decency had won through and she had decided she couldn't go through with the deception after all, or perhaps it was a trick to try to get him to contradict her. He told himself it was essential he should stand firm and say nothing to dissuade her. 'You're not going to take Filippo there, are you?' he asked her.

'No. I bumped into Sarah, my old nanny, in the market. She's got a new job now, but her employer's gone to France for two weeks, so she's free. She's very sweetly offered to come and look after Filippo for me while I'm here. It'll make a huge difference to me. I must say.' Jane hadn't planned to tell anyone she was back, so had been absolutely stunned to see Sarah, and in the absence of any prepared story, had ended up bringing her back to the studio with her for coffee and blurting out the truth. Sarah, in her element at anything to do with gynaecological problems had been agog with amazement and sympathy and immediately pledged her undying support.

'I'm glad,' Alex said, 'and you must let me know if there's anything I can do as well. Would you like to borrow my car, perhaps? I don't usually bother to take it to work with me because there's nowhere to park.' She might have tried to deceive him, he thought, but she genuinely seemed to be trying to make amends for it now. The least he could do for her was to try and make it all as easy for her as possible.

'Thanks.' Jane was touched. 'I'm not sure what I'm doing tomorrow, but it would probably be very useful.'

'I could bring it round to you tonight after work,' he said, 'if you want to see me, that is.'

'Of course I want to see you.' Jane was startled. Didn't he realize how impossible it would be for her to survive the dreadful ordeal which lay ahead without his support?

'What time would you like me to come?'

'Could you make it about seven thirty,' she asked, 'so I'll have time to give Filippo his supper and put him to bed before you arrive?'

Alex was punctual to the moment. He had changed from his office pinstripe to the velvet suit he had worn on New Year's Eve. Jane recognized it and felt an immediate pang. Underneath he had on a black, open-necked shirt. There must have been some good weather in London since she had been away, because he had a slight tan which made him look foreign and gypsy-like, and more attractive than ever.

She had dressed carefully in a long, royal-blue corduroy skirt and matching silk shirt with a blue cardigan, delicately embroidered with pink roses. Her hair was newly washed and her cheeks were glowing with rose blusher, which she had applied more liberally than usual to disguise her extreme pallor.

As soon as she had shut the door behind him, they fell into each other's arms. Jane found herself wishing passionately that words had never been invented, and that they could just stay holding each other like that for ever. All the bitterness and resentment she had been feeling towards him for his apparent change of heart fell away now she was in his presence again, and she admitted to herself with absolute certainty that, like it or not, she was still hopelessly and irretrievably in love with him.

He, on the other hand, was quite surprised at how pleased he felt to see her again. He had forgotten how beautiful she was, and found it almost impossible, looking at her, to imagine her as the amoral schemer of Verge's description. He felt that the confusion of her sexual life was more likely to spring from fecklessness and warm-heartedness than from a desire to trap people. And who could blame her, he thought, for losing count of the men she had slept with when she must, in her time, have had so many at her feet? If it wasn't for the inside information that Verge had so thoughtfully provided him with, he might even yet, he reflected, have found himself in danger of making a fool of himself.

'It's so good to see you again,' he told her. 'I've been feeling so lost and uncertain since you phoned me. I wondered if I wasn't in danger of behaving like Dostoevsky's Idiot.'

Jane smiled. 'I haven't read it,' she said. 'What did he do?'

Alex looked a bit embarrassed. 'Oh well, I'll lend it to you if you like,' he said.

'All right. Thanks. It's strange you should mention Dostoevsky, because I've been feeling a bit like Raskolnikov in *Crime and Punishment*. You know, thinking I could commit adultery because I was a superior being to whom laws didn't apply, and then making a terrible hash of the whole thing and being driven to confess because I had such awful pangs of conscience.' She smiled ruefully, and he took her in his arms again and hugged her, while her head found its old resting place in the hollow of his shoulder.

Later she poured them both some wine, and sat on the sofa beside him, clasping his hand tightly, but unable to meet his eye as she described the afternoon's events.

'First I had to go to the offices of the Bureau near Regent's Park and give all my details to this lady. I'd been sort of hoping they might agree to operate without knowing whether I was pregnant or not, but they said I'd have to do a test, and if it was negative this time I'd just have to go away and wait until it was positive.' Jane swallowed. She remembered the wild mixture of hope and fear that had seized her at these words. If the test was negative now and went on being so for some weeks, she would be unable to have an abortion. It would give her time to consolidate her relationship with Alex and, hopefully achieve her aim of keeping the child. But what if at the end of that time he still didn't want it? How could she bear to get rid of it once she was several weeks gone? And if she were to stay in England now, waiting till the test should prove positive, she would be bound to lose Giorgio and deprive Filippo of his father. 'Anyway,' she went on flatly, 'it was positive.'

Alex squeezed her hand. So this doubt at least had been removed. But what about the even greater doubt over the child's paternity? If Verge and Sandra were right and Jane was lying, she would be bound to betray herself eventually. He told himself it was essential that he should wait until she spoke.

'There was a gynaecologist there,' Jane went on, 'who examined me and confirmed that I was pregnant. I then had to go on to Harley Street to see another gynaecologist. There was a young Italian couple there too, who didn't speak a word of English, so the receptionist asked me to take them with me and interpret for them. I was feeling a bit weepy at that point,' she stopped and smiled at him to show she wasn't reproaching him, 'so it was really rather a lifesaver for me to have them to look after. It wasn't very far to Harley Street, so we walked together. The girl told me she was twenty-two, and that she and her boyfriend were planning to get married anyway, but that she couldn't bring herself to tell her family she was pregnant because her mother had always been so proud of her, and it would have humiliated her so much if her daughter had had to have a shotgun wedding.' Jane shook her head.

'I said to her that surely if she told her mother the choice was between a shotgun wedding or an abortion, she'd opt for the former, but they both just stared at me, and the girl said: "Oh no, I couldn't possibly say that to her." It seemed so strange to me in this day and age –' she trailed off. And who was she to talk of strangeness, when she was preparing to kill the child she wanted so desperately in order to please the two men in her life?

'Anyway,' she said, 'we got to Harley Street at that point, and I was examined by a Dr Fink. He reminded me a bit of Jacob in the Bible – you know – "Esau my brother is a hairy man and I am a smooth man." He was incredibly smooth.' She shuddered slightly. 'Completely hairless, but smooth in manner as well. He told me – she hesitated – 'that he'd be the one doing the – operation.'

Alex held her hand tighter.

'We've fixed it provisionally for Friday,' she said. Today was Wednesday. She could actually have had the operation tomorrow if she'd wanted, but she'd given herself one more day. Twenty-four hours to see if she could persuade Alex to change his mind.

'Have you got a baby-sitter?' he asked her after a long pause. 'I thought we could go back to my house for dinner and I could show you how the car works, and you could maybe drive yourself back in it later.'

'Yes,' she replied. Liliana was, as usual, busily marking papers in her room. She had seemed totally unfazed by Jane's unexpected arrival the previous night, and mercifully unquestioning about the 'minor operation' story. 'The only problem is,' Jane hesitated, 'that I promised to ring Giorgio tonight to tell him how – I got on, and I haven't been able to get through yet.' At every attempt to dial, she had been greeted by a maddening, head mistressy voice proclaiming, 'Lines from London are engaged. Please try later.'

'Would you mind awfully,' she asked, 'if I tried once more now?'

'Of course not,' Alex said untruthfully. 'I'll go and sit in the car, shall I, while you do it?'

'Oh there's no need to do that,' Jane assured him. 'I can go upstairs.'

'No, I think I'd rather sit outside,' he said firmly. 'I'll see you in a few minutes,' and he finished his wine and went out.

For the next hour, Jane tried frantically and vainly to call Giorgio, keeping Alex abreast of the situation with periodical visits to the car. She knew that neither of them would be able to enjoy their evening together if she went home with him without having made the call, but eventually, at nine, they left for his house and ate a snack together in his dining room, before going upstairs to his bedroom to watch the ten o'clock news.

After this Jane nipped down to the kitchen again, and finally got through to Giorgio, who having been all honey and sweetness the previous night, was now moody and suspicious, especially when she told him the operation was not going to take place until Friday. Jane was struck once more by guilt, and by the feeling that Giorgio, unpalatable as it might seem to her, was the voice of her conscience, and that perhaps for that reason it was her duty to stay with him.

It took Alex hours of cuddling and comforting her before she felt ready to make love, and by then it was too late, and she was too tired for it to be more than quick and functional. Afterwards they fell asleep exhausted in each other's arms. Jane woke in panic at four, and he got up and drove her home, telling her he would be round with the car at 9a.m.

When Alex had gone, Jane sat on at the breakfast table, lingering over her coffee, and trying to make a plan of campaign.

Brief and unsatisfactory as their lovemaking had been the previous night, it had been enough to prove to her conclusively that Alex was the man she loved and wanted to spend the rest of her life with. That meant she had one night left to tell him she wanted to keep the baby. The abortion clinic was in Streatham. Jane had to be there at eight o'clock the following morning, so it had been arranged that she would spend the night with Alex and be driven there by him while Sarah and her daughters stayed at the studio to look after Filippo, whose temperature had returned to normal and who, apart from having rather a poor appetite, seemed back to his old rumbustious self. Alex would collect Jane on Friday evening after the operation and bring her back home.

Sarah was at the house now, dressing Filippo for a short outing to the market. She had just missed Alex, who, after delivering the car keys, had stayed for a quick coffee with Jane and Filippo. Jane had been delighted to see how well the two of them had got on. Alex had been gentle and deferential to Filippo, treating him as if he were a sage of fifty rather than a child of two, while Philly, generally shy with new adults, had soon been chattering away confidentially to his new friend, whom he addressed firmly as 'Lix'.

Jane, watching them together, was conscious of a stab of happiness all the more poignant because it was so inextricably mixed with pain. When Alex left, she walked to the door with him, and he kissed her goodbye like a husband going off to work.

'I'll see you tonight then, at seven thirty,' he said.

'Yes,' she agreed, and thought that she would save all her powers of eloquence for then.

'You do promise me, don't you,' he said suddenly, 'that whatever happens you'll come round tonight?'

'Of course I do,' she said in surprise. She had to, she thought. Tonight was the most important night of her life. It was her last chance to save her baby.

Sarah poked her head round the door and interrupted her reverie. 'We're just off,' she said. 'I won't keep him out long, but it's such a lovely day that I think we might just venture as far as the swings.'

'I'll drop you there,' Jane offered. 'It'll give me a chance to try out the car. I suppose I might as well get some use out of my ill-gotten gains.'

After dropping Sarah and Filippo at the swings in St

Helen's Gardens, Jane drove to the market to stock up on food, then decided to wander down as far as the flyover and cheer herself up by looking at the antique clothes. Opposite her favourite dress shop was a newly opened shop called Moonshine which, as well as books on astrology, sold tarot cards, ouija boards and pendulums. Jane couldn't resist going in.

The shop smelt strongly of incense. A dark girl in a midnight-blue dress, with long curly hair tied back, gypsy-style, in a red scarf, sat behind the counter stroking a black cat which perched on her knee, and smiling at Jane encouragingly as she browsed round the shelves. Behind her was an archway with a beaded curtain and a sign beside it saying, 'Crystal Ball and Tarot Readings'.

Jane glanced at the sign, looked away, hesitated and then returned to the counter. 'Would it be possible for me to have a tarot reading?' she asked.

'I'll just see.' The girl stood up and let the cat drop lightly to the floor. She disappeared with a clank of beads to the nether regions, to return a few moments later.

'She's got someone coming in ten minutes so if you want a full reading you'll have to come back in an hour's time, but if you'd just like one question answered she can do it for you now and it'll cost you one pound,' she said.

'One question will be fine.' Jane followed her through the beads to a back alcove where a surprisingly ordinary-looking middle-aged woman sat waiting for her behind a table on a bench covered with Indian cushions.

'Hello, dear.' She motioned to Jane to sit opposite her. 'I'm Maureen. You have a question to ask me, I believe?'

'Yes, please.' The words were barely audible. Jane was quite surprised to feel her heart pounding madly against her chest.

'Shuffle the cards for me will you and then I'll spread them out for you and you can pick out any five. You don't need to tell me what the question is. Just ask it in your head and I'll read the cards for you and tell you what they mean.'

Jane took the pack and started to shuffle. She felt as if she was in a sort of trance. It was only after she'd handed the cards back to Maureen that she realized what an important decision might hinge on the order in which they were spread and had a wild impulse, which she resisted, to demand them back and start all over again.

'Now pick five.'

Jane's hand moved forward as if of its own volition and chose five cards. It seemed to know exactly which ones it wanted.

Maureen spread them out in the shape of a cross. One card each at the top and bottom, and three across the middle.

'And now ask the question,' she said.

Jane took a deep breath and clasped her hands. Am I going to keep my baby? she asked silently.

'Well, what we've got here,' Maureen said, pointing to the bottom card, 'is the Ace of Wands. That symbolizes birth, or a new beginning.' Jane gave a little gasp. 'But over here on the right,' she pointed, 'is the Queen of Cups. This is the card of rivalry, so you may have a rival in this project. It's your growth and new development, but there may be someone who wants to challenge you about that and have it for themselves or destroy it.'

Jane slumped backwards. Could it be Georgina? she wondered wildly. But no. So far as she knew, Georgina didn't even know of her existence. It must be someone else. She forced her mind back to the present so she would hear what Maureen was saying.

'Over here on the left is the Devil.' She shook her head. 'A lot of problems here. A Devil will intensify whatever it touches, and it's in this middle line here, so there's intense sorrow, and over here with the Queen, intense rivalry. You've got to watch out. This is no run of the mill rival. This is someone who can do damage – who wants to do damage – and the Devil's someone who's intensely tied up within themselves and doesn't know what to do.'

Could it be Alex? He *had* seemed very strained since her arrival in England. Could it be something to do with this mysterious rival? But Maureen was speaking again.

'Up here at the top,' she said, 'is the Knight of Wands. That means escape. There's someone here who wants to escape or leave. It can be, too, a card of foreign travel.

Someone in this situation who wants to travel abroad or wants to change or move away.'

Me? thought Jane, or Alex?

'But the final outcome is here,' Maureen pointed to the central card, which was of something soft and tender-looking, a red fruit, Jane thought, or a heart, with three crossed swords running through it. 'This is the Three of Swords,' Maureen said, 'and it symbolizes sorrow.'

Stumbling out into the daylight after her reading, Jane ran slap into Verge's mother, Maria. She made a some-what incongruous figure, teetering along the road among the hippy traders in a full-length wild mink coat and stiletto heels.

First Sarah, Jane thought wildly, and now Maria. The situation was so awful that there was really nothing to be done about it except laugh.

'Janie!' Her foreign accent almost imperceptible now after so many years spent in England, Maria sounded absolutely delighted to see Jane as she enveloped her in a mixture of soft fur and Calèche. 'How lovely to see you. I am on my way to have lunch with Virginia. She asked me to buy her some bread at Ceres. But what are you doing here? I thought you had gone back to Venice.'

'I had,' Jane admitted, 'but now I'm back again.'

Maria put her hands on Jane's arm. 'My dear,' she asked seriously, 'are you back for good?'

Jane shook her head, wondering wildly what Verge had told her mother. 'Oh no.' She tried to sound casual. 'Just for a few days.'

Maria then proceeded to astonish her by saying kindly, 'Well, you know my dear, that if you are in any trouble you can always come and stay with me.'

'Thank you.' Jane was so taken aback by this unexpected display of feminine solidarity that she felt her eyes fill with tears. 'That's very sweet of you. How's Trevor?' she went on politely.

Maria pursed her lips disapprovingly. They were painted defiantly scarlet in a cupid's bow, but there was no disguising the thinness of the upper lip, which Verge had so unfortunately inherited. 'I'm extremely cross with him at the moment,' she said confidentially.

Jane could barely suppress a smile. She had heard the story from Verge. Maria, she knew, had recently undergone a face-lift. She had given her age as forty-five, but Trevor, Verge's father, hearing of this at the last moment, had rushed over to the anaesthetist just as Maria was about to be wheeled into the operating theatre, and begged him to modify the dose because in fact his wife was over sixty. It was quite possible that in acting thus Trevor had saved Maria's life, but it was equally possible, according to Virginia, that Maria would never forgive him.

'But I'm sure you'll get over it, won't you?' Jane asked.

Maria waved an elegant, red-tipped claw in a gesture of deprecation. 'Do you want me to tell Virginia I've seen you?' she asked confidentially.

'Oh yes.' In her embarrassment, Jane felt suddenly very upright and British. 'And please give her my love.'

'But of course.' Maria kissed Jane once more and disappeared into the bread shop. It had been obvious to her instantly that Jane was in deep trouble, and she felt quite surprised by the depth of compassion she had found herself still capable of feeling for a fallen sister, especially considering the fact that she had spent most of Jane's childhood resenting her furiously for having been born prettier and cleverer than Virginia.

Since growing up, however, Virginia had become the perfect daughter. Apart from the brief hiatus with Robin, which everyone now pretended had never happened, she had never put a foot wrong or disobeyed her parents in any way. Therefore it was really quite eccentric of her, Maria decided, perplexed, to feel so acutely irritated by her at times, and to find herself wishing, most unreasonably, that she could have grown up slightly less perfect and more human and affectionate like Jane.

It had been immediately evident to Maria that, despite what she'd said, Jane wished to keep her visit to London a secret. Virginia, she decided, would hear nothing about it from her.

* * *

Jane put off calling Virginia until the evening. Maria, she thought, was bound to have told her of their meeting, and however much Jane would have preferred to remain incognito, it would now seem both unfriendly and cowardly of her not to contact her friend.

'Verge,' she said, 'it's Janie.'

'Janie?' For a moment Virginia sounded almost frightened. 'Where are you?' she asked.

'In London. Didn't your mother tell you? I bumped into her this morning.'

'No.' Virginia's surprise sounded entirely genuine. 'No she didn't. What are you doing here?'

'I've come over for an abortion.' Jane said. In her vulnerable position she couldn't afford to make enemies. Alex had told her that Virginia knew she might be pregnant and she felt instinctively that this was the best way to mollify her. To admit that she still hoped to convince Alex to allow her to continue with the pregnancy would only be, Jane was sure, to inflame her.

'Well, thank God for that at least,' Virginia said truculently. 'Honestly, Janie, I couldn't have believed you'd be so stupid.'

'I know,' Jane said dismissively. Yes, she thought, it was true she'd been stupid. She'd never tried to deny it. But did that one blissful moment of stupidity when she had been sufficiently carried away by passion to dare to make love to someone without counting the cost really entitle the whole world to scream at her? She was the person, after all, who was going to suffer for it. She was the person who was going to pay the price. 'I'd had my coil removed that morning, you see, because I'd been to Bobby and found out from him that Giorgio'd had a vasectomy without telling me. Then Alex called, and I agreed to see him, and I suppose I was just so confused by all that had happened, and so used to being safe with the coil, that the whole thing just went out of my head.'

'Giorgio had a vasectomy?' Jane was surprised to hear Verge sounding so startled.

'Yes. Didn't Alex tell you? He had it more than a year ago, and didn't tell me a thing. Did you get my letter, by the way?'

'Oh, yes.' Virginia answered. Jane had written to her a few days after hearing of Giorgio's accusatory phone call. She had apologized for involving her and tried to explain how the accusation had come about. 'I haven't replied to it actually. I didn't know what to say.' She didn't know what to say about the vasectomy either. She supposed she ought to tell Alex but if she did, he and Janie might yet go ahead and have the child. If only she hadn't told me, Virginia thought.

'Don't worry about it,' Jane said. 'I just wanted to be sure you'd got it.'

'How long are you here for?' Virginia asked.

'Well, the operation's tomorrow,' Jane told her 'but then I couldn't get a flight back until Tuesday morning, so Alex is taking Philly and me to Suffolk for the week-end to recuperate.'

'How nice.' Virginia who, for a moment, had been feeling almost ashamed of herself, was once more bitterly jealous. How on earth, after all the lies she had told Alex about Jane, had she managed to persuade him to invite her to the country? Alex's country house was *her* domain, she thought resentfully, not Jane's. She was damned if she'd do anything to further their relationship. 'Get him to show you the place where he made a pass at me,' she said spitefully.

The full force of Virginia's jealousy struck Jane at last. To bring up that old story at a moment like this showed such crass insensitivity that Jane could almost feel compassion for Verge, especially as, having talked to Alex about the incident, she was now convinced that he had never intended to make a pass at Virginia at all. When she had mentioned it to him he had looked blank for a moment.

'I do remember,' he had said at last, 'ages ago when Verge and Robin were staying the weekend with Julie and me, saying that I wanted to walk across the old wreck. It's about a mile out from the beach. It takes about twenty minutes when the tide's out. Julie and Robin said they didn't want to come, so I went with Verge. We talked a bit about Julie's illness, and Verge was being terribly sweet and sympathetic, so I took her hand, I remember, and said something about how lovely it was to be able to talk to her and she snatched it away and said, "I'm not going to have an affair with you, you know." I remember being terribly surprised, because that wasn't what I'd intended at all. I'd just thought of her as someone I could confide in, so I said something like, "Oh no, of course I realize that would be impossible, wouldn't it, as we're all such good friends?"'

Jane had believed him implicitly. The whole incident reminded her of one which had taken place in Venice the previous summer when a rather silly English spinster in her sixties, whom Jane had met at a cocktail party at the British Consulate, had confided in her, on hearing of her friendship with Helmut, that she had once had to resist his advances during the course of a drink at her *pensione.* Her face, as she described the incident, had taken on the same foolish expression of gloating false modesty as Verge's had when she described Alex's so-called pass. Jane, knowing as she did from Helmut, that he had never slept with a woman in his life, had hardly been able to meet the woman's eye. At the same time she had felt a deep pity for her foolishness.

'All right,' she said quietly to Verge. 'I will.'

'Well I'm glad you're being sensible enough to have an abortion, at any rate,' Virginia said, slightly mollified. 'It would have been extremely stupid of you, you know, to have pinned any hopes on Alex.'

'I know he's got to resolve the situation with Georgina still,' Jane agreed.

'Oh it's not just Georgina,' Verge said hastily, 'he's had about four other women besides her this month, you know.'

Jane could never remember afterwards how she had managed to end the conversation. All she could hope was that Verge hadn't fully realized the extent of the wound she had inflicted on her with her last random thrust of the rapier. So Alex had lied to her. He had told her clearly that since they had been together there had been no one else, but now it seemed not only as if Georgina had come back to him after all, but that there had been others as well.

Many women might have dreaded Georgina's return, but until now Jane had always felt convinced that it was essential for her own happiness with Alex that Georgina should reappear. Jane was experienced enough to realize that what she and Alex had shared together was exceptional, and had been sure that once he saw Georgina again he would quickly discover that there was nothing left between them. Georgina's chief weapon was her absence. A flesh and blood rival could be dealt with and despatched. A legend held an unfair disadvantage.

Now it seemed as if she had been mistaken in this. It made her doubt everything. Could she have been wrong about the bliss they had experienced together as well? One read of cases where deluded women were convinced that their lovemaking had been something exceptional, whereas to the man it had been no more than a casual fling. It had never happened to her before, but that didn't mean it couldn't be happening now. She got up and paced round the room. The whole thing was too humiliating and horrible to contemplate.

It didn't cross her mind to doubt Verge. Verge lived opposite Alex, and, as Jane already knew to her cost, made it her business to find out exactly who he was seeing. No one, especially not such an old friend as Verge, would be wicked enough to invent such a story at such a time. It therefore followed that the story was true and that Alex was false. Charming, sweet, seductive, and utterly, utterly false.

As Jane put the phone down she decided she would not speak to Alex that night. How could she risk having a child with someone who had proved to be such a liar? For the sake of peace he might well agree to her going ahead with the pregnancy, only to abandon her at some later date when she was in an even more vulnerable position than she was at present. Giorgio had been unfailingly kind to her in this crisis. She might not love him any more, but it was her duty, for Filippo's sake, to put any thoughts of Alex aside and return to Venice as soon as possible.

She went to Alex's house punctually at 7.30. Now that she knew him to be so treacherous, she abandoned any attempt at words for fear of where they might lead them. Instead they spent the whole night making love. If she could only have enough of him, Jane thought desperately, perhaps she could slake her appetite and thus begin the dreary process of getting over him.

She had a moment of clarity in the night while Alex dozed, his arm resting tenderly across her breasts and his lips nuzzling against her ear. Do I have the right she asked herself, to murder my child purely in order to protect myself from being further hurt by a man I know to be false, or is it my duty to save the child even if I thus doom myself to being abandoned by both Alex and Giorgio?

She moved restlessly. Alex snuggled closer towards her and her arm moved upwards involuntarily to caress his dark curls. The answer came to her almost immediately. But I already have a child, she reminded herself and my duty to him is greater than my duty to the child I'm expecting. If I deprive Filippo of his father's support, I'll be sacrificing my living child for my unborn child, and this I have no right to do. If I go ahead and have this child, I won't be able to feed either of them. Alex could possibly be forced into paying child support but Giorgio, being foreign, could not. I have no alternative, therefore, but to go ahead with the abortion.

CHAPTER TWELVE

They set the alarm for 6.30. On the way to the clinic, rather touchingly, Alex showed Jane the Knightsbridge mews house he had lived in as a child and the flat in Fulham where he and Julie had first set up home together after their marriage.

There were a stream of arrivals at the clinic which, had it not been for the sign outside, might easily have been mistaken for a respectable suburban villa. Alex was hard pushed to find a parking space, but insisted on coming in with Jane, and waiting with her, clasping her hand, until the last possible moment, when she was whisked away by a stout sister with a refined accent, who had the same smooth, reassuring manner as the abortionist Jane had met two days before. She took Jane to a double room, already occupied by a very young upper-class girl, and told her to take off all her clothes and put on her dressing-gown.

'Hallo,' said the girl, sounding far more assured than Jane felt, 'I'm Belinda. We're going to be sharing a room tonight.'

'Well actually,' Jane told her, feeling quite apologetic, at spoiling the fun, 'they told me I could go home this evening if everything went OK. I wanted to, you see, because I have a little boy.' She started to undress.

'Are you married then?' the girl asked.

'Yes, but this baby isn't – isn't my husband's. What about you?'

'Oh no.' Belinda stared at her. 'I'm in the middle of my O levels. I chose today because I don't have another exam till Monday. My parents think I'm at Wimbledon.'

The sister returned and eyed Jane's dressing-gown covetously. It was an expensive green velvet one she'd bought about seven years before to take to rather a grand house party.

'Isn't that absolutely gorgeous?' she said silkily. 'Do tell me where you got it.'

'Harrods, I think,' Jane replied.

'Oh yes.' The sister's eyes flickered over the dressing-gown once more, and when she spoke again her accent seemed to have climbed at least two notches up the social scale. 'It absolutely *screams* Harrods at you, doesn't it?'

Alex, driving to work through the rush hour, had a sudden almost overwhelming desire to turn the car round, dash back to the clinic, force his way into the operating theatre and remove Jane from the hands of the executioners.

He had dreamed last night that the child was his, and that he and Jane were getting married, and he had woken up feeling small, ashamed and desperately, desperately sad. On his way to the clinic with Jane he had had a strange sensation that fate was taking over, that it wasn't them doing this thing, and that the whole matter, for reasons he could neither understand nor explain, had been taken out of their hands.

This sense of powerlessness reminded him suddenly of his childhood. Was it then, he asked himself, that the brainwashing had begun? The rigid public school training that had taught him never to follow his own instincts for fear of ridicule, but always to take the path mapped out for him by his superiors in order to be seen to be doing the right thing in the eyes of the world?

He remembered how, when he was at Eton, his household had been thrown into turmoil by a letter from his housemaster to his father which complained that 'Alex seems to think it more important to sit listening to a symphony by Mozart than to practise for the rugger team.' His father had written back that his son needed 'toughening up', and his housemaster, by way of doing this, had read the letter aloud to the assembled house before evening prayers. It was then that Alex had started to retreat into himself, rather as his mother, a singer before her marriage, had cut herself off from her theatrical friends and turned herself into the perfect county hostess in order to please his domineering father, before drinking herself to death a few years after Alex's marriage to Julie.

On leaving Eton, Alex had wanted to go to art school. This had been refused categorically, as had his subsequent request to read history of art at Cambridge. His father had informed him, 'No son of mine will ever go to Cambridge,' and sure enough Alex had ended up being packed off to Oxford to read PPE.

The next crisis had come with his choice of career. An old friend of his father's had offered him the chance of becoming a partner in his management consultancy business. Alex had refused politely, until confronted by his almost apoplectic father who had convinced him that no young puppy in his position could possibly afford to turn down such an excellent offer.

By then Alex had become involved with Julie. He didn't really like county girls, but they were the only ones he ever seemed to meet apart from tantalizing glimpses of the actressy set who performed with the OUDS at Oxford. He'd dreamed sometimes of auditioning for their productions as a set designer, but his father had persuaded him to join the cricket team instead. This took up all his free weekends, so he never really had time to meet anyone he liked or felt at home with at Oxford. He already had his work cut out to end up with a cricket blue – at the attainment of which his father had cried with happiness – and rather a disappointing second.

He had drifted into marriage rather as if he had been sleepwalking. He was so conditioned by then to never getting the things he wanted that it had hardly seemed worthwhile to put up a struggle. He had the same sort of feeling today. Last night, when he was with Jane, he had felt that she loved him and that it was true the child was his and that all he had to do was say the word and she would go ahead and have it and they could live happily ever after. But Verge and Sandra had told him that it wasn't his and that Jane couldn't be in love with him. They had said she was just using him, and that if he married her he would be ruining his life for ever, and because Alex had never known love as a child, but had been left totally in the care of nannies apart from the one afternoon a week when his mother reluctantly took charge of him because it was the nanny's afternoon off, he found it easy to believe them. More importantly, Jane had said nothing either, which she surely would have if the child had really been his. It would never have occurred to Alex that a woman might love him enough to allow herself to be dragged in silence like a lamb to the slaughter in order not to inconvenience him. All he could imagine was that she had decided after all that Giorgio was a better bet. He had been a fool, he told himself now, to believe even for a minute that someone like Jane, an actress, beautiful, intelligent, and wonderful and generous in bed – everything in fact that he had ever dreamed of in a woman – could ever really be serious about someone as insignificant as him.

A car hooted at him and Alex jumped and glanced at his watch. He must stop dawdling. He had a 9.30 meeting in his office, and he mustn't let the other partners down.

When he collected Jane that evening, she was very white and looked as if she had been crying. He rushed up the steps of the clinic and put his arms round her. 'Oh Janie, was it so dreadful?' he asked.

'No. They were very nice.' She tried to smile reassuringly 'No.' she went on. 'It's Filippo. I rang Sarah just now to say I was about to leave and she told me he'd got much worse this afternoon and she had just taken his temperature and found it was 104°.'

'Oh Janie –' he hugged her to him for a moment – 'so you want to get back to him as soon as possible, of course. But what about you? Will you be all right to look after him?'

'Of course I will.' She broke away from him and started to climb into the car. He followed her hastily. 'There's nothing wrong with me,' she said determinedly as they drove away. 'Everything went absolutely fine. But I couldn't help thinking,' she went on in a low voice, 'after I'd made the phone call, how ironic it would be if anything should happen to Filippo just now, when I'd got rid of this baby.' She started to fumble in her bag for a cigarette. Alex grabbed her hand and held it until it relaxed in his.

'Nothing's going to happen,' he said.

'No.' She appeared to be blinking back tears. 'It's not, is it? I'm not going to let it.' She squeezed his hand briefly before relinquishing it. 'I'd better let go of you now, hadn't I, so you can drive?' she said.

'Does this mean,' he asked her, when they had gone a bit further, 'that you won't be able to come to Suffolk tomorrow?'

'Oh Alex – yes. I suppose it does, and I was so looking forward to it. But that doesn't mean,' she said slowly, 'that you have to stay in London. You can always go to Suffolk without us.'

'Oh but I'd rather stay,' he said at once. 'I can be some help to you surely, can't I. If you have to stay in with Filippo?'

'Well, yes, you can,' she admitted. She would have died rather than tell him, but she didn't know how she would manage if he went to the country. 'Liliana's away this weekend, most unusually, and I'd told Sarah I was going to Suffolk with you, so she's made other plans.'

'I'll come and stay with you,' he offered. 'Filippo won't know. I'll come round after he's gone to bed and leave before he wakes in the morning, then just reappear casually later. I can do your shopping for you and get his medicines if he needs them.'

'It's very good of you.' She was touched. She thought how unusual it was for a childless man even to be aware of such things. 'I'm afraid I won't have much time for you,' she added. 'Children can be incredibly demanding when they're ill, you know.' She talked on a bit about the arrangements she would have to make and the things she would need to bring Filippo's temperature down. Alex had always thought of her as rather diffident and indecisive, but all that had disappeared now, to be replaced by a quiet strength of purpose. She seemed to have entirely forgotten both herself and him in her concern for her son and Alex found himself thinking with a pang that under different circumstances she would be exactly the sort of person he would have chosen to be the mother of his children.

The weekend only served to confirm him in this opinion. In fact, Filippo recovered very quickly once he knew his mother was safely back, and Jane and Alex spent long hours together while he slept, watching the tennis on television and having the sort of conversations they ought to have had at the beginning of their relationship if Virginia's intervention had not propelled them prematurely into clandestine sex.

'I haven't told anyone this,' said Alex on the Saturday, 'but I've been going to art classes three times a week since you've been away, and my teacher seems to think I'm reasonably promising. I've had a talk with the people at my office, and they've agreed to allow me a year's sabbatical – the economic climate's so bad at the moment that I think they're actually quite relieved not to have to pay my salary – so I can paint full time and see if I'm any good. A friend of mine owns a gallery and he's promised to give me his honest opinion of my work at the end of that time, and if he likes it at all, he's going to give me my first exhibition.'

Jane hugged him. 'Oh Alex, how exciting for you.'

'Yes, and if that goes at all well I shall sell the London house.'

'But won't you mind that?' Secretly Jane though it would be all to the good if he severed some of his claustrophobic closeness with Verge.

'It'll be sad, of course,' he replied, 'but it's a small price to pay, after all, for a really satisfying career – if I can only get started.'

'You will, I'm sure,' Jane assured him, 'and, since we seem to be confessing things, I've got a play shoved away in a drawer, which I wrote before I discovered I was expecting Filippo and then did nothing about because I was in such a state of shock. I've been thinking these last few days that perhaps I should pluck up my courage and show it to somebody.'

At all costs, Jane thought, she must start to earn some money so she would never again be trapped into doing something she didn't want because she was financially dependent on a man.

'Oh you must.' She was quite taken aback by his enthusiasm. She had become so conditioned by now to the Italian idea that anyone who looked the way she did couldn't possibly have a brain. 'Where is it? Can I read it?'

'It's in Venice,' she told him. 'I'm going to dig it out when I get back and see if I think it needs anything done to it, and then bring it back with me when we next come and show it to an old friend of mine who directs plays. Oh – was that Filippo?' She froze. 'No,' she said a moment later, 'he's having a wonderful sleep, isn't he? I'm so glad. That cold sponging really seemed to bring his temperature down.'

Jane had run the bath with lukewarm water and filled it with Filippo's favourite bathtoys. Then, when he was thoroughly engrossed with them, dabbed his forehead and wrists surreptitiously with a cold flannel for ten minutes to bring down his fever.

'He's been awfully good, hasn't he?' Alex said wonderingly, 'I can't get over it, I'm so used to Ben and Joshua smashing the place up when they come to stay that I thought all children behaved like that. Or is Filippo just being good because he's ill?'

'Oh no,' said Jane indignantly. 'He's always been good. He's more languid than usual, of course, because of the fever, but he's never gone around smashing things for no reason. He's too intelligent for that. He knows that once they're broken they can't be played with any more.'

'Well I suppose Ben and Josh think that if things get broken, their mother'll just go out and replace them,' Alex said.

Jane looked at him sideways. Was she imagining it or did he seem a trifle disenchanted with Virginia? 'Do

Verge and Robin bring the au pair when they come and stay with you?' she asked curiously.

'No, never. The house isn't really big enough.'

'I'm quite surprised they can cope then,' Jane confessed.

'Well actually, they can't,' Alex replied, and they looked at each other and laughed. 'Did I tell you,' he went on, 'I ran into Robin this morning when I went home to change?' He asked if we'd like to come over to tea later, but I'd better ring him, hadn't I, and say Filippo's not well enough to go out?'

'Yes, please,' said Jane. 'They say twenty-four hours at home after the temperature's returned to normal. It's important', she went on, her face clouding, 'that he should be well enough to travel on Tuesday.'

At Verge and Robin's house the phone rang.

'That may be Alex,' Robin said. 'I saw him this morning. He seemed a bit down at not having been able to take Janie to the country so I invited them over for tea.'

'I can't see them,' Virginia said hastily. 'I'm not well.' The au pair had been inveigled into working on Saturdays and had taken the boys to the park while Virginia had her afternoon rest. Robin looked at her sharply before going over to answer the phone.

'You're in luck,' he said a few minutes later. 'They can't come anyway. Filippo's not up to it. I'd better leave you then, hadn't I, as you're not well?' He walked out of the room.

Virginia collapsed back on the pillows. Her morning sickness had already begun, and the trouble with it was that it seemed to go on all through the day. She told herself that she had won at last. She had destroyed her best friend's child, the child she had wanted so desperately, and at the same time paid Janie back in full for presuming to try and steal her good friend Alex. It had been the perfect crime. She had played on the insecurities of two shy people who had never had high opinions of themselves and manipulated each of them into believing that the other was indifferent to them. She could never be brought to trial for her crime, and if she were ever accused of it, all she would have to do was maintain that she had believed she was telling the truth. It was the moment she had been waiting for for nearly fifteen years. The moment of her revenge on Janie for having rejected her love as a teenager. She couldn't understand, therefore, why she didn't feel happier about it.

On Jane's last night Alex took her to the opera. Filippo was fully recovered and Liliana had agreed to babysit. Jane hadn't brought a dress with her, so Alex took her to buy one in the Portobello Road. It was long and white and very romantic, with a drawstring neck and wide sash, and delicate flowers embroidered on the bodice and skirt.

'I can't take it back with me,' she told him, as she emerged from the changing room to sycophantic cries of admiration from the French assistant. 'It's too unlike my usual style, Giorgio'll know.'

'Then I'll keep it for you at my house until you come back.' Alex's eyes were soft. 'But you must have it. You look so beautiful in it. It's somehow just the way I imagine you looking when you're not here.

They gazed at each other, and the hardened assistant felt quite a pang for a moment at seeing a young couple who were obviously so madly in love with each other.

The opera was Janáček's *Jenufa*, the harrowing story of a mill owner's granddaughter whose stepmother drowns her illegitimate baby without her knowledge in order to save the family from disgrace. Neither Alex nor Jane had seen it before, and they held hands very tightly during the second act when the stepmother, full of agony and indecision, enters the bedroom where Jenufa is sleeping and returns with the child, wrapped in a shawl, before disappearing with it into the night.

Almost more unbearable to Jane was the later scene, where Jenufa, still half-drugged, wakes to discover her child is missing. As usual Jane had forgotten to bring a handkerchief, and having been so resolutely stoical until now, felt she would die rather than ask Alex for his. To sniff, she knew, would be even worse, as it would also alert all their neighbours, so she was forced to sit immobile while the cold tears ran down her cheeks leaving a black trail of mascara which she was fortunately able to wash off without Alex noticing by making a hasty dash for the ladies' room before the lights went up.

The friendly barman felt quite sorry to see them looking so cast down in the interval. He didn't wait to ask them what they wanted, but poured them the same drinks they had had in the first interval and slid them silently across the bar. Jane was most impressed by his memory, and actually managed a watery smile.

Alex put his arm protectively round her shoulders as they returned to their seats in the stalls. It was unthinkable that they should walk out. The piece was far too good. But they both wondered in secret how they were going to survive the last act. Jane smiled up at him, grateful for his support and oblivious, as he was, to everyone else in the crowded theatre, and especially to a small, plumpish woman of about forty in an expensive black lace dress who was sitting with her husband and a party of his friends in a grand tier box, watching them both intently through her opera glasses.

And now the moment of their parting had arrived and Alex was standing on the observation platform at Heathrow, surrounded by families waiting to wave goodbye to their relatives' planes. Jane didn't know he was there. They had already said their goodbyes inside the terminal and Jane had given him a last searching look in which, for a moment, he'd caught a glimpse of unshed tears behind the brave smile put on for Filippo, before she took the little boy by the hand and disappeared with him through the departure doors, not turning even when Philly dragged at her arm and repeated insistently that he wanted Lix to come with them.

Alex had been trying to tell himself all morning that since he, as an intruder in Jane's life, had brought her nothing but disaster, the best thing he could do for her now was to withdraw without a struggle so she could attempt to stick the pieces of her life together. He hadn't realized how hard it would be to let her go. The last few days had contained some of the loveliest, and at the same time some of the worst moments of his life, but it wasn't until now, at the moment of parting, that Jane had let her guard slip for a moment and allowed Alex to realize fully the extent to which she too had been hurt. She had reminded him at the end of some brave wounded animal, dragging herself off with dignity to die in the undergrowth, and suddenly, desperately, he realized how much he needed her to stay so that he could comfort her and she could comfort him in their mutual bereavement over the child which might have been theirs.

Desperate to get one last glimpse of her he walked rapidly down the long corridor to the observation platform, peering through windows as he went to make sure he had got the gate number right. It helped that she was flying Alitalia. If it had been British Airways he doubted very much if he would have been able to pick out the right plane from the long line snaking towards the runway. For a moment it disappeared behind some buildings, and then it was there again, its distinctive red and green colouring making it possible for him to pick out even at that distance, as it paused for the last time before hurtling its way along the tarmac for its effortless soar into the sky. He watched until it was a small speck in the distance, and continued to imagine he could see it long after it had disappeared. He felt rather as if she had gone to heaven and he was left on earth, alone and most unutterably sad.

Alex sensed something was wrong as soon as he walked into the house. It was shortly after 10p.m. He had gone straight to his office from the airport, and from there to his evening class, where, in making charcoal sketches of Rob, the bejeaned, earringed model, he had found for the first time that day, if not happiness, at least a total absorption in his work and a merciful measure of oblivion. He had hardly slept the previous night. Jane had been forbidden sexual intercourse for six weeks after the operation, so they had to find other ways of making love, caressing and kissing each other for most of the night, which they had started at his house, and then, not able to bear being parted for even the few hours which remained before he picked her up to take her to the airport, finished at her house, chastely, in the bed she had shared with Giorgio. He was feeling very tired now. He had planned to take a Mogadon, just for tonight, and to go to bed immediately.

Nothing in the house seemed to have been disturbed, and Alex was just beginning to relax again when he found the note lying on his pillow.

Darling love,

I saw you last night in the second interval, and didn't hear a note of the last act. I felt so ill that I'm not sure how I lasted till the end.

Dear oh dear oh dear, what a muddle and mess everything is. I was desperate to grab you and kiss you and bury myself in your body.

I leave my letter on your pillow, but I have that awful feeling that you're not coming home tonight and I might miss you. I feel a total panic and can't pull myself away. I've touched everything you touch to get a bit nearer, and rested my head on your pillow for a minute to warm it. I feel so lost and empty and just can't move from this seat in case we slip away further. I love you so very, very much. A truly physical pain. I can't tear myself away. Whatever happens I shall haunt you forever, waking and sleeping, not to speak of myself being haunted by you. Should you come home tonight, please, please, come to me, whatever time. I need you so much, the warmth, the touch, the love – you gentle beautiful creature.

Darling, I'm feeling cold. Please come. But I know you are away. If only I knew where I could reach you in thought and spirit. My darling darling darling, I'll love you forever with more love than you know or even want. Can people die of love?

Forever yours, Georgina.

This was highly inflammatory stuff, Alex reflected. It was odd, therefore, that on this occasion it should leave him so utterly cold. Was it because such an excess of passion after a three-month silence somehow struck a false note? It was obvious, even to Alex, that this sudden return could only have been prompted by jealousy of

Jane. Or was it that Georgina's letter, for all its flowery, romantic style, failed to move him even a tenth as much as Jane's silence and the look of love in her eyes when they parted from each other at the airport?

He was just trying to decide what to do when the telephone rang.

'Oh my darling, thank God you've come home at last!' It was Georgina.

'I was going to ring you,' he heard himself sounding polite but slightly defensive, 'but I've only just got in, and I was feeling rather tired.'

'Shall I come to you then?' she asked eagerly.

Oh God, no. Alex hadn't thought about it before, but he felt certain suddenly that he would find it impossible to perform adequately in the bed he had shared last night with Jane. 'Well, actually I really am very tired,' he repeated. 'Do you think it could possibly wait until tomorrow?' It was the first time he had ever said no to her in his life.

'It's that girl, isn't it?' she said suddenly.

'What girl?' he stalled.

'The one you were with at the opera. Henry pointed you out. He looked at me with such a cruel smile and said: "Isn't it nice to see Alex again, and with such a pretty girl?" Is she with you now?'

'No she's not,' Alex said wearily. 'As a matter of fact she's in Venice. I saw her off this morning.'

'Venice?' For a moment Georgina was sidetracked. 'But nobody goes there in June, do they? Why don't you come to me then?' She lowered her voice seductively. 'And let me show you how much I love you?' When he didn't respond immediately her voice became sharper. 'I'm only here for one night,' she said. 'You must see me. You simply can't refuse me after all this time.'

'Oh all right,' he said wearily. He felt a sudden bitter resentment at her bossiness and the fact that it was always she who dictated when their meetings should take place. On the other hand, it was a unique chance for him to find out what he really felt for her, and he supposed he ought to take it. If he didn't it might well be another three months before she came to London again and placed herself so categorically at his disposal. 'I'll be round in a few minutes,' he told her.

She opened the door to him in full makeup and a diaphanous peach-coloured negligée, and taking his hand, led him straight up to the top floor of the house. All the rooms up there had been knocked into one, and converted into a sort of seductress's boudoir with a bar, sofas, and a large brass bed, the looming presence of which was somehow impossible to ignore.

Alex turned his back on it and sat down on the sofa, while Georgina opened a bottle of wine for them both and sat down beside him. On her questioning him, he started to tell her about Jane – not the abortion, of course, merely the fact that he'd met her through mutual friends, been very happy with her, and was probably going to spend his summer holiday in Venice so he could see more of her. As he talked, he was aware that Georgina, obviously aroused by the fact that he had been unfaithful to her, was edging closer and closer to him. When he had finished she reached out her hand and put it on his cock.

'But I'm not ready to let you go,' she said.

He looked at her dispassionately. One of the reasons he had initially been attracted towards her when they had first met ten years ago, was because of her superficial resemblance to Jeanne Moreau who, in *Jules et Jim,* he had, as a pimply undergraduate, found to be one of the most seductive women he had ever seen. Now, cruelly, the years had rolled on, and for the first time he was aware of the slight slackening of skin under her jaw. When she smiled at him seductively, he noticed that her mascara had smudged and left a row of black dots on the puffy area above her eyes. He wished for her sake that she had not insisted on his coming round tonight. If she had been prepared to wait, the contrast with Jane's youth and beauty would have been less painfully marked.

'I've been thinking that perhaps we shouldn't see each other for a while,' he said to her. 'Three months, say, so we can both decide what we really feel.'

She undid his trousers and started to play with his cock. 'But it's been three months already,' she replied softly, 'and I feel exactly as I did before. I'm certainly not prepared to wait so long again.'

He started to speak, but she silenced him by bending over and kissing him on the lips, massaging his penis as she did so.

'Let me show you how much I love you,' she breathed. 'We'll have a wonderful night of love together and then if you still think you shouldn't see me in the morning, I'll let you got without a murmur. But I'll guarantee,' she continued with a seductive laugh, 'that by then you'll have changed your mind.'

It was beginning to seem to Alex by then that the simplest thing he could do would be to comply. He still couldn't bring himself to move towards her, but she saved him the trouble by flinging her negligée over her head and kneeling naked at his feet to suck his cock.

Alex closed his eyes. Until Jane, Georgina's talents as a fellatrix had reigned supreme. It was hard to define exactly what it was that Jane did better. Perhaps it was just that Georgina was too predatory. There was always the slight feeling that she was hardening him up so she could use him as a vibrator, whereas Jane had seemed so gentle and loving when she sucked him, as if giving him pleasure was an end in itself.

Thinking of Jane, he grew hard. Georgina raised her head and smiled victoriously. 'Come and lie on the bed,' she said, 'and let me do it all to you.'

Alex allowed himself to be stripped and led to the bed and mounted by the naked Georgina. Just for a moment, the sensation of entering her again was exciting, and he started off by quite enjoying it. Soon, however, it began to pall. She had left the light on, which was a big mistake, because he was unable to help comparing her body to Jane's, and noticing for the first time that, undressed, Georgina was undoubtedly rather squat and short-waisted, and that the position she was in had caused the skin of her face to flop forward, giving a slightly jowly effect.

His erection began to wilt. Georgina, feeling it, started to ride him harder, while massaging her own clitoris furiously with one hand. On her face was a look of increasing desperation. Unfortunately it didn't work. The harder Georgina tried, the softer Alex became, and the more certain he felt that for the first time in his life he was simply not going to be able to come.

As Georgina rode on and on, Alex became more and more bored. He started to compose polite sentences in his head that would persuade her to relinquish her seat and end this embarrassing ordeal for them both. In the end his body did it for him. His penis, completely limp by now, simply flopped out of her, and she got off him and lay beside him and asked him humbly if he would lick her clitoris for her so she could go to sleep.

Alex, feeling he owed her one, agreed politely and satisfied her quickly and efficiently, but without becoming in the slightest bit aroused. Afterwards, she snuggled up to him and started to caress him again and ask him what he would like her to do to him. He insisted once more that he was extremely tired, and she, seeming frightened and sad now, let go of him finally, and allowed him to turn over and go to sleep.

Several times in the night he was aware of her fondling and attempting to arouse him with kisses and caresses. The phrase 'using every trick in the book' came into his mind as he lay awkwardly beside her, steadfastly feigning sleep. In the morning he awoke to find her sucking his cock. This was better, because he was able to keep his eyes shut and imagine it was Jane. This time too, Georgina managed things more cleverly. She sucked him until he had almost come, and then climbed on top of him at the last minute so he was able, by a supreme effort of will, to come inside her, knowing with absolute certainty as he did so that he was never ever going to be able to bring himself to make love to her again.

Normally she would have brought him some coffee in bed, but Alex, anxious to get out of the house as quickly as possible, pleaded an early meeting.

'But you've got to have something,' she insisted, trying to waylay him.

'Oh, I'll just grab something in the café on the way,' he told her.

'Then I'll come with you,' she said determinedly,

starting to fling on her clothes from the night before, which she had left on a chair. These consisted of a long black lacy dress and a red fox stole, which by night had no doubt been very romantic and *fin-de-siècle*, but which at 9a.m., after a failed night of passion, Alex found faintly tawdry and embarrassing. It was as if she had to grab the first thing that came to hand, regardless of suitability, because she was afraid that if she turned her back on him for a moment he would make his escape without her.

They ended up going to Parsons in the Fulham Road. Georgina ordered a coffee, and Alex, feeling better now they were on neutral territory, some freshly squeezed orange juice, scrambled eggs, and two rounds of toast and marmalade. As soon as the waitress had gone, they started to negotiate how long it should be before they saw each other again. Alex held out for three months, Georgina a week. Finally they compromised on two months, Alex thinking that with any luck he could arrange to be in Venice when the time came.

Seeing that Alex was adamant, Georgina started to harangue him discreetly in a low voice. 'I really don't know how you can treat me like this,' she said, 'after all we've been through together –'

The waitress came with their drinks. Alex smiled at her gratefully. What have we been through together? he thought. When we started our affair we agreed I'd leave Julie and you'd leave Henry. I did leave Julie, but you didn't leave Henry, did you? He drank some orange juice.

Georgina looked as if she were about to cry. 'And all the love I've shown you –' she went on.

Alex felt totally unmoved. What love? he thought, remembering all the nights he had lain awake waiting for her to call, and the evenings spent standing outside the Opera House like a tout trying to sell his tickets. He looked at her steadily, and she dropped her gaze and seemed to grow slightly uncomfortable.

'And now,' she said huffily, 'just when I was on the point of making up my mind to leave Henry and come to you –' she raised her eyes in what was intended to be a devastating combination of wronged innocence and accusation and met his gaze fully.

Alex smiled. 'Bullshit!' he said pleasantly, and finished his orange juice.

Georgina flushed angrily and rose to her feet. 'I'm going now,' she said, 'because I don't want to quarrel with you, but I warn you, I'm simply not going to accept being dumped like this.' She waited, but he failed to react. 'You know I really don't understand you.' Her voice grew shriller. 'For nearly two years now you've been telling me how much you love me—'

'I did love you,' Alex interrupted her. 'But you killed my love with your unreliability and broken promises.'

'But you *can't* kill a great love,' she argued. 'Not if it's a really deep and sincere emotion.'

Alex just looked at her. At that moment the waitress arrived with his food. Alex thanked her warmly and reached for the pepper mill. Georgina tossed her head and walked out of the restaurant, pausing for a moment at the door so he would have plenty of time to follow her if he wished to.

Alex, left alone, didn't even turn his head to see her go. He was conscious only of a blissful sensation of relief at being free from her at last. He reached for a piece of toast and buttered it thickly before tucking hungrily into his scrambled eggs. This afternoon he would call his travel agent, and tonight he would write to Jane.

Jane's homecoming hadn't gone off too badly. Giorgio had met her at the airport and, rather to her relief, brought Franco, his young assistant, with him in the boat. Throughout the day he had seemed reserved but friendly enough, going to the gallery in the afternoon while Jane unpacked, and announcing that he had invited Helmut to dinner that evening to welcome her back.

Jane's momentary coolness with Helmut seemed to have blown over, though she had not told him the true reason for her visit to London. At the end of the evening Giorgio offered to walk Helmut home and went upstairs to get a sweater. Jane took advantage of his absence to ask Helmut whether her letter from Alex had arrived yet. It was the only letter he had ever written to her and Jane was pathetically anxious, now they were apart, to have something of his to keep as a talisman. Helmut, however, replied that it had not. It had only been a week since Alex posted it, so Jane accepted this readily enough.

She went to the bathroom and got undressed. Filippo was sleeping peacefully in the next-door room. She couldn't help feeling relieved that she and Giorgio couldn't make love for six weeks, as she would have found it too brutalizing to go straight from one man to another. Her despairing love for Alex had in no way diminished her affection for Giorgio, however. Since her return, her heart had gone out to him for behaving so well towards her, and she hoped desperately that they could start to rebuild their relationship. She looked on her love for Alex as a sort of violent sickness which had not yet run its course, but which she hoped she would be cured of in time. The flat, which Giorgio had taken on the Lido, had been theirs from the first of the month, and Giorgio was going to take her there the following day. As far as she could look forward to anything in her lovesick state, Jane was looking forward to her two months at the sea. It would be a desperately needed period of calm in which to heal her mental and physical wounds.

She heard the door slam as Giorgio returned. A moment later he had entered the room and grabbed her by the arm. Jane saw to her dismay that he appeared to be trembling with rage.

'What is it, Giorgio?' she asked him, trying desperately to remain calm.

'Helmut told me', he said angrily. 'that you asked him if he had received a letter for you from your dear Alex. Why did you ask him this?'

Jane swallowed. Thank you, Helmut, she thought. 'Because Alex told me he'd sent me one,' she said steadily, 'and I wondered if it had arrived.'

'So you saw Alex, did you?'

'Yes I did. I told you I couldn't promise not to.'

'And did you fuck him as well?' he asked aggressively,

poking his face close to hers so she recoiled from the smell of garlic on his breath.

'What's the point of asking me that?' she said wearily. 'You know you wouldn't believe me even if I said I hadn't.'

'Oh but I would believe you.' His voice was softer now, and full of spite. 'Little Gianna who is always so honest and so kind to animals. It is only human beings that she hurts, is it not?'

Jane tried her best not to be irritated by his lack of logic. She reminded herself of how hurt he must be feeling and spoke to him gently and appealingly. 'But, Giorgio, I've done what you wanted,' she said. 'I've got rid of the baby and come back to you. Please be kind to me on my first evening.' Her eyes filled with tears. The attack had been so unexpected.

'Ah yes. You get rid of the baby. And you say you do that for me, do you?'

Jane tried to think. All she really knew was that she certainly hadn't done it for herself. 'Partly,' she said honestly, 'and also for Filippo –'

'And what about for Alex?'

'Also for Alex,' Jane admitted. 'I didn't feel it was right to force him to have a child when it was entirely my fault I got pregnant.'

'Or was it', his face was close to hers once more, 'because he refused to have anything to do with you or the child?'

Jane moved away from him and sat on the bed. 'He didn't refuse to have anything to do with me,' she said. 'He – paid for the operation and was very helpful in making all the arrangements.'

'Oh yes,' Giorgio said sarcastically. 'He was very helpful in getting rid of it, wasn't he, because he didn't want it, no?'

'No.' Jane was doing her best to keep her voice steady. If she could just succeed in hiding from him how much he was hurting her, perhaps he would grow tired of it in the end and give up. 'He didn't want it. But I think that was quite natural under the circumstances. Considering he hardly knew me.'

'So you think that if he had known you better he would have wanted your child?' Giorgio asked sneeringly.

'I don't know,' she said wearily. Did he really think she was going to fall in the trap of saying yes?

'So this was why you went to England? So he should know you better, as he suggest in his letter?'

'In his letter?' Jane repeated stupidly,

'Yes. He say in his letter that he wish to know you better, but then when you come, and he does know you better, he decides he does not want you after all. Doesn't he?' he shouted suddenly.

'But how do you know what the letter said?' Jane was still dazed at first, but then suddenly she understood. 'Helmut gave it to you, didn't he?' she asked accusingly.

'I went to his house yesterday and saw it lying on the table.' Giorgio told her. 'He tried to stop me reading it, but I had to. My whole future might have depended on that letter –'

'Yes, I can see that.' Jane was trying desperately to be fair, while at the same time adjusting to this new set of circumstances. In his place she might have done the same thing, she realized, but afterwards she would have confessed to it immediately, not just pretended the letter hadn't arrived. 'But what were you going to do about it if I hadn't asked Helmut?' she asked curiously. 'Just keep quiet about it for ever?'

Her incredulity seemed to enrage him further. 'I do what I want,' he shouted. 'What right have you to criticize me after what you have done? Why do you care so much about this letter? You are still in love with him, aren't you? Why then did you come back to me?

'Because I thought', Jane said, unconsciously summing up the whole tragedy of her life so far, 'that you needed me more than he did.'

'Not because he threw you out?'

'No.' Jane said wearily. 'He didn't throw me out.'

'I think he did. You are twenty-seven now, you see. That is old for a woman. He prefer someone younger.'

Jane gaped at him. It didn't seem worth pointing out that Georgina, her chief rival for Alex's affections, was over forty. He was obviously too far gone for logic and was just trying to strike out blindly and hurt her as much as possible.

'I could get someone younger myself, you know,' he went on. 'Oh yes. I have many opportunities. You were already too old for me when we met. If you had been younger I could have formed you and taught you myself, but it was too late. You were too spoiled and set in your ways.'

Jane rose to her feet and started to walk out of the room, but he grabbed her and threw her on to the bed. She was wearing just a T-shirt, which rode up, exposing her body. As she tried to pull it down she saw to her horror that he was undoing his belt and trousers, and advancing towards her as if to rape her.

'No, Giorgio!' she screamed. 'I'm not allowed to have sex for six weeks. The doctor said so.'

'Ah the doctor say so!' He stepped out of his trousers and climbed onto the bed, grabbing her as she tried to escape at the other side. 'So how did you manage with Alex last night? Did you give him one of your beautiful blow jobs? Did you lick his balls and stick your finger up his arse? Did you? Ah! Little Gianna the great sex expert!' and he grabbed her by the hair and forced her mouth over his cock.

At first, as he thrust vigorously into her mouth, Jane could hardly believe what was happening. She began to struggle with all her strength, certain that in a moment she would prevail and he would let her go. As he continued she started to choke and gag. She remembered reading once of a mass murderer who had suffocated his victims in just this way. At the time she had wondered if it was really possible, but now she could see only too well how it might be. She had stopped struggling by now and was concentrating all her efforts on getting gasps of air in between the cruel thrusts which were obstructing the back of her throat. The blood, pounding round her brain, seemed to have caused everything in her line of vision to turn scarlet. Just as she became convinced that she was about to die, the thrusting stopped and he started to twitch convulsively. He let go of her head, and for the first and last time in their five years together they achieved a macabre form of simultaneous orgasm as Giorgio's sperms mingled inextricably with the stream of vomit which gushed uncontrollably from Jane's throat.

Jane couldn't leave the house because of Filippo. She walked in silence to the linen cupboard and took out a blanket so she could sleep on the sofa. Giorgio watched her, silent and brooding.

The following day they went off early to the Lido for the start of their summer holiday.

Alex was just finishing his morning's work when the receptionist buzzed him.

'Are you free, Alex?' There's a lady here to see you. A Mrs Sandra Bailey.'

On the whole Alex was quite pleased. He had been feeling very churned up emotionally that morning. The momentary euphoria he had felt at freeing himself from Georgina's clutches had faded, and he had been forced to face the fact that he was utterly alone once more.

Sandra, he felt, would be a sympathetic listener. He decided to invite her to eat with him in the local trattoria. He would feel safe with her there. She could hardly rape him in a restaurant.

He noticed that she had dressed up for the occasion in an ankle-length brown crepe skirt and boots, with a floral silk shirt. Over her shoulder she carried a large straw basket.

'What a nice surprise, Sandy,' he said, kissing her. 'Have you been shopping nearby?'

'No.' She seemed unusually serious, but as yet he felt no stirring of alarm. 'I came to see you specially because I've got something important to tell you.'

Alex longed to ask what it was, but sensing rather than seeing the receptionist's eager eye, steered Sandra hastily out of the office and towards the restaurant, which was just off Sloane Square.

'So – what's the important news?' he asked her as they walked along.

'I'll tell you when we get there,' Sandra replied. 'Don't worry about it.'

Alex immediately did worry. He could only think that

somehow Martin had found out. Perhaps Sandra had confessed to him in a fit of jealousy. The thought made Alex quite angry. If Martin knew the lengths to which Sandra had been prepared to go in order to seduce him, he felt he could hardly fail to exonerate him from guilt in the matter.

'How's Martin?' he asked anxiously as they sat down.

She shrugged. 'I don't know. Whenever we have a quarrel nowadays he just says he can't stand any more and walks out of the house. I think,' she said bitterly, 'that he's started up again with Seamus. I found a ferry ticket to Ireland in his pocket after his last disappearance.' She sat back in her chair and lit a cigarette. Alex relaxed a bit. It didn't sound as if Martin knew anything after all. The waiter came and they decided to have just one course each. Sandra smoked too much to have any interest in food, and Alex didn't have a good appetite after his enormous breakfast.

'So, what was it you were going to tell me?' he asked when the waiter had gone away.

Sandra took a puff of her cigarette and looked at him defiantly. 'I'm pregnant,' she said.

'But that's wonderful!' Alex exclaimed. He reached out and patted her arm. 'I'm so glad for you both, Sandy. What a lovely surprise. Especially as you thought Martin – well – might not be able to –' Recent tests had proved that Martin had a low sperm count, and that although not absolutely out of the question, his chances of fathering a child were considerably reduced.

'I don't think he can,' Sandra replied. 'After all, we've been trying all this time without any success. This child's not his at all, although he doesn't know it. It's yours.'

Alex's hand went rigid. Sandra grabbed it before he could withdraw it.

'I know you're going to regard this as a terrible shock,' she said, 'especially after what happened with Jane, but please remember that for me it's something wonderful. It's what I always wanted. I already knew before you came to lunch that Martin probably couldn't have children, so I decided I'd try to have your child instead. Martin and I had been talking about adoption or artificial insemination, so can't you see that it's much better for both of us that it should be the child of someone we know and like?'

Alex felt rather like a boxer who, having received one stunning blow to the right side of his head, staggers upright again only to walk into a stunning blow to the left. 'But are you going to tell Martin it's mine?' he asked.

'No,' she replied. 'He's very fond of you, and I think the knowledge that we'd made love together would make him extremely jealous. I'm letting him think it's his. It's not impossible, after all, and it'll be better for the child.

'By the way, Alex,' she went on. 'I want to assure you that I'm not asking you for anything. I'll take care of the whole thing. Whatever happens, you won't have to worry about it at all.' She smiled at him. Her skin was very sallow today, and Alex thought she looked rather like a witch.

The waiter came with their food. Alex stuffed a forkful of tagliatelle into his mouth. At least eating gave him a pretext for freeing his hand from Sandra's.

'But I asked you if it was safe.' he said, bewildered.

'Yes, I know you did,' she said patiently, 'and I told you it was. I tricked you, Alex. I'd selected you as the person I wanted to be the father of my child, and the day of our lunch was the most fertile of the month.'

Alex was too intelligent not to see the bitter justice in the situation. It was painfully obvious to him now why Sandra had been so vicious about Jane's motives. She had obviously been judging them by her own.

'So you just used me?' he said.

'Oh no, Alex.' Her face was serious now. 'I love you. Surely you must know that? I've loved you almost since I met you, although I could see you were never really interested in me or you would have made a pass at me ages ago. I know I pretended it was just sex so as not to scare you off, but it was love I was giving you that day, even if you didn't want it, and in return you've given me the best present I've ever had in my life.' She smiled at him beatifically and took a mouthful of her pasta.

Alex felt faintly sick as he remembered all the times Sandra had interfered in his relationships under the guise of friendship. The time she had told him of Julie's deception over her illness – information which had precipitated his affair with Georgina. The time Sandra had offered to lend him her flat for sex with Georgina, and then prevented it by taking an overdose. The way, when he and Georgina had finally got together, Julie had mysteriously known about it the following day, and finally Sandra's terrifying hostility towards Jane. Could all this interference really have been motivated by love? His head swam. Surely love was supposed to be about wanting the other person's happiness – not destroying it at every turn in order to gain possession of them for oneself?

He made one last appeal. 'I really don't think I can cope with this, Sandy,' he said earnestly. 'Deceiving Martin like this, I mean. After all he's my best friend.'

'Well, I'm very sorry, Alex,' she said angrily, 'but perhaps you ought to have thought about that before you screwed me. Can't you see that it's too late now? It would spoil everything if you told him. I couldn't bear it. I think,' she said slowly, 'I might even kill myself.'

Alex couldn't face going back to the office. Instead, hardly knowing what he was doing, he hailed a taxi and went home. Virginia came out of her house just as he was paying the driver. She hesitated and then came up to him. Alex noticed dispassionately that she was looking almost as awful as he felt.

'Oh Alex,' she said without preamble. 'I just want you to know that you mustn't ever believe anything I say to you about Jane. I've always had a very emotional relationship with her. It – it goes back to when we were teenagers. I'm afraid I get far too angry with her at times.' She paused. 'I found out that Giorgio did have a vasectomy after all,' she said in a rush. 'I think, you know, that it must have been your baby she was expecting.' Her eyes filled with tears, and she looked at him pleadingly, as if begging him for absolution.

Alex knew immediately that she was telling him the truth and his sense of despair increased. Of course, he thought. He had allowed himself to be persuaded by the voices of 'reason' into letting Jane have the abortion, something he had known instinctively was wrong, only to be instantly and cruelly punished. A child conceived in beauty and bliss had been sacrificed for one conceived in duplicity and betrayal by a woman with serious emotional problems whom he didn't even fancy. He was still so full of the horror of what Sandra had told him that at first he hardly took in Verge's culpability in the matter. He patted her on the arm and told her not to worry, then went into his house and unplugged the phone and went to bed.

For both Jane and Alex, the next six weeks were among the worst of their lives. Jane found some comfort in setting up home in the bright modern flat they had taken near the Quattro Fontane beach. It stood in a large garden full of palm trees and Gauguinesque flowers, and had a spacious balcony on which to eat meals and sunbathe.

At first Giorgio came every evening to check up on Jane, hurl pornographic insults at her, and demand details of Alex's sexual performance. Gradually she managed to persuade him gently that it might be better for both of them not to see each other for a while. He claimed to hate the beach anyway, so he could use the time to catch up on business and think calmly about what he wanted to happen to their relationship, while she would do the same. He eventually seemed to accept this, though he still felt it necessary occasionally to assert his masculinity by turning up late at night when she was least expecting him. Sometimes on these occasions she felt convinced that he had come with the express intention of killing her, but knowing she must protect Filippo she always managed, by displaying a strength and serenity she was far from feeling, and by making constant references to their son, to calm him down.

Jane found salvation during this period by devoting her days entirely to Filippo. They would go to their cabana on the beach each morning with a picnic lunch, which they ate in a highly civilized way at their little table under the verandah. Afterwards Filippo would take his siesta on the *lettino*, well protected from the sun, while Jane read Dostoevsky's *The Idiot*, seeing the point now of the comparison Alex had made between himself and Prince Myshkin, but seeing also that Myshkin's impulsive proposal to the beautiful Nastasya Filippovna was to be regarded as a worthy action stemming from his nobility of character rather than, as Alex had seemed to think, something to be sneered at.

In the late afternoon she would take Filippo to the main shopping street on the back of the bicycle she had hired, and watch him as he went on interminable rides in the little fairground or buy him crescents of fresh coconut from the stall by the beach.

The would eat their dinner together on the balcony, and later, when he was in bed, Jane would work on her play. She had salvaged it from its drawer in fear and trembling, but had been pleased, on reading it, to find it much better than she had imagined. Her chief fear now was whether she could write anything so good again.

She decided to re-type the whole thing, making small corrections as she went along. Often she worked far into the night, grateful to have an occupation that would take her mind off Alex and the fact that he hadn't written.

She knew she could always contact him, but they had agreed that he would write first, and she felt very strongly that this time the move should come from him. As the weeks dragged on with no word from him, she felt increasingly stunned by his betrayal. She had committed murder for him, she thought, and never uttered a word of reproach to him for going back on his word. He in return was not even prepared to accord her the courtesy that any normal person would be prepared to show to the most casual of his friends.

After his lunch with Sandra and the subsequent conversation with Verge, Alex felt totally aimless and pathetic, as if his life had lost all purpose. For over a year he had been sustained in his loneliness by the vision of a future with Georgina. Now she had proved to be merely a mirage, and, by his own lack of self-confidence which had led him to listen to false advice, he had thrown away his chance with Jane. It was impossible to go and see her now, he thought, with this sword of Damocles hanging over his head, and equally impossible to write her a false letter pretending that everything was normal. On the other hand, how could he tell her the truth? That her best friend had betrayed her, and that he had got another woman pregnant – a woman whose poisoned advice had been one of the factors which had contributed to the murder of their child?

Not only had he lost both Georgina and Jane, but the Baileys and Askews as well. Sandra seemed to realize that it would be too dangerous to bring Alex and Martin together now – that Martin would be bound to see something was wrong and might well cross-examine Alex until he revealed the truth. Verge, too, seemed to be avoiding him. There was something shamefaced and shifty in her attitude to him now, and though he was equally relieved to avoid her, he couldn't help feeling a bit nettled by it. After all, she, surely, was the one who had wronged him. He had only done exactly what she had told him to do.

When his art school closed for the summer holidays, Alex put his London house on the market, left his job, and moved down to Suffolk. He played golf, had dinner with old friends of his parents, and spent hours sitting at his easel studying the endless variations of light which played on the creeks.

CHAPTER THIRTEEN

July 1974

Six weeks after the abortion, Jane came quietly into Venice to attend a clinic attached to the Ospedale Civile for her post-operative check up. When she told the doctor the nature of her operation he looked at her coldly, examined her for about fifty seconds and dismissed her abruptly, telling her disapprovingly that she was in perfect health.

Inevitably she thought of Alex, and wondered again why he hadn't written to her. She had done everything he had asked her to do all along the line, she thought bitterly, and in return he had abandoned her and left her to face the hostility and contempt of the doctor.

Afterwards she went to collect Filippo from the friend's house where he had spent the morning. She had planned to go straight back to the Lido, but instead, feeling a sudden rush of affection for Giorgio, decided to pay him a visit at his shop. As she walked there, she thought guiltily of how very much she had hurt him. Bad-tempered and occasionally violent as he was, he had never betrayed her or let her down. She longed desperately to sever the invisible thread which still bound her to Alex, unworthy as he was, and throw all her energy into rebuilding her relationship with Giorgio who had proved himself without question to be the better man of the two.

She arrived at the shop just before one and found the door locked. She knew that while she was away Giorgio often had lunch at the café in the Campo San Fantin, so she made her way there, pushing Filippo in his chair.

There was no sign of Giorgio in the café either. Jane was just wondering whether to have a snack there or go straight back to the Lido when Franco, Giorgio's assistant, a boy of sixteen with dark blond hair and a thin, sensitive face, passed by on his way to the shop. Jane hailed him and asked him if he knew where Giorgio was.

'In the gallery, signora. He asked me to come at one to take over. He likes to keep it open in the lunch hour because of the tourists.'

'Well, the door was locked just now.' Jane told him. 'He must have left early. What a pity.'

'Are you sure?' Franco looked surprised. 'He doesn't usually leave before I return. Was his boat there?'

'I forgot to look,' Jane confessed.

'Shall we go back and see?' Franco suggested. 'If he has gone I can let you in to the gallery with my key. Perhaps he has left some message to say where he has gone.'

Jane and Filippo walked back to the shop with Franco. It was on the right-hand side of a long, narrow *calle*. At the other end was a hump-backed bridge over the small canal where Giorgio parked his boat. When they were still about twenty yards from the shop, the door opened and Giorgio came out with a girl in a blue cotton dress who, as he turned to lock the door, flung her arms playfully round his shoulders and stood on tiptoe to kiss him on the side of his head.

'Papa! Papa!' said Filippo, pointing.

Jane whipped the chair round so he was facing her. She crouched down and put her finger urgently to her lips.

'Hush, Filippo,' she said. 'Don't disturb Papa. He's with a customer.'

Filippo subsided, obedient to the familiar command. Jane raised her eyes to meet Franco's. The expression of acute misery and embarrassment on his face told her everything she needed to know.

'We'll just go back to the *campo*, I think,' she said evenly, 'and give Giorgio time to finish his business,' but before

255

she could turn, Giorgio had straightened up and put his arm round the girl's shoulders. Jane had read that it was possible to tell just by the way a couple walked together, whether or not they were lovers, but she had never been convinced of the truth of it until now, as Giorgio and the girl in blue, their figures seeming to shimmer slightly in the midday sun, walked slowly towards the bridge and disappeared down the steps together into his boat.

Jane rang Helmut when she got back to the Lido and learned that the girl was an American tourist who had been sighted on Giorgio's arm several times during the past few weeks. As far as he knew, she was with a group of art historians who would be staying on in Venice for at least another ten days.

Armed with this information, Jane rang Giorgio that evening. Furious at having been caught out, he at first tried to deny everything, but when she told him what she had seen, he shouted that what he had done was perfectly justified, and that she was the last person in the world who was entitled to criticize him.

'All right,' said Jane calmly. 'So can we agree that we're even now, and that when she goes back to America we'll try to make a fresh start?'

'No we can't!' he shouted, seeming further enraged by the reasonableness of the suggestion. 'You were the one who began it, so I am entitled to a thousand infidelities for your one!'

The following day Jane rang Alitalia and booked a ticket to London. Giorgio, contrite now that she was actually going, but even more terrified that she might stay and cause a scandal, accompanied her to the airport and pressed a large sum of money into her hand. He told her he would come to London in the autumn to discuss the future with her.

Martin rang Alex in the country from time to time to see how he was getting on. In the past, the Baileys had spent many happy weekends in Suffolk with Alex and Julie, and, after the divorce, with Alex alone. Now Alex felt Martin was half hoping to be asked again, and that he was growing increasingly puzzled by Alex's lack of response to his friendly overtures.

He rang again on a particularly lovely day at the end of July. Alex was able to tell him that he had received a satisfactory offer for his London house, and that if all went well, contracts would be exchanged at the end of the following week.

'Julie's agreed that I can give her a lump sum from the proceeds and stop paying maintenance.' Alex told him. 'That way I can forget all about financial pressures and just concentrate on painting.'

'Good for you,' Martin said. 'I'm sure it's much the best thing for you both to make a clean break. After all, she's working full time now, isn't she, and seems to be completely better?'

'Yes, thank God.'

'Well, if you're coming up to London next week to exchange contracts,' Martin went on, 'why don't you come and have dinner with us? It would cheer Sandy up. She's been feeling very depressed recently.'

'Oh dear,' Alex said insincerely, wondering what right Sandra had to be depressed when she had supposedly achieved her heart's desire. 'I suppose pregnant ladies do get a bit down from time to time, don't they?'

'Oh but she's not pregnant,' Martin said.

Alex felt quite light-headed. 'But she told me about six weeks ago that she was,' he protested.

'She did think she was for a while,' Martin agreed, 'but then her period came on about a fortnight ago. She's always been a bit irregular, you know. It was a perfectly normal period so we think the pregnancy must have been a false alarm. She's been extremely cast down about the whole thing, I must say.'

The sense of relief Alex felt was so exquisite that he could even find it in himself to pity Sandra, while fully realizing now how completely untrustworthy she was, to forgive her for not having told him she wasn't pregnant. He promised to let Martin know exactly when he was coming to London, and hung up, using the excuse that he had to go out for a drink.

The sunset was particularly beautiful that day. Alex

poured himself a glass of wine and sat down at the wrought-iron table in the garden, watching as the sky grew slowly darker and writing an affectionate letter to Jane.

In August, Jane took Filippo to stay with her father, who had retired to Devon and was living near Lyme Regis with his widowed sister. She made light of her separation, saying merely that Giorgio was extremely busy at the moment, but would be coming to London later on when he could get away. To her relief, Filippo seemed just as happy, if not more so, playing on the Spartan English beaches as he had on the well-manicured sands of the Lido. Jane might shiver at the contrast in temperature but Filippo didn't even appear to be aware of it. Jane was delighted. It seemed to bode well for their future life in England.

They returned to London at the end of August, to find a letter from Verge which had been sent to Venice and forwarded by Giorgio.

Dearest Janie,

I'm writing primarily to find out how you are. I've heard from Sarah that things are not too good, and that you're expected home (Freudian! I mean England) soon, although I don't know if that just means a visit. I'm anxious about you and Philly, and although I'm too inexperienced to offer useful advice, I sense that to live in an atmosphere where there are quarrels or even just bad vibes must be incredibly depressing and destructive and also makes it impossible to judge the situation rationally and fairly to all. Perhaps you need to step outside for a bit to work things out.

I do feel I'm to blame for most of all this. I was far worse than naive. Something I stupidly and thoughtlessly thought would be amusing has turned out extremely serious and damaging to all of you and maybe has even broken up your family. Although obviously things between you and Giorgio must have been pretty bad, you did after all love each other not so very long ago and maybe you could have, after this bad patch, restored everything. But now I feel that something too disruptive has intervened and possibly prevented that forever. I seem to have been terribly insensitive and not to have cared enough about you all to have worked out the pretty obvious repercussions. Anyway, enough of petty moralizing and recriminations!

All goes well here. We're expecting a baby towards the end of February. It's been pretty good this time. The sickness passed off very quickly and as I've put on less weight I can still wear everything except trousers and very tight waists.

We've just come back from the best holiday in years. We went to Corfu, to a heavenly hotel right on the sea with a marvellous beach, food, water-skiing – everything. It was so successful that we stayed on an extra week, and for three weeks I didn't lift a finger in any direction. We took Carmen, who rose to the occasion like an English nanny. I explained to the children that I was on holiday for three weeks and she'd do most of the work. They slept separately with her, and we met on the beach after breakfast. We also had dinner alone, and every time there was any shit or whining she leaped up to deal with it – it honestly made the holiday.

Otherwise no news. We haven't seen Alex since before our holiday. His house is sold and he's moved to Suffolk. Georgina lives there too, of course, so it's much easier for them to see each other now, and I gather there's been another renewal of promises from her.

I've written too much. I'm not used to it and my head's swimming. Write to me.

Lots of love, Verge

Jane smiled wryly at this. Naturally it would not even occur to Verge to have any qualms about announcing that she was expecting a baby just when Jane's child by Alex would have been due. How typical of her also to say in one breath that she was having a child, and in the next extol the joys of a holiday, the chief success of which had lain in seeing as little as possible of the children she already had. Still, the apology at the beginning had been a handsome one, and had melted the anger and bitterness Jane had been feeling towards her friend. Verge might have been unnecessarily cruel at the time of the abortion, but she had probably only done it to save Jane from making a fool of herself over Alex who, in the event, had proved to be every bit as faithless as Verge had said he was.

She decided that she would ring her. The news that Alex had moved to the country and was back with Georgina had caused her a distinct pang, but at least it meant that she would be safe from further temptation from him. Perhaps she and Verge could patch up their friendship. It would certainly be useful to have someone to advise her on the merits of the various nursery schools in the area. Thanks to Giorgio's financial generosity she would be able to take her pick of them, and once Filippo was settled, she could see about getting a part-time job. She had sent her script off, with rapidly beating heart, to her director friend. He was away on holiday at the moment, but expected back imminently. She was also thinking of converting a second upstairs gallery which Giorgio had used for storing objets d'art into a spare bedroom. If she could find another lodger as satisfactory as Liliana, her financial problems would be solved, even if Giorgio should decide to defect later.

She rang Verge that evening and arranged to go to tea with her the following week. Alex was not mentioned by either of them.

Alex sat on the window seat of his empty house drinking some tea from a paper cup. It was September and today was completion day, although the removal men had actually finished yesterday, scattering their load between Julie, Suffolk, and the auction rooms. There was really nothing further that needed to be done in the house, but he had come anyway, without telling anyone, for a last sentimental look at the property which he had purchased with such high hopes only two and a half years ago, and in which he had since experienced such varying extremes of bliss and misery.

He glanced idly across at Verge's house. She and Robin had been generous in their offers of help during the removal process, and he had visited Verge the previous afternoon for a final cup of tea – Robin having unfortunately been away. Alex was still painfully conscious of the sense of aversion he had felt towards Verge since the start of his affair with Jane, while she too seemed curiously awkward and embarrassed in his presence. He wondered if it had something to do with her pregnancy. She could no longer get into her jeans now, and had been dressed in a snake-green smock from Elegance Maternelle.

Jane had never replied to his letter, so he assumed that she must have succeeded in making a go of it with Giorgio. It had occurred to him, of course, that she might never have received the letter and he had wondered if he shouldn't write again, just to tell her he had sold his house and was moving to the country.

'Have you heard from Janie at all?' he'd asked Verge abruptly yesterday, when it became apparent that no information was going to be volunteered from her side. He hadn't meant to ask, but suddenly the sense of *déjà vu* had been too much for him – the tea tray, the sofa where he had sat beside Jane as she fed Filippo, the sight of his own house, curtainless and unadorned as it had been on the day of their first meeting.

Virginia busied herself furiously with the tea strainer. 'No,' she said, 'but Sarah, our old nanny, says she seems to be settling down again OK.'

Alex said no more. He had no right to be hurt, he told himself. It was just as well Verge had saved him from making a fool of himself by writing again. Jane could always contact him if she really wanted to. She already had his country address, and the Post Office would be forwarding all his London letters there for the next six months.

'So this is goodbye then,' Verge had said to him on the doorstep.

'Well, not really.' He had made light of it. 'I'm going to look for a *pied-à-terre* here, as you know, to spend a couple of nights a week in so I can carry on with my classes. I'll invite you round as soon as I find somewhere.'

He knew he ought to ask the Askews to Suffolk, but somehow he couldn't quite face it. Bitchy urban gossip and uncontrollable children had somehow lost their charm now that he was doing what he wanted for the first time in his life. It seemed only just to him, after all the harm he had done, that the price he should have to pay for this satisfaction was acute loneliness.

Suddenly he leaned forward, hardly able to believe his eyes. Verge's front door had opened, and Jane was standing at the top of the steps, slim and smiling and dressed in blue jeans, exactly as she had been on the day they had first met. Were it not for the fact that Filippo, bronzed and sturdy, was very far from being the helpless infant he had been on that previous occasion, Alex might have thought he had summoned up some ghost from the past.

He sprang up, planning to run across the road and greet her, but then checked himself. Verge must have known yesterday that Jane was coming, but had chosen to keep the information to herself. Did this mean that Jane was here with Giorgio and had sworn Verge to secrecy?

Still keeping his eye on Jane, he picked up the telephone and dialled her London number. For today the phone was still his and he could call whom he liked.

A foreign woman answered, and he asked to speak to Count Orsini.

'He's not here, he's in Venice. I don't know when he come,' she said.

Alex took a deep breath. 'Is Jane here by any chance?' he asked.

'Oh yes. She went out. She should be back very soon. Can I give her a message?'

'No, thank you,' Alex said. 'I'll try her again later.'

Jane was descending the steps now, and unfolding the pushchair for Filippo. She turned and waved to Verge and started to walk towards Ladbroke Grove. Once again Alex was about to follow her when he stopped, transfixed suddenly by the expression of despair and longing on Verge's face as she stood on the steps looking after her.

But she's in love with her! he thought spontaneously, and felt a thrill of shock. Was this then the explanation of Verge's prick-teasing, the frigidity at which Robin had sometimes hinted, the exaggerated condemnation of Jane's affairs with men? Made crafty by this new knowledge, he waited with fast-beating heart until Virginia had gone into her house and shut the door behind her.

He decided that he would go to Jane and throw himself on her mercy. He would tell her all about Sandra and

Georgina, and repeat everything that Verge had said to him. The time for lying was over. It was essential for Jane's sake that she should know the truth, even if he lost her in the process.

He decided to give her ten minutes to get home. He would need that time anyway to calm himself down. What could he take her as a peace offering, he wondered? She had brought him lilies, but now the shops were shut.

Suddenly he had an inspiration. He rushed into his back garden. For today at least the roses were still his. He had planted them himself shortly after moving in, and they had grown rampantly up the side of the house, quickly covering the trellis he had so painstakingly erected, and cascading joyously over the top. Taking off his jacket, he set to work, gathering the fragrant white armfuls of his favourite banksiae – the rose without a thorn.

Jane had just finished bathing Filippo when the doorbell rang.

'Me go! Me go!' he said eagerly.

Jane smiled at him and tied the belt of his towelling robe. 'All right, darling,' she said. 'Be very careful on the stairs and tell whoever it is that I'll be down in a minute.'

She gave him a kiss and watched him run off. It was probably one of the neighbours. She would be glad to see them. She was feeling full of love for the whole world. Her director friend had rung that morning and told her that her script showed a lot of promise. He wanted to set up a lunch as soon as possible with another writer who specialized in TV adaptations. She let the water run out, then folded Filippo's towel and placed it on the radiator before going down.

When Filippo opened the door he saw Alex standing on the step, his arms full of white roses.

Alex squatted down so they would be the same height. 'Hello, Filippo,' he said smiling. 'Is your mummy home?'

'Yes, she is. She said just a minute.' Filippo was full of self-importance at getting the message right. 'Hello, Lix,' he added, and showing unusual demonstrativeness, he

flung his brown arms round Alex's neck and kissed him
on the cheek.

Jane emerging from the passageway, saw them there
together and paused, transfixed suddenly, on the landing
at the top of the stairs.

END

Class No. _F._   Acc No. _C/52855 88_

Author: _Dunhill · A_   Loc: ~~1 APR 95~~

LEABHARLANN
CHONDAE AN CHABHAIN

1. **This book may be kept three weeks. It is to be returned on / before the last date stamped below.**
2. **A fine of 20p will be charged for every week or part of week a book is overdue.**